This is a work of fiction.

All speaking characters in the novel are entirely fictitious.

Secret Spanish Colours

Tom Pearson

'It appeared that even in Barcelona there were hardly any bullfights nowadays; for some reason all the best matadors were Fascists.' George Orwell — 'Fighting in Spain' — April 1938

Chapter one

Saturday, December 5th, 1936,

Five months after the start of The Spanish Civil war,

Barcelona, Spain.

Nineteen-year-old Emily Edelman was halfway down La Rambla, the tree-lined, one-kilometre-long street in the centre of Barcelona and right outside the Boqueria market. She's read that La Rambla got its name came from the old Arabic word *ramla* which meant sandy riverbed. When the local government in the fifteenth century wanted to divert a sewer beyond the city walls, the gully left behind was filled in and became an important axis for transport and markets. It was quite a sight in the bright sun of this chilly afternoon.

She was struck by the heady spell of a worker's city at war. She knew that Madrid had already been bombed and was continuing to be bombed and there had been a lot of casualties with buildings damaged and destroyed. But here the place had an almost carnival atmosphere to it.

She had to step to one side as a tram scuttled down from Plaza de Catalunya rattling between the six-storeyed, grand imposing buildings on either side. The street was crowded with hundreds of people strolling about the cobbled paths or browsing through the dozens of weekend market stalls and kiosks. Groups of tricorn-hatted, blue-coated, civil guard policemen wandered under the massive, iron Gothic street lamps and they were joined by heavily armed assault guards brought in to keep the peace with so many young men in the city coming from all over the world to help the republic and the fight against Franco.

Any spare expanse of wall was covered with bright posters, mostly in the republican colours of red, yellow and purple along with defiant slogans in Spanish, Catalan, French and English, and portraits of muscular men and women with raised fists and raised rifles, waving flags showing the hammer and sickle. Groups of khaki clad men wove their way through the crowds. The clatter of horses' hooves and cartwheels and general clamour of the street threatened to drown out the speeches on every street corner where mainly young men and women harangued the small groups that had gathered to hear them, passionately laying out the next strategy for the city and the war and urging people to join their cause or encouraging donations to the party or union. The communists, the anarchists, the socialists, the unionists and even peasant farmer land reformers stood on upturned beer crates or small sturdy tables preaching to the already converted.

The light snow on the ground was mostly gone but some still remained along the bare grey branches of the elm and poplar trees lining the edges of the walkways, making them glint and glisten in the sun like fairy lights strung up for the impending Christmas festivities.

Emily pulled her thick scarf closer to her neck, tugged the bright blue woollen hat further down and pushed her blonde hair under it. She was beginning to feel cold and anxious. She was completely lost and had been for the past half an hour. *What the hell do I do? Which way do I go? Where the hell am I?*

She noticed two young women across the street standing outside a café, smoking and laughing. They were joined by a third woman and they hugged each other. All wore long coats and were swathed in scarves. One had a slouch hat, one a knitted cap and the third wore a green forage cap with a red star pinned to the front. All three were

6

wearing loose-fitting trousers covering their chunky short-heeled shoes. She watched them for a few seconds before making up her mind and walking across, dodging between a horse drawn cart and a tram as they passed each other and then threading her way between fresh piles of horse manure. She arrived just as the three were going into a side street and put a hand on the arm of the tallest one. All three turned around at once and stared at her.

Should I be pathetic or detached and casual thought Emily. *I'm certainly not feeling detached and casual. Let's hope they take pity on me.* She gave them the biggest smile she could manage then took off her hat and held it to her chest. She tutted to herself and felt her shoulders sagging. *This is stupid, I'll be curtseying next.*

Emily crammed her hat into the deep pocket of her thick, brown corduroy jacket and from the inside pocket took out two pieces of paper. She held one of the papers up, smiled again and began reading slowly and methodically from it, giving each syllable close attention. 'Excuse … por favor …excuse …soy Inglesa … puede ayudarme por favor … donde es … donde es … oh bugger, I'm getting this all wrong.' She pointed to the other piece of paper which had a roughly drawn map. 'Aqui … here … this place … can you help please … por favor.'

The three young women looked at each other, pulled puzzled faces and shrugged. They gave Emily a careful full inspection, looking her up and down and then back again as slow as they could. They shook their heads and looked at each other again, this time accentuating the shrugs and then flicking their hands and shaking their heads again. Their attitude just this side of indignant at being bothered by this person.

7

Bloody hell, I'm only asking. I just need some help, that's all. Sod it then.

'Okay ... sorry,' Emily said. She gave another short defeated smile and then began walking back to the crowds on La Rambla, wondering what she was going to do. The anxiety still there, but magnified now and crawling around her chest coming further up, up. *This is crazy. I'm so stupid, getting lost. What the hell do I do now?*

She had only gone a few yards when she heard a voice calling out, 'Hey, English. Hey English girl.'

Emily turned and saw the three young women looking at her with broad smiles and then the smiles breaking out into loud laughing.

The tall one said, 'Only joking English. You are English right? Only joking. We can help you of course. What do you need to know?'

Emily let her head fall to her chest, pulled it up again to reveal another smile and blew out a long breath. 'Oh, thank goodness. Thank goodness. I'm lost. Completely lost.' She produced the map again and pointed to a cross drawn on it with pencil. 'I have to get to this hotel. Here, this place. Do you know where it is.'

The tall girl took the map from Emily and considered it. She grinned at Emily. 'Yes, yes of course. I know where this is. We can take you there. It is not a long way.'

'Thank you. I was with a group but we somehow got separated in the crowds and I haven't a clue where they are.'

'International Brigade?'

'Yes.'

'Excellent… and thank you, thank you so much for coming,' said the tall girl. 'You come with us.' She pointed to her friend with the knitted cap. 'This girl is called Carmen. This one with the fancy hat is called Maria.' Maria took off her forage cap and gave a deep theatrical bow. 'My name is Isabel. And you are?'

'Emily.'

'Okay, English Brigadista Emily. You come with us first,' said Isabel. 'We don't have to walk far. We will take you to our favourite café.'

'But I haven't the time. I really need to get to the –'

'Don't worry, we will get you there,' said Isabel. 'But at first you must come with us. We must show our hospitality to you. We need to thank you for coming to help.'

Maria and Carmen linked arms with Emily. She could smell Carmen's strong perfume and felt the gentleness of her grip as they all walked along Calle de la Porteferissa for two minutes before turning into Calle d'en Roca and stopping at a large, blue double door at the end of the street. The left-hand door had a crack running the entire length of it and the paint was peeling with whole patches missing so that you could see the sun-damaged brown wood underneath.

'Here we are,' said Maria, her voice was dense and husky and matched perfectly her muscular frame and easy way of almost gliding along. She pointed to small wooden sign above the doorway. 'Comercio Gratuito. Best café in Barcelona. Not the most elegant … but the best.'

Carmen pushed the heavy door open and they went into a large mahogany-panelled room with a long, dark wooden counter running along the entire length of one wall and an enormous mechanical cash register at the end, with glistening brass decorations and metal keys that gave off snicking sounds as money was counted in preparation for the loud ding of the cash tray when it was opened. Shelves with dozens of bottles were behind the counter on either side of the huge ornate mirror, some thick with dust. Draping the mirror was the red and black flag of the anarchists. A fireplace at the far end of the room provided a warm glow. Brass wall lights lit by gas and with elaborate, fluted glass covers and bulbous mantles provided most of the light as the two windows looking out into the street were very small. In between the lights were newspaper articles pinned to the wall alongside faded posters advertising concerts and sherry festivals. The wooden floor was sagging and cracked, with an old threadbare rug in the middle. On the ceiling a long white-painted plank was nailed between two cracked plaster boards. Emily found out later that no-one could remember if it was there for decoration or support. Most of the ceiling was stained with dusky black patches from years of cigarette smoking and the space from head height to the ceiling was filled with lazy, wispy, swirling trails of hanging smoke.

The room was in an L shape with more than twenty tables in the main area in front of the counter and then a further twenty tables around the corner. Nearly all of the tables were occupied, with a mixture of elderly and young couples, groups of old men with flat caps and berets and young men in military uniform and forage caps. The tables were laden with an assortment of jugs, large and small carafes, and wine glasses glistening, reflecting the light from the gas lamps. The room was filled with noise: talking, laughing, shouting, the clinking of glasses as toasts were made and the scraping of chairs on the wooden floor.

Sitting on three separate tables were obvious new arrivals to the city, all young men, at their feet brown paper parcels tied with string. They were wearing a jumbled assortment of khaki trousers, shirts, jackets and outsize berets. It was a muddled confusion of first world war surplus uniforms and it was difficult to see anything that fitted perfectly. All wore the red bandanas around their neck that were everywhere in the city. They were to a man, well-meaning courageous amateurs strengthened and boosted by the belief that the world's freedom depended on them. An allusion or not it bolstered them greatly.

'Here,' said Maria. 'Let's sit here.' She motioned to an empty table and waved at two older men on the other side of the café. The four young women took off their coats and hats and slung them over the chairs. Emily took the time to have a good look at her new friends. They were all about her age or maybe a year or two older. Maria had short, wavy brown hair with big dark eyes and a perpetual smile. Carmen had a broad face, thick dark hair with a red ribbon tied at the back and a dimple at her chin. Isabel had short dark hair with blue eyes and a wide mouth. Isabel and Maria wore bright coloured blouses under sleeveless sweaters and Carmen wore a green roll neck sweater. Emily looked down at her loose brown shirt and wide khaki trousers. She pulled at the shirt and made a face.

'Ha. You look beautiful, English,' laughed Maria, leaning forward and banging on the table with both fists. 'The perfect Englishwoman. Perfecta. Excelente.'

'So,' said Carmen, 'What would you like to drink?'

'Coffee?' said Emily.

'No, no, no.' Carmen opened her mouth as wide as she could in mock surprise. 'No coffee for our International Brigadista. What kind of wine? Red or white?'

'It's four o'clock in the afternoon. This is madness,' laughed Emily.

'Ha, this is war. White wine war. And it's Saturday. No work tomorrow.' Isabel threw an arm around Emily and laughed with her.

A waiter appeared at the table and said something in Spanish which Emily didn't understand. The three girls laughed and Isabel turned to Emily. 'This is our good friend Miguel.' She looked at the others. 'He has a limp. It keeps him out of the war.'

She explained what she had said to Emily. Miguel pulled a face and made a fist pretending to hit her, then smiled and put on an exaggerated limp back to the counter.

'He knows what we want,' said Carmen. 'We are in here many times … very often.' She grinned and pulled out a pack of cigarettes.

A few minutes later Miguel returned with a tray. He placed a large carafe of white wine and four glasses on the table and then a large dish with plump green olives in herb-scented oil, slices of pale manchego cheese and chorizo sausages. He put some chalk marks on the table letting him know how much wine and what type had been ordered.

Emily stared at the food with a surprised look. 'I haven't any money to pay for food … or wine,' she said.

'Don't worry. Free food … tapas,' said Maria. 'Little dishes but enough. And we pay for the wine. You are our guest. It's the least we can do.'

'You'll find you will not have to spend a lot of money in Barcelona,' laughed Carmen. 'Everybody is thankful to you and glad that you are here.'

Isabel picked up an olive. 'This café gives extra tapas. It tries to help out those who can't get enough to eat. The war has not helped supplies of food so this place … it does what it can to provide a little to those people who need it.'

'Also, it's good advertising for the café to make more customers,' said Maria smiling.

Isabel wagged a finger at Maria. 'This café does what it can to help. Any food left over goes to the *CNT*.' She looked at Emily. *'The national Confederation of Labour,* and they give it out to the people who need it.'

'This is a socialist café, like so many in Catalonia in these days,' said Carmen. 'And we are friends with the anarchists here.'

Isabel poured the wine from the carafe into the four glasses. 'And another thing you need to know my friend Emily – no tipping. The waiters would be deeply insulted if you give a tip. No socialist waiters will accept tips.'

Emily took a long drink to keep up with the others who threw the wine back lustily and quickly refilled their glasses. 'How come you all have such good English?' she said.

'We're clever,' said Maria, grinning.

'Don't listen to her,' said Isabel. 'We made deal – el pacto – a pact? We have known each other before we were five. We decided we would help each other to speak another language. It was between French and English. We flipped a coin.'

'Which one won,' laughed Emily.

'Bah,' Maria laughed too and wagged a finger in Emily's face. 'You are funny English Brigadista.'

After a few minutes another carafe was ordered. Miguel came with the wine and more tapas and put another mark on the table with his chalk.

Isabel lit another cigarette, deliberately blew the smoke into the air in a long thin stream to disperse the wafting clouds hanging above her head. She shifted in her seat so that she was a little nearer to Emily. 'So, Emily. I am interested … we all are interested … to know how you came here.' She waved a hand at the others. 'I think we know why you came here. But it is fascinating to us to find out how all these people are coming to help us. How do you do it? How do you get here? I know your government is not helping you. If it was up to them, you would not be here at all. How do you all do it?'

Emily smiled at them. 'Oh, you know, just jump on a train …'

'No,' said Isabel, managing to frown and smile at the same time. 'Serious. We want to know. If you come here to risk your lives we at least need to know where you all came from and how you got here. We find it quite amazing. How did you get here? How did it start? Where exactly are you from?' She pointed a firm finger at Emily and gave her a stern but friendly look. 'Exactly.'

'Well,' said Emily, looking at the three expectant faces in front of her. 'If you must know, then I'll tell you.' She took a long drink. 'I come from Newcastle which is a town right up in the north of England by the Scottish border. My family were originally emigrants from Germany. They were very conservative. There is only me, no sisters or brothers. I decided a couple of years ago that I need to be more independent. I was training as a nurse ... only a few months in ... when I decided to join the Labour party, the major left party in Britain. When the civil war started the issues were perfectly clear to me ... Franco was being used by Hitler to form part of an international fascist league and unless it was stopped her there would probably be another war. So, I went to a lot of open-air meetings at a place called the Bigg Market in Newcastle. I started reading a lot of books about politics and economics and eventually went to Communist Party meetings ... in a bookshop on Westgate Road at the other end of town. I joined the Young Communist League and we used to have dances as well as meetings at rooms in Blandford Street.' Emily broke off and looked at the others. 'Sorry ... is this what you want. These places mean nothing to you.'

'It is exactly what we want,' said Carmen. 'Please, please continue. We want to find out all about your journey. We are related to this.'

'Okay then,' said Emily, she looked at each of the three faces in turn. 'So, I decided to see if I could help out here. I went down to the Communist Party headquarters in London. There you were quizzed about any military experience or any particular skills. I had a little nursing training so they accepted me. Party membership wasn't necessary but everyone would be asked why they wanted to fight in Spain. I know that some were considered unsuitable because of their age or ... lack of ideology I suppose These were sent home. Although the majority of the British volunteers that I knew were communists, others were members of the Labour Party or small left-wing groups,

15

even some from the Liberal Party. From London they passed me over to Birmingham where I was to wait until a group was ready to come over.

The party funds covered most of the money needed and I had saved a little bit. There were about twenty of us in that group. I was one of three women and the rest were mainly Welsh lads. We were sent back down to London. I had a passport ... which is quite unusual ... so when we boarded the night ferry from Dover to Calais I went straight through. The others had detectives asking them what they were doing and where they were going. The British police had orders to discourage anyone wanting to come to Spain. Those applying for new passports or visas at the post office would be refused if it was thought they were going to Spain to fight. The Welsh lads said they'd won some money on the horses –'

'Horses?' Carmen broke in.

'Gambling. Betting on horse races,' said Emily. 'So, they said they'd won some money and were off to Paris for the weekend to celebrate. You don't need a passport for a weekend so it was a standard story I believe. In Paris we were met by comrades and sent to various hotels run by trade unions for a couple of days. The hotels weren't what you might call luxurious. All money was confiscated there and returned later or sent back to your home to ensure there was no drunkenness. We were issued with ten francs a day to make sure that all you could buy was some Gauloises cigarettes and a couple of drinks.

When we arrived at the Gare du Nord station, the taxi drivers, who were all left-wingers, recognised us at once for what we were and gave us free rides to the Bureaux des Syndicates which was an assembly place for foreigners coming from all over Europe and beyond. Then we were sent by train to Perpignan. It was funny because at the station in Perpignan, again people knew exactly who we were. They could see that we were going to Spain to join the International Brigades. And there were crowds of ordinary people: railway workers, men in overalls, men in suits, women office workers, housewives, cheering us and singing. At Perpignan we transferred to buses and went off to Spain. We crossed to a small Spanish village near Gerona at the foot of the Pyrenees ... can't remember the name ... where we stayed in some stables for two days.

There were volunteers arriving there from all over the world. I think one of them was from Iceland and even some from Hitler's Germany. Then we were sent by train to Albacete just on the coast here ...which is the headquarters of the International Brigades.' Emily looked down at her clothes again. 'We were given uniforms there ... if you can call them that. We had a bit of training for about a week and then a few of us were sent here to meet up with some more volunteers from Britain and show them were to go.' She looked at the others, absolute concentration on their faces. 'And that's where you come in, rescuing a lost brigadista.'

The three Spanish girls eased themselves back in their chairs still looking at Emily. 'Thank you, Emily.' Isabel's eyes gleamed. 'As I said before, we are always very interested in these things.' She nodded slowly and looked away but flicked her head back to look at Emily as a sudden thought struck her. 'But what about your parents? What do they say about all of this?'

Emily took a cigarette off Carmen and lit it. 'She sat back in her chair. They didn't like it when I joined the Labour Party. They hated it

17

when I joined the young communists and more or less gave up on me. I don't blame them ... I suppose it's just as much my fault. We never really tried to discuss things ... and so, when I said I was coming here, that was the last straw. I haven't heard from them since.' She stared at the wine glass in front of her. 'No, I haven't heard from them since ...'

Two sets of chalk marks later Emily was deep in conversation with Isabel about Isabel's role as a teacher when Maria nudged her and pointed with her glass to the table at the end of the counter. 'Listen Emily. Now we begin the singing. I love this place. Always singing.'

Two, well-dressed older men started a song and then the whole café joined in. The slow, lilting, hypnotic melody filled the room. The words cascading, flowing between the tables, holding the singers together with something more than just a tune or words.

Emily looked around the café at the solemn faces, giving the song the seriousness it deserved. She turned to Isabel. 'Is it Spanish? It doesn't sound Spanish.'

'No, this is Catalan language song,' said Isabel. 'It's a Catalan love song *Muntaya de Conigo*, an old song full of ... sentimentales, you know ...' She thought for a moment. 'It has nostalgia, yes? It is about mountains and a nightingale. We sing in Catalan here.'

More songs followed. The songs went on for twenty minutes and then there was a short gap and Maria grabbed her opportunity. She nodded to Isabel and smiled. '*Els Segadors?*' she asked.

Isabel laughed and raised her glass as Maria pushed her chair back suddenly and had to hang on to the table to regain her balance.

'You'll like this one,' Isabel clinked glasses with Emily. 'Everyone likes this. The best Catalan protest song. *Els Segadors – The Reapers.* It describes how in sixteen-forty the Catalan reapers revolt against the Spanish army that enter Catalonia to fight the French but instead were abusing the local population. The chorus is *Bon cop de falc,* it tells the reapers to use their sickles against the enemy.'

Maria climbed unsteadily on to her chair but then stood up with her forage cap raised high above her with a straight right arm. '*Els Segadors!*' she pulled her head back, and then shouted through the clouds of smoke to the ceiling, '*Els Segadors!*'

Emily expected loud cheering at the announcement but instead there was a deep, hushed silence for a moment as dozens of faces turned to look at Maria. One man called out a greeting, quickly followed by another and then there was a mass banging of fists on tables, thumping out a steady beat, softly at first but soon getting louder and louder. Maria brought her right arm across her chest and raised her left hand in a clenched fist salute. The banging stopped and the silence rippled through the room again. Then she started the song, singing in Catalan and beginning slowly, her husky, rich, rasping voice wrapping itself expertly around the words. Her captivated audience sat absolutely still, listening intently, willing Maria on. The whole room seemed to become smaller.

Catalonia triumphant

Shall again be rich and bountiful

Drive away these people

Who are so conceited and so contemptable

The words were not lost on this audience: they understood everything that was being sung to them, what it was about and what it meant, particularly at this time. Maria's throat bulged with the effort of control and she screwed her eyes tight shut as the words flowed around the walls and the hushed tables until the words themselves became almost irrelevant and the song developed a lilting ethereal quality, solemn, almost like a hymn. A song of praise and worship and hope. She waved both hands, still with her eyes closed, beckoning her audience to join her.

Emily gazed around the room spellbound as everyone joined in instantly, quietly at first following Maria's lead for the first few verses until the final chorus came. Maria's gritty tone could just be heard above the mainly masculine voices thundering out the words which meant so much to them, accompanied by the thumping of fists on tables beating out the rhythm until the panelled walls resonated with the fervour of the singers. The power of their voices funnelling the grey layers further up into the ceiling in a swirling whirlwind of smoke. The discordant voices only added to the dramatic quality of the song.

Strike with the sickle

Strike with the sickle

Defenders of the land

Strike with the sickle

And when it was over there was a pause as everyone recovered their breath and looked around the room and at each other knowing that what had just happened was a special thing even for this time and for this place. They had all sung the song over the years and the singing of this particular song had always had great meaning for them but in these difficult times for Barcelona and Catalonia the song had greater relevance and the intensity and devoutness of the singing was more passionate than ever before.

They clapped and roared their cheers and stood to salute Maria, her face glowing and her chest heaving with the effort and emotion of her performance. She stepped down carefully from her chair and the room echoed with the clattering of scraping chairs as her audience resumed their seats.

And then the fighting started.

Three men, dressed in khaki and wearing red bandanas around their necks stood up from a nearby table and came alongside Maria. The first one, a thin tall man, about thirty years old with straw-like fair hair began speaking to her in Spanish. Fast Spanish, belligerent, heated.

Emily couldn't understand what was being said but she could detect the anger in the voices. The words soon got louder until Maria, now joined by Carmen, started shouting back. The men began to jab their fingers aggressively, first at Maria and then Carmen and then at Emily.

Emily put a hand on Isabel's shoulder. 'What's going on?' she said.

Isabel stood up. She glared at the men and didn't take her eyes off them as she answered Emily. 'They did not like the song,' she said trying to concentrate on the angry exchange as well as answering Emily. 'They don't like us. They are saying we are Trotskyist fascists. They overhear you talking and they don't like you because you are English and your government won't help. And they don't like this café because it has anarchists.'

Emily pulled herself up from her seat knocking her chair over. 'I thought we were all on the same side. I knew that the –'

Everything started to happen very fast.

The man with the fair hair leapt forward and pushed Maria with both arms, forcing her to fall back against the table next to them, spilling drinks and knocking bottles over in a sprawling clattering mess of arms and legs as she fell to the floor. Maria stumbled clumsily to her feet and the four young women stood motionless for a few seconds stunned by the violence of the push and wondering what to do next. The café became silent again, watching. The men had stopped shouting and began to turn, satisfied that they had made their point.

Emily ran past Isabel to stand in their way. 'Don't bloody hit my friend!' she shouted and aimed a punch at the man who had pushed Maria. It would have been an impressive sight and had it been successfully completed would certainly have given him a bruised cheek at the very least. However, if she had attempted it before the last two glasses of wine it would have been better, as it was, the punch evaporated into a long, lazy swing which landed Emily's fist eventually against the man's neck. Nevertheless, it stopped him in his tracks, giving Emily and Isabel enough time to launch themselves at him.

The next sixty seconds were a blur of flying fists and glasses and bottles and hurtling ashtrays and upturned tables, accompanied by cracks and splintering and grunts and dull thuds. One chair and one stool came to bounce and crash amongst the furious whirling bodies as more and more of Maria's audience came to help the four young women: running across the room and reaching into and over the tangle of bodies to grab hair or ear or arm or whatever they could and then yank and heave and twist and punch.

Eventually sheer weight of numbers managed to pull them apart and the three men were manhandled roughly across the room through the door and into the street. The door was slammed shut behind them and the café became a babble of excited voices with hands being shaken, nods of thanks and back slapping.

'Good punch,' said Isabel, looking at Emily. 'I didn't know who was going to start it. I'm glad it was you. Always nice to have a guest feel happy to join in.' She gave a loud laugh and imitated Emily's slow swinging punch.

'I didn't realise you could handle a bar stool so well,' said Emily.

The girls began laughing uncontrollably, exhilarated by the adrenalin rush of the fight. Miguel crunched over two broken bottles as he brought over another carafe and replacement glasses. He pulled out his chalk but then smiled, shrugged and put it back into his pocket.

Carmen filled everyone's glass and then held hers up. 'To the reapers!' she shouted, and all of the people within hearing raised their glasses too.

'So, tell me Isabel,' said Emily, wiping a smidge of blood from her nose. 'Are we on the same side as those three or not?'

'It all is very compleja, complicada … complicated,' said Isabel. She brushed some broken glass over the edge of the table with a sweep of her arm. 'A civil war within a civil war.'

'Well,' Emily replied. 'I knew there were different factions. I'd been warned about it. But that was crazy.'

23

'You ha to ... he fery careful in ... arcelona,' said Maria, wincing and sucking in blood as she tried to speak without touching her split bottom lip.

Isabel smiled at Maria and pulled a sad face. 'Since the victory in the elections for the workers unions in Catalonia at the start of the war,' she said, 'there has been a lot of in-fighting among the leftist groups.'

Carmen leaned forward to catch Emily's attention. 'The Spanish Communists are pro-Soviet, pro-Stalin and Leninists. And they hate the revolutionary socialists.' She waved a hand. 'Like most people in here, revolutionary socialists who support Trotsky's ideas.'

'Also,' said Isabel. 'There are Soviet spies and agents everywhere, helping to try and take control of the cause. They hate it that the Marxist Unification Union have sided with the anarchists, so they have people like those three who are told to cause trouble and arguments wherever they can. But,' she added, 'I like it that you don't argue with them – you just punch them.'

'Yes,' laughed Emily. 'It was slow but well meant. I enjoyed that. I liked the look on his face.'

'But now English Brigadista,' said Carmen. 'We need to get you to your hotel so that you can meet up with your British comrades.'

A few minutes later they left the café to ripples of more applause as they passed each table and stepped out in to the darkness of Barcelona. On the next street they saw the burnt-out wreck of the church of Santa Maria del Mar. Its walls blackened and roof collapsed. The walls daubed with red paint showing the communist, socialist and anarchist symbols and slogans.

Emily pointed to it. 'I've heard about this,' she said. 'How many were burned down in that night in July.'

'So,' Isabel said coolly. 'We had fifty-eight churches here in Barcelona. We burned down fifty-seven. Only the cathedral was spared.'

'They call this the *Red Terror*,' said Carmen. 'But we only respond to the *White Terror* when mass executions were made by the Francoists. This was revenge for the Catholic church collaborating with the nationalists. Some nationalist priest collaborators could make decisions on life and death depending on if you were a socialist or just a supporter of the republic.' Carmen nodded to a section of wall with one-metre-high words painted across it in red. 'It says: *the only illumination we need is from a burning church*.'

'The priests from this church,' said Emily. 'What happened to them?'

Isabel shook her head. 'Let's get you to your hotel. We can't have a lost brigadista wandering around at night.'

Chapter two

Emily's Funeral

Saturday, 27th August 2016,

Newcastle, Northern England.

The coffin was brought in on the shoulders of six pallbearers and as it turned into the nave a spontaneous burst of applause came from a small group of ten people at the back of the church. The hundred or so other members of the congregation turned to find out what was going on and then just as quickly turned back as the coffin came past them and was carefully placed on a stand.

The priest then mentioned a few things he had gleaned from the members of the family and said a few words intended to comfort them. He stepped down from the pulpit and gave a long deep bow to the simple wicker coffin next to the font, directly in front of the main aisle. He nodded to Xavi. It was Xavi's turn to represent the family and say a few words about Emily Edelman. It was to be a revelation to many there.

Xavi climbed to the pulpit. He was slightly bowed but moved easily for a man of eighty-four years. He was tall and slim with thick, almost white hair and a tight, well-clipped grey beard. The deep creases on his broad forehead wrinkled, framing his dark brown eyes and the loose skin under his chin flowed as he took some papers from inside his jacket and placed them on the lectern. He glanced at them and realised at once that the words were stale, wouldn't work and couldn't compete with the oppressive intensity of the air around them all. It was very hot inside the church and he gave his nose an involuntary wipe with a single finger to brush away a bead of sweat. He took out his glasses, put them on and straightened, surveying the black rows in front of him. He felt a tightening at his throat and took his time looking at them, contemplating; wondering what they would make of what he was about to say. Of course, he couldn't tell them everything. He couldn't tell them what she'd really done. That would be far too dangerous and would have serious and far-reaching consequences for the whole family. He wouldn't do that. He loved them all too much.

He gave a small cough to clear his throat and took a quick deep breath.

'Hello everyone. I think I know a lot of people here but for those who don't know me, my name is Xavi Santiago Rodrigues.' His gravelly Spanish accent could still be detected, even after living in Britain for decades. He began quietly and slowly to calm himself and disguise the slight wavering he felt in his voice. He needed to get this right; it was important that they understood. 'And I am here to talk about this wonderful lady, Emily Edelman.' His long leathery hand shook slightly as he waved it at the coffin to his right. 'Emily, even at her great age, her death was still so sudden and took us all by surprise.'

He coughed again and took a firm grip on the edges of the lectern.

'Emily was like a big sister to me. That's how it seemed and how it always felt.' His eyes drifted from the page and the carefully scripted words and scanned the walls for inspiration. 'Well, she was … and she wasn't … she somehow …' The pause was too long. Awkward. He couldn't find the words. He abandoned the search and returned to his notes. 'And she too was an immigrant, at first an outsider … like me.

In her case it was that her parents came from Germany just before the first world war. And I think it is important not to gloss over the fact that there were certain … hostilities … towards her and her family just like there were certain hostilities towards me and my friends, at least from some quarters, when we arrived from Spain in nineteen-thirty-seven, in fact, just before the Second World War.'

Xavi gave a small tight smile and glanced down at the absolute silence.

'Emily was born in nineteen-seventeen. And as I say, faced some difficulties in her childhood. But this did not deter her … probably made her more determined to fight for social justice … and all the other causes she embraced during her life.'

He looked around the church again and settled his gaze on a carved stone pillar at the back. The light grey giving some relief from the black rows and blank faces with their sombre stares. Xavi needed this counterpoint to help steady him. He crinkled the corners of his eyes to keep the tears back. He felt his heartbeat quickening and made his decision at last. He allowed his shoulders to drop, took off his glasses and pushed his notes to one side still staring at the column.

'You see, Emily was only nineteen, just nineteen, imagine that … when she went to Spain … against the wishes of her family. She was a devout socialist, if I can use that word in context in such a place, all of her life. At home she was … what's the word … cantankerous, a bit of a rebel. Fiery. To be honest, her parents always said she was a little devil.' Xavi stopped briefly as a ripple of nervous relieved laughter drifted up from the rows in front of him.

'Never doing what she was told, always arguing, never giving way. Her mother and father tried to stop her going to Spain … but she went anyway. And for those of you who are not aware, eighty years ago, in nineteen-thirty-six, when Emily went, Spain was in the grip of a terrible civil war. A war fought between the nationalists and the fascist powers of the right, under general Franco, against the republicans and leftists. Franco, supported by Mussolini and Hitler always outgunned the republicans. Thousands from across the world joined the fight to help the democratically elected republican government and formed International Brigades. Emily joined the British International Brigade and arrived in Barcelona. It was a horrible, cruel war for all of us involved. I was six at the time and my family was killed in a bombing raid. My entire family. All of them. In an instant. Wiped out.'

Xavi didn't dare look around but he could sense the thickening of the silence flowing into every stone in the church.

'Emily was in the front line for many months before her brigade was disbanded, but not before more than half had been killed. During that time, according to all accounts she performed her duties bravely. In the early days she used a rifle and fought alongside her comrades and then later worked as an auxiliary nurse in the medical service units. She saw terrible, terrible things. She helped to put together broken people … those that could be put together. She survived. The pressure was relentless. But she stuck to her task and served and supported and struggled and survived. She was one of many. And I am so very proud of her. Proud of her selflessness. Proud of her courage. Proud of her dignity and beliefs. Proud to have known her. She carried hope with her … everywhere … all the time. She was one of the heroes although she wouldn't like me saying that.'

He halted for a few seconds and stared straight ahead, then reached for his notes and glasses and took a piece of paper from the bottom. 'I'd like to read part of the famous speech, *La Passionara,* given by Dolores Ibarruri, co-founder of the Spanish Communist Party in her farewell speech for the International Brigades as they marched through Madrid in nineteen thirty-eight, after being disbanded.' He cleared his throat and held on too tightly to the paper so that it crackled in his grasp. He remembered to drop his shoulders and loosened his grip, *relax, relax, take your time.* He pulled his chin up lengthening his neck to better control his breath and words. 'In her speech she said: "For the first time in the history of people's struggles, there was the spectacle, breathtaking in its grandeur, of the formation of the International Brigades to help save a country's freedom and independence – the freedom and independence of our Spanish land. They gave us everything – their youth or their maturity, their blood, their lives and their aspirations, and they asked us for nothing. Communists, socialists, anarchists, republicans – different colours, different ideologies, yet all profoundly loving liberty and justice. They came and they offered themselves to us unconditionally. They gave up everything – their loves, their countries, home and fortune, fathers, mothers, wives, brothers, sisters and children. And they came and they said to us: *We are here. Your cause, Spain's cause, is ours. It is the cause of all advanced and progressive mankind.*

Comrades of the International Brigades, for political reasons and reasons of state you are being sent back, some to your own countries, some to exile. We shall not forget you. And when the olive tree of peace is in flower, entwined with the victory laurels of the Republic of Spain

– return! You can go proudly. You are history. You are legend. Long live the heroes of the International Brigades!"'

Xavi folded the paper and placed it in his pocket. 'This is Emily,' he said, his voice soft and slow. 'She can go proudly. She is history. She is legend.' He pulled back a little from the lectern, shook his head and smiled at the coffin.

'She came back to Newcastle after her time in Spain … when she had been injured … and just before the brigade volunteers were sent home. I was part of a group of twenty refugees brought to Newcastle and then sent to Tynemouth on the coast. It was there that I first met Emily. She was a regular visitor to the home we were in. Because she knew what we had gone through, because she could help with translation and because she still wanted to do her bit. At the end of the civil war in early nineteen-thirty-nine all of my friends went back to Spain but I had nowhere to go. Our village had been virtually wiped out. There was no-one for me back home.' He caught his breath and gave a tiny hiccupping sound.

'I had nowhere to go. Emily took me in and looked after me … as she has done for the past seven decades and more. She was my friend … my confidant … my surrogate sister. And I am proud to call her all of those things.'

'During the second world war she again served as a nurse, this time for the British army, and could have been promoted several times, but preferred, as always, to be on the frontline, *at the sharp end* she would say. She again helped with refugees after the war and then went to work for the National Health Service when it was formed in nineteen-forty-eight, and there had a distinguished career, eventually becoming a trainer of other nurses.'

'She was always a calm, dignified figure who liked to laugh a lot. Her family were always very important to her and she was devoted to her daughter Rosa, sadly unable to be here today. Also, her granddaughter Ana, and Ana's children Amber and Axel.'

Xavi looked up and caught the eye of Ana in the front row only a few feet away. Ana was fifty-four, tightly wrapped in a long black coat, short cut unruly brown hair flopping over her brow. Dark-rimmed spectacles perched on the end of her nose with green grey eyes peering out and bright red lipstick in a taut line. Ana held his gaze, nodded and then turned to her left to her twenty-three-year-old daughter Amber, and to the empty seat next to her where her twin brother Axel should have been sitting.

'She would have loved to be here herself,' Xavi continued. 'You all know, she loved a good party.' Small murmurs and lots of smiles. 'And we all know she liked a good drink, *just to keep the tubes oiled* she used to say.' This time, laughter echoing around the thick stone walls. 'And to be honest, there were times when we thought the gin would get the better of her, but she always pulled through.' Heads nodded and more laughter.

Xavi smiled and waited for the laughter to stop. 'It is unbelievable that we will never see her again. And that there is an Emily-shaped hole in the world.' He looked at the coffin. 'Adios mi luz maravillosa … goodbye my wonderful light. We will never forget you or your struggle.'

'Bollocks,' Amber said under her breath and lowered her head.

Some heads looked around as it wasn't obvious where the voice came from, but Ana knew. She frowned, mouthed, 'What!?' and glared at her daughter.

Amber glared back, twisted her lips and adjusted the zip of her black leather jacket. Then flicked at a purple hair on the thigh of her jeans. 'Load of crap,' she whispered to the floor.

Xavi could sense some distraction but chose to ignore it and looked again at the coffin. 'We will never forget you or your struggle,' he repeated. 'It is what made you what you were. It is what gave you a reason to live: your caring, your compassion, your bravery. You are truly legend. As you and many others said all those years ago, *no pasaran*. The republican cry, *no pasaran* – they will not pass.' Xavi pointed to the very back of the church. 'And I must thank the members of the International Brigade Memorial Trust who have made the journey here today to say farewell to Emily.'

From the main door at the entrance to the church a lone voice rang out, startling the rows of black coats and dresses. All eyes turned to see a well-dressed, older man standing at the back with a raised arm and fist. 'No pasaran!' he called again, and then walked quickly out of the church.

*

Hours later, in the early evening, the last of the mourners from Emily's funeral had left Ana's house.

Ana poured herself another large wine and went looking for her daughter. She found Amber in the back garden on the steps of the decking, half hidden by a fuchsia bush, sitting cross legged. Ana

33

stepped warily across the grass as if it were ice and small cracks were already beginning to show. She wasn't sure how to do this.

'There you are,' said Ana. 'At last. I've been looking all over the house for you. I haven't seen you all afternoon.'

'Well, you found me.' Amber pushed herself back and stared at the bush. 'Go on then, say it.'

'Okay then. You shouldn't have said that at the church.'

'Why not?' Amber snorted, twisted her thin frame around and played with a strand of her long purple hair.

'You know why. You shouldn't have said that. It was embarrassing and tacky.' Ana spoke softly trying her best to make her words sound reasonable.

Amber shrugged and gave a sucking sound with her mouth.

Ana sat beside her daughter and took a long drink from her glass. 'It *was* embarrassing. I thought you had more sense than that. I don't think Uncle Xavi heard it. Good job. He would have been very upset.'

'Well, he shouldn't say such stupid things then.'

'What do you mean?'

'All that International Brigade stuff. Socialist crap.'

'What's wrong with that? It's what defined her. It meant a lot to your Great Grandma Emily. I didn't know a lot about it. But I knew it meant a lot to her.' Ana pointed at Amber with her glass. 'Just because you didn't like her.'

'I didn't say I didn't like her,' Amber snapped.

'Well, didn't like her politics then. We can't all believe the same things you know. You have to be a bit more tolerant of different views.'

'Do I?' Amber pulled her head back. 'Was *she*? Really? *Was* she?'

This was going exactly the way Ana didn't want it to go. The way it had gone so many times before.

'Well, was she?' Amber glared at her mother and continued. 'No, she wasn't tolerant of different views. Left, left, left. Half the population doesn't agree with her, but she didn't care. Couldn't care less. As long as everyone knew she was *socialist*.' Amber spat the word out and twisted her lips down. 'As if that would solve all the problems.'

'Some people think it might.'

'Yeah, loony lefties brainwashed by intellectuals and their unworkable ideas.'

'So, what's your solution then?' Ana tried to grab the words back, but it was too late. She didn't want a debate with her daughter. Not today. Not anytime. There was never common ground to be found. She always came away with her mind in disorder and then later spending too much time on too much self-examination about their relationship.

'I don't know if I have a solution,' Amber pulled her words together slowly and deliberately, softly snarling. 'But at least I'm willing to listen to other views, to other ideas. Just in case, just in case mind you, that the left might be wrong … and someone else has the audacity to come up with a plan … the cheek to put forward different policies that would help this country.'

'That's probably a big thing. A big thing to say … *this country*. Grandma Emily never thought of the problems of this country. She always talked about trying to help everyone, no matter which country you came from. She was international. An internationalist. She knew all about two countries – Germany and Britain. But she always said everyone is having a hard time, in every country. She said we're all just the same ... powerless. And it's no good sorting out one nation. Every nation has to be sorted out. We are not in isolation. We should always have –'

Amber jumped up, one whole arm waving, swiping the air, then punching the words. 'What's wrong with helping ourselves first? What's wrong with nationalism? Never mind other countries. We can help them later. What about us? Let's get our own act together first. What's wrong with thinking about your own country? What's wrong with nationalism, eh?'

'I don't know.' Ana looked away from her daughter, shook her head slowly, swirled the wine around in her glass and stared at it. 'I don't know the answers. I wish grandma Emily was here to explain it all. She had it reasoned out. I'm not as clever as her. You know I'm not as clever as you. I don't have the answers ... but it seems to me that it's sensible to want to help everybody, regardless of where they live and what language they speak.'

'But you have to start somewhere,' said Amber, her voice rising. 'If great grandma believed that we are powerless ... and I agree with her ... then we have to take control of our own situation, our own country, first. The place is cracked, broken, it needs to be put back together.'

'Haven't we already started to do that with Brexit. And look what's happened. The whole country's divided.'

'Oh no, not this again!' Amber shook her head and pulled her lips wide apart in a derisive grin. 'It's what the people wanted. They wanted to take control. To make their own decisions.' She gave a long slow smile. 'The result probably finished Great Grandma Emily off.'

Ana looked up quickly. 'That's not a nice thing to say. Horrible. An awful thing to say. And not all the people wanted it, only half.'

'Have to start somewhere.'

Ana shook her head. 'I don't want this.'

'What?'

'This arguing. It's not good. It's not good at all. We shouldn't do it.'

Amber stared at her mother for an uncomfortably long time. 'So, we just shut up and say nothing.'

'Might be better.'

''Cept you always seem to side with Great Grandma Emily.'

'No, I don't.'

''Course you do. All the time.'

'Well, she was brave. In the things she did and the things she said.'

'I'm not doubting that. That's not what I'm saying. I'm saying there might be other ways to do things, to think about things, but you always try to shut me down.'

'Well,' said Ana wearily. 'I'm sorry you feel like that. I don't think I do.'

'You do.'

'I'm your mother. I'm supposed to look out for you.'

'You take over. You criticise me. You're nosey. Always poking your nose in. Always criticising. I think you enjoy making me feel inadequate.'

'Don't be ridiculous. How do I do that? How can I do that. You're very clever. You've been to university. You've got your degree. You're much cleverer than me.'

'Know what? I think you're jealous.'

'Don't be stupid.'

'What else then? What is it? Why do you hate me so much?'

'This is ridiculous. Of course, I don't hate you. I love you.'

'Ha! That's a laugh.' Amber pulled at a lace of her boot. She glared at her mother, defiant, combative. 'I hate this family. No-one says what they really mean. It's so weak. Everyone's so weak. It's just verbal incontinence.'

Ana stiffened. She wished she hadn't had so much wine. Emboldened by it she said. 'Weak? Weak, are we? This family? This family that supports you. I'm not perfect but I'm trying my best. I'm trying to come to terms with my imperfections.' It was too late now. 'And what about you Amber? What do you do for this family? Not a lot. You're always grumpy. Always complaining. I think you enjoy it. You're selfish, manipulative and unkind. You … '

'Wow, keep it coming mother,' taunted Amber. 'This is great. I can see the love shining through.'

'I just don't know where you get your attitude from. I've always tried to help. Even at school. The times I had to go to that school for bullying.

Oh, if only once it was you being bullied, but no, it was you – you were the bully. I had to plead with them to let you stay.'

Amber gave her mother a long blank-faced look 'What can I say? I like picking on weaker people. It's fun.'

'That's a horrible nasty thing to say. You can't think like that. You don't believe that?' Ana wanted to stop now but this seemed an important moment and she had other things to say, get off her chest. 'And I've seen the posts you put on the internet. Horrible. I can't believe you think it's right. Quite vicious. You seem to think it's fun saying those things to hurt people. Even your friends.'

'So-called friends.'

'You've known some of them for years ...'

Amber gave her mother an overly indulgent smile. 'It's wise not to tell me your secrets.'

'Know what? You seem to have a distorted view of yourself. You seem to think that the way you behave is positive ... the right way to do things. Can't you see it's just plain nasty? You're callous and self-absorbed.'

Amber smiled again. 'I do have a tendency to go over the top ... but the drugs help.'

Ana shook her head. 'It's too dark Amber. Way, way too dark.'

'Ah, but darkness has great sex appeal ... don't you think ... *mummy*?'

Ana looked around the garden, looking for help, trying to work out to how to end this amicably. But instead, she waded back in, unable to stop, the anger encouraged and stiffened by the alcohol. 'I don't get you Amber. I don't understand you. *We* don't understand you. You seem to have a heartless insensitivity to the feelings of others. Even when you were young you always had to spoil things. Always complaining, whingeing, moaning. Like back there at the service for your great gran … you have to try and spoil it. You seem to take some kind of perverted pleasure in spoiling things. And you seem to think that you're the good guy … raging against the world, trying to right the inadequacies of the world. Well, you're not. I can tell you, you're not. You're not the good guy. You can be nasty and hard. You just stick two fingers up at the rest of us. Anything goes.'

'Mmm … oh well, a bit of everyday sadism can be very invigorating. I've spent a good deal of time researching dark tendencies.'

'Unbelievable. You're unbelievable. I don't know what went wrong. Your brother –'

'Oh, no, no, no,' Amber gave a big explosive laugh. 'Please, please, please don't let's talk about my lovely, sweet innocent brother. We wouldn't want to taint him with all this. It's far too truthful for his delicate ears.'

It was Ana's turn to stare at her daughter for a long time,

Amber stood up and brushed some imaginary flecks of soil from her red jeans. 'Well, thanks for the chat mother. Thanks for the constructive criticism. It's been a revelation.' She walked back to the house. 'I'm going out,' she said, over her shoulder.

'Where to?' said Ana. 'What about …?'

But Amber was already gone. Ana watched her stomping through the back door into the kitchen. She knew she'd heard her. For a fleeting second, she wanted call after her, 'You know I love you.' But the thought scuttled away in a hurry. Instead, she gave a small shake of her head and forced a half smile which quickly turned into a dejected look with a dark shadow falling across her face.

Ana sat in the garden for a long time. It was getting quite late now. The day was cooling and she rubbed her arm to warm it. She sat very still, staring straight ahead, put a finger to her mouth and chewed on the nail. She pulled her hand away, wiped the finger on her cuff and took a long drink of her wine. She gazed around the small garden with its three, red rose bushes, assortment of empty plant pots, probably twenty in all, half of them cracked and broken. The two long rows of raised flower beds stifled with weeds, untended for months now, adding to the general chaos. She scowled at the apple tree to her left from which four handbags hung: a blue, leather tote bag, a pale blue, satchel bag and two barrel-bags, one red and one bright green. All four overflowing with dried soil and decaying lobelia, begonia and geranium. She had thought they were clever and arty and fun. But that was before her world started falling apart.

She picked at a loose sliver of decking. It came away easily, a piece the full length of her arm. Underneath, a frenzy of woodlice scuttled for safety and a centipede crawled over her finger, too fast for her to shake it off, before wriggling down and disappearing between the boards. The decking should have been stained in the spring. She flicked the piece of rotting wood towards the largest plant pot heap in the corner. It smacked against it and shattered into three pieces.

She just couldn't be bothered with the garden these days. Too busy coping with Grandma Emily's sudden illness, and then the funeral, and the frustrating visits to her mother, deteriorating in the care home. And those two, Amber and Axel, biological twins but worlds apart. And all the bickering.

She tried to think back, as she had done many times before, to discover what had changed. What had she done. What she could have done better. Or was it something else? Was it someone else? She wasn't perfect, she knew that, but she had always tried hard, always put them first. *What happened?* Amber was … well, she wasn't sure what Amber was. She couldn't understand how she behaved the way she did, had the views she had, could say the things that she said. Maybe she was just a bit too boring for her daughter. Maybe a bit too safe? *Safe?* *Doesn't everybody want to be safe?* And she had given them a safe place to live. Where they could grow. Maybe that was it … maybe they had too much space to grow. Maybe she should have been more controlling, *no, not controlling*, maybe more boundaries or more willing to be decisive, give direction. But that was difficult when you weren't sure which way to direct them to … and weren't any good at it. They both knew more than her. They were both intelligent, more intelligent than her … she realised that at least.

Surely it wasn't the father thing? They had talked about that. They both seemed okay with that. It was a drunken one-night stand. A one off. She had been honest. When they were old enough to know. They both seemed okay with it. *Were they okay with it?* She'd had men friends over the years. When it didn't work out it just seemed to make her stronger. Make them all stronger. At least that's what she thought. And there had always been Xavi. He was always there for them. *Maybe it was that. The father thing.* But they never said anything really. Yet they still seemed to blame her for something. And surely if it was that it would make them hate something else. Not themselves. They seemed to hate themselves. At least Axel did. Amber hated herself and everyone else as well. She sighed, as deep a sigh as she could muster, wanting to physically feel her body ache with frustration and remorse as a kind of self-punishment. 'I don't know. I just don't know,' she muttered.

A red admiral butterfly flitted about in front of her, quivered as if wanting to land but then flew off. Ana watched it fly away and then called after it, 'Yeah. Not much here for you, my friend.' She took another sip of her wine. 'Best to go somewhere that smells a bit better. It's all death and decay here.' *Wow, getting a bit too morbid now, better have a coffee,* she thought to herself.

She shuffled about, twisted round and then pushed herself up with one hand. She took a second to steady herself, throwing out both arms for counterbalance and spilled some of her wine on the decking, washing away the slowest of the woodlice with a tsunami of pinot grigio.

'Hello.'

The voice came from behind Ana. It was a man's voice. She wanted to whirl round but though better of it and instead took three steps to turn and then looked at the man standing behind the half gate at the bottom of the garden.

'Hello,' the man said again. 'I'm sorry to bother you.'

'It's no bother,' said Ana, walking towards the gate. The voice had jolted her out of her stupor and she looked again at the man trying to work out where she had seen him before. 'Come in, come in. What can I do for you?' She pulled the latch up and opened the gate. 'I'm sorry, do I know you?'

'No,' the man smiled as he came into the garden. He was tall and fair haired, about the same age as Ana, wearing a dark suit and carrying a backpack on one shoulder. 'You don't know me but you have seen me. Back at the church …'

'Oh yes, yes, of course.' Ana pointed her glass at the man. 'You were at the church. You shouted something and then you left.'

'No pasaran. Spanish. It was a slogan used during the Spanish Civil War. No pasaran, *they shall not pass*. The man at the pulpit giving the obituary mentioned it.'

Yes, didn't get that, thought Ana, *I was a bit too preoccupied with my crazy daughter at the time*

'It was used by the republicans,' continued Richard, 'fighting Franco …' His voice trailed off, he smiled again, nodded and raised both hands to acknowledge Ana's puzzled expression. 'I'm sorry. I should start again and introduce myself.'

'I think that would be a good idea.'

'Okay … my name is Richard. Richard Stevens. My grandma was Isabel. My mother, Isabel's daughter, married an Englishman and came to live in England. So, here I am. Still living in England. London to be exact.'

He waited for Ana to react but she continued with her puzzled expression, accentuating it with raised eyebrows and a small wave of her glass before taking another sip.

'Isabel?' she asked.

'No,' Richard pulled his head back and then shook it. 'You haven't heard of Isabel?'

'Sorry.'

'Like I say, she was my grandma … and a great friend of your grandmother. A very dear friend.'

Ana looked down at her empty glass. 'I think you'd better come inside, have a drink and tell me all about Isabel.'

'No, thank you, thank you so much but I won't intrude. I realise it must have been a tough day for you. I just came to give you something.' He pulled the backpack from his shoulder and began to unfasten it.

'But I don't understand. How did you know about the funeral? How did …? This is all a bit confusing …'

'I know. I apologise for turning up like this out of the blue. But I had to do this today. I knew about your gran's death from the International Brigade newsletter. Because of the Spanish connection and my grandma's story I still subscribe. I found where the church was online but I didn't know your address so I had to follow you from the service. I waited until everyone was gone.' He pulled a bundle of envelopes from his bag. 'I really need to give you these.'

'What are they?'

'Letters. Correspondence. From your grandmother to my Grandma Isabel and from Isabel to your Grandmother Emily. They were great friends during the war in Spain. Isabel was a teacher in Barcelona … that's where they met … right at the start of the war. When the Basque region was heavily bombed a lot of refugees, mainly children, were

45

taken to Barcelona. My grandma looked after them and later volunteered to accompany them when they were evacuated to Britain. Hundreds of them. And thousands more to other countries. Isabel came with twenty children to stay in Tynemouth just at the coast, about ten miles from here.'

'Yes, I know where Tynemouth is.' Ana failed to keep her words kind. She was still upset about the conversation with Amber. She was intrigued but also beginning to get slightly irritated, and the wine wasn't helping. She made a mental note to try harder, not to sound too harsh.

'Of course. Yes, of course you do,' said Richard. 'Anyway, Isabel and the children stayed here until they were repatriated,' he looked up quickly, remembering the service, 'except the man at the pulpit of course. Isabel had to accompany the children back to Spain … there were problems tracking down families … I don't think Emily and Isabel met after the war but they kept in regular contact.' Richard widened the top of the backpack to show Ana the inside. 'Five hundred and thirty-two letters. My grandma died in nineteen ninety-six. They kept in contact for sixty years. These were all kept at my mother's house. Apparently, my grandma and your grandma agreed that Grandma Isabel should keep them in Spain. My mother died last year and I found them in a box when we were sorting out her house. Been gathering dust in the attic. I've only had a chance to read them in the last couple of months … takes some doing I can tell you.'

Ana leaned forward to get a better look inside the backpack, crammed with neat piles of letters. 'I see what you mean.'

'I know it seems a bit off … reading private letters. But in a sense, it's a record, an historical record … and fascinating reading.'

'But why give them to me?'

'I suppose because it has a certain symmetry to it. You and your grandmother are the other half of the story. You need the letters to understand the history. Oh, and by the way, they're all in chronological order. A few gaps naturally, some went missing over the years.'

Richard held out the backpack, Ana took it and gazed inside again. 'Well, thank you, thank you very much,' she said. 'I'll certainly try and read some. I don't know when though, I've got a lot on at the moment you understand.'

'Yes, of course. Okay then,' Richard took a step forward and shook Ana's hand. 'Nice to meet you and so sorry about your grandmother. I'd better go now.'

'What? But you can't go yet. Come inside. Tell me more about your grandma.'

'No, really. Like I say, I think I've intruded enough. I think you need this evening for yourself.' He turned to go but then stopped. 'But I would like to see you again sometime. When you've had a chance to read the letters. It would be nice to chat about them.'

He walked to the end of the garden, waved and smiled back at Ana as he pulled the gate shut behind him.

Chapter three

Saturday, 27th August 2016,

Newcastle, Northern England.

Ana watched Richard disappear through the gate. Meeting him had been a welcome, intriguing distraction from Emily's funeral that morning and the weariness of hosting friends and relatives later. She was exhausted but now they were all gone Ana stood for a few moments gazing around the garden and then stared at the backpack he had left and slowly shook her head. *Isabel*, she thought to herself, *who on earth is Isabel?* She walked back to the house and went into the kitchen with the bag. She put the bag beside an old well-worn chair next to the smart light-wooden table in her modern kitchen then went to the fridge poured herself another large glass of Pinot Grigio and flopped down in the chair. She took a long drink and then another one, placed the glass on the solid oak flooring and opened the bag. She pulled out a pack of letters, dog-eared, some torn, with sellotape holding them together and with an elastic band around them over a piece of paper with a large *one* written on it in thick black felt tip.

Ana widened the elastic band and tugged out the top five letters. She placed the pack back into the bag, reached for her reading glasses on the corner of the table, slunk further into the chair and opened the first letter.

Monday, December 7, 1936

Dear Isabel,

I hope this note reaches you. (sorry my Spanish is nowhere near as good as your English – in fact it's non-existent so I'll have to write in English, sorry)

I looked for you and your friends, Carmen and Maria yesterday afternoon, in that café just off La Rambla but couldn't find you. What a night it was! I just wanted to say how much I enjoyed talking to you all. You were all so friendly and full of life. I bumped into your friend Miguel who you introduced me to at the café, he's helping at the International Brigade Reception Centre and he said he'd give this to you.

It was good to have some female company to chat to. These are hard times and it's so sad what is happening to your country. But we will win. Many more comrades are coming each week to join the fight. I have a lot to learn about Spain but already I love the land and the people and of course Barcelona.

I remember you said you were a teacher, muy importante – see, I'm learning already. We are leaving in a few days for training to a place called Tarazona de la Mancha in the Albacete region.

Please write or contact me if you can. I'd really like to see you and your friends again.

Regards, Emily Edelman.

Ana read the letter again then put it on the floor beside her glass. She picked up the next one.

Thursday, December 10, 1936

Dear Isabel,

Thank you so much for yesterday. I enjoyed the evening very much. Miguel said he'd deliver this. I completely forgot to ask for your address. You and your friends were in fine form again.

Tovey un grand tiempo (I'm learning). Got a Spanish chap who brings bread to check the spelling but he didn't seem too sure either so I just spell what it sounds like. And I really did have a wonderful time (that's what it's supposed to say).

I love your café and the tapas and of course the wine. Although alongside the stylish dress you were wearing this time I felt quite out of place (only joking). The jackets and shirts we've been given are very stiff and itchy. I'm glad I brought my own boots and trousers.

The new recruits bring news from Britain. Back home the right wing spread propaganda that we are all misfit adventurers and unemployables. Our foreign secretary Sir Anthony Eden told the House of Commons (our parliament) that "drink was a factor" in our recruitment. Nothing could be further from the truth. We are all glad to be here to help build a socialist movement and defend democracy.

We leave tomorrow for training. Please write when you can, if you want to of course, and send me your address. You can contact me at the 15th International Brigade centre at Tarazona de la Mancha, Albacete.

Regards, Emily Edelman

Ana had a sip from her glass and took another letter from the pile.

Tarazona de la Mancha,

Albacete,

Tuesday, December 15, 1936

Dear Isabel,

Thank you so much for your letter. It arrived this morning. It means a lot to receive post. Everyone gets very excited when the post arrives from Barcelona.

I'm sorry to hear that the children in Madrid seem to be suffering so badly. They must be still in shock at the bombings. But I'm sure with you as their teacher they will get through it. I know how much you care about them.

You ask about the camp. The food is bearable with lots of meat and beans. Tents are a bit cramped. Our tent was near the lavatory which was blocked for a whole day and didn't work. The smell was overwhelming. We moved our tent! But smells of one kind or another can't be avoided. There are about 150 of us here up to now. About twenty or so women, three of the men come from the same area as me in Northern England. The main language spoken seems to be German but more English speakers are arriving every day: British, American and Canadians and even some Australians. Sometimes the camp can be bewildering as we go from one supposed authority in charge to another. Also, we had a big surprise when we were invited to a concert. Paul Robeson the American singer came to entertain us. We could hardly believe it. He was fantastic and just what we needed.

We have been training. If you can call it that. Seems to be lots of marching about. I suppose it's to keep up the appearance of a military unit because we didn't have enough weapons for everyone. We had three old Colt machine guns. No ammunition. And we'd practise taking them to pieces and putting then back together.

Today however, joy of joys, ninety Soviet rifles arrived and we were allowed to fire ten rounds each.

We had a bit of a setback yesterday when about ten Irish volunteers, who were already unhappy with the British officers, discovered that one of the senior officers had played a part in covert, undercover operations in Ireland just after the 1916 Irish uprising. Following a stormy meeting the Irish lads decided to leave and join the American volunteers in the Abraham Lincoln Brigade who are training in the next village.

The camp is a real mixture of intellectuals, workers, communists, socialists, and anarchists. There are lots of different trades represented. We have clerks, painters, salesmen, electricians, miners, labourers, bricklayers, dockers, carpenters, seamen. And believe me there are a lot of lively discussions, sometimes too lively. Also, quite a lot of Jewish volunteers. Our brigade is the 15th and we also have the Hungarian Risolski brigade with us.

Our British brigade is commanded by Wilf McCartney who had previously served 10 years in Parkhurst (a British prison on the Isle of Wight) for spying for Russia! He's a good leader though and a really decent chap.

The weather is getting worse. I didn't realise it could get so cold. We have been given extra blankets courtesy of the women from the Spanish Defence League volunteers in Albacete town. We were extremely grateful.

Write soon if you can,

Take good care of yourself,

Kind regards,

Emily

Ana put the letter with the others at her feet. It was hard to imagine the cold her gran was going though all those years ago on such a warm day as this. And how exciting for such a young girl. 'Nineteen?' Ana said out loud, 'Nineteen? How?' She shook her head slowly and looked around her kitchen. A few empty bottles of beer on the table and counter alongside a dozen or more teacups and mugs and wine glasses. Plates, some neatly stacked, some with half eaten sandwiches and cakes. 'They all came for you,' she said. 'They all came for you. But we didn't really know. We never really knew.' She looked at the cluttered table again, and shook her head again. 'That can wait.' She tilted her head and smiled, realising that she was talking to herself. 'Oh well.' She picked up the next letter. 'Let's see what you're up to now young Emily. Let's see where you're going with this.'

Tarazona de la Mancha,

Albacete,

Monday December 21, 1936

Dear Isabel,

Que gran sorpresa! And it really was a great surprise when you turned up, (we are having Spanish lessons in the camp every other night).

It really was a lovely weekend. I am so glad you and Carmen and Maria came to visit. You all made a great impression on the lads. And thank you again so much for the lovely shirt you brought me, muy bonita. Also, the chocolates you all brought for us. They did not last long I can tell you. I will buy you something special when next I see you.

I know how long it would have taken you and your friends to get here. Thank you so much for taking the time, I know you must be very busy at this time of year. You have all been so very welcoming and I cannot tell you how much it really helps to know that we are appreciated. I very much value your friendship.

It seems that our training is coming to an end, thank goodness. We will be returning to Barcelona for a week or so for a break before they send us on again. We have heard that the Francoists are gaining ground in the west, ready for another crack at Madrid and that there is a big concentration of their forces near Jamara valley to try and cut the road from the west to Madrid and then on to Valencia.

A French comrade gave me an address of a room in Barcelona where he has stayed before. You can contact me there it you wish. The address is, 37 Calle de Sant Anna. The street joins La Rambla, on the right, near the top by the Place de Catalunya.

Really looking forward to seeing you all again.

Take good care of yourself,

Feliz Navidad,

Kind regards, Emily.

When Ana opened the next letter, she noticed the signature at the bottom. 'Oh … Isabel,' she said. 'So, here you are.' She took a long drink from her glass and put it down by her feet. As she sat back and adjusted her reading glasses a wave of warmth flowed across her face.

138 Calle de Nueva,

Plaza Segovia Nueva, Madrid

Monday January 4, 1937

My dear friend Emily,

I just have received your letter yesterday. It was brought by Carmen. I am so very sorry that I miss you but we had to leave quick to come to Madrid. There are even more refugees here and a lot of children to look after. They are scared and have been seen terrible things in the Basque region. Whole villages have been destroyed. I have to come, along with other teachers to try and bring some sense of normal to the children. Carmen and Maria also are here. They have joined the POUM Marxist militia and are now soldiers! I wish I could join with them but it is not possible with so many children coming. My place is with the children. Carmen and Maria are looking strong with the uniform and red berets and rifles. They look very serious. Most times they look serious but then we start laughing. Everyone looks serious. As you taught me, everyone is keeping their eye peeled and using their loaf (I love your crazy sayings).

The situation in Madrid is quite bad. There has been a lot of fighting in the streets but everything is calming now. As you know even the republican people fight among themselves, the socialists against the communists and the anarchists against both of them. We need to be together if we will win this war. We cannot fight each other. We also hear about the fascista forces who include Moroccan regulares. They are collecting just east of the city in the Jamara valley. But we are ready, the republican tanks are here, the republican armies are here and more International Brigades coming.

Would it not be a strange thing if you were sent to the Jamara valley and were fighting along with Carmen and Maria. I do not know when I will see my friends again. They have to obey the military organisation now. I do not know when I can see you again. I hope that I do.

Keep safe.

Keep your eye peeled.

We will meet again,

Your friend Isabel

Ana took off her glasses and dabbed at her eyes with the back of her hand. She let her head fall against the back of the armchair. Her right hand relaxed, Isabel's letter drifted to the floor and as Ana sank gratifyingly into an unconscious state which she often referred to as sleep, her right foot slumped forward and knocked over her glass. The wine spilled out and began seeping into Isabel's letter, diluting the ink and beginning to blur the words: spidery threads of black creeping over the page.

Chapter four

Saturday, 30th July 2016,

One month before Emily's funeral,

Welling care home, Newcastle.

'Rosa,' said Xavi breathlessly through the intercom. 'We've … come … to see Rosa Edelman. This is her grandson … Axel.' Xavi and Axel huddled for shelter under the small roof of the care home doorway. It was raining heavily and they had run from the car at the far end of the crowded car park.

The receptionist looked up from her computer, recognised Xavi, reached across to a switch at the edge of her desk and buzzed them in.

'Ah, yes … of course, of course … Rosa,' said the receptionist, giving a sympathetic smile. 'Nice to see you Mr Rodriguez. Not too good today I'm afraid.'

'Okay,' said Xavi, returning the smile although his was an automatic reaction, a quick pull on the lips, eyes not involved. He nodded to Axel.

They walked across to the big double doors and the receptionist pushed another button to let them through.

'Third floor now,' said Xavi. 'She's been moved up.'

Axel gave him a questioning look.

'Third floor is not so good,' said Xavi. He gave a low grunt and left it at that.

Xavi glanced at the noticeboard as they passed, filled with children's pictures from the local school, crayoned and felt tipped, colourful, cheerful… and incongruous thought Xavi. But then he checked his thinking, *not fair,* he said to himself.

Axel had stopped and was looking at the noticeboard. He needed to contribute something, some small talk, but didn't really know how so he smiled vaguely.

'Children from the local school,' said Xavi. 'They visit from time to time. Talk to the residents. Try to cheer them up I suppose. I think they do.' He looked at Axel. The baggy skin on his face tightened. 'But they don't go to the third floor.'

'How bad is she now?'

Xavi turned the question over in his head. 'When was the last time you visited your grandma?'

The words hit home although they weren't meant to. 'Dunno',' said Axel quietly, the smile faded. 'Maybe six months or so.'

'Well … to be honest, she's deteriorated quite a bit in the last few months, even after all these years … so …' Xavi flicked a hand, spreading the fingers and passing on the unspoken warning to Axel of what he would find.

Axel nodded his acknowledgement. 'Y'know, it's strange. I can hardly remember her not being here.'

'Yes, it …'

Axel stared at Xavi, waiting for him to complete the sentence but Xavi's eyes had wandered away, somewhere far off.

'Should we ...?' Axel walked a few feet along the tartan-patterned carpet. And then turned back. 'Uncle Xavi?'

'Yes, yes, of course,' said Xavi.

They moved on along the corridor, picking up the pace, walking purposefully now. Past the closed doors, each with a plaque: Sandra, Jeanette, Sarah, Francis. All women, and each with a photo of a smiling, vital, animated woman staring out into the lavender-coloured walls. Past the posters of old film stars and popstars, past the Beatles and Queen and Fleetwood Mac. Doris Day, arms spread wide in a buckskin jerkin beaming out from the Calamity Jane poster. Sean Connery, gun in hand, Audrey Hepburn, cigarette holder and big floppy hat.

'Know any of these?' said Xavi, nodding at the famous faces as they passed.

'One or two.'

'New owners. Brightens the place up. Trying to trigger memories. I remember them all.'

At the end of the corridor a woman wearing a pale blue health care tunic came out of one of the rooms walking alongside a resident who was using a walking frame to negotiate the turn, leaning into it with tight-lipped determination. 'Come on Francis, let's get you back. Wrong room again.' The care worker gave a knowing look and slight roll of her eyes to Xavi and Axel. 'We'll be late for tea at this rate. We'll need to get you cleaned up.' Francis gave a puzzled look to the care worker and brushed a hand at the oily cream dripping down her cardigan. 'You know you've got your own cream, don't you, Francis? Let's get you tidied up and I'll sort out Betty's bed later.'

Francis stared at Xavi and Axel as they came alongside. Unnerved by the two tall strangers, she left the walking frame and took a firm two-handed grip on the handrail running the length of the corridor, glared at them and then stuck her tongue out. The care worker smiled, rolled her eyes again and showed the palms of her hands apologetically, but Xavi shook his head, waved the apology away, dismissing it with his own half smile, and then turned to the door leading to the stairs.

'Still broken,' said Xavi pointing to the notice on the lift doors. 'Two weeks now. Need to get that fixed. Lot of old people visit here. Probably putting people off coming.'

'How often do you come?' asked Axel.

'Every week now. Used to often come twice or maybe three times a week.'

'That's a lot. That's very good of you.'

Xavi gave a shrug, held the stair door open for Axel and then followed him up the stairs to the third floor, Xavi's boots with slow heavy steps thudding around the corridor, Axel's trainers and light steps providing quick, soft beats as a contrast. Neither of them mentioned the smell from the corridor: bleach and disinfectant, but still sometimes unable to cover the slight stale smell coming from one or two half open doors. Although the staff kept on top of it, it was difficult to get rid of the smell completely. Anyway, Xavi was used to it and didn't give it a second thought.

The third floor was quite different. The walls were empty apart from notices showing what to do in the event of a fire and three landscape paintings of the local area. Four spare chairs were spread out along the corridor. The smell was more pervasive, accompanied by something else which Xavi had never been able to work out.

Axel turned left but was stopped by Xavi. 'No, This way Axel. We're looking for number thirty-eight. At the end.'

The door to thirty-eight was wide open. Xavi went in first and when Axel came in and stood to one side, he noted the change in Xavi's face as it lit up. There was a big, broad smile, showing even teeth, slightly yellowed with nicotine stains, wide eyes and bushy eyebrows reaching as high as they could.

But it wasn't enough. Axel saw Xavi's smile slip for a split second as the figure in the chair turned to watch them with no recognition and then the pain almost shone through – almost – but it was quickly replaced by the smile again. Genuine or not, it worked, thought Axel, trying to think what it meant and also what expression he should use.

'Hola, Rosa,' Xavi stepped forward and touched Rosa lightly on the knee. 'How are you today?' He turned to Axel and flicked his head beckoning him forward. 'Axel is here to see you. You remember Axel, your grandson. Come to see you. See how you are.'

Axel placed a hand on Rosa's shoulder. 'Hi, Grandma Rosa, nice to see you. How are you doing today?'

Rosa didn't move. She continued staring straight ahead. Staring at the far wall. Her grey hair was tied neatly back in a bun and she wore a heavy green cardigan buttoned right up to her long neck. Her small open face had only shallow wrinkles and she held her head high, lips clamped shut, long thin hands crossed on her lap. Her skin had a bluish white tinge to it that seemed to overly reflect the light from the large window to her right.

Xavi motioned to the single bed in the corner. 'Have a seat, Axel.' Axel walked across and sat down gingerly on the bed. It was neatly made with the duvet folded and he didn't want to mess it up.

'I'll get a chair,' said Xavi. He went into the corridor and returned seconds later with a low-backed wooden chair. He placed the chair next to Rosa, sat down, then reached across to hold her hand. 'So, Rosa, old girl. How are you doing? Food still okay? We had trouble parking. Lots of cars here today. Got wet too. Quite a walk across the car park. Actually, we ran because it was raining and nearly got soaked. Another few seconds and we would really have got soaked. Much better day yesterday. Hot though. To be honest, too hot even for me. And you know how I like the heat. I see the flowers are doing well.' He turned his head to look at a vase of white lilies sitting on a chest of drawers. Axel followed his gaze. 'Brought them last week and they're just coming out now,' said Xavi, searching for some symbolism of hope for Axel's benefit.

Rosa sat still, unblinking.

'Have you been down to the community lounge today, Rosa?' Xavi said. 'Are you okay for sweets? I know you like your mints. Nice big television in the community lounge. I bet they have a good film on this afternoon.' He looked at the window. 'Still raining. Going to get soaked again, Axel and me. Good for the garden though, eh? Wish I had a garden. I'd like to dig and think about what to plant. Think about the seasons. Not too much digging though, eh? Nice to sit out in the garden. Not today though. I think I might bring some roses next time. What do you think? Roses? Nice big red roses.' The sentences nearly outrunning his tongue in their hurry to fill the space with big emphatic syllables jostling for position, stalling the awkwardness of dead silence.

Axel looked from Xavi to Rosa and back again. So, this is what you have to do, he thought to himself, just keep the words coming.

Rosa pulled her hand away gently. She continued staring straight ahead but began a gurgling noise deep down in her throat.

Axel leaned forward, frowning. 'You, okay? Grandma?' He looked at Xavi, relieved at having something to say. 'Is she okay Uncle Xavi?'

'Yes, okay,' said Xavi. 'She gets like this from time to time.'

'What is it?'

'She has difficulty breathing sometimes.'

'She's a lot worse than the last time I saw her.'

Xavi nodded. His nostrils flared for a moment.

'I ... I never really found out what it is you know,' Axel gazed at his grandmother. His words ached out and he felt his cheek burning. 'I mean, I know it's some kind of dementia but she's always been ill as far as I can remember.'

'Huntington's disease.'

'What's that? I mean I've heard of Huntington's disease but don't really know ...'

'It's inherited. Causes neurons in the brain to degenerate. Usually diagnosed between the age of thirty and fifty.' Xavi looked at Rosa. He'd explained this a thousand times. 'People with it progressively lose their ability to basically look after themselves. Seems that the neurons in the brain lose their way to communicate with each other. She's ... unravelling ... bit by bit.'

'It's inherited?'

'Yes, but not definitely inherited. There's a fifty per cent chance of passing it on to children. And twenty-five per cent to grandchildren. And it usually doesn't affect the carrier.'

'I'm not thirty yet, I –' Axel stopped, embarrassed at his self-interest in front of Rosa.

'It's okay Axel. You've been tested when you were a baby. You're okay. And your mum. And your sister Amber. You're all okay.' Xavi flashed Axel what he hoped was a discreet comforting smile.

Axel let his gaze roam around the room, thinking, deciding what to say.

'So, it's down to that time in Spain. In the civil war,' Axel eventually announced to the duvet. 'Great Grandma Emily and that affair that no-one talks about. That's where she must have got the disease that she passed on to Grandma Rosa. From the guy she was having an affair with. That's right, isn't it? Lots of affairs in our family.' He looked at his grandma. 'And one-night stands that produce my mum.'

'Lot of things happened back then in Spain.' Xavi said quickly. 'Tough times. Dangerous times. People didn't know if they would survive. So, some people found comfort from wherever they could get it.'

'So, Edergran Emily fell for a guy in Spain. We still don't know what happened to him, eh?'

'No, nobody knows. It happened so quickly. He was on the front line. He went away and didn't come back. Probably killed.'

'Probably?'

'Well, definitely then. Thousands died. Hundreds of thousands.' Xavi shifted in his chair and turned his head to stare pointedly at Axel.

'Do we know who he was?' Axel asked. 'Where he came from?'

'No, we don't know.' The words came out spiked and tight. 'Your great grandma didn't speak about it.'

Axel glanced at Rosa and frowned again.

'It's okay,' said Xavi. 'She doesn't know what's going on. She can't understand. We can talk over her. Been like this for months.'

'Will she …? How long?' A lump rattled in Axel's throat making the words scrape.

Xavi tilted his head and gave it a little shake. 'To be honest, no one really knows. This could last for years.'

Axel scrunched his face up. 'Who pays for all this?'

'Your great grandma and me … and your mum. We help out.'

'Do *you* get help?'

'A little.' Xavi flashed a smile at Axel and then straightened his face quickly. 'No need to worry. We can manage. We have to.'

Rosa moved her hand and raised her head a fraction. 'Blue, blue, by blue, by blue.' She mumbled the words and dribbled a little as she spoke them but they were discernible. 'Blue, blue, by blue.'

Xavi watched the surprise on Axel's face as he turned to his grandma. 'She often says this,' said Xavi. 'Over and over again. They think it can be for security or reassurance … or something. They think it could be the last stages of familiarity … or so they tell us.'

'By blue, by blue, by blue. Blue, by blue, by blue.' Rosa continued. Xavi pulled a tissue from a box at her feet and wiped her mouth. She started gurgling again, still staring straight ahead.

'You know who she was named after don't you?' said Xavi.

'I think so. Some philosopher or other, wasn't it?'

'Great Grandma Emily's favourite. Rosa Luxemburg. German. From the old country, obviously. Jewish, obviously. A great socialist revolutionary, obviously. Assassinated in Berlin in 1919.'

'Obviously.'

Xavi gave a small laugh. 'Just seems to fit the story of your great grandma, doesn't it? Naming her daughter after a Marxist agitator. Just like her.'

'Suppose so.'

'I often think of Rosa Luxemburg when I come to visit your grandma. Not that she was anything like Rosa Luxemburg, or even your great grandma.' Xavi wiped Rosa's lips again. 'I looked her up. A famous saying of Rosa Luxemburg was: "Those who do not move do not notice their chains". That saying goes around my head all the time when I am here. Seems ironic now, eh? Since your Grandma Rosa hardly moves at all.'

Long seconds passed silently, apart from the deep-throated gurgling of Rosa. Xavi was comfortable with it but Axel fidgeted at first and then joined his grandma in staring at the wall.

'Did nobody try?' said Axel, his voice falling to a whisper. 'Did nobody try to contact the guy?'

'Do you mean Great Grandma Emily's ...?'

'Yes, him.'

'Of course.'

'What happened?'

'Nothing happened. He couldn't be found. Lots of people couldn't be found. You remember I was very young at the time but from what I can remember, I think letters were sent, military units were contacted.'

'But they gave up.'

'I don't know what you mean by *they*. Your great grandma was by herself. Her parents wanted nothing to do with it. People were just ... not found. Even to this day there are still mass graves being uncovered. People spend lifetimes looking for their loved ones: fathers, brothers, sisters, mothers.'

'Was he British? Spanish?'

'I don't know.' Xavi spoke with slow deliberation, trying to hide his exasperation. 'Your great grandma never really spoke about him.'

'All those years you were living with her.' Axel shrugged and opened up the palms of his hands. 'You never talked about it.'

'Good Lord, no, no, she never wanted to.'

'Maybe he was an International Brigader. They must have records.'

'We never talked about it Axel. We *never* talked about it Your great Grandma Emily tried to forget it.' The spikiness returned.

'Wasn't she upset about the disease. He must have passed it on to her and then Grandma Rosa?'

Xavi raised both eyebrows as far as they could go. 'Of course she was. But it was no use. He couldn't be contacted. Like I said, he disappeared like thousands of others. Impossible to trace. She tried to forget. It's better than having something eat away at you all these years.'

Axel wanted to say, like Grandma Rosa, but he stopped himself.

'Blue, blue, by the blue, by blue, by the blue.' They both turned to Rosa. Her gaze had dropped to the floor.

They sat in silence again. The only noise was the traffic outside and the rasping, gurgling of Rosa

'Maybe we can go now,' said Xavi, smoothing down Rosa's cardigan. He turned to Axel. 'Is that okay?'

'Yes, yes, okay. Fine by me.'

Xavi put the chair back in the corridor, came back into the room and bent over Rosa. He took her hand. 'We have to go now Rosa. We're off to see your mother, Emily. I'll come again soon.' He kissed Rosa's forehead and walked to the door.

Axel placed a hand on Rosa's shoulder. 'Bye then grandma.'

Rosa stared through them as they left.

Once outside in the corridor Axel gave Xavi a puzzled look. 'I didn't know we were going to see Eldergran Emily.'

'Seemed to be a good idea. She doesn't live far from here.'

'So, it's visiting old folks' day, is it?' Axel tried a wide-eyed lopsided grin.

Xavi stopped and Axel had to turn to face him. 'No, it's not.' Xavi pulled himself up. 'It's paying respect to your relatives. To the people who love you and care about you. What's wrong with that?'

There was a glint in Xavi's eye that Axel hadn't seen before. He'd never seen Xavi angry. Never. Something had happened in the last few minutes and he knew his next few words would have to be the right ones.

'No, nothing wrong at all,' Axel began. 'I was just a bit surprised. I didn't know I was...' He was going to say *summoned* but just in time changed it, '... expected.'

'You haven't seen her for a long time either.' Xavi gave him a judgemental stare.

'Yes, you're right, we're in the area we should ...'

'She asked me to bring you after we've seen Rosa.'

'She did?'

'Yes, she did. She wants to give you something.'

'What?'

'I'll let her tell you.' Xavi nodded to him, letting Axel know that whatever had happened in the last few seconds was now over.

*

Twenty minutes later Axel and Xavi were standing outside the door to Emily's small terrace house in the Jesmond district of Newcastle. The rain had stopped and was replaced by searing heat. The garden was completely covered in flagstones with six large plant pots filled with hardy, tall evergreen shrubs.

Axel waited for the doorbell to be rung but instead Xavi produced a key from his jacket pocket and opened the front door. Xavi noticed Axel's slight surprise. 'We agreed I could keep this when I moved out years ago. Good to have a spare, saves a lot of time in case we need to get in quickly ... oh, and...' Xavi jabbed the key at Axel, 'best not to mention the... affair. She doesn't like to think about it too much.'

Axel nodded and followed Xavi into the long entrance hall. Cream coloured walls, two coats hanging on bright, silver hooks just by the staircase and stairlift.

'That you Xavi?' A strong, firm voice came from the end of the hallway.

'Good Lord, I hope so. If it's not me then it's probably a burglar,' Xavi called back.

'I'm in the lounge ... I'm all alone ... and I've got nothing to steal.' The voice was even louder, followed by a deep chuckle.

Xavi opened the lounge door, led Axel in and then the two of them stood facing Emily who was sitting in a brown leather armchair with a small table to the side. She was fiddling with a huge Rubik's cube but put it down on the table when they came in. Axel noted her slim figure and how white her hair was, pushed back from a round, remarkably smooth face. She looked nothing like ninety-six years old. Similar to Rosa the wrinkles that were there were not deep, and bright blue, only slightly rheumy eyes darted about looking each of them over. She was wearing a red T-shirt with a picture of Yggdrasil the mythological Norse sacred tree on it and a long-sleeved blue work shirt open over a pair of green jeans. Her feet were bare. She gave both of them in turn a wide, full lipped smile, then fluttered a hand about in welcome and several silver bangles clinked and caught the light.

'Good, good, you got him to come then?' said Emily. 'Sit, please sit.'

Xavi motioned to a sofa for them both to sit on. Axel sat furthest away from his great grandma and stared about the long rectangular room. Bare beige walls, tall indoor thin leafed wide plants, a heavy dark wooden table in the far corner. A tall set of drawers to one side of the window. Two brightly coloured rugs in front of an enormous television bracketed on the wall where the fireplace should have been. The room had a distinct smell of cigar smoke and was very warm.

'So, how do you like my room, Axel? You haven't been here for quite a while?' She waved her hand again. 'Sorry ... that wasn't meant as a criticism.'

'Well, you're right eldergran. I haven't been her for a long time. I should come more often. And the room is ...'

'Bare?' said Emily.

Axel smiled. 'Well, yes, I suppose bare sums it up. I don't remember it being as bare.'

'Good. That's just the way I like it. Can't be bothered with a lot of fuss and frippery. Too much dusting.'

'No photos?' Axel said.

Emily tapped her head. 'Got my memories up here. I remember everything. The memories are always there. Admittedly, sometimes I don't want the memories. But they're always there. Filling me up. Saturating. I don't need reminders on the wall. I don't like to dwell on old photographs ... they just make me sad mostly. So, I'll just keep remembering what I want to remember. Until I can't … but not just yet anyway, eh Xavi?'

Xavi gave an indulgent laugh. 'No, not just yet. Still got all your marbles.'

'So, how are you, Axel? I hear you're going through a bit of a rough time. Your mum says you're a bit depressed. Not wanting to go out. Not wanting to see anybody. A bit lost? That's not good. Young lad like you should be out and about having fun.'

Axel looked up quickly. 'Wow, you don't mess about do you eldergran? Straight to the point.'

'What's the use of not getting to the point?' said Emily. 'Just wastes time. Might as well get on with it … and at my age… I haven't got time to waste.'

'So, what's mum been saying then? I must be in a terrible state. Coming apart at the seams.'

Emily gave him a big smile and then laughed. 'She's just concerned that's all. She wants to help but I don't think she knows how. At least that's what I think. She says the house is a bit difficult with you and Amber these days. You, with your head all mixed up and Amber going around like a gangster's moll.'

Axel shook his head and twisted his mouth. 'What?'

Emily pointed at him. 'It's true is it not? She seems to be getting some very strange ideas these days from what you mother says. I don't know where she gets them from. Maybe you could help your mum and talk to Amber.'

'Me!'

'Yes, of course you,' Emily said, using the softest voice she could find. 'You're both the same age. Talk to your sister. Engage. See if you can help. And maybe Amber can help you.'

'I don't think that'll work. She hates me. She makes that perfectly clear.' Axel stared hard at the floor.

'That's not true,' Emily frowned. 'She's your own flesh and blood. She doesn't hate you.'

'She does. She hates everybody.' There was a slight hiss to Axel's voice. 'To be honest, I would help if I could but she's way out of my league.'

'Out of your league? That's a bit defeatist Axel. You're equals. You're just as good as her … or just as unhinged … or just as lost.' Emily leaned forward and stared at him from under knotted eyebrows. 'But what about you?

Axel looked at Xavi and then at Emily. He pulled his head back. 'I thought this was a nice family visit. I didn't realise I was going to be cross-examined.'

'We just want to help, if we can,' said Xavi, unfolding the words rather than speaking them.

'Are you still taking those pills?' said Emily. 'You know that's not good.'

Axel shuffled in his seat and gave a tiny two centimetre shake of his head. 'No, I've stopped taking them. They didn't help. Didn't help at all.' He held Emily's gaze. 'I'll be okay. You don't need to worry. I'll get myself sorted out. You don't have to worry about me.'

Emily settled back, blinked once and then brought out her words with soft deliberation. 'But that's the thing you see. We do worry about you. You shouldn't keep everything bottled up and secret. Try and tell us what's happening so we can help.'

'Bottled up? Secret?' Axel stared at Emily. 'That's rich.'

'What do you mean?' said Emily widening her eyes and pulling a face.

Xavi put a hand on Axel's arm. 'Axel, no.'

'What do you mean? Say it,' said Emily, not unkindly.

'I mean … I mean … the secrets in this family. The things we never talk about.'

'What things don't we talk about?' said Emily. 'Specifically, what things?'

'You know what!' Axel's voice was rising. The words spilled out jaggedly. 'Specifically. Affairs in Spain. Specifically. And no-one seems to want to know or find out about it. It's all just hidden away. Specifically. One-night stands. Put to one side. Specifically.'

Emily reached down to the small table by her chair and picked up a pack of Hamlet cigars. She took one from the pack already unwrapped then put it to one side of her mouth and lit it with a lighter from her pocket. She sucked hard on the cigar, blew out the smoke and took another drag before holding it up and tapping the ash onto a small white plate on the table.

Emily turned to Axel. 'Would you like some biscuits?' she said. 'I've got custard creams and Viennese whirls. I ate the last of the chocolate hobnobs yesterday. I love them, everything's just a bit tighter, don't you think – like a digestive that's been to the gym.'

'No,' said Axel, expressionless. Slightly annoyed, he wasn't going to indulge her by laughing at her joke. 'I don't want a biscuit … thank you.'

Emily took another drag on her cigar and then laughed. A great, big bellowing laugh which bounced around the room looking for some place to land but couldn't find one so continued ricocheting around. Xavi and Axel looked at each other, unsettled.

Emily recovered and began staring into space, still smiling. 'He died Axel,' she said, finally. 'He just died. That's what happened in those days. A brief fling. Weeks. And then he died. And that was that. Nothing to get all hung up about. That's what happened. Nothing to talk about.' She shovelled in as much pathos as she could muster.

Axel stood up, walked to the end of the room and looked out of the window. 'But we don't know anything about him. Don't even know where he came from.' He twisted round. 'And you must have been upset and furious. When you found out. When you found out about Grandma Rosa and the disease he'd given her.'

'Of course, of course I was angry. I *was* bloody furious' Emily glanced at Xavi. 'But it was too late then. It was years later when we found out. Your grandma must have been thirty or more when we found out about the disease. Nothing could be done about it. And he was gone.'

Axel spread his arms wide. 'But who was he? We don't know his name? You never mention him.' His voice was becoming even louder, staccato and shrill.

Emily stared at Axel. Her face suddenly became younger and she smiled rapturously at him. 'He was just a man, Axel,' she said slowly. 'I can't even remember much about him. It was hundreds of years ago. Lifetimes ago. He wasn't British. We were together for a few weeks and then he was killed.'

'You know that for definite, do you?' grunted Axel.

'Of course,' said Emily. 'At the battle of Brunete. In July '37'.

'You remember where he died,' Axel snorted. 'You even remember the month that he died ... but you can't remember his name or which country he was from.'

'You should let it be Axel,' said Xavi quickly. 'No sense in dragging up the past. This is about you and how we can help if we can.'

'But that *would* help!' said Axel, his voice quavering with the effort of trying not to shout. 'Knowing where I came from. Knowing where mum came from. Knowing who we came from. It's not too much to ask, is it? Eldergran - partner? Don't know. Grandma - partner? Don't know. My mum - partner? We don't know. Not very good at hanging on to men in this family, are we? Where've they all gone – abducted by aliens? '

Emily laughed again, barking out a loud, uproarious roar, making her choke on the cigar smoke in her mouth and forcing out an inadvertent fart that sounded like a squeaking clarinet. Axel and Xavi twisted round to look at her with surprise and Axel finally managed a smile.

'Oh, I do beg your pardon,' said Emily still giggling. 'I'm terribly prone to bottom burps. Not an age thing either. I've always been prone. Can be quite embarrassing.'

'Well, at least it seems to have broken the ice,' said Xavi.

'I do hope so,' said Emily. 'We can't have bad feeling in the family.' She looked at Axel. 'Especially with the men. There's not many left to go around.' She gave another rowdy, mischievous laugh.

Axel shook his head. 'It actually isn't that funny. You're hiding something, aren't you? We deserve to know. We deserve to know everything. You can't keep pushing things away. You can't keep pushing us away. We deserve to know.'

'That's better Axel,' said Emily. 'This is what you need to do. Come out fighting. When the flames are all around you – eat the fire.'

'Oh, never mind all that eldergran. It's not metaphors I want. It's just what I've been saying. Always secrets. How am I supposed to know where I came from. Who I'm related to. Nobody talks. That's what gets to me. Nobody talks about it and everything is covered up.'

'But does it matter that much?' said Emily. 'It's who you are now that counts. And if you really –'

'It's not just that though, is it Axel?' Xavi interrupted.

'What d'you mean?' Axel, scrunched his face up, bracing himself.

'You can't blame the family all the time,' continued Xavi. 'You have to stand up for yourself. You have to decide what you want to do. I don't mean to be harsh. Good Lord, you must know we all love you. But you don't seem to be able to settle. You can't hold down a job. You decide to leave college. You seem to blame everything on family history —'

'Pfff … what family history?' snapped Axel. 'We haven't got any family history.'

Emily smiled at Axel and pointed her cigar at him. 'You're frightened.'

Axel puffed his cheeks up and blew out a long breath. 'What? Of what?'

'Of everything,' said Emily. 'And I can't blame you. Life can be very frightening. Just living can be scary but like Xavi says, you have to take control. You've got freedom of choice and that can be both appealing and terrifying … you know it's often said that man was never so free as under the Nazis.'

Axel straightened. 'That's just crazy.'

'Not really,' Emily leaned forward. 'You didn't have to think under the Nazis. Under any totalitarian regime. People were actively encouraged not to think. People were told what to do. Choice was taken away. Your mind was clear, uncluttered. Day to day actions were thought out for you. Your mind was free. As long as you didn't tell what you were thinking about your mind could wander off to wherever it wanted. Everyone thinks they want to be free. But do they really? Is it such a good thing? You had total –'

'So, you want me to join the army!' Axel broke in, nodded to her and gave a sarcastic smile, then came across to sit on the sofa again.

'No, of course not,' said Emily. 'Unless you want to. And that's the point. I'm … we're … just saying that … we all have anxieties about being free because of all the responsibilities of having the power of choice and the worry of making the wrong choices. We don't know which way to turn. And I'm afraid that seems to be you, Axel. It appears that you have a good dose of the angst, bless you. You need to find your guilt. What a relief it is to find out what is hurting and driving you.

What it is that you think you're culpable of? That's the question you should be asking yourself. You can't keep living in the dark. It might make things disappear for a while but it won't make them go away.'

There was a long silence broken only by Emily sucking hard on her cigar and blowing out smoke, lips pursed, forming a small round hole to control the stream, pushing it away from her face.

Axel watched the smoke column for a few seconds and then turned to Emily. 'And what about you eldergran?'

'Me?'

'What about all those years? Why didn't you find someone else? Did you find *your* guilt? What about your choices?'

'Exactly. It was my choice. I wasn't frightened by any choice. I embraced it. It was what I wanted to do. It was how I *chose* to live.' She pulled her head up searching for something. 'We are condemned to be free … but some of us can cope better than others. I think life is made unbearable by lack of meaning. Doesn't matter what your circumstances are you have to have some meaning in life.'

Axel folded his arms and looked at her pointedly. 'And were you happy?' It was an important question for him.

A long pause.

'Not necessarily,' Emily said eventually. 'Not all the time. It's probably good not to be happy all the time. You can become complacent. But I was content most of the time. Anyway, I had the family. They made me happy. And I suppose the beauty of that kind of situation is that I could retreat when I wanted to. Also, I had my work … and I had my memories of Spain. That was the most wonderful time of my life.' She looked at Xavi and he gave a small, almost indiscernible nod. 'The memories are with me always.' She flicked a hand at the bare walls. 'I don't need any aide memoires. Sometimes they can crush the memories. Images can trick. I have it all in my head and in my heart. All the voices.'

Axel stared at her. He hesitated for a moment. 'But what about love?'

Emily pulled her head back. 'Love? Love? Depends what you mean by love. Oh, I've loved Axel. And been loved. I've loved the family. I've loved my work. I've loved all the people I've met. I've loved that I've … tried.' She tilted her head and smiled almost coquettishly, disarming him.

'*Tried?*' said Axel. The word she used was long and feather soft to go with her smile. It was quite a combination. He knew it was difficult to rage against her when she did that.

'Tried to be kind. Tried to do the right thing. In Spain we tried to stop bad things happening. We didn't succeed but we showed everyone that some people were willing stand up and fight. *You* have to stand and fight. For yourself. You have to. You need a purpose.'

'That's okay for you eldergran.' Axel looked at her and blew off a tidy snort. 'You're hard. It's all a bit much for softies like me. It's all a bit overwhelming. I'm not sure that I can.'

Emily looked across at Xavi and caught his attention. 'In the top drawer, Xavi. The blue leather box.'

Xavi pulled himself up and went across to the set of drawers. He opened the top drawer and took out the box then walked back to Emily, gave it to her and stood by her chair.

'I've got this for you Axel,' Emily put down her cigar on the white plate, unfastened the brass catch and pulled back the lid, then stopped and looked at Axel. 'If you'll accept it. I'd really like you to take it.'

'What is it?'

'Two flags, Axel.' Emily brought out a silk cloth from the box and held it up. It was about the size of a small towel. 'Two flags sewn together. Two flags to show a connection. To show what can be achieved when people come together to help each other. Two flags to show that people all over the world will always come together to do the right thing.' She looked at Axel again. 'I'm sorry, I had a better speech prepared but I can't remember it. Anyway, you get the picture. It's very important to me. It was given to me in Paris when I left the brigade.' She glanced at Xavi. 'Muy importante. On one side is the flag of the Spanish republic, the flag of the people.' The flag had three broad horizontal stripes, the top red, the middle yellow and the bottom dark purple.' She turned the cloth over. 'On the other side is the flag of the International Brigades.' This side showed a red background with a yellow three-pointed star in the middle. Above the star was written in bold yellow capitals *BRIGADA INTERNACIONALE.* Below the star was a clenched fist in gold surrounded by the words *15th battalion volunteers,* also in gold.

'But why do you want to give it to me?' said Axel. 'Why don't you keep it if it's that important to you. Or why don't you give it to Amber or my mum … or Xavi?'

'Because *you* need it. You. I'm sure it will help you. Think of it as a totem. A talisman. *Your* aide memoire. Something to remind you that you always have a choice. And all you can do is choose the best way you can. Don't get too hung up on your decision … but make a decision. Sometimes you just have to jump and hope for the best. These flags are about decisions made, ways chosen, good decisions, or at least good intentioned decisions. That's all we can do Axel … have good intentions. Make mistakes. When you make a mistake, it shows everyone that it's okay to be vulnerable. You can help other people to be free, to be vulnerable, to be more relaxed. If you won't think of yourself, think of what you can do for others… just by trying. We can all be… mutually supportive. Just by being light. By being vulnerable.'

'I'm … I'm not sure,' said Axel. His face dulled.

Emily laughed and produced another broad smile. 'That's exactly my point Axel. Nobody's sure of anything. Jump in. Jump in and I promise you you'll start swimming. Take it and look after it. At the very least it'll remind you of today and what we were talking about.'

Axel pushed his hands deep into his pockets. 'If it's that important to you, maybe you should keep it.'

'It *is* very important to me,' said Emily. 'It's one of the most important things that I have. Almost sacred. It has been my talisman. It has helped me … and protected me. But I want you to have it. Specifically. Specifically, you.' She smiled again. 'You care about this family. And I think you need these flags. You need them now. They need to be looked after and be able to look after someone else. To help them. To help them remember which way to go. It has to be now. Please take it now. I'm worried that it will be lost when the house is cleared. I don't want it to be just thrown away.'

'What d'you mean? Are you moving?' Axel said quickly, frowning.

'You could put it that way,' said Emily.

'But where to? You've always lived here'

Emily put her head to one side and softened her eyes, but this time not flirtatious. The smile was still there but deeper now, comforting and explaining all at the same time. Her eyes drilled into him, sad and intense and reassuring.

'What? Oh!' The sudden understanding slapped into Axel. Like having a door slammed in his face. He stared back at Emily. Trying hard to think of something to say but unable to. 'What?' was all he could manage. He noticed everything was quite still, as if the room was holding its breath. He heard a grating noise, throaty, stifled, and looked at Xavi. Xavi's eyes gleamed and he was staring hard at the wall.

'Don't worry about him,' said Emily, matter of fact. 'He always gets like this these days. Never used to be like this, I think he's grown into it. Very emotional is Xavi. Hates talking about it, bless him. Water oozes out of him. Weak tear ducts and a weak bladder. Never willingly passes a toilet these days, do you Xavi?'

Xavi let the cough go, quickly rubbed his eyes with a finger and thumb and placed a soft hand on the back of Emily's chair, too afraid to touch her. 'But it's my choice Emily. My decision.' He mimicked a cross face and laughed lightly. 'I can't help it. It's the way I am. I haven't got a stone for a heart … like you.' He tried another laugh, louder, but it didn't quite work.

Emily turned to smile at him and placed her hand gently on his. 'I know Xavi. I know. But you'll have to try harder. Boxes of tissues are expensive.'

Now they both laughed and Xavi rubbed his eyes again.

'But you're looking fit,' said Axel. 'You look fine. Well. Fit. Fit and healthy.' The words sounded metallic as if he'd forgotten what to say halfway through and relied on predictive text.

'Well, appearances can be deceptive,' said Emily. 'We can't go on for ever. I do feel fine but that's not what the doctors are saying.' She paused again to allow Axel and Xavi to compose themselves. 'Anyway, back to business …'

'I'm sorry, I didn't know,' said Axel.

'No, we've kept it quiet,' she said looking at Xavi again. 'No sense dwelling on it … and when one gets to a certain age one doesn't want to make a fool of oneself. Just get it over with. And it's our secret.' She nodded slowly at Axel, slowly and deliberately. 'No sense in other people getting all upset. Your mum for instance, right?' She made a point of staring at him for too long without blinking to help emphasise the meaning. 'No sense in getting your mum upset, *right*?' she repeated. She waited for him to nod and then folded the flags again and held them out for him. 'Please take them Axel. It would mean so much to me if you take them and promise to look after them.'

Axel made to shrug but then thought better of it after what had just been said. He realised how important this was for her. He moved the tip of his nose up and down, a tiny movement, reached across and took the flags from Emily. 'Thank you. I will look after them. I promise.'

'No, no. Thank you Axel.' Emily's face tightened and became unreadable. 'Thank you for looking after them. I know they will help you.' She straightened and gave Axel another steely look. '*It's not a trivial thing.*' The words came out with delicate, low precision, almost a whisper. She allowed a few seconds to pass and then quickly reverted to her broad smile. 'Well then, you'd best be off. I've got one or two things to do.' She picked up her cigar, smouldering on the plate. 'I hope I see you again soon.'

'Oh, the audience is over then.' Axel said, hoping to end on a bright, light-hearted note and hoping that his eldergran took it the way it was intended.

'Bah,' she laughed. 'And take this soppy old man with you.'

'Okay, this soppy old man will drive you home Axel,' said Xavi as he walked to the door and then waited for Axel as he gave Emily a kiss on the cheek

'See you later eldergran,' Axel said quietly. He stopped for a moment and gave her a long look so that she totally understood what he wasn't saying. 'I've enjoyed my grilling and ... I'll take good care of your flags.'

'They're your flags now,' said Emily. 'They'll take good care of you. And just as important, take good care of yourself.'

Axel followed Xavi along the corridor and out into the street.

Xavi stopped suddenly. 'Oh, nearly forgot, here's the key, just wait in the car Axel. I need to remind your great gran about something.'

'What?'

'Oh, it's nothing. Just about some shopping I'm doing for her next week. I won't be a minute.'

Axel walked back to the Volkswagen Polo parked on the other side of the street while Xavi went back into the house.

Emily was standing by the window watching Axel and smoking her cigar when Xavi came into the room. 'Hello Xavi, long time no see. What's the matter?'

'That was tricky.'

'You mean, *the affair*.'

'Of course, that's what I mean.' Xavi shrugged. 'And your great grandson isn't stupid. He can see you're hiding something. He had you talking about it. I was worried you were going to go too far.'

Emily laughed. 'I think the timely fart diverted his attention.'

'He'll continue.'

'You think?' Emily blew out smoke.

'I do think.' Xavi frowned and stared about the room. 'Good Lord, I do think … all the time.'

'Well don't. Don't worry.'

'But I do worry.'

'Don't. Everything is fine. No-one will ever know. It was a long time ago. It's all forgotten with. It's our secret.'

'If you say so. But we have to be careful. You have to be careful.'

'Bless you, always looking out for me.'

'Okay then,' Xavi said. 'I'd better go. Axel is waiting for me to take him home.' He went to the door then stopped and called over his shoulder before leaving, 'I'll see you in few days.'

Emily watched through the window again as Xavi's car pulled away. She looked up and down the street: cars passing; two young women, probably students, ambling along wearing shorts, big sunglasses, easy, enjoying the baking hot day; an elderly man with his dog, standing by the corner, taking a rest, the heat getting to them. She took another drag on her cigar and blew the smoke on to the window pane. The glass fogged up, obscuring the boiling hot street.

She always hated hot days. The suffocating, sweltering, dazzling air. The glass cleared and her mind drifted back as it often did to the baking hot day almost eighty years before. She stood for a long time gazing with unseeing eyes out of the window. She sucked hard on her cigar and pulled her lips back into what looked like a smile. A long, luxurious, satisfied smile. Her eyes however were still and cold.

Chapter five

Monday, 26ᵗʰ July 1937,

Brunete town, 24 kilometres west of Madrid, Spain.

'Okay, that seems fine. Just keep the arm up You can go now – and hurry.' Emily Edelman cut the frayed edge of the bandage around the boy's arm and tested his forehead for any signs of fever. Her hand came away wet and she wiped the perspiration off on her pants. He was even younger than she was but the scars on his cheek and neck made him look much older. His khaki shirt was torn, stained with sweat patches and he stank. But then again so did she and she couldn't tell who was the worst. He stared back at her blank faced and uncomprehending. 'Oh, sorry, sorry. I'm tired. Vamos, vamos, Rapidamente, rapidamente. Go. Go.' The boy nodded, gave a quick smile. She wanted to say 'mi camarada', a small thing but indicating shared fellowship and hopefully giving encouragement to fellow frontliners. But it was too late, he was gone.

Emily put the scissors back in her pocket and walked to the back of the makeshift medical unit which was only two kilometres behind the front line. The battle for Brunete had ended indecisively the previous day and the republicans were pulling back to Madrid after nationalist counter attacks. Thousands had died and there were an equally huge number of casualties. She was the only one left of the team of three nurses and one doctor in her sector. Her job, sixteen hours a day, was to patch up the less seriously wounded. The rest of the team had been taken to Madrid to help with more urgent cases needing surgery.

The place had been thrown together in the last few days of the battle as the frontline changed. A few wooden beams reaching across walls of sandbags and covered with tarpaulin. Two squares had been cut out to act as windows but not too large because it got very cold at night and then they had to rely on a fire and lanterns for light. The room was long enough to lie four men end to end and three end to end across the width. There were no beds. A large table was in the middle of the room with two chairs and spare sandbags to sit on. An empty, metal cartridge box held bottles of disinfectant. In another corner a smaller table held some enamel plates and mugs along with rolls of bandages and items of painkillers, some spare packets of cigarettes, a few cocaine tablets for pain relief and even fewer bottles of morphine, most of which had been taken back to Madrid. Another metal cartridge box was upturned and a fire was still burning inside. A small hole had been cut in one end and the steaming kettle on top was used to sterilise the equipment along with the fire itself. The disinfectant was saved for open wounds.

Emily took a drink of warm water from a mug and then picked up a hard, corn husk broom and began sweeping the floor. An explosion could be heard in the distance, maybe three or four miles away she thought, but she took no notice and continued sweeping the grasses and soil from the earth floor out through the doorway. It was stifling inside the unit. She wore her khaki military shirt loose over her trousers with a red bandana tied around her neck to catch the rivulets of sweat from the broad forehead of her oval face, now with darkened baggy eyes through lack of sleep. She flicked at her short, blonde wavy hair to chase away the flies and gave a yelp as she stood on a stone, wishing she had kept her boots on even though they made her feet hot, her woollen socks now dripping wet with sweat.

Emily brushed the last few pieces of grass away and then turned back into the unit to see to the sterilisation of her knives and needles. A sound behind stopped her and she turned to see the canvas cover being pulled aside. A tall thick-set man stooped at the entrance and then came in to the room adjusting his eyes, accustoming them to the gloom inside. He looked around for a long time, deliberately ignoring Emily.

At last. 'Hola, como estas?' said the man. His smile was far too big.

'Muy bien. Are you okay? Can I help?' said Emily, gesturing lazily, too tired to drag up the little Spanish she had learned. 'Do you need a dressing?'

'Oh, English speaking,' he said, taking off his cap and throwing it on a chair. It fell off but he didn't bother to pick it up. 'British?' He spoke with a heavy accent.

'Yes. What can I do? Are you injured?'

'No, no I'm fine. You with the British? The Saklatavla brigade?'

'Well … yes, fifteenth British International Brigade. No-one can pronounce the brigade name you mentioned, so we never use it.' Emily leant heavily on her broom, keeping a firm grip on it, wary. 'Your English is very good.'

'Thank you. Lived in London for five years. Studying to be a lawyer. Then travelled about for a year.' The smile was still there.

'I'm from Newcastle. Northern England. Do you know it?'

'No, but I've heard of it.'

'The world seemed enormous then. Tiny now. So, where are you from?'

'Budapest.' He looked at her for a response. When none came, he bent slightly forward. 'Hungary.'

Emily gave a small, tired shake of her head. 'Yes. I know.'

There was another silence as Emily looked at him, waiting for him to speak, but he avoided her gaze and looked at the clear sky through a square hole in the roof. She noticed his light green eyes framed with long eyelashes and with a slight scar at the corner of his right eye. Apart from that his face was unblemished, nearly handsome.

'Lazlo. Lazlo Kovac. Captain.' He gave another big smile, showing perfect but slightly discoloured teeth with just one canine missing from the bottom jaw. She wished he wouldn't use that smile. 'Hungarian Risolski International Brigade.' He tilted his head as a question.

'So, I'm Emily. Emily Edelman. Nurse, I suppose. Though I've had very little training. They moved the women from the frontline combatants after a directive from the republican council. The communists disagreed but were overruled.' She waved her hand. 'So, I found myself here.'

'Kept busy, eh? Hard work?

'Mostly long work,' Emily tried to study him without him noticing, wondering where this was going. 'Minor cuts and wounds. But lots of them. Serious cases are taken further back and then on to Madrid.'

'Frontline. So, you were …?

'At Jamara, back in February.'

Lazlo looked at her more carefully and raised an eyebrow. 'The battle of Jamara. Impressive.' He looked around the room again. 'And now you're here. Doing a good job no doubt, but in very primitive conditions. How old are you?'

'Nineteen.' She was beginning to feel awkward. 'I've been a postman also. Important to get the letters to and from the front. Keeps morale up.'

'Nineteen? Half my age. Yes, of course. Morale. Very important. And letters, *Muy importante para la moral.*' He widened his eyes and waved his arms wide in a flamboyant gesture. 'I like to practise my Spanish … and English, and fortunately some of it is easier than others. A piece of cake. Is that the right phrase?'

'That would do I suppose.'

'What is it called again? Forgive my English. Idiom?''

'No idea. Probably.' *What the hell do you want?*

'Anyway, postman, nurse or whatever, you're doing a good job. We need more people like you here. They need to send us hundreds more.'

'We could do with more equipment. But it has to be easy to move. We have to move fast. New policy. We have to be as near to the frontline as possible. But we get good medical information from Madrid and Barcelona.' Emily needed to keep talking. Keep everything normal. 'Our death rates are lower than in the first world war. Blood transfusion techniques and blood banks are being developed for the first time. *Muy importante para moral.*'

Lazlo grinned again. He pointed to a jug on the table. 'Is that water? May I have some? It's hot outside but it's boiling in here. I don't know how you stand it.' He poured himself some water into a mug without waiting for a reply and then frowned when he took a sip and realised how warm it was.

'We get used to it.' Emily flicked at the earth floor with her foot. She realised she was standing too still. Too stiff. And by herself. 'We have to have the fire going constantly. We don't know what's going to come through that door so I ... we ... have to be ready.' She corrected herself to show that she wasn't alone. She was. And she didn't want to be right at this moment.

'Very good. I really admire your dedication and enthusiasm ... and fearlessness. Here... all alone.'

He gave her a look which she couldn't work out. A too confident, searching look. Everything about him was over confident she thought. Maybe it was because he was much older, or maybe he just wanted to talk. But he shouldn't be here anyway if he wasn't injured. She didn't like him and she wanted him to go.

Emily took a drink from her mug on the table and stared at the fire. It needed more wood but she didn't want to turn her back to gather the sticks She was beginning to be unnerved. 'I don't think I'm capable of enthusiasm anymore ... or even to be frightened. I still believe in all this but I wish it were all over.' *What the hell does he want?*

'Yes, so many young men throwing their lives away.'

'And women.'

'Of course. Many lives wasted.'

'No. I don't want to believe that. This is good cause. The right thing. If we can stop the fascists here then we won't have to fight them again.'

Lazlo stared at her, a few seconds too long. He gave a lopsided grin. 'So … are you a Trot or a Marxist?'

She noted *Trot*. She'd heard it many times, normally used as a term of abuse by the Stalinists in the republican army. 'All Trotskyists are Marxists,' she announced

'But not all Marxists are Trotskyists.' He saluted her triumphantly with the mug.

No need for smugness at this stage of the game, thought Emily. *Why the hell doesn't he just go?*

'I'm both,' she said. 'Continual revolution. Trotsky's ideas. We can't just have a socialist state in one country. It has to spread and grow worldwide. It has to be global and it has to be permanent.'

'Very idealistic. But you do realise of course that we can't win this war.'

'We *will* win,' said Emily, taken aback slightly, although she had met defeatists and defectors before. 'We must win.' She could feel a little twitch at the side of her temple.

'We must win but we won't win.' Lazlo, blank-faced now, serious. 'Bravery like yours … is not enough. Germany and Italy send troops and planes and weapons to Franco but your country and France sign non-intervention pacts.'

'Russia helps.'

'Yes, but not enough.'

'So, why are you still here then?'

'Good question. And I don't really know the answer. I suppose I started out with ideas like yours ...' His voice trailed off. He looked up through the hole again for a few seconds and then continued. 'Anyway, we're leaving this sector immediately, falling back to Madrid. The last lorries are loading up. They said there was a medical unit here with one nurse left so I said I would come and get you.'

Emily nodded. 'Okay then. I'll try and take as much as I can. Would you be able to help me carry some things?'

'Unfortunately, no.'

'No? Why not?' She winced and darted a surprised look at him. She needed help. They were both on the same side. She searched for some kind of expression of outrage but found herself helplessly, idiotically shrugging and shaking her head. A sudden awareness was forming in her head. A bad awareness. She felt a sudden rush of blood swirling through her body and the hairs on her arms began to tingle. *This was not good.*

'Because ... because we all have needs.' He was talking very quietly. 'And there is something else I need to do. You said yourself, morale is very important. We have to keep morale up. It's a beautiful July day. Things should be creative, not destructive.'

The room became ice cold.

She wanted to be busy now. She didn't want any more of this. 'Where exactly are the lorries?' She forced the words out.

'Do you have a boyfriend back home. Someone waiting for you.' He kept his eyes on her, unwavering, his lips pulled back to something resembling a smile and she noticed his long fingers rolling backwards and forwards against his thumb.

'A husband,' she lied. 'If the war spares me.' She needed to say this because she wasn't sure what was happening. She needed empathy, some kind of rapport with him. 'The doctor will be back soon. He'll help me if you can't' A rising tide of panic was starting to come in rushing waves. She put on a huge puzzled expression and tried staring at him indignantly. Ridiculously. She knew this wouldn't be enough.

Lazlo walked towards her. He moved slowly, like a cat prowling, never taking his eyes off her, and stood centimetres away. 'Well,' he said. 'Here we are.' His gaze oozed over her, brushing against her chest, gripping her neck, forcing her to stiffen and pull her head back. She felt her skin tighten.

She thought he sounded almost apologetic. She was going to say, what do you mean? But she knew well enough what he meant. And he looked massive to her, an impossible size: huge shoulders and head, thick neck, broad chest. She forced herself to breathe. He smelled of something. Strawberries she thought for some reason.

'Don't be stupid,' she said, and then pathetically she thought, she added, 'My husband ...'

Lazlo loomed up. He spoke quietly. She hated the way he spoke quietly. It would have been better if he snarled. 'Don't scream,' he said. 'If you scream it will get very messy. And anyway, there's no-one around. We're quite alone.'

'I'm not going to bloody scream you utter bastard – *comrade*.' But a lump rattled in her throat and her voice clogged spoiling the effect of her words. She knew she was too tired to scream even if she wanted to.

She pulled the broom up across her chest, thinking of how best to use it but Lazlo lunged forward, wrenched it from her grip and threw it into the corner of the room. He was even closer now. His breath came fast and heavy and warm and she saw the fevered exhilaration in his eyes. The excited green eyes, boring into her. She could feel his gaze creeping through her veins. The eyes were all she could see now.

She tried to push him with her left hand but he was far too heavy to be moved so she backed off two paces, reached into her pocket and pulled out her scissors. She wanted to yell at him and her lips arranged themselves into word movements but no signal came from her brain. A cold terror came crawling through her stomach and tried to reach up to her throat but she was just too tired … couldn't be bothered to complete the feeling. What she really wanted to do, for some reason, was laugh. Out loud. Break the mood. It was worth a try.

Lazlo looked down at the scissors and gave that excessive smile. 'Really? You think so?' he said with a light, silk smooth voice. 'This could get messy then.' He leapt forward again, slapped her hard in the face, stunning her, and wrenched the scissors from her grip. He stared down at the scissors in his hand then back at her and gave her a long up and down look, starting with her face and then moving down to her legs and stockinged feet and then back up again, taking his time, all the time in the world. He twisted his face, not quite masking his leering lips and then walked around her, scrutinising, inspecting every detail of her. He placed the scissors very precisely on the table, gently and deliberately positioning them, giving them meticulous attention, playing with them and her. Then he turned back to her, relishing the moment. His whole body seemed to fill the room and she detected other smells for the first time: his, excited and feverish; hers, simple stark fear.

This time she allowed the terror to continue and complete its work, wanting it to numb her. The most important thing for her at this moment she realised was not to run out of things to think about. She could feel hot liquid behind her eyes. He was making her cry. How cruel, she thought. This man's cruelty was unending. On top of everything else he wanted to make her cry. She bit her tongue to stop the tears and tasted blood.

There should have been a frenzied flurry of arms and legs, kicking and punching and fighting. But she was exhausted and knew it was useless. He came forward again, put his leg behind hers, heaved her round and threw her down on to some sandbags. She forced herself to relax her whole body, making it a dead weight, and stared at him deliberately and impassively as he fumbled and tore at her shirt, not wanting to give him the satisfaction of seeing her dread and disgust. Above her she noticed that one of the wooden beams holding the roof had a crack in it almost stretching to the other side. She could see the bright blue sky through it. *That's dangerous*, she thought to herself, *could bring the whole thing down. Need to get that fixed.* And then she buried her gaze into the beam, deep, and then deeper, as deep as she could, until her eyes blurred with the effort.

Twenty minutes later she came to her senses. She hadn't passed out but was in a dazed sort of dreamlike, post anaesthetic state. She was completely naked apart from her socks. Lazlo had gone. She rolled over on to her side and found her trousers and torn shirt under the table. She was aching all over, with bruises already starting to show on her legs and arms. She forced herself up and pulled on her clothes, wincing at the effort. Suddenly feeling nauseous she turned back to the sandbags and retched over them, and kept retching.

She wiped her mouth with her sleeve, found her boots and realised that she didn't know what time it was. She knew she had to get to the lorries before the sector was overrun by the nationalist soldiers. She didn't want to fall into their hands as well.

Pulling herself up by the table she staggered across to the doorway steadying herself on a chair halfway across. There was no-one to be seen. No sign of any lorries. No sign of help. He had left her to the tender mercies of the enemy.

She went back into the unit, pulled out all of the bottles of disinfectant and painkillers and emptied them on to the floor. Then she tipped the bandages, towels, cardboard boxes of linen and arm slings from the cartridge box and made a pile in front of the fire. She kicked the fire box over and the pile was soon alight. Nothing for the nationalists to use. She took a burning roll of bandages and jabbed it at the tarpaulin, then watched for a few seconds to make sure that the blue flames were spreading across the whole of the sheet.

She grabbed the jug of water from the table, stumbled out of the unit and started walking the twenty-four kilometres to Madrid. When she got back to her brigade, she wouldn't tell the British comrades what had happened. She worried about what they would do and what revenge they would extract in her defence. It would be bad for morale.

She would re-join her medical team, and in a few weeks, in a small boarding house on Calle de Santa Ana, in central Madrid, she would learn that she was pregnant.

Chapter six

Wednesday, 26th October 2016,

Newcastle, Northern England.

Axel had a quick look around and then threw his backpack over the low stone wall at the end of the swing bridge. He climbed after it into the darkness, away from the street lights, started up the steep bank and pulled the hood of his jacket tighter. He shivered as the freezing rain splattered all around, drenching him. Slipping on the saturated loose soil, he grabbed at some branches to steady himself. It took him a couple of minutes before he reached the top.

Overhead, the huge stone arches of the two hundred metre long High Level Bridge loomed into the midnight sky as it soared high above the River Tyne, spanning Newcastle and Gateshead, one of seven bridges within two kilometres to do so. The bridge was a road, rail and pedestrian link between the two towns. It provided a continuous rail link between Edinburgh and London. The upper railway deck, forty metres above the water, was carried on six arches supported by stone piers; the road section suspended from the arches by massive iron ties. It was opened in the heyday of Victorian engineering and considered to be one of the most notable engineering feats on Tyneside. It was also Axel's home and had been for the past few weeks.

Axel looked back at the narrow river with thousands of splashes catching the lights of the bars and restaurants on the quayside and turning the black water into an ever-changing pattern of disc-shaped pools. He tucked the bottom of his jeans into his socks so that they wouldn't catch on the spikes, blew on to his hands to warm them and took a firm grip on the two-metre-high fence blocking entry to the base of one the arches. The iron fence was fastened to the side of the arch and Axel knew exactly where to place his feet to climb up. He threw his bag over and heaved himself to the top of the fence, carefully placing a foot in between the spikes on the railings. He swung his other leg over, pushed off with his right hand on the damp concrete, then landed heavily on the other side.

The space he landed in was about eight metres long by five metres wide. It caught some light from the street lamps down below and from the full moon which highlighted the glittering rivulets running down the wall from the cracks in the concrete. The floor was cemented, and spattered with leaves from the bushes and small trees which helped to partially conceal the place. The high ceiling of the arch gave good protection from the rain but even so puddles had formed just inside the fence. Empty beer cans and cider bottles were strewn about alongside crushed pizza boxes and a variety of discarded plastic bags and wrappers, old blankets, bits of tarpaulin, flattened cardboard to sit on and a plastic heap which used to be a pop-up tent. Three half bottles of vodka, two of them empty, were positioned neatly against the wall of the arch next to a circle of a dozen bricks forming a hearth, the remains of a fire still warm. Beside the hearth was a wooden crate completely covered in tin foil with a door fashioned out of cardboard covered in foil which had fallen open. There was one metal grill shelf balanced on four bricks inside the box, a metal dish of hot coals was still on the bottom of the box heating the can of beans above which were now congealed into a gluey brown mess and which had obviously been forgotten about.

There was a thick, musky sweet smell in the air.

'Bit late tonight dear. What kept yer?'

Axel picked up his bag and nodded to the voice. 'No reason mum. Thanks for waiting up though.'

The voice sniggered.

Axel nodded again, sat down on a plastic bucket near the hearth and took out two chocolate bars from his bag. He threw one across. The bar bounced off the top of large cardboard box and fell on top of the bottom half of a sleeping bag poking out from it. A cloud of smoke emerged from the box followed by a head with a thick beard and bobble hat pulled down over the ears. 'Ooh, Mars bar,' said the head. 'My favourite. That's very kind of you, my friend.'

Leon shuffled forward in his sleeping bag and picked up the chocolate bar. He took another deep draw from his joint, then ripped the paper off and took a big bite of the chocolate. Axel didn't know how old he was because Leon refused to tell him and teased him repeatedly to try and guess. Axel thought about thirty-five but he could easily be five or six years either side of that figure.

'That okay for you?' said Axel. 'You forgot about your beans.'

'Ah yes … divine … just what I needed for supper. You are a prince my friend. A prince among men. Couldn't be bothered with the beans. Bit worried they were past their sell by. Couldn't tell how old they were. Going to start dating the cans. Got a stick of glue and I'll label everything so we know what's what.'

'Trouble with dating the cans is that they'll soon forget about you and find somebody new.' Axel waited for at least a smile if not a laugh and when it didn't come, he said, 'How's the smoke?'

'Marvellous, absolutely splendid.' Leon dragged himself further forward and then propped himself up with one arm. 'How went the day, old pal?'

'Not bad,' said Axel, taking a bite from his chocolate bar. 'Looks like you've had a good day?'

'I always have a good day,' said Leon. He wiggled both eyebrows.

'Been anywhere?' said Axel.

'Town ... for a bit of a nose around. You?'

Axel thought for a moment. 'Nah'. He walked across to the vodka bottle picked it up, took a swig, grimaced and put it back. 'Just the same as every day. Rambled about a bit.'

'Bit of beggin'?'

'A bit,' said Axel looking out over the river. He never liked to admit it.

'Ah well, that's not good enough young man,' said Leon. 'I, Sherlock know your vile secrets. And I will reveal them when the time is ripe.'

'Reveal away,' said Axel.

Leon pulled himself up and sat with his hands on his knees. 'Man, you'll give us beggars a bad name.'

'What d'you mean?' Axel turned around only half feigning being affronted and tilted his head lightly as a way of telling him to get to the point.

'Well ... your heart's not in it, man. You have to be committed. You have to be passionate about it. It's not a hobby.' Leon took another wheezing suck on his joint. 'You have to approach it like it's a vocation.

It's a career. Otherwise, it's just like any other job. You have to give it everything you've got. Passion. Passion. That's the key me old mate.'

Axel smiled. The biggest smile he'd had for a long time. Then the laugh burst out. 'Okay,' he said. 'I'll try harder.'

'Aye, do that. We can't have folk round here thinking we're amateurs, can we?'

They were quiet for a long time looking at the rain, wafting and slanting across the front of the arch.

Leon leaned back, stretched out to retrieve a can of beer from the cardboard box and took a sip. 'You shouldn't be here y'know.' He offered the can to Axel.

Axel shivered, rubbed his hands together, then walked over, took the can and went back to his bucket. He took a long drink. 'Ah, man, you always say this. Every time. Every time you've had some dope. It sets off some kind of reflex action. You'll be saying what you usually say in a minute.'

'Say what?'

'You know what. All that stuff about expectations and good jobs and settling down … letting people down.' Axel shook his head at Leon. 'I'll not let anyone down here.'

Leon blew out a long plume of smoke, followed by an impressive litany of swearing and then laughed as loud as he could just to emphasise his ridicule.

'What's the matter with you?' snapped Axel.

'You. You're the matter. Yer just kidding yerself man. Not letting anyone down. Man, yer letting everyone down including yerself. Expectations ... good jobs ... settling down. You sound ridiculous. I never said that. I wouldn't say that. It's something you've thought of yourself. Some kind of defence to convince yourself.' He opened another can of beer and jabbed it at Axel. 'You know why you're here and I know why you're here.'

'Really? Why's that then?'

''Cos you can't hack it out there. You give up too easily. It's true. I'll keep on saying it. You don't belong here. You don't need to be here. You should go home man. This is not for you. Just because yer having a hard time with yer family. It'll pass.'

'I've stuck it so far.' Axel took a longer drink. 'You don't need to worry about me.'

'I'm not.'

'Well, what about you? You could go back, couldn't you?'

'No, no chance. Too stuck on these things,' He waved the joint triumphantly in the air. 'As well as other things. She'd never have me back. That's why she kicked me out in the first place. And I quite like being free. And I quite like doing whatever I want. And I quite like being wherever I want to be. And unlike you I can put up with this. I don't mind a bit of slummin'. So, I'm quite happy ... but you ... you seem to enjoy being miserable. And you could – should – go back.'

'No, there's nothing there for me now. I'll not go back.'

'You prefer it here, do you? You can stick it, eh? Having fun?'

Axel didn't answer. He took another drink from the can, crushed it in his hand and tossed it against the fence.

'Hey, careful,' Leon shouted in mock outrage. 'You'll damage the furniture.'

There was a movement from the far corner. A piece of tarpaulin was pushed aside revealing a sleeping bag, and then a figure sat up. Even in the gloom of the arch Axel could see it was a female figure, swaddled in scarves, with a red coat covering her.

Axel jumped then stood up to get a better look. He turned to Leon. 'Eh? Who's this?'

'This, my friend ...' said Leon, 'is a girl. You might have seen them before. They're a bit different to us, they –'

'What's she doing here?' interrupted Axel, interested, not hostile.

'What do you mean, *what's she doing here?* Same as us. She had nowhere to go. So, I said she could stay here ... if she wanted. I didn't know we were getting all territorial. I mean, I know it's a nice place and all that. I know she's got a different skin colour but I'm sure she'll not bring the neighbourhood down if that's what you're worried about. Hindu. Exotic, eh? She seems like a nice girl. I thought the place could do with a woman's touch.'

Axel sat back on his bucket. 'I'm not getting all territorial. I didn't realise we were taking in tenants.'

'I should hope not,' said Leon. 'Anyway, she's a guest, not a paying tenant. And she jumped at the chance when I told her about the place.' He put both arms up and swung from side to side. 'Affordable city studio apartment. Panoramic views across the river. High ceilings, large balcony – actually nearly all balcony. No noisy neighbours … if you don't count the cars overhead. Not forgettin' the trains.'

'Open plan living room,' said Axel joining in, tapping his bucket and pointing to the brick hearth beside him. 'Fully furnished, with open range cooking facilities.'

'Lots of natural light,' said Leon.

'Free spiders and slugs included.'

'Ah,' said Leon. 'She's not too keen on spiders and creepy crawlies. She saw some before and wasn't impressed.'

A rustling sound caught their attention as a sleeping bag was pushed aside. The female figure struggled to her feet, walked across with her long red coat wrapped around her and knelt beside the hearth, warming her hands.

Axel nodded to Leon. 'I see you've given her the en suite.'

'You'll just have to pee on the other side,' said Leon.

'Ugh, what?' said the female figure.

'Just joking,' said Leon.

'Do I get an introduction?' said Axel.

'Well, you would … if I could remember her name,' said Leon.

'Samira,' said the female figure. 'Samira Bakshi. I usually get Sami. And you are?'

'Axel. Axel Edelman. Pleased to meet you. How do you like the place?'

'Love it,' said Samira. 'Love what you've done to it. Very cosy.'

'Good,' said Leon. 'Now that the formalities are over … anyone fancy a joint?'

'Not for me thanks,' said Axel, still looking at Samira. 'So, how did you meet him?'

'Just … saw him sitting on the corner … not sure which street … I'm still new here. Only been here a few days. Stayed in a hostel in the centre of town for the first two days but the money soon ran out and I had to find somewhere to stay that was safe.' Samira gave Axel a steady look. 'Leon assured me I would be safe here.'

Axel nodded. 'Of course. You've only got the spiders and slugs to worry about here.'

'And the cold and the wind,' said Leon. He pushed his chest out and began calling out in a dramatic stentorian voice. 'Oh, the wind the wind, the cold and the wind.'

Samira looked at Axel with a blank face. 'Is he always like this?'

'Always,' said Axel. 'Hard to get a sensible word out of him. I think you'll like it here.'

'Mazel toft,' said Sami, and then smiled at Axel's surprised look. 'Your name sort of gave it away.'

Chapter seven

Tuesday, 30th August, 2016,

Antoni's apartment,

115 Calle de Segovia, la Latina, Madrid, Spain.

'I don't think it will work. In fact I know it won't work. It's not what we need right now. In fact, it's not what we do. I thought you knew that. It won't work.' Antoni strode the floor in his small apartment in the old town district of Madrid.

It was hot and muggy. The air conditioning had broken down and the atmosphere in the room was stifling enough as it was.

Antoni was 56, very tall, completely and glisteningly bald with a slight paunch but powerfully built. He spoke with a pronounced Catalan accent, having lived in Barcelona for many years as a child and always pronounced Madrid as *Madrit*. He was seen as an elder statesman now by the younger members of the organisation and had mellowed since his street fighting time. He kept his temper well these days. Someone to listen to. The pacing helped him concentrate on his thoughts and his breathing.

Six faces watched him as he paced between the low coffee table and the three sofas. All the faces were half his age. Camilla and Marco sat on the long, leather sofa in front of him. Ramon, Felipe and Valentina on the battered leather sofa nearest the door. Javier watched from the back of the room, arms folded, lounging against the bare brick wall near the large window, three storeys up from Segovia Street. The window blinds pulled down against the sweltering heat. Six, young smart faces recommended and recruited over the last few months for their different talents. Different but well-coordinated for the special tasks they had undertaken and would continue to undertake for the far-right cause. Recruited because of their ideological strength, their skills and adaptability in modern technology and their ability to carry out well hidden cyber-attacks on the government establishment, the unions and particularly the left-wing political parties.

'No,' Antoni continued. 'I don't see it working. I'm not taking this to the committee to sanction. It's not what we do. It's foolhardy and can put everyone at risk. It's just exhibitionism.' He blew out a short exasperated breath and stared at the ceiling. His voice rose slightly and he flicked away a small bead of sweat trickling down his neck. 'And ... if it goes wrong ... which it will. It would expose us.' He glanced at Ramon. 'That's not the business we're in. We have to be careful. Careful and ready ... and hidden.

Ramon smarted and went to stand up but Felipe held on to his arm and pulled him back, not taking his eyes off Antoni who had noted the movement.

There was a knock at the door. A well-practised knock. Four short taps then a gap and two more short taps. Antoni nodded to Marco and he walked across and opened the door. A small, slim man with long brown hair tied up into a pony tail and a well clipped beard came into the room. He wore a brown three-piece suit, white shirt and brown tie and stood just inside the door with his hands in his waistcoat pockets. He was about the same age as Antoni and gave a big smile to the others in the room.

'Vincente,' said Antoni, frowning and looking at his watch. 'Glad you could make it.'

Vincente broadened his smile at Antoni's slight irritation. 'Sorry. Apologies,' he said. 'The metro was bad. Nuevos Ministerios line was down. What's all this about? What's all the rush to have a meeting?'

'Well,' said Antoni, producing a smile to match Vincente's. A smile with his broad lips but not with his eyes. 'I think Ramon should tell you Vincente. It will be good for the rest of us to listen to this ....' He stopped himself from saying *madness*. 'To listen to this again.'

Vincente looked at Ramon. He raised his eyebrows to emphasise the puzzlement in his expression. 'So, what's it all about Ramon? What's so important?'

Ramon pushed himself forward on to the edge of the sofa, put his hands on his knees and straightened his back. He was twenty-nine years old, stocky, a square kind of shape, average height, combed back blond hair, dark blue eyes. Always neatly dressed with a shirt fastened to the top. Always with a slight, carefully trimmed and managed stubble, and aftershave with a strong smell of lavender. Somewhat diffident and slightly insecure with a tendency to keep to the background and keep his thoughts to himself although when roused he could speak candidly and fervently. 'Joan Miro', he said quietly, ready to go on the defensive.

This time Vincente's eyebrows formed a v shape. He leaned his head to the right and looked at Antoni and then back to Ramon. 'Joan Miro?' he said.

Ramon straightened even further. 'Joan Miro the famous surrealist painter. He was –'

'Yes, I know who Joan Miro was,' said Vincente. 'What about him? He's dead. Been dead for a long time. If I remember correctly, he was no friend of ours.'

'Exactly,' Ramon stood up and glanced around the room. 'During the civil war in the thirties, Miro was on the side of the left, the republicans. I've researched him. In 1937 he painted a huge mural called "The Reaper", also known as "Catalan Peasant in Revolt". He said his painting represented the *dream of a nation that wanted freedom from oppression.*'

'Fascinating,' said Vincente, widening his eyes. Antoni gave a snort and a shake of his head and smiled at the faces on the sofas, some grinning back, some blank.

Ramon scowled as much as he could without losing his way, then pulled first on his ear and then his nose. 'The mural was based on the Reaper war in the seventeenth century between the Catalan peasants and the ruling classes. And although Miro was not all that political, the civil war inspired him to criticise the Franco regime. At the time of the civil war Miro was working in Paris and he exhibited his mural at the Paris world exhibition in 1937 in the Spanish Pavilion along with other impressionists and surrealists like Modigliani, and Picasso with his *Guernica* painting. Miro's mural was massive, five metres high and four metres wide. Spain's other great painters collected in Paris to show solidarity with the republic and the fight against Franco.'

'Very nice,' said Vincente. 'Good for them. But it didn't do them much good did it? They lost.' Derisive snorts and sniggering came from most of the room.

Ramon glared at Vincente. 'The point is –'

'Yes, what is the point?' Vincente cut in, adjusting his tie and smoothing down his beard.

'The point is … the mural went missing.' Ramon pulled his arms behind his back. He wanted to poke the air with an aggressive finger but knew he had to keep calm. 'The mural went missing and there are rumours that Franco's agents destroyed it, but no-one really knows.'

'Again. What's the point?' said Vincente.

'Yes, tell him your point,' Antoni jabbed the air. He had no qualms about doing it. He had heard all this earlier and was getting even more irritated at hearing it again.

Ramon took a deep breath but turned as he did so to hide it from Vincente and Antoni. He didn't want them thinking he couldn't handle this. He turned back and looked at both of them in turn, slowly. 'No-one really knows what happened to the mural.' Ramon kept his voice low and soft. 'Some black and white photographs exist but no-one knows the true colours that were used. However, a smaller version of the mural was painted by Miro on silk. A practice version where he experimented with the colours for the whole thing. An exact copy. It's important because the original painting disappeared. It's believed that the smaller practice version was smuggled out of the exhibition by Spanish Republican sympathisers to keep it safe so that the painting could be replicated. In his book, written at the time, "Art through the Spanish Civil War", Hugo Aguilar mentions this and also says that a seamstress used by the Spanish Pavilion suggested that the smaller painting had been sewn between two flags, the Spanish Republican flag and an International Brigade flag, to avoid detection by Franco's agents. It would obviously have been a major coup for them if they could find it and publicly destroy it.

If we find it,' continued Ramon. 'We can destroy it, make a public demonstration of it, show everyone that we have a long reach. That we have a history too. That we will confront the left in any way we can. We can say we destroyed the original and now we destroy this. We can burn it in front of the media. The great symbolism of the painting for the left will be no more. And we could do it just before the Catalan independence referendum scheduled for next October.'

'You know this for a fact,' said Vincente.

''Course he doesn't,' Marco shouted from the sofa. Too loud, he knew. He folded his arms against the stares of the others. 'He doesn't know for certain where it is or even if it exists. It's like Antoni says – exhibitionism. He's going for glory.'

'It's his theory,' added Antoni. 'There's no actual facts or truth.'

'So, this is what we're all here for,' said Vincente, throwing one hand in the air. 'A theory. A theory about something that happened eighty years ago. A theory that –'

Ramon seized on this and saw his opportunity. '*Something that happened eighty years ago*. Isn't that why we're all here anyway. To right the wrongs of the last few years. To right the wrongs of the republic.' He could feel his voice quivering. 'To make sure that what happened eighty years ago is never forgotten. To make sure Franco is never forgotten.' He stared around the room for a few seconds and then settled on a crack in the wall in front of him giving him time to control his thoughts. 'We owe it to that generation. We owe it to those who fell. All those who fought the communists and socialists …'

114

Antoni prowled across and stood directly in front of Ramon. An easy reach across. He gazed into Ramon's face, considering him. Looking him up and down, inspecting his legs, his feet, his chest, his neck. Slow. He kept very still, marking the moment, another bead of sweat skating down his neck. Making sure that everyone understood the moment too. Then he leaned into Ramon and whispered. His voice subdued, almost tired. 'You don't have to lecture us about the fight against the communists. You don't have to remind us about those who gave their lives for liberty. You don't have to tell us what we're here for.' The soft words became solid, clattered around the room and then rammed themselves into Ramon's throat. Antoni took a step forward; Ramon could feel the hot breath on his eyes. The room became deathly still and the thick silence filled the whole space, expectant, waiting.

'Antoni.' It was Vincente. He moved across into Antoni's peripheral vision, gliding, slow and deliberate, slow, slow. Like approaching a dangerous guard dog. No sudden movements. He had known Antoni for more than thirty years. He had seen what he was capable of. 'Antoni. Leave it.'

Antoni rolled his head slightly towards Vincente without taking his eyes off Ramon. He took a packet of cigarettes from his trouser pocket, flicked out a cigarette and lit it with his lighter in one smooth movement. Vincente was expecting him to blow the first smoke in Ramon's face but he didn't, instead he turned, gave one last short smile to Ramon then sauntered across the room to the window and stood beside Javier.

'Ramon. This is not what we do.' Vincente shook his head slightly. 'We've moved away from all that kind of thing. Let the others do that. It's not what we're about. We're trying to be a bit more cerebral, a bit more intelligent, cleverer. A bit more secret. We exist undetected. I thought you knew that. You do know that. This is what we've been doing since our organisation was founded. We still agree with the others about the outcome but we disagree about the methods. If you went ahead with this it would damage the people we align ourselves with. It would damage our credibility with them. They see us as being more subtle than this. They rely on us to damage the republicans without causing problems with strongarm tactics. That's what they set us up for. That's why they pay us. If you need to do things that way perhaps it's time you chose a different group to be with.' He let Ramon take this in. 'You're clever Ramon. And since your recommendation to join us you've been a great help in our social media campaigns, but this idea could cause us real difficulties with the party and particularly with our backers. They would fail to see the point of us if we're just going back to the old ways.'

Antoni took a deep drag from his cigarette and blew the smoke out through his nose. 'Oh, you haven't heard the best bit yet.'

Vincente looked at Ramon. 'Well?'

'I know where the painting is,' said Ramon. A cloud passed over his face when he heard his own words. They sounded like a child desperate to please.

'Okay,' said Vincente, pulling his head back in surprise. 'This is your gamechanger is it? So, where is it?'

'I've shown the others already, said Ramon, reaching inside his jacket and pulling out a piece of paper. 'I can tell you now —'

'England,' Antoni shouted across the room. 'He says … thinks … it's in England. Bloody England.'

'England?' said Vincente.

Ramon handed the paper to Vincente.

'What is it? What am I looking at?' said Vincente.

'This,' said Ramon, 'is a photo I took of a Facebook article from a few days ago. It mentions the International Brigades which fought in the civil war for the leftists. Anything which mentions the International Brigades I am interested in, for many reasons. This was brought to me by a friend of mine who knows of my interest. It's about the funeral of an old woman named Emily Edelman. Two pictures. In the first one, when she was younger you can see she's holding up an International Brigade flag.'

'Yes, I see. So what? I've seen lots of people holding up these rags,' said Vincente.

'But can you see ... the side of the brigade flag has flopped down ... and there's a Spanish Republican flag on the other side. You can make out the colours. Also, can you see the date and place it was taken. It was Paris, 20th October 1937. The Paris exhibition, when the Miro mural went missing, was held from 25th May until 25th November 1937. This woman, Emily Edelman was being discharged from the British brigade. On the other side of the article, you can see a photo of a friend of hers, apparently a refugee she took in from the civil war, at her funeral, and behind him beside the coffin is a framed photo of her as an old lady, again holding up the flags.' Ramon looked around the room. 'It exists.'

'Agreed,' called Antoni from the window. 'A double-sided flag exists. But it proves nothing.'

'Nothing,' echoed Vincente. 'Antoni's right. It's a double-sided flag. No doubt there were lots of these. It doesn't prove that the Miro mural copy is between them.'

'But … the date is exactly at the right time …' Ramon said. A final plea. The child was back.

'No doubt there were lots of foreign lefties being discharged at the same time … and we know a lot of them went through Paris. That was the normal route.' Vincente looked again at the photo. 'So, what exactly do you want us to do?'

'He doesn't want *us* to do anything,' said Antoni. '*He* wants to go to England and find the mural … the imaginary mural … of course it will be handed over easily, no questions asked, or perhaps he'll steal it … from a foreign country, causing an international incident. and embarrassing our donors. I can't believe we're even discussing it. And get this …' He pointed a fist at Vincente.

'What?' said Vincente.

'He wants us to pay for it,' Antoni raised his voice but kept it level. 'To fund his crazy adventure. For his glory, just like Marco says. He wants a thousand euros to spend a couple of weeks in England chasing this stupidity. A nice holiday.' There was a murmur in the room. Antoni looked at the others. 'Yes, you heard right, a thousand euros. He told me last night. That's why I called this meeting.' He looked around the room, scowling and pointing at each face with his cigarette. 'We need to know who we are and where we are and what it is we do. We can't have individual elements. We have to be together. Like Vincente says, this is not what we do now. We have to be smarter. We have to get the electorate … yes, the electorate … I know some of us don't like that term but that's the game we're in … at least for the moment. We have to get the electorate on our side. We have to be squeaky clean. A folly like this would just distract from our real work.'

Ramon shook his head. He knew he was beaten. He looked down as if he was talking to someone on the carpet. 'It's not a folly. It's a big mistake not to take this opportunity to strike a big blow.' He was fading inwardly. Thwarted. Broken. His skin suddenly became too big for him.

'No,' said Antoni. 'It would be a big mistake to do it … and a waste of money. So, as your director of operations, I'm saying this will not go to the national committee … and I think you Ramon should have a long, hard look at us and remind yourself of why you joined this organisation. And if you don't like what you see, you can go, always remembering that we rely on … and expect … total secrecy. And if we don't get it then there are consequences. Now, thank you for your time, everyone. This meeting is at an end.'

The sofas were emptied as everyone silently left the room. Ramon was first to leave ignoring the surly looks of Marco and Javier. At the end of the dark corridor Felipe and Valentina carried out a hushed conversation before leaving the building. Vincente stayed to talk to Antoni.

Out on the busy Segovia Street Ramon turned left and headed for the Viaducto de Segovia bridge. He sloped along, hoping to be repaired by the air but the heat drained even more of him.

He had only gone fifty metres.

'Ramon! Ramon! Wait up!'

Ramon turned to see Felipe and Valentina walking quickly to catch him up. 'Wait,' repeated Felipe. 'We need to talk with you.' Felipe, leather jacketed and wearing a black baseball cap, was twenty-five years old, thin framed, black hair, slim, with a wide mouth and slight lisp. His dark eyes darted about, unable to concentrate on anything for more than a few seconds. His face too handsome, almost pretty. He had been an activist since university and had been with Antoni's group since they were formed. Always provocative, he was known for his passionate, radical views; too intelligent for *fanatical* but some would say almost too clever for his own good.

'What about?' said Ramon.

'You know what about,' said Valentina. 'We need to talk about your project. I know you don't really know us yet but –'

'What about it?' snapped Ramon.

'Let's find somewhere quiet … and cool.' Felipe flicked a hand towards Calle de San Pedro. 'There's a café down there.'

Minutes later the three of them were sitting in the café de Nuncio. Ramon and Valentina with coffees, Felipe with a long glass of cold lemonade.

'We think you were treated badly back there,' began Felipe. 'You were trying to bring something extra to the table but you were dismissed out of hand. That didn't sit well with me. Mainly because I think you're right. I think we do need some kind of grand gesture.'

'And this could be just what is needed,' said Valentina, lounging back in her chair, easy and relaxed, complementing Felipe's intensity. She had struck up a friendship with Felipe right from first meeting him.

She was twenty-seven, tall and just slightly overweight, sunglasses pushed back over dyed blue hair cut short on one side. She had been with Antoni's group for five months and had impressed everyone with her technology skills: hacking into e-mails a speciality. She had a long scar down the left side of her face from the corner of her eye to her cheekbone, that was the part of her hair that was cut short. She never spoke about the scar but didn't mind showing it.

'You know what I think,' said Ramon. 'So, tell me your thoughts… and by the way … are you two …?'

'No,' said Valentina quickly, she glanced at Felipe. 'Fellow falangists.'

Felipe took a sip of his coffee, ignoring Ramon's question. 'The referendum in 2014 to gauge support for Catalan separatism independence was a disaster. As you said back there, there will be another in October next year. We need all the ammunition we can get to spoil the referendum, stop the cause of the Catalan Peoples' Party, stifle the desire for an independent state.'

'There'll be no national unity if the referendum goes badly,' said Valentina

'Exactly,' said Felipe. 'We need a whole Spain. I don't think the likes of Antoni and Vincente realise how dangerous the times are that we live in. They think long term, but the danger is here, right now. We need to follow the British example of Brexit. My country right or wrong. To hell with Europe. We need a whole Spain. We don't need Europe.' He spoke rapidly with the pious zeal of a new convert.

Valentina looked for a response from Ramon but there was none. He gazed impassively from her to Felipe. She twirled her cup between her fingers. 'We have a right and a responsibility to intervene. The radical right need a push. We can provide that. The political party and all their friends have gone too far with their need for social acceptance and legitimacy. The Catalan referendum will give credence to all those liberals and leftists. We need extreme nationalism. We need to be united as one nation. No compromise.'

Felipe leaned back in his chair and stared at Ramon. 'It's like what you said back at Antoni's, we owe it to those who fell eighty years ago, all those who fought the commies, all those who fought for liberty.' He looked about the room, searching for the words. 'Spain is the future, not Europe. We need a patriotic alternative. The left doesn't have moral superiority. Our main pre-occupation is the unity of our country, for our families, for our children. They'll follow us. They just need strong leaders, just like our first leader Jose de Rivera. Remember the Falange party slogan in the thirties, "Somos como somos. Somos como tu. Ponsamos como tu." We are how we are. We are like you. We think like you.'

'Of course,' Ramon kept his face blank. 'I don't need a history lesson.'

'Remember what Rivera said,' continued Felipe. '"We must have political unity and the elimination of regional separatism. We must have the abolition of political parties". *That's* what we should be aiming for. The public demonstration of the burning of Miro's mural would be a good start.'

'It's a long shot,' said Ramon abruptly. He took a sip from his cup. 'That's one thing I agree with Antoni about. It's a long shot.'

'But worth it ... and necessary,' said Valentina. 'And we could get some help from the far-right groups in Britain. They would support this.'

'Absolutely they would,' said Felipe. 'I already have some contacts I can talk to. I'm sure they'll help with accommodation and transport.'

'No money,' said Ramon flatly.

'What?' said Felipe.

'I have no money,' said Ramon. 'That's why I wanted Antoni to ask for funding. I'm not working and I don't have enough to go.'

Felipe and Valentina exchanged quick glances. 'I have a little money,' said Felipe. 'And I can take time off work, but we'll need a few weeks to prepare. We need to go as soon as possible'

'I can get some,' said Valentina. 'It's important we do this. Vital.'

Felipe folded his arms and leant heavily on the table, smiling 'And if we need anymore,' he said. 'We can *borrow* some in England.'

Valentina laughed and raised her cup. 'Una grande y libre,' she said and then repeated the motto of the Falange Party in perfect English. 'One, great and free.'

Chapter eight

Thursday 20th November 1976,

Xavi's flat,

Heaton Road, Newcastle, Northern England.

Xavi walked across to the kitchen worktop and flicked the switch on the kettle. A cup of coffee would do the trick. He'd finished his deliveries early today and returned the van to the warehouse before two o'clock. He'd gone for a swim at the pool in Byker and his face was still a little flushed from the forty lengths and the thirty-minute walk back to his small, downstairs, two bed, Victorian Tyneside flat on the main street. The kitchen smelled of chlorine from the towels and swimming shorts draped over the back of one of the three plastic chairs tucked under the blue, rectangular, Formica table, and still dripping wet even after being wrung out tightly. He sniffed his hand. He smelled of chlorine even though he'd taken a long shower after the swim. His hair was wet from the sudden cloudburst which had made him hurry to get back. He'd used the swimming towel to dry it but the towel was already damp and it hadn't really worked.

He was forty-five years old with thick, dark hair, greying slightly, untidy goatee beard, baggy eyes, a heavily lined forehead and round shoulders which gave him a tired, world weary sort of look. He countered this intentionally by straightening every few minutes (or when he could remember), and with wide open eyes and a deep smile, both of which unfortunately weren't sustainable for a long time but enough to give him a surprised, open-faced, welcoming expression. He had a slight paunch but his body was in pretty good shape from the regular swimming sessions and the effort of loading and unloading his deliveries for the bookstore in the centre of Newcastle.

The doorbell rang and Xavi turned quickly towards the sound, almost slipping on a wet patch on his grey and cream squared linoleum flooring. It was unusual to have somebody calling at this time, at any time really, so he went to the front door pulling his shoulders back and lifting his eyebrows.

He found Emily on the doorstep, rain dripping from her short, blonde hair. Xavi relaxed, lowered his eyebrows and smiled.

'Good Lord, Emily Edelman. What brings you here. Come in. Come in out of the rain.' He ushered her along the short, pale blue corridor to the kitchen. 'Here, let me take your coat. Let's get you dry. I'll get you some coffee.'

Emily slipped off her kagoule and Xavi put it on the back of one of the chairs. She felt her jeans and dark blue sweater to see how damp they were and then sat with her elbows leaning on the table.

'Have you heard?' Emily began, although she could tell from his manner that he obviously hadn't.

'Where's Ana?' asked Xavi, heading towards the kettle which was throwing out clouds of steam as the off switch was broken.

'She's at a neighbour's … Jean. Dropped her off straight after picking her up from school. Jean often looks after her… likes little kids. Rosa's still not up to looking after Ana by herself. I had to come round straight away as soon as you finished work.'

'Why? What's so urgent?'

'He's dead,' said Emily, fixing Xavi's back with an urgent look. 'Haven't you heard?'

'Who? Who's dead?' Xavi could tell from the excitement in her voice and the *he* that it wasn't anyone they knew well enough to get overly upset about.

'Franco.'

Xavi stopped at the worktop. He made a sound like an – oh – with a tiny panting breath. His whole body became rigid. He stood immovable like an ancient standing stone. He stayed frozen for several seconds, then his shoulders sagged and his head stooped so low that it looked like he was melting.

'He's dead,' repeated Emily quickly, her voice heavy now. 'Haven't you heard?' She felt suddenly sad. He should have been the first to know.

Xavi pulled himself up but then his shoulders slumped again, giving up. He reached forward to turn off the kettle. There was an ocean of silence. 'When was this?' he said quietly. 'Today?'

'Yes. Today.'

'How?' Xavi stared at the wisps of steam from the kettle and gripped the workbench, resting his whole weight. The air around them stilled and went cold as if time was taking a breath.

Emily still couldn't see his face to judge his reaction. 'Heart failure,' she said quietly. 'Just after midnight. Apparently, he said on his deathbed that he regretted all the killing.'

'Oh, that's good then,' said Xavi. 'That's good of him.' The words came out slow and impassive, shrivelled together.

Finally, Xavi turned and Emily could see his eyes glistening, a tear slowly falling to his cheek. She saw the little boy she had taken in after the war. The ragged little boy, shocked and upset at what he'd seen. Traumatised by the bombing, by the loss of his village, the loss of his family. The little boy abandoned, adrift, alone. She could see all the years of grieving and the unbearable pain in him again. She felt the heat behind her eyes and the stinging flow of her own tears as they cascaded in to the side of her gasping mouth and lodged in her throat. She felt the thud of her chest and her body tingled with thousands of tiny shockwaves. She tried to say something but it got lost in the ripples of her skin as her face struggled to slow down. She needed to smile and cut through the tears but the smile wouldn't come.

'So, he's dead,' said Xavi, his voice uneven. 'Finally dead.'

'Yes.'

Xavi leaned against the worktop. He folded his arms and then unfolded them. He took both palms and wiped his eyes. He shoved his hands deep into his pockets and then took them out and folded his arms again. He looked at his hands flat against his chest. He didn't know what to do with them. He didn't know what to do with his body, with his face. He looked at Emily expressionless.

'So, he's dead,' he said again.

'He's gone Xavi. He's gone.' She wanted to go across and hug him but there was an unbridgeable gap between them. An unsurmountable wall of sadness best left alone until it passed and the world could move again. There was a long silence and the room became very small. Emily focused on a thin crack on the table with a speck of crumb caught inside.

She was afraid to say anything. She knew the words would smash the space between them and shatter a precious, irreplaceable moment.

There was a sudden single explosion of laughter rupturing the silence.

Emily looked up quickly and saw Xavi's head back, mouth wide open. The laugh roaring out, filling the corners of the kitchen. He laughed again with his eyes tight shut. His fingers pulled into fists against his cheek as if trying to stop it. He shook his head violently from side to side so that his hair flopped about and the deep creases in his brow became corrugated and cavernous. And then his head fell to his chest and the laughing turned into a gurgling, gasping, breathless gulping. He sucked in air so hard that his face shuddered and his whole body began rocking and jerking uncontrollably. The tears came again, spurting out almost cartoon-like, flooding down, down and past his cheek and chin and overflowing on to his neck and the collar of his shirt.

Emily ran to him.

The chair spun across the floor as she kicked it away and threw herself around him and hugged him and hugged him and hugged him. She was blinded by tears and so she felt for his cheeks and kissed his face and his neck and tasted the saltiness of his tears. She folded herself into him and around him, her body taut and aching with the power of the embrace.

Xavi buried himself into her. 'It's over. It's over,' he murmured. 'He's gone. At last, he's gone, thank God, he's gone.'

They gathered themselves and pulled apart but still Emily clutched Xavi's hands. Finally, she had to let go to thumb away her tears. She smiled at him and at last she laughed. She turned and looked across the kitchen. 'Looks like I've been throwing chairs about in all the excitement. We should do something else to celebrate rather than breaking furniture.'

Xavi nodded and pushed himself away from the worktop. He cleared his throat. 'I think this calls for something other than coffee.' He opened a cupboard door by the side of the fridge and brought out two glasses and a tall bottle of whisky.

Emily sat back at the table. Xavi moved the towel and swimming shorts to another chair and sat at the opposite end of the table. 'Jameson's, okay?' he said, still breathing deeply.

'Perfect,' said Emily. She wiped away more tears with her sleeve as Xavi poured two large glasses of whisky.

Xavi raised his glass. 'Here's to the future of Spain.' His voice cracked and thin, like burnt newspaper.

'Amen to that,' said Emily. 'And here's to you Xavi. My dear friend. May you find peace now after all these years.'

'May we all find peace,' said Xavi, and then added. 'But I think it might be too much to hope for completely.'

Emily gazed at him. 'You know, Xavi, I can't remember seeing you cry. Not even when you first came here. You didn't cry then even though you'd lost everything … everyone. You were too stunned to cry. You seemed to live in shock for a long time. But I think when you came to live with me as a little boy you were at least … comforted. I think I did a good job.'

'Of course. Of course, you did. I owe you everything. If it wasn't for you, I don't know where I'd be.'

Emily nodded, smiled and raised her glass in salute. 'You should cry more often Xavi, it suits you.'

They sat for an hour talking about the civil war, something they hadn't talked about for years. Something always avoided. They even talked about what Xavi remembered about his family in the Basque region and they talked about his adopted family of Emily and Emily's daughter Rosa and now Rosa's daughter Ana. They talked about Rosa's illness. They talked about what this day meant for the future of Spain. They cried and laughed some more and they drank some more.

After a full two minutes of silence, when they had each found a different part of the kitchen to look at and rest their thoughts Xavi looked pointedly at Emily. She stiffened. It hadn't been mentioned yet and she knew it was coming.

'And what about you Emily?'

'What about me?'

'We toasted peace a few glasses ago.' Xavi fixed her with a searching, whisky fuelled, overly sympathetic look. 'Will you find peace. I know that it burns away inside you still. Will you find peace.'

Never. Never. Never. Emily rolled the word around in her head. The repetition ensuring there was no going back on her resolve.

'I don't know,' she said, looking carefully at Xavi, gauging him. 'What do you think?'

'Maybe it's time. Good Lord, we all have to come to terms with things. You never speak of it … and him … but I know that it is still with you. I know that it still eats away at you. The fact that you don't speak of it shows me how much it still hurts you. Will you finally let it go? Will you finally find peace?'

Emily pictured a twisted smile, fevered eyes and powerful arms. *Never. Never. Never. There can be no peace.*

'So, you think I should just … put it behind me,' she said.

'It was a terrible thing to happen. I understand. I do. But at least Rosa came out of it …' The words slipped out involuntarily and collided with each other seemingly in their rush to find somewhere to hide before they completely offended. Xavi wished he could erase them. He took another sip to hide his awkwardness and then put the glass to his forehead and rolled it across a few times as if trying to put the words back in their rightful, unspoken place.

A long, awful pause.

'When did you see last see Rosa, Xavi?'

'I saw her about just before the job in Scotland,' said Xavi. 'I've been away for about a month.'

Emily sat back heavily and also took a sip of whisky. 'It's getting worse day by day. She finds it difficult to look after Ana now. Her hands are shaking more; she stumbles about; she's clumsy; can't seem to think straight; can't concentrate. And now she says she can't swallow properly,' she said, addressing the glass and concentrating on the swirling amber liquid. 'The disease is crippling her.' Her mouth became a tight thin line. 'The disease he gave her.' She tried softening her face and smiling, but couldn't quite get it right. 'And he doesn't know that. He doesn't know what he's done. He only knows what he did to me.

He doesn't know about Rosa and what he's done to her.' She looked at Xavi. 'He needs to know … after all … it's every father's right, isn't it?'

Xavi shuffled in his seat. Uncomfortable. 'What do you mean?'

'He needs to know what he's done to two lives. How he's destroyed and crippled them.'

'How? How could you possibly tell him. You can't let this hurt go on for ever.'

Emily leaned forward, her eyes gleaming and forcing Xavi to stare back. 'I wanted to talk to you about Franco but I also wanted to talk to you about him … Lazlo Kovac.' She hadn't spoken the name for years and Xavi could see how much it hurt her to say his name, the whisky unable to mask her hatred at the mention of him.

'Lazlo?' Xavi wanted to say it too. He said the name sharply. He wanted to show her that he was still an accomplice. That the shared secret gave them both an equally repulsed intimacy. He wanted to show her the abhorrence he also felt. But he also knew that perhaps it was time to leave the past behind. 'You can't possibly find him after all these years.'

Emily ignored the last comment. 'It seems an appropriate time. A new beginning for Spain. An ending for me.'

'But you can't possibly find him to tell him.'

'Ah, but, my dear friend, I *have* found him.' Emily tilted her head and widened her eyes. She saluted him with her glass. 'I've known where he is for three years.'

'Good Lord, how? How did you find him?'

'I keep in touch with old comrades from different countries. Those who were there. They give me information about events, reunions and such like. Then there's the International Brigades veterans' newsletters. I found out that a certain Mr Lazlo Kovac has been made chairman of the Hungarian Brigades veterans' group based in Budapest.'

'But you can't go to Budapest. They wouldn't let you in. There are still strict border controls for foreigners.'

'Well, I think you're right. I probably couldn't get there. But I don't need to. The Hungarian Communist Party are taking a different route now. They're trying out a policy of liberalisation, but still with Soviet blessing of course. They've already allowed some Hungarians to travel to the west for business and tourism. Since nineteen-seventy the Kadar government in Hungary has made it easier for their citizens to travel, to celebrate the twenty fifth anniversary of Hungary's liberation at the end of the second world war. My old friends call Hungary the merriest barrack in the socialist camp.'

Emily waited for Xavi to take this in.

'So, what does this mean for you?' said Xavi. Then with sudden realisation. 'Ah, so you think he might be allowed to travel abroad.'

'He definitely will be allowed to travel abroad. To Paris in fact.'

Xavi shook his head and gave a puzzled look. 'Why Paris?'

Emily's eyebrows shot up. 'Because my dear friend, in the French veterans' newsletter, Lazlo Kovac is down to lead an Hungarian International Brigade delegation of Spanish Civil War veterans to Paris on February the sixth next year. There's to be a conference to celebrate the fortieth anniversary of the battle of Jamara valley which took place just west of Madrid. One of the most important battles. That's why the date was chosen.'

'Jamara,' said Xavi. He knew of Jamara and gave the word the reverence it deserved.

'It wasn't my most pleasant experience of Spain. A lot of killing. A lot of pain and misery. But we stopped them taking the road to Madrid. Our brigade was in the thick of it, thirty per cent casualties. In fact, all the International Brigades were in the thick of it. It seems we were the shock troops ... though we didn't know it at the time.'

'Even though you weren't military trained.' Xavi was listening carefully. Emily hadn't talked like this before.

'That didn't seem to matter in those days,' said Emily. 'The Spanish Republican leaders just wanted some meat up front.' Emily gazed around the room and smiled without looking happy. 'The British and American Brigades had to merge afterwards: they had taken so many casualties on ... on ... oh, yes, the hill. Murder hill we called it.' She pulled at a straggle of hair and pushed it behind her ear. 'I remember them all Xavi. All the International Brigades. Can you imagine it? People, men and women from fifty countries. More than forty thousand of us from all over the world ... more than ten thousand died. The Italian column, the Matteoti brigade; the Canadian Mackenzie-Papineau battalion; The French Henri-Barbusse, the Commune de Paris 11th battalion; The German Thaelmann brigade; The American Abraham Lincoln brigade ... and of course ... the Hungarian Risolski brigade. All formed by the Comintern, the Communist International. All went as volunteers. Of course, there were adventurers but most went because they believed in something. They had an idea of something better or at least the thought of an idea. But they certainly didn't want what Franco had to offer.'

Emily sat back and studied Xavi. 'I'm going to be there,' she continued. 'I've still got my veterans' membership. But I'll not travel with the British delegation. I'll travel independently. I'll be –'

'And do what?' broke in Xavi. 'When you travel to Paris. What will you do then? He must be well into his seventies.' He took another quick drink and placed his glass too forcefully on the table.

'He has to know. Don't you think he should know? He's probably leading a comfortable retired life now. But he needs to understand what he's done.'

'So, you'll actually talk to him?'

'Of course.'

'It's a long way to go by yourself if you're not travelling with the Brits.'

'I've done it before.'

'A long time ago. When you were much younger. And you travelled with other party members, didn't you?'

'A few.'

'It's too dangerous. You don't know how he'll react.'

'Well, not too fast I would have thought,' smiled Emily. 'Like you said, he must be quite old now.'

Xavi shook his head slightly, exasperated, and folded his fingers into his hands. 'I can't imagine it would be a pleasant meeting and a nice, friendly chat. Situations like this ... passions can be aroused.'

Emily gave a sudden, loud, snorting guffaw. 'They certainly were forty years ago,' she laughed.

Xavi measured his voice. 'No Emily. Passions *can* be aroused. Who knows what could happen. Everyone gets too excited and then anything can happen in the heat of the moment.'

Emily twisted her mouth as if to say something but then clamped the words and the giggle and sent them back. She saw that Xavi was being serious and not in the mood for any funny comments. But she knew also that she wasn't getting too excited. She knew she *wouldn't* be excited. She wasn't going to get nervous or hysterical. She had considered this for a long time. She knew what she had to do. She had a plan and she meant to stick to it, coolly and dispassionately.

'I'm going,' she said.

'He's an old man.'

'What's that got to do with anything?'

Xavi shrugged. 'I don't know.'

'You're not trying to *defend* him, are you?' Emily tried to look at him with harsh outrage but had too much to drink to pull that off so had to settle for mildly offended.

'Of course not. I just think it will be probably worse for you than for him. If he's still that sort of person that you... *met*... all those years ago. Then probably he won't care. He'll probably laugh at you. Why put yourself through all this. You're sixty years old.'

Emily stood up and glared at Xavi. She sucked in air through pursed lips and steadied herself to summon up as much rage as she could. 'I'm only fifty-nine, actually!' she bellowed. 'I was nineteen years old!

Nineteen! I've had forty years of all of this! Rosa is thirty-eight. She's just starting her term, but she definitely won't get forty years of it. He has to know! And he will bloody know! And he will bloody understand what he's put us through!'

She sat back down with a bump nearly knocking the chair over. There was a short silence. 'I'm sorry old friend,' she said presently, quieter. 'Whisky talk. I've had too much. I'm sorry I raised my voice. We shouldn't argue on such an auspicious day as this. I know you're only trying to help me. You're just looking out for me as you've always done. But my mind is made up. You won't stop me.'

Xavi waved away her apology. He nodded in resigned acknowledgement and his face tightened in concentration. They sat for a few seconds each collecting their thoughts.

'I'll go,' said Xavi finally. 'I'll go with you.'

'Now who's using whisky talk?' said Emily flatly.

'I owe you. I owe you everything Emily Edelman. Good Lord, I owe you absolutely everything. And I'm coming with you. To make sure you don't get yourself into trouble.'

'I don't need anyone to look after me. You don't have to come. I don't want you involved.'

'Of course, I do. I have to.'

'You don't need to.'

'I do. Just like you. I do. I have to. I have to repay you. It's something I have to do.' He looked away from her. 'I don't have to convince you. I'm coming and that's an end to it.'

'Well then,' said Emily, she softened her face and worked up to a smile but then changed her mind and turned it into a grave astute nod. 'I understand. I understand completely. I know what you're saying Xavi and I'll be glad to have your company.' She raised her glass. 'We'd better have another drink on that.'

Chapter nine

Friday, 4th February 1977,

Rue Rodier, Montmartre, Paris, France.

Emily and Xavi opened the shutters and looked out of the window of Emily's third floor room in the hotel Rodier. Xavi's room was on the fifth floor and facing the trash cans and discarded broken chairs at the back of an Italian restaurant. They pulled the window pane up to get a better look. They had arrived late last night and wanted to see what the place had to offer. On one side of the street below there was a busy market and the shoppers hurried about trying to get under the awnings as quickly as possible to get their fruit and vegetables as it was raining heavily. French voices boomed out along the pavement as the market traders announced prices and what they had to offer.

Across the other side of the street, they watched an old Citroen 2CV pull up alongside a much sought after parking space between a Peugeot 404 and a Volkswagen beetle. The Citroen began manoeuvring to park between the two cars although the space was very tight and looked impossible.

'No, look,' said Xavi, pointing to the Citroen. 'Impossible. He'll never do it. That's far too small a space.'

The Citroen reversed into the Peugeot, pushed it a few inches, then straightened a little and pushed it a little more. It straightened again and gently moved forward to push the Volkswagen a wheel's length towards the car in front. This continued for four more pushes backwards and forwards until the Citroen finally settled into its newly enlarged space. A man got out of the Citroen, locked his door, pulled his coat collar up against the rain and strolled off along the street.

'Excellent,' said Xavi. 'So, that's how you get a parking space in Paris.

'Looks like it,' said Emily, grinning. 'If you haven't got a space — make one. Very interesting.' She grabbed her kagoule from the bed. 'Let's go. We've got a lot to do today. You've got the address written down for the meeting, haven't you? I've been there before, a long time ago, but I can't remember how to get there from here.'

'Got it here,' said Xavi pulling a piece of paper from his duffel coat pocket. 'F.C.P. French Communist Party headquarters, 2, Place de colonel Fabien 75019. Nearest metro from here is the Abbesses station, about a ten-minute walk.'

Emily nodded. 'I'm looking forward to seeing it again. That's where we all came in thirty-six. The French Communist Party organised everything for us. Got us set up with the brigades. There were so many coming then that they could be organised into similar language brigades and battalions. They gave us a little money. Got us across the Spanish border on the night train to Girona. And then organised transport to Albacete.'

Xavi took out a guide book from his other pocket and opened it at a marked page. 'It says here that the place has been completely transformed by the Brazilian architect Oscar Niemeyer, in the sixties. It's now a large, curved glass-fronted building.'

'Well, things change, but it'll be good to see it again whatever it looks like now.'

Xavi put the guidebook back in his pocket and gave her a stern look. 'You'll see him again too. He's probably changed. Will you recognise him?'

Emily glanced at him but didn't answer. She knew she would recognise him. She just hoped that he was here and that nothing had stopped him coming. She put on her kagoule over her red shirt, zipped it up and walked to the door.

They left the hotel and hurried through Rue Rodier, splashing along the old cobbled streets of Montmartre and the beautiful Rue de L'Abreuvoir. They stopped for only a few seconds to gaze at the gleaming dome of Sacre Coeur, looking silkily cream, bleached by the calcite in the stone as the rain poured down. The stone gutters by the kerbs at the edge of the worn pavements were overrun with streams of water flowing down the hill.

They entered Abbesses station, pulled back their hoods, shook their coats and bought their tickets at the square window of the ticket office. The elevators weren't working and a sign said they would be out of action for a week so they began climbing down the steep spiral staircase. The Abbesses station on the Place des Abbesses was the deepest of all the Paris metro stations: thirty-six metres down and one hundred and seventy-six steps to the platform. Some ceiling lights weren't working so they had to take care, holding on to the cold metal handrail and squeezing past passengers climbing up, pressing against the wall with its bright posters, advertising adventurous events and places to see in Paris, plastered over the cream-coloured wall tiles.

After a short journey of fifteen minutes and seven stops on Metro line two they stepped on to the platform at Colonel Fabien station. They used the elevator to take them to ground level, took a short walk along the Boulevard de La Villett and in a few minutes arrived at the French Communist Party headquarters at the Place de Combat. It had a large, blue-tinted, curving glass wall and along the street the pavement turned into a flowing, blue concrete ramp guiding visitors to a sunken entrance.

Emily and Xavi walked to the desk at the entrance and Emily showed her International Brigade membership card and the tickets which had been sent to her in England. She introduced Xavi as her guest and they were both given plastic passes to clip on their clothes. The passes would give them entry for the next three days of the conference. The woman at the desk spoke to them in perfect English, gave them a sheet of paper outlining the itinerary for the day and pointed the way to the main hall where the meetings would take place.

They walked along a smooth, vibrant green carpet with long, rectangular windows just above their heads providing natural light. The carpet continued, leading them into a five hundred and fifty seat auditorium under a huge fifteen-metre-high concrete canopy in the shape of a dome, covered with thousands of light-reflecting aluminium blades. The green carpet continued to the front of the auditorium before fanning out, framing and enclosing the stage. The place was already filling up and the chattering swirled around the room rattling against the dome.

They took two seats at the back of the hall. In front of them at the end of the rows were notices on tall flagpoles showing the members of the various delegations where they should sit. The British delegation was six rows in front and to their left. Xavi nudged Emily and pointed to the front of the hall and the Hungarian members sitting two rows from the front.

Emily scanned the row. Fifteen men and two women. But all she could make out were the mostly grey or greying heads and two men completely bald.

Xavi leaned into her. 'Can you see him?' he whispered.

'No, I can't make him out. They've all got their backs to us.' Emily caught her breath and noticed a tightness in her chest. *He must be here. We can't have come all this way and not find him. Don't say he hasn't come.*

The hall went quiet as a short stocky man walked to the front and made an announcement from the stage, first in French, then English and finally Spanish, making brief opening remarks and asking for the various delegations to name their country and brigade. A portable microphone was passed between the rows, starting from the back of the hall so that the delegations could introduce themselves. The leader of the French delegation stood up to long applause and said a few words which Emily and Xavi couldn't understand. The microphone was passed forward to a German delegate who spoke in English, again with loud applause. Then an American delegate spoke on behalf of the fifteenth Abraham Lincoln Brigade, thanking the Commune de Paris eleventh battalion and the French Communist Party for hosting the event.

Finally, the microphone was passed to the front rows and came to the leader of the Hungarian delegation. He stood and rolled the microphone in his hands before turning to face the hall and give his introduction in Hungarian.

Emily caught only three words … Budapest … Lazlo …. Kovac.

And there he was. After all this time. Decades. Tall with full grey hair. Slim and erect, he carried his age well, looking more middle aged than old. A gold tooth flashed behind his bottom lip as he spoke. His face seemed to glow, showing how proud he was to be there. After reading a prepared introductory speech he removed his reading glasses and spoke in flawless English. 'It's nice to be among friends again. Comrades, we are all thankful to be here as so many gave their lives for a just cause.' He looked pointedly around the hall. 'And now it seems so many of us have given our hair.' He grinned at the faces in front of him and waited for the laughter from those who understood English to die down. 'Some of the battles may have been lost, but the war goes on. We will carry on. We carry on for our comrades who fell and we carry on for Spain and we carry on for all people who want freedom,' he raised one arm with a clenched fist and called out, 'and we carry on for the *Internationale*.'

There was huge applause around the hall for a full half minute and then the French delegation members were on their feet and began singing the 'Internationale'. Soon every delegate was standing and joining in. The words echoed around the hall until finally there was a great cheer as the song finished and everyone resumed their seats. All except one. Lazlo Kovakz remained standing, waving to the hall and taking a final triumphant accolade.

'So, that's him,' said Xavi.

'That's him,' said Emily.

'Sure?'

'He's had a gold replacement tooth where his was missing. That's him.'

'How are you feeling?'

'Not sure.' She stared at Lazlo, now handing back the microphone and taking his seat again with his back to her. 'But, strangely enough … happy.'

'Happy? I wasn't expecting that.'

'No,' murmured Emily, sitting back and folding her arms.' Neither was I.'

With the introductions over, several speakers came to the stage, most giving their talks in English. At the end of the session there was a three-piece band playing a Spanish folk song and then a lone American with his guitar singing the 'The Battle of Jamara valley'. Most of the delegates joined in to this well-known brigade song but Emily sat quietly, staring at the back of Lazlo's head.

The meeting broke for lunch at twelve. Emily and Xavi followed the other delegates to the restaurant and queued for sandwiches and coffee.

'Are you going to say anything to him?' said Xavi, having to raise his voice slightly above the clanking of the dishes and cups and the constant excited voices.

'No, not now,' said Emily. 'It's not the right moment. Too many people about. I want to do it in private. Just him and me.'

She noticed two of the Hungarian delegates leaving the restaurant by the side door.

Emily tapped Xavi on the arm to get his attention above the noise. 'I won't be a moment,' she said. 'Wait here.'

'What? Where are you going?'

'I'll not be long.' She nodded towards the door. 'I just want to get some information.'

She walked quickly to catch up with the two Hungarian men and was gone for ten minutes. When she returned, she smiled at Xavi and then gave a puzzled look at the two cups in front of her.

'Got you another one,' said Xavi. 'Your first coffee went cold. How did it go? Find out anything?'

'Lots. One of them spoke a bit of broken English so we managed to communicate. I told them I was writing a newsletter for the British International Brigade Veterans' Association and wanted to know how everyone was looking forward to the rest of the conference and the trip to Paris. I wanted to know where they were staying? What they were doing in their spare time? And especially ... who their leader was?'

'And?'

'Turns out they're staying in Montmartre too, at the Victor Mass hotel. They were given the same list of suitable hotels as us from the conference organisers. That would have been interesting, eh? If we were staying at the same hotel? They use the same metro as us, the Abbesses. They've been here three days already and they're enjoying seeing some old comrades from the war. And of course, they're enjoying the drinking, apart from, interestingly, the leader of their delegation. Chief Marshall Kovac, they call him. An honorary title, I think. He spends time with them but he likes to go sightseeing around Montmartre with his camera in the early morning.'

Xavi leaned forward. 'Okay, so we wait outside his hotel and follow him. Get him alone and you can talk to him. I'll be there in case he gets awkward.'

Emily held up one hand and tried to keep her voice down, though it was difficult to be heard above the clamour in the restaurant 'No, sorry Xavi. I have to do this by myself. It's important for me. Do you understand?'

Xavi pulled at his goatee beard. 'Of course, if that's what you want. But wouldn't it be better for me to be there with you when you tell him.'

Emily shook her head. 'I'll be fine old friend. You don't have to be concerned about me. You enjoy the sights of Paris and we'll meet up in the evening at the hotel. He doesn't scare me. There's no need to worry. I might not even say anything tomorrow. Maybe wait a bit longer. We'll see.'

A buzzer announced the start of the afternoon session and Emily and Xavi filed back into the main hall with the rest of the delegates and took their seats.

*

The next day was Saturday. It was six thirty in the morning and Emily was sitting at a covered bus stop opposite the hotel Victor Masse. There was a slight drizzle and there were only a few people about. Two workmen with long brushes were sweeping the pavement opposite and heading towards their cart. Two women strolled past her and a young man in a tracksuit was running steadily along the street. The door to the hotel had opened twice since she had been there but only for some uniformed staff to leave with their shift being over.

She had already been there for thirty minutes and was wondering if she had missed him or if he was going to go out later or if he wasn't going to go out at all. She put these thoughts to one side and decided to hang on and wait. She rehearsed some words in her mind, going over and over what she would say to him. She kept changing them. She wanted to get this just right. Hit the correct tone. No hysterics. Just the facts and see what he would say. And she had other speeches ready depending on his reply. Although, already she knew she had more than enough trains of thought to handle. And she should have gone to the toilet before she left her hotel. It was getting cold now and she pulled further back into the bus shelter to keep out of the slight breeze and also so as not to be too conspicuous. Two buses had already stopped but she had declined to get on. Anyone watching her would think it a little strange that she had been sitting there for a long time, seemingly not going anywhere.

She knew that the next session was due to start at ten so he would have to come out soon and start his sightseeing if he was to make it back to the conference. She was rewarded fifteen minutes later when the front door to the hotel opened again and Lazlo came out wearing a dark green flat cap, a long tan-coloured raincoat and a camera slung over his shoulder. Emily's heart sank as she noticed he was with another man.

They started walking along the street, bending into the rain, and she followed them at a discreet distance with the hood of her kagoule pulled firmly over her head. At the corner of Rue Duperre she saw them stop and shake hands. Lazlo continued by himself along the Rue Houdon and then into the Abbesses metro station, through the dragonfly-style entrance with its beautiful art nouveau glass roof, green wrought iron arches and amber lights. She hurried to catch up to find out where he was going. She stood two steps behind him by the ticket office and watched him point to his street map and ask for a return ticket for the nearest metro to Notre Dame. The woman at the ticket office window told him, in English, to take the metro for Saint Michel on line four as it was direct. He would easily see Notre Dame and be able to take a walk along the Seine.

Widening your sightseeing Lazlo? Emily thought to herself.

After Lazlo had collected his change and left the window Emily bought her ticket and followed him down the steps to the platform. When the near empty train arrived, she took a seat in the next carriage making sure she could see him through the glass of a connecting door. Twenty-five minutes and seven stops later the train arrived at Gare de Saint Michel. Lazlo took the elevator up but Emily didn't want to get too close so raced up two flights of stairs to ground level. She arrived at the top breathing hard and could just make out his dark green cap as he made his way across the street heading towards the cathedral of Notre Dame.

She tracked him for a further half hour in the drizzling rain as he studied the angles carefully and took his photographs all around the cathedral. Then he walked a little way along the river to the Pont Neuf bridge spanning the Seine with its creamy coloured stonework. He took pictures of the semi-circular bastions jutting out along the pier and the twelve arches decorated with hundreds of grotesque stone masks. He crossed on to the left bank and sauntered among the book stalls, the early morning joggers and the street artists just setting up for the day with the brightly-coloured, huge umbrellas protecting their canvasses.

He took more photos of the bridge and still more of Notre Dame across the water before turning into the Latin Quarter along Rue La Grange and going into a café. Emily stood outside for a few moments, watching through the window to see where he was going to sit. And then she went in.

It was a small café with ten, round, light-wooden tables, a long glass counter half way along the back wall with pastries and cakes displayed, and a black and white tiled floor. Lots of photographs of well dressed, handsome men and women featured on two walls. Five of the tables were taken, mainly with couples and Lazlo sat in a corner table at the front of the cafe with his back to the window. He was looking at his camera and taking the occasional sip from a small cup, adjusting his glasses to see more clearly.

Emily bought a coffee and then walked across to Lazlo. She wasn't sure why, and she hadn't meant to, but her legs made their way across the floor and then arrived at his table. She hadn't planned for this today. But here she was.

'Pardon? Excuse-moi?' She smiled and pointed at the chair.

Lazlo smiled back. 'Mais oui. Yes, of course, please.' He waved a hand.

Emily pulled the chair out, dropped her shoulder bag to the floor and sat down.

Lazlo straightened, put his camera to one side, looked around at the empty tables and gave Emily a puzzled look. 'I'm sorry. I don't speak much French. Je ne parle pas Francais.'

'Oh, that's okay,' said Emily, unzipping her kagoule. 'I'm not too good at it myself. A little school French that's all.'

Lazlo continued with his puzzled look and opened up his hands spreading out the fingers. 'Can I help you?'

Emily didn't know what to say to that so she took a drink of her coffee to buy some time.

'English?' Lazlo continued. 'You are English?'

'Yes. And you?'

'Hungarian. Budapest.'

'Oh, Hungarian. Tourist?'

'Yes and no.' Lazlo pointed to his camera and took off his glasses. 'I like taking pictures. But I'm here for a conference … just for a few days. And you?'

Emily glanced at his green eyes with the slight scar by the right one, that she remembered so well. She broke away and adjusted her chair, bring it closer to the table. 'Yes, yes,' she said. 'Holiday. Little break. Just for a few days.' She was surprised by her voice. It sounded creaky and brittle and she realised she was shaking. She took a deep breath to recover. She could feel the back of her eyes heating up and bit the inside of her mouth.

'Are you okay?' he asked. 'You look a little flushed. Can I get you some water?'

No, no, not that. Don't do that. Don't be kind.

'No, thank you,' she said. 'I'm fine. Just get a little dizzy from time to time.'

Lazlo started to wind the strap around his camera. She sipped at her coffee and took the opportunity to have a good look at him over the rim of her cup. Her eyes opening and shutting as if seeing him for the first time. *After all these years. Now you're an old man. Enjoyed a full life. And enjoying your later years with your camera and your sightseeing. Not a care in the world.* She wasn't sure how she felt: somewhere between a sense of accomplishment at being here at all and nervousness at the expectation of what might happen.

'Nice camera,' she said. She coughed to get rid of the lump rattling in her throat. 'Looks new.'

'Bought it here. Cost half a year's pension,' he laughed, giving his big smile 'But it's worth it. It can bring back a lot of memories.'

Emily gave a small shake of her head. *That's it. That's the smile. The over-confident horrible smile.*

'Memories are very important,' Emily said, stretching out the words, savouring their connivance and intrigue. *If only you knew what memories I have. What memories you made for me.*

'Absolutely. And this little thing here can bring them all back. Nikon F2, easy to use, lots of different lenses. Makes me feel like a professional.' He laughed again.

'That's nice.' Emily took cover behind her own best smile, trying to remain calm. 'And who will you share your memories with?'

'Oh, my children. All grown up now with children of their own. My wife died a few years back.'

'And are they all well?'

'Yes, yes, thank you, they are all healthy and doing well. Better than I did at their age. He laughed again and relaxed into the conversation. 'And you? Do you have a family back home?'

'I have a daughter and a granddaughter.'

Go on. Go on. Ask if they're well. Ask. Ask.

Lazlo sipped at his drink. 'Are they here with you?'

'No, they're back home,' she said, and then added slowly. 'In Newcastle.'

Lazlo twisted his mouth as if to say something but then changed his mind. He looked at her more carefully and for a split second she felt a prickle of excitement race through her chest.

Emily let him consider this for long seconds. Eventually she said, 'So, this conference, is it for European pensioners who are camera enthusiasts?'

Lazlo came back from seeming to try to remember something, something from a long time ago. He laughed. A curious sort of uncertain laugh. 'No, not exactly,' he said. 'Although, some of them are pensioners now, like me.'

'So, what is it?'

'It's a conference for International Brigade veterans of the Spanish Civil War.' His voice became steady, tinged with satisfaction and pride. *'The heroes* as they were called.'

The words ignited something in Emily and she hated his imperious, boastful tone. 'Oh, I see,' she said. 'Which side?'

Lazlo pulled his head back 'The republican side of course.'

'Oh yes. You lost, didn't you? 'She produced a short sardonic smile.

Lazlo stared at her, slightly frowning. 'We were there to help save a threatened county's freedom and independence … the sacrifice … the banners of Spain were lowered for so many heroes …' He tried to remember some more of Dolores Ibarurri's farewell to the brigades but it wouldn't come so instead he repeated, 'there were so many heroes.' Then he tried to look away.

Emily reeled him back in. 'So … you were one of the good guys, were you?' she snapped. The words were scornful, intended to get a reaction.

Lazlo repositioned himself in his chair and leaned back. She could see white below his green pupils, the light flickering between his ridiculously long eyelashes, the grey hairs in his nostrils. Then, with a deep breath he gradually brought his head down and scratched at the light stubble on his chin.

'Why did you sit here?' Lazlo said slowly. 'Is there something I can do for you?'

'I doubt it. You wouldn't even help me carry some things to load on to the lorries.'

'What?' Lazlo's mouth began to open and shut rapidly. Eventually his jaw went slack.

'And I'm glad your family is well.'

It took him a long time to answer. He nodded. 'Mmm,' was all he could manage. And then. 'Thank you.'

'Your English is very good.'

Lazlo nodded again, she watched him concentrating hard, trying to work out what was going on.

'You lived in London for a year studying to be a lawyer,' said Emily.

Lazlo still did not answer but forced himself even further back in his chair and folded his arms.

Emily looked down at her hand and rubbed at her index finger. Then she stared at Lazlo. Taking as long as she could. Forcing him to stare back. Without taking her eyes off him she leaned down, took out a photo from the top of her bag and placed it in the middle of the table.

'This is my daughter. She isn't well like your family. She's thirty-eight and very ill with Huntington's disease. Have you heard of it?'

Lazlo sat motionless. He glanced at the photograph briefly. His face was blank. 'And? Why are you telling me this? You seem to know me. How did you ...? Oh, never mind.'

You're not going to care, are you? You're not going to give it a second thought. How horrible. How vile.

'I was in the International Brigades too,' said Emily. 'At Jamara and Brunete,'

'Impressive,' said Lazlo, staring at her.

'That's what you said then. When you wouldn't help me load the lorries.' Emily glared into Lazlo's still impassive face.

'I am sorry,' said Lazlo. 'I don't know how I can help you. I am sorry for your daughter.'

'Your daughter too,' Emily said. She leaned forward and gripped the arms of the chair. She could feel the blood surging through her body throbbing at her neck and throat.

Lazlo pulled his lips together and shook his head. 'Sorry. I don't understand,' he said, looking away, his gaze flicking about among the pictures on the wall.

Emily put her elbows on the table, rested her chin on her hands and stared at him with wide unblinking eyes. 'My name is Emily. I was a nurse in the forward dressing station at Brunete. We were retreating. Everywhere was confusion.' She took in a deep breath and kept her voice low. 'You took advantage of the confusion. You came into the shelter and raped me.'

Lazlo took a long drink from his cup and gave her a steady look. He put his cup down carefully and turned the cup so that the handle was pointing to his right. Then he turned it again so that the handle now pointed towards him. He unfolded his napkin and delicately wiped a sliver of liquid from his mouth. Without taking his eyes off the napkin as he replaced it, he said softly, 'I don't think so. I think you are mistaken.'

Emily wanted to slam both hands down on to the table but she held them across her stomach and gulped in more air. 'You raped me.' She said under her breath, her voice shaking with the strain of controlling it. 'You raped me and impregnated me with the disease that my daughter has. And now she can't drink or eat properly or even walk properly.'

My God. You can't even remember, can you? You can't remember.

Emily pulled her head up and narrowed her eyes. 'Go on say it, Lazlo Kovac. You can't remember, can you? You don't care.'

'Extreme situations,' said Lazlo.

'What?'

'Extreme situations,' said Lazlo. He waved a derisive hand as if swatting a wasp away. 'It happens. It happened many times. A necessary comfort.' Emily thought she saw the beginning of a smile on his lips but then it quickly changed into an indulgent frown. 'We all get over it,' he continued, as if explaining a problem to a child. 'We have to. And you have me mistaken.'

'So, you've done this many times.' All she could hear was the rapid thumping of her heartbeat. 'A comfort for who?'

He didn't answer. He put his elbows on the table and rested his chin on his clasped hands mimicking her. He blinked and stared at her and kept his face impassive, unmoved: displaying a stolid, unruffled indifference. But she could see his knuckles whitening with the effort.

She tried to remember her speech again. The one she had rehearsed outside his hotel. The one she thought about for the last few months, ever since she had discovered he was still alive and was coming here. Finding the right words then rearranging them. Finding the right words to show what it had meant for her, how it had shaped her life and how inhuman he had seemed at the time. She had vowed to herself that she wasn't going to scream. She wouldn't give him the satisfaction of seeing her lose control but at the same time she would let him know that he had made a big mistake: a huge error of judgement, if he thought she would just let him off the hook.

There was a long silence. Long and stiff and deep. The gap between them thickened. She wanted him to say something. She wanted him to remember at least. He had to say something. It was his turn and she needed his words to trigger her speech but she knew that she was struggling to compose herself enough and remember it. The walls were closing in, squeezing the light and the space until all that was left was Lazlo's blank face surrounded by a grey fog and his green eyes darkening, fixing her with a frozen stare.

Emily scraped her chair back and stood up quickly. 'I need to go to the toilet,' she said. She didn't want to leave but she needed to be away from those eyes. Five steps away she turned back and levelled her voice, taking careful aim. 'My God. You were a bastard then,' she railed at him, her voice firm and strident. 'And you're still a bastard now.'

The young couple at the table behind turned and looked at Emily as she swayed between the tables and disappeared through one of the two red doors at the end of the long glass counter. They glanced at Lazlo and then turned awkwardly to continue their conversation.

Emily came back four minutes later and looked around but Lazlo was nowhere to be seen. She sat down and sipped at her coffee. The same couple whispered something to each other and gave furtive glances again. Emily looked across at them and stared pointedly. *Don't look at me like that. You don't know. You have no idea.* She wished she had said more to Lazlo. But she would meet him again, she was certain of that. Although of course, she thought, he might decide not to risk bumping in to her again. He might decide to leave, go home, not wanting to have to deal with her again. But was he really like that? He didn't seem like the sort to be embarrassed, certainly not by a woman. He looked confident and unapologetic and sure of himself. Even in his seventies now he still had that air of arrogance she thought. The swagger and conceit of someone who doesn't give a damn. *He doesn't give a damn. He knows he can get away with it. It was too long ago.*

Emily stared down at her cup. She wished she had said more. It hadn't been enough, nowhere near enough. She had thought she would be more dispassionate but she had been more nervous than she had imagined. *No, not nervous. It was hate. The hate got in the way and stopped me thinking clearly. I should have said that I* ... A door closed quietly behind her and Lazlo suddenly appeared and sat down opposite.

'I thought I had better go to the toilet too.' He smiled at her. 'At my age you need to take every opportunity.' He leaned right across the table and gazed at her for seconds, forcing her to stare back. 'Sometimes it's better to leave the past behind us,' he whispered. 'That's why it's called the past.'

Emily pulled back from him. She had been caught off guard. She knew she needed to say lots of things but all she could think of was screaming out *rapist* to the whole café and sending the word crashing around the place making as many heads turn as possible. But she knew she couldn't do that; she shouldn't draw too much attention to herself in case she was recognised later.

Instead, she said quietly, almost conspiratorially, as if disclosing a closely kept secret between friends. 'You don't care, do you?'

'No.'

Blunt and chilling, Lazlo left the word hanging between them, waited for a few seconds and then and stood up.

He adjusted the camera strap over his shoulder and gave a small, very slow bow, disdainful and unpleasant, mocking her. He pushed his chair under the table and then made to leave. Emily fixed her gaze away from him to the back of the room. She tried to think of something to say but perhaps, she thought, she could save that for another time. As Lazlo came alongside Emily he reached across gently, picked up her cup and saucer and flicked them on to her lap, spilling coffee over her sweater and jeans. Emily jerked back, gasped and stared at him, shocked and appalled in equal measure. She saw the corners of his mouth pull up into a brief smile. She pulled the cup up but the saucer fell to the floor and bounced once without breaking before rolling off and trundling loudly cross the room. The wooden floor amplifying its journey as it rebounded off the leg of the young couple's table.

Lazlo was already at the entrance to the café as the saucer spiralled to a clattering halt in the middle of the room. Every face in the cafe turned from him to Emily and back again as he pulled up his collar and stepped out into the rain.

*

That night Emily met Xavi for dinner at the hotel at their prearranged time. He was already at the table as Emily came into the hotel restaurant. He waved at her and she went across and sat opposite him, a gleaming white tablecloth, an opened bottle of red wine and two sparkling tall glasses between them. The place was already nearly full and the buzz of chatter and the clink of metal and glass filled the large room.

'Where've you been?' said Xavi urgently. 'I waited for you at the conference hall.'

'Yes, sorry about that,' said Emily.' Did you go in?'

'Only for about an hour. Then I came back here. I thought you would be in your room.'

Emily ignored the implied question. 'Was he there?' she asked.

'Lazlo? Yes. He was with his delegation.' Xavi leaned forward. 'Where've you been? Did you see him? Did you talk to him?'

'Yes, yes, I saw him. I followed him to a café by Notre Dame and I spoke to him. Spent the day wandering about afterwards to think things through.'

'Well?' Xavi's eyes gleamed and he tensed his face. 'What did he say?'

Emily took a moment. She looked around the restaurant and then back at Xavi. She knew that he loved her and would do anything for her. And she loved him. He was a good man and she didn't want him involved in this.

She gave him a wide smile. 'He apologised.'

'He did?'

'Yes, he did. He said he was very sorry. He said he wished he could make it all better. He wished he could have the time again to make amends. He was sorry about Rosa and hoped that she would get better.'

'Good Lord,' said Xavi. 'That's good news then. Very good news.' Then he pulled back. 'I mean, you know, it doesn't alter anything but … it's good news, right?'

'Yes,' Emily nodded.

Xavi reached across and touched her hand. 'You can rest easy now, yes?'

Emily smiled again. 'I suppose so.'

'This is very good news. Very good. News worthy of celebrating.' Xavi poured two glasses of wine and held his up. 'You can put all of this behind you. It's not necessarily a happy time, I know, but at least he has shown some kind of human kindness. After all these years you have some kind of closure.'

'Of course,' said Emily. 'Closure … that's right.'

*

The following morning Emily was up early again. She slipped a note under Xavi's door *'See you later. I hope you don't mind. I'm going for a long walk to clear my mind after yesterday. I'll see you tonight.'*

It was still raining. It had rained all night and there were lots of puddles around as she walked quickly to the Victor Mass hotel and took up her position at the bus stop huddling into a corner to avoid the rain dripping down through a broken tile in the roof.

At exactly six forty-five Lazlo came out of the hotel wearing his green hat, tan-coloured raincoat and holding a large umbrella. He was alone. Obviously, none of his delegation wanted to join him and stroll about in the wet. Indeed, they were the only two people on the street, the rain keeping everyone indoors on this Sunday morning. Emily leaned further back into the shelter and watched Lazlo hurry along the street and turn the corner. She followed him into Rue Houdon and then across the empty road into Abbesses metro station keeping a good distance from him although he seemed too preoccupied with clutching his camera to his side under the umbrella to keep it dry rather than looking about.

She stood behind the big wrought iron gates as Lazlo bought his ticket. Then when he had left the ticket window she went in and bought a ticket to Pigalle, the next metro stop. It didn't matter where Lazlo was going, she wouldn't be following him today.

She caught up with him halfway down the deserted, steep spiral staircase as he slowly and carefully negotiated his way in the dim light. The soft shoes she had deliberately worn allowed her to get two steps behind him without being noticed. Emily had a quick look behind and then strained forward to see beyond him to the empty steps stretching down to the platform still several metres below.

'Lazlo Kovac,' she said.

He turned awkwardly, one hand on the wall still steadying himself and looked up at her.

'You,' growled Lazlo. 'You again. What do you want this time?'

'Nothing.'

'You have no more funny stories to tell me?'

'No.'

'Then, what do you want?'

'Nothing. I just want you to know who it was. Who I am.'

'What the hell are you talking about? Are you completely mad?'

'Back at the café yesterday, you didn't seem to remember me. But I think you did.'

'So, what if I remember you? What does it matter? It was a long time ago. Who cares if I remember or not?' He let go of the wall and turned to face her, steadying himself on his umbrella. 'What does it matter eh? Get over it. And get the hell away from me.'

'I just want you to know who it was.'

Lazlo shook his head and spat at her feet. 'What does that mean? Have you gone soft in the head? What the hell are you talking about?'

'My name is Emily Edelman and I just want you to know … in these last few seconds … who it was who killed you.'

'Don't be stupid,' Lazlo shouted. 'You're completely mad.' His head stooped low and his shoulders stiffened. His face seemed to darken and she saw fear in his eyes as he looked about to see if anyone was on the stairs to help. He knew he was vulnerable where he was standing and he turned to try and reach across and hang on to the iron stair rail.

He was already off balance when Emily took a quick step forward and pushed him on his left shoulder as he turned. It didn't take much and she was surprised at how easy it was. What was most pleasing to her was the look of absolute terror in his face as he stared back at her when he began falling backwards down the stone stairs, crashing and clattering off the curved wall and tumbling down, down. He was soon out of sight and Emily stepped quickly down the stairs after him. It took a full twenty seconds for him to reach the platform level and she arrived at the bottom to find his body a tangled, broken mess of twisted limbs set at impossible angles. The tightly wrapped umbrella at his side.

She rushed across to his body and reached into her pocket for the empty syringe. His mouth hung open and a pool of blood covered his gold tooth. But as she bent over him and felt the carotid pulse at his neck, she realised she wouldn't be needing the syringe to inject air into his vein and block a blood vessel. His camera was by his side, Emily picked it up and slung the strap across her shoulder. She stood over him and was soon aware of two figures running along the platform. Emily looked at them, a middle-aged man and a younger woman, and shook her head to indicate that it was no use. Then she pointed to the stairs and made a tumbling motion with her arms. The woman ran back along the platform to try and find help while the man stood staring at the body and said something in French which she nodded at although not understanding. Emily touched him on the arm and made a telephone sign with her hand to her ear and then pointed again to the stairs. The man nodded and Emily hurried off, climbing back up the stairs as quickly as she could.

When she was near the top she took the camera from its leather case, wrenched the roll of film out and ripped it apart. She placed the camera on the step and smashed it with her heel until the lens glass was completely shattered and jagged bits of plastic spread across the concrete. Then she stamped on it again. And then again. She took a moment to stare at the mangled pieces. 'No more memories for you, comrade,' she muttered.

*

By eight o' clock Emily was back at the hotel Rodier. She took the lift up to the third floor and let herself in to her room. She took a bottle of warm red wine from her suitcase and poured some into the glass in the bathroom. She drank deeply and then poured another one and drank that. She went back to the suitcase, changed into another sweater and dark trousers and put the coffee-stained clothes from the previous day into her bag. Then she sat on the bed and tried to think of what to do next but all she could see was Lazlo's face as he fell backwards and then the sounds of bone hitting concrete.

A knock at the door brought her back. When she opened the door Xavi came in with her message in his hand. 'What's going on?' he said. 'I thought I'd catch you before you went out. Where do you have to go now? Aren't you going to the conference?'

Emily suddenly felt like crying. It seemed the right thing to do, given the circumstances, although she fully realised Xavi would want to know why. It wasn't something she did much but she was aware of thinking clearly about it and she was relieved to be thinking clearly about anything at the moment. She felt her ears burning and her eyes stinging and thought for a brief moment about stopping the tears but decided at the last moment that they were needed. The first tear trickled down he left cheek and was soon followed by streams flowing down and dripping on to her chin and neck. She kept perfectly still and made no sound.

Xavi stared at her. 'What? What's going on? Whatever is the matter? Why are you crying?' He stood motionless with his arms by his side.

Emily brushed the tears away with the back of her hand and gave a gasping laugh. 'I knew you wouldn't know what to do. You're supposed to give me a hug.'

Xavi, still nonplussed, repeated his questions. 'What's going on? What's happening?'

Too late now, thought Emily.

'Lazlo's dead,' she said. Her voice was cracked and faltering.

'Good Lord. What? How? How did it happen?'

'Apparently he fell down the stairs at the metro station.' She tried her best to sound as matter-of-fact as she could but the words came out overly frigid.

'When?' Xavi frowned.

'This morning. Early.' She immediately knew that was a mistake.

'This morning? But, how do you know? Did someone tell you? I haven't heard anything. We don't know anyone here who could tell us.'

Emily used a sleeve to dry up the last of the tears and then gave her full attention to the light fitting in the centre of the ceiling.

Xavi threw up his hands. 'Emily! Speak to me. What's going on? How do you know?' He suddenly stiffened, tilted his head and waited for a few moments. 'Were you there? Is that why you left the message?' The words were terse and hesitant and Emily could tell he didn't want to say them.

Much too late now, thought Emily.

'I was there,' she said, not taking her gaze from the light fitting.

'Emily, you're getting me worried now. So, you saw him slip? I thought this was finished. He apologised. I thought that was the end of it. Why did you go and see him again?'

Emily twisted her mouth, trying to think of what to say. All she could manage was, 'I was there. I went to see him again.' The words slid out slow and mechanically.

'But why? You said he apologised. You said he was sorry. Did you talk to him, before …'

'Yes.'

Any moment now, thought Emily.

'So, you saw him slip. Were you on the stairs beside him? I don't understand why you went … I thought that … and how did he slip? I thought… oh no! *Oh no!*' Xavi sat down heavily on the wicker chair by the far wall. 'Oh no, don't tell me. Good Lord don't tell me …'

'He was a monster,' Emily stared at Xavi. 'An absolute monster. I just –'

'Don't tell me.' Xavi held up both hands trying to block her words and push them back. 'I don't want to know. Don't tell me.'

'You already know,' Emily lowered her voice. 'I don't need to tell you. He was a monster. Worse than what I imagined. He didn't care. He didn't care about me or Rosa. He didn't care about all the others he's done this to. He admitted it.' She scrunched up her eyes. 'What do you think I was coming here for? I told you he was sorry because I wanted to keep you out of this. But he wasn't sorry. Not at all. I did … I did want to keep you out of this.'

Xavi rubbed at his neck, rolling the wrinkles around and blew out a breath. 'Too bloody late now,' he whispered.

'I pushed him Xavi. I pushed him for all those others as well. It was justice.'

They submitted themselves to a long searching examination of each other.

Xavi's finger crept up to his forehead and slid to his temple before settling on massaging his eyes, taking a moment to arrange his thoughts. He pulled his hand down to his side, stared at the floor and slowly shook his head, over and over, with long, wide measured movements, backwards and forwards, backwards and forwards. She wanted to tell him to hurry up. They needed to get this over with: it was unbearable. She wished he hadn't come to the room. It would have given her a few hours to work out what to say, to keep him out of this and try to stop the ear-splitting whirlwind in her head.

'It was justice Xavi.' Emily snapped. 'What would you have done? He ruined my family. He deserved it. I wish I could have done it years ago. It was justice. He thought he could get away with it but there's always consequences. We all have choices to make. If you make the wrong choice then you should pay for it. He forced this choice on me.'

Xavi looked up. 'And what about his family?' he said, his voice still quiet. He didn't say the words to antagonise but that's how they sounded to her.

It was Emily's turn to stiffen. She pushed her head back. 'He didn't care about *my* family! Why should I care about his!' The words came out too quick and too loud and too heavy, cutting, almost snarling. She wanted to take them back. This wasn't the person she wanted Xavi to see.

Xavi took a deep breath and gave her a look she hadn't seen before. She couldn't read it but she knew she didn't want to see it again.

He stood up and pushed his hands deep into his pockets. 'So … was it justice? Or revenge?'

Emily thought carefully and gave him a steady look that she hoped would reinforce her words. 'It was justice Xavi. Pure and simple … justice. And I would do it again. I would do it a hundred times.'

'Okay,' said Xavi. 'Justice then. You had a choice and you chose justice. Justice is better that revenge. Revenge is toxic.' He stared about the room. 'But what about the law? What about morality?'

Emily allowed her shoulders to relax and took a long time to answer. 'Believe me Xavi, I've thought about this for years. This is the law. This is morality. He deserved it. He made his choice and he had it coming. If it wasn't me then I hope it would be someone else.' She looked around the room trying to find the right words. 'And ... I would have thought that this fitted in with your Humanist theories. This is all about common humanity, isn't it? Moral values based on human nature. Ethical decisions based on reason and concern for other human beings. Giving our own lives meaning. Getting justice for others.' She fixed him with a self-assured, resolute stare. 'Justice delayed is justice denied. His justice was delayed far too long.'

Xavi stared back and bowed his head slightly giving a tiny nod.

'But what about you?' Emily continued. 'You now have a choice. Between the law and friendship. And I didn't want to give you that choice.'

The words fell heavily on to the floor between them.

Eventually Xavi looked up. 'No. You're wrong my dear friend.' His face was expressionless. 'I have no choice.'

Chapter ten

Monday, 24th October 2016,

Newcastle, Northern England.

Ramon, Felipe and Valentina stepped on to the platform at Newcastle Central station and made their way to the large station clock where they had agreed to meet Felipe's contact. They each carried backpacks and looked, as they intended, like three student backpackers travelling around Britain. It had been a long journey from Madrid's Adolfo Suarez airport in the early morning and then a long train journey from London's King's Cross station which should have taken four hours but actually took six because of a downed power line.

'Me pregunto donde estara,' said Ramon. 'Yo quiero – '

'No! English!' Felipe said quickly. 'We agreed. Just English. All the time. Even when alone. You keep forgetting Ramon. We don't want anyone guessing where we're from. And no cell phones. They're easily tracked. And yes, I wonder where he is too. This was the meeting place but we're two hours late. Maybe he's been and gone.'

'Felipe' A voice came from behind them.

They all turned together and saw two men. One, dark-haired and tall and wearing a leather jacket with a smart shirt and a huge toothy smile. The other one much shorter, wearing a grey suit, slightly balding with not quite as broad a smile.

'Yes,' said Felipe. 'That's me.'

'Marvellous,' said the leather jacket. 'You made it then. Well done. Brilliant. I'm Arthur,' he turned to his partner, 'and this is George. Not our real names of course. Last month George was Odysseus. Keeps Special Branch on their toes when they're phone tapping and listening in to conversations.' He looked at the three blank faces. 'No? Oh well, not to worry. It keeps us amused. Lightens the tone, y'know. Anyway, good to meet you.' He spoke with a soft southern English accent and had a cheery open face with a ruddy complexion.

'I'm happy that you waited,' said Felipe. 'Sorry we're late, the train was delayed.'

'No problem,' said Arthur. 'Anything to help our international friends … and it gave us the opportunity to have a beer or three while we waited. So, it's not all bad.'

Felipe introduced Ramon and Valentina.

'It's good of you to help us,' said Valentina.

'We'll do anything we can to help,' said Arthur. He lowered his voice. 'Your cause is our cause. The English Arrow Alliance is here to give any assistance we can. We know the importance of friends in other countries. We're all falangists at heart, eh? And don't worry we won't get in the way. Felipe has given us the essential facts on why you're here. Anything to mess up the Catalan independence elections can't be a bad thing, can it? We're all on the same side and maybe you can help us in the future.' He smiled at each of them in turn. 'Anyway, we've got you somewhere to stay for a few days … and we've got the address of the bloke Felipe mentioned. We've been keeping an eye on him for you, seeing what he's up to since that commie friend of his croaked … Xavi, I think his name was. Is that right?'

'That's him,' said Felipe.

'Good,' Arthur turned to his friend. 'We've got a car.' George disappeared to get the car. 'We can take you to a friend's house not far from here, it belongs to Will Roddy. The house is empty for a bit while he's ... detained for a few months.' He gave an even broader smile. 'We've put some beer and food in it for you. You can use his car, Honda Jazz, he won't be needing it. His laptop too. I've got the codes for you. It's pretty central so you shouldn't have any trouble getting about.'

Twenty minutes later they pulled up outside a house in Walker Road. Arthur waited until they had pulled their rucksacks from the boot and then handed over an envelope and two sets of keys, one for the house and one for the car.

'Okay,' said Arthur. 'Have fun. Anything you need just give us a call. Felipe's got my number. The bloke's address is in the envelope. It's not far from here actually. We can catch up with you in a couple of days but for now it's best if we're not too visible. Special Branch like to keep tabs on us to see what we're up to. Happy hunting.'

Arthur and George went into another car parked beside the house and drove away. It was nine o' clock in the evening and the three Spaniards were very tired. 'Let's go in and get some rest,' said Ramon. 'I think we're going to have a busy few days ahead of us.' It was the first time he had spoken since they had arrived at the station. 'We should visit this Xavi character tomorrow. Hopefully we can do this quickly and get back home.'

*

The following morning at his flat in Heaton, Xavi was just finishing his third cup of coffee when the doorbell rang. He ignored it. He didn't want to see anyone. It was eleven o' clock and he was still in his pyjamas. He felt all of his eighty-four years today, though people would say he didn't look anything like that age. Emily's death two months ago had really affected him and he was drinking way too much. He felt alone and always sad, not wanting to go out, not even wanting to swim which was his favourite thing. He tended to sleep late these days and today felt especially tired after staying up drinking gin and tonic and watching television until the early hours. And he certainly didn't want any visitors.

The doorbell rang again. 'Hell's teeth,' Xavi muttered to himself. He pushed his cup to the centre of the small table beside his chair, turned awkwardly in his seat and stared at the front door, willing it to go away. He waited and then pulled himself up and went to the living room window where he could see outside the front door. The curtains were still closed and he drew them back slightly to get a good view. He could see three figures on the doorstep. 'Hell's teeth,' he muttered again. 'Bloody hell.' *Why can't they see that the curtains are closed? Why don't they just go away? I don't need any canvassers here. I know who I'm voting for.*

The doorbell rang again this time accompanied by three, rapid loud knocks. Xavi walked back to his chair and was just about sit down when he heard the letterbox opening.

'Xavi! Xavi Rodrigues! Are you in?'

Xavi swung round. He rubbed the three-day old stubble on his face and tried to concentrate. He took a sweater slung over the back of chair, discarded from the night before and pulled it over his pyjama top.

Who is it? How do they know my name? Why don't they just go away and not bother me?

'Xavi! Xavi are you there? We just need to talk to you for a few minutes.'

Xavi stared at the door again. There was a definite accent to the words. He wasn't sure what to do. He was curious but he definitely didn't want to speak to anyone. He knew he should just go back to his chair until they had gone away but he found himself standing by the front door and turning the key.

Xavi blinked as he opened the door and looked at the three figures huddling on his doorstep trying to shelter from the wind. Two young men and a young woman. Small misty clouds were coming from their mouths and the two men rubbed their hands together warming them. The woman's blue hair was being whipped across her face to the short cut hair on the other side, flicking across a long scar, reddening with the cold. He took a careful note of the scar. *Where are you from?* thought Xavi, remembering the accent he'd heard. He noticed their lightweight thin jackets. Only the woman had a scarf. *Why aren't you dressed for this cold Autumn weather?*

One of the men stepped forward and held out his hand. Xavi shook it. It was freezing.

'Hello,' said the man. 'I'm Felipe. Very pleased to meet you. These are my friends Valentina and Ramon.' As he spoke more clouds of freezing breath covered his mouth.

'What can I do for you?' said Xavi.

'May we come in and talk to you for a few minutes?' said Valentina, clawing at her hair, her eyes shining with the cold.

'No,' said Xavi. He didn't want them getting all cosy and having long conversations and him providing biscuits and tea. He looked at each of them again. 'You can stand inside the doorway if you like. Keep out of the wind.'

Felipe led the way and then Valentina and Ramon came in and all four crowded together in Xavi's small hallway. Xavi half closed the door, *just in case*, he thought. The long scar still on his mind.

'Why do you want to speak to me?' said Xavi.

'Yes, please excuse us,' said Valentina. 'We should have written to you first but there wasn't a lot of time. We are all from Lisbon. We are international students of politics at University College London. We have a short break in lectures for a few days so we thought we'd do some travelling around the country. Our lecturer knew that Felipe here was studying the role of Portuguese members of the International Brigades in the Spanish Civil War. He knew that one of the last remaining British International Brigaders had unfortunately just died and asked if we would be interested in interviewing anyone who knew her for Felipe's thesis and also for the university history department's quarterly broadsheet. We decided to combine travelling with helping our friend.'

'Well,' said Xavi. 'I'm sorry you've come all this way but I don't think I can help you. The lady in question, Emily Edelman, didn't like to talk much about the war or her time in the brigades.' *This would definitely be a bad idea,* thought Xavi. 'Again, I'm sorry,' he continued. 'I haven't anything to add than what you have probably read in the newspapers and on the internet. It isn't long ago that she died so it's all a bit raw you understand. She was a very dear friend.'

'Yes, of course, but is there anyone else we can talk to?' said Ramon.

'No, I'm sorry. I don't think so,' said Xavi. *You don't seem overly sympathetic.* He didn't want anyone else bothered by these three and he certainly didn't want them digging about and finding information about Emily's past and their secret.

'Surely, there must be,' said Ramon. His voice had an edge to it that Xavi didn't like. Valentina flashed a look at Ramon and frowned.

'Okay,' she said, giving Xavi a smile. 'Maybe this is a bad time. Perhaps we could come back when –'

Ramon broke in. 'We've come a long way. It would really help us if you could let us know who to speak to.' He held Xavi with a blank stare.

Xavi felt a tingling sensation at the base of his neck. He wondered at first what it was. A draught coming in through the front door? Then he realised exactly what it was. Not fear exactly but the beginnings of a kind of alarm. He was alone inside his house with these three and he didn't like it.

'No,' said Xavi flatly. 'I can't help you.' He returned Ramon's stare and this time he didn't apologise.

Valentina stepped in again and gave a disarming shrug, intended to relieve the situation and signal an agreeable end to their meeting. 'Okay, that's fine Mr Rodrigues. We'll leave you in peace.'

Xavi glanced at her and nodded.

Valentina turned to go but Felipe took a half step forward. He put up both hands. 'Please Mr Rodrigues, just thirty seconds of your time to explain.' He looked at Ramon and Valentina. 'One of the chapters in my thesis is on the in-sig-nia ...' he turned to Valentina for confirmation of the word and she nodded, 'and the meaning behind the slogans used in the civil war and in particular the meanings of the design and colours of the flags.' He produced a newspaper photograph from an envelope in his jacket pocket. And showed it to Xavi. 'We have this newspaper picture of your friend Emily holding up a double-sided flag, one side the International Brigade flag and the other looks like the Spanish Republican flag, but it's not very clear. I'd really like to take a photo of this for my thesis.'

'Only one photograph,' said Ramon squeezing between Valentina and Felipe until he was directly in front of Xavi. 'It would mean a lot to us.' He lowered his voice and spoke slowly but couldn't disguise his voice sufficiently. The words sounded cold and unfriendly, even threatening.

Xavi stood as still as he could. He could feel his heartbeat catching and missing a beat. He wanted to rub at his chest and take a deep breath but he kept his arms by his side. He managed a quick glance at the half open door and knew it would only take a gentle nudge and then, *click*, he would be cut off and completely alone. He could feel the tiny tendrils of panic starting to flow up through his stomach. A lorry sped past outside; its booming engine broke the silence and Xavi realised the three of them were staring at him. It had been a long few seconds and it was his turn to speak.

Xavi coughed, sniffed and pushed himself up as tall as he could. 'I don't know where the flags are now. I haven't seen them since Emily passed.' He flicked a hand towards the door. 'I'd like you to go now. I have things I need to do.'

'Did she give them to anyone?' Ramon persisted, still with the same blank stare.

'I just told you,' said Xavi.

'But they are in the photograph,' said Ramon, the words tumbling out, brittle and cutting. 'She's holding them up. They look important to her. She would not just get rid of them. She must have given them to someone. If not you, then someone in the family. There must be someone else we can talk to. It's very important.'

Xavi took a moment to decide what to do. *I can't just stand here letting my nerves get the better of me.* He leaned towards Ramon. 'You speak English very well so it can't be that you don't get what I'm saying. Or is there something wrong with your hearing? I told you once and I'll tell you again. I – can't– help – you. Do you understand?'

Ramon blinked once and narrowed his eyes. He was about to say something when Valentina put a hand on his arm and looked at Xavi. 'Thank you, Mr Rodrigues. We're sorry to have bothered you. Thank you for your time. We'll let you get on with your day.' She gently turned Ramon around and waited for Felipe to follow him out into the street before giving a smile to Xavi and then closing the door behind her.

Xavi finally took the deep breaths he needed, walked back to the living room and slumped into his chair. He rubbed his brow trying to calm himself down, lay back and closed his eyes. *This is not good*, he thought to himself *something tells me this is not good at all.*

He picked up his mobile phone from the arm of the chair. He would let Ana know he had had visitors but apart from that what else could he say … that he was frightened? That he *thought* they were dangerous. Wouldn't that just scare Ana? She didn't know that Axel had the flags. He might be worrying her needlessly. She already had too much worry in her life: Axel was missing and Amber was going off the rails. And were these three really dangerous? One of them was a bit weird but the other two seemed reasonable. But the student story? That didn't seem right. He'd have to think this through before he made a fool of himself. He put the phone back on the arm of the chair.

Valentina, Felipe and Ramon walked to the end of the street where Valentina stopped them with a raised hand and launched into Ramon, her eyes blazing. 'What? What the hell was that all about? You were getting very aggressive.'

A woman passing by glanced up at the raised voice and then hurried on.

Ramon scowled at Valentina, annoyed. 'Nosotros necesitamos –'

'English!' hissed Valentina quickly looking around.

Ramon shook his head and blew out a long icy breath. 'We need to get information.'

'He's old! You can't handle him like that.' said Valentina.

Ramon jabbed a finger at her. 'He knows. He knows where the flags are. Why is he not telling us? He knows something. Maybe he's already discovered Miro's painting between them.'

'Even so,' said Felipe. 'We have to be careful. We can't just play our hand all at once. What you did was not very clever. To be honest I was a bit surprised. We need to be cleverer than that.'

'Exactly,' Valentina pulled her scarf further up around her neck. 'You've made him nervous Ramon. It was counterproductive and damaging to our task.'

Ramon stormed off ahead for a few yards but then shook his head again and returned. 'Okay,' he said. 'You're right. I was pushing too much. But we do need information.'

'This is important, very important,' said Felipe. 'And we have to be smart. If we can get that painting and burn it in public like *you* suggested Ramon then it could be just the help our people need. Every small step is important in reminding people of just what they will lose if Catalan breaks away with the lefties. One nation together, a strong Spain. And also, it would give us more respect from Antoni and the Madrid group. Maybe then they would listen to us more.'

'I get it. I know,' said Ramon through tight lips. The other two both noted the twitching of a muscle at his jaw and realised how tense he was.

Valentina pushed her hands into her coat pockets as a sudden gust of wind made her shiver. 'Okay then, let's just make sure we all know what everyone is going to say next time.'

Felipe looked up quickly. 'What next time? How can we possibly talk to him again? He's suspicious now. You spooked him, Ramon.'

'He knows where it is!' snapped Ramon. 'I just know it. He was her best friend. He'll be looking after it for her or making sure it's safe somewhere.'

'So, what do you suggest?' said Valentina slowly, trying to calm things down. 'He won't help us now.'

Ramon looked back at Xavi's house. 'First of all, we need to make sure he hasn't got it.'

'And how do we do that?' said Valentina.

Ramon looked at her. 'We'll just have to search his place for ourselves.'

Felipe shrugged and looked at Valentina. 'I suppose we don't have much choice.'

'And then what?' said Valentina. 'What do we do then?'

'Hell, Valentina,' Ramon snorted. 'We'll just have to find out where it is and who has it. You don't expect them just to hand it over, do you? We're going to have to be a little bit naughty sometimes.'

Valentina widened her eyes. 'I know that,' she said. 'But we don't want to get caught. It would look bad for the Madrid group and I don't think they would be too happy about it. Remember, they don't even know we're here.'

'We'll just have to be extra careful then,' Ramon smiled defiantly at Felipe and Valentina. He turned and looked back. 'Come on. Let's see what we have to do.'

They walked a little way along the street, turned the corner, went around to the back of Xavi's flat and looked over the low stone wall into the yard. Beside the overflowing bins they noted five empty gin bottles and a wooden back door with its panels topped by a leaded glass window.

'We need to buy a good glass cutter,' said Felipe.

*

They returned when it was dark and took turns, one watching the light in Xavi's living room while the other two kept well out of sight and out of the cold in the nearby Free Trade Inn. At eleven o'clock Valentina drove back to tell them that the living room light had gone off and a bedroom light was on. Ten minutes later Ramon, Felipe and Valentina sat in the car just up the street from Xavi's house.

'The bedroom light has just gone off,' said Valentina pointing to the house. 'Let's give him some time to get to sleep.'

They drove off and then returned ten minutes later, sitting outside Xavi's flat for another few minutes before closing the car doors quietly and walking around to the back of the flat. Felipe cringed when he began opening the gate and it gave a rasping, squealing sound which seemed to echo all along the back lane in the stillness of the night. He didn't try the gate anymore but motioned to the others to climb over the low brick wall. They were out of sight of the rest of the flats now and they kept to the shadows as Felipe produced a roll of thick masking tape and fixed three long lengths to the leaded window and then took out the glass cutter and scored a hole the size of a fist in the glass. The tape held the glass in place until Felipe tugged it free and then put his arm through the hole and opened the door leading into the kitchen. He gave the others a surprised look. 'It's open already.'

'Check the kitchen first,' whispered Felipe. 'Then the living room and then the bedrooms. Let's hope he's fast asleep so we can check his bedroom. Remember it could be folded up small or it could be in some sort of display box or maybe hanging on the wall.' He inched the door open and then turned to the others. 'No more talking when we're in.'

Once inside they closed the door quietly, turned on their torches and searched every drawer and cupboard, taking their time and opening doors slowly and carefully. They moved into the hallway, their beams of light slashing through the darkness along the wall looking for any sign of the flags. Felipe shook his head and pointed to the living room. The door was open and they each crept to a different part of the room.

Felipe examined a bookcase, Ramon a set of drawers and Valentina combed through another tall set of drawers which held dozens of CDs. She gave up after a few minutes and then turned her torch across the room looking for something else to search. A gentle rasping noise like the sound of air escaping from a balloon caught her attention and then she heard a gurgling sound like water swirling down a plughole. She pointed her torch towards the sound.

The light fell on a large armchair and Valentina could make out a pair of legs. She gave a stifled gasp which alerted the others and flicked the beam further up until it landed on the face of Xavi, fast asleep, mouth hanging open, an empty glass tumbler still in his right hand resting on his lap and a half empty bottle of gin on the small table by his chair.

She immediately switched off her torch and backed away. Felipe and Ramon turned off their torches and then waited at the door to see if Xavi would wake. When he didn't, they gently closed the door and went into the first bedroom leading off the hallway. A few minutes later they came back to the hallway and went into the second bedroom. After a thorough search and being careful to replace anything they moved, they stood around the bed.

'Okay, nothing here,' said Felipe in a hushed voice. 'Let's take some things and get out.'

It had been agreed that they would make it look like burglary by taking some things from Xavi's flat. They split up again and started taking anything expensive that they could carry. They would dump everything in the river on the way back to their house.

Ramon took a radio from the kitchen and was picking up a clock from the hall table when he noticed a photograph in a silver frame. It was a picture taken at Christmas time. Ramon recognised Xavi and Emily and there was another woman about Xavi's age and then a younger woman and two older teenage children, one boy and one girl. He pulled out his phone and took a picture of the group. Then he joined the others at the backdoor. They left the door slightly open and walked quickly to their car.

Ramon showed the others the photo he had taken. 'If the flags are not at his flat then one of these must have it. It looks like a family celebrating. She would surely have kept them in the family.'

Valentina was sitting in the back, she leaned forward to get a closer look. 'It certainly looks like a family group. It's worth a try but how are we going to find them? They could be anywhere, not even in this town.'

'And we haven't got enough money to hang about her for too many days searching for them,' said Felipe

Ramon looked at Felipe. 'What about that Arthur guy we met at the station. He said his group would give us any help they could. We could ask him.'

'Okay,' said Felipe. 'I'll contact him.' He turned the key in the ignition and they set off into the night back to Will Roddy's house.

Chapter eleven

Wednesday, 26th October, 2016

Newcastle, Northern England.

A few hours after the break-in at Xavi's and just two miles away, Ana sat at her kitchen table with a large cardboard box in front of her. She hadn't looked at her gran's letters for a while. There were so many, almost two or three had been written every week and it was taking a long time to get through them. She had decided to stick strictly to the chronological order and so she took out the next batch and untied the string holding them together. She lay the letters in a neat line at the side of the table put on her glasses and started to read.

Tuesday, February 2, 1937

Tarazona de la Mancha, Albacete.

Dearest Isabel,

I am safely back at camp after a long drive in one of our brigade trucks. The seventy-two hours leave seemed to fly by. It was very cold and raining hard all the way back but it was worth it. It was worth every frozen mile. I can't tell you how much I enjoyed seeing you again. And all of your friends of course especially Carmen and Maria. You must be worried about them as they told us all they were being sent to Jamara with the army. I don't know when they will let us have another break as we are being deployed to the Jamara valley too to link up with the republican army. I hope I see your friends Carmen and Maria there. Wouldn't that be something!

I will remember the evening at your favourite café for a long time. The vermouth with the cubes of honeycombed grey ice was so delicious. The waiter was so proud of that ice. It's strange how people can be so joyful when everything is being destroyed around them. Strange days indeed! The main impression on walking about Madrid is that nobody seems to even think about danger. Nevertheless, I could see for myself that the majority of those beautiful houses in Gran Via had been hit by the German and Italian bombers. Although the guns roar almost continually and sometimes they are quite deafening, the people are very courageous and they all put on a brave face.

As you said, my Spanish continues to improve and I appreciate you helping me and being so patient when I completely mess things up. I love it when you speak slowly and pronounce the words with elaborate movements of your lips and use your eyes for emphasis.

I can't believe I have been here for more than five months already. I think I am coping well although conditions at camp are pretty primitive. I know that it is hard in Madrid for you all too. I have been given driving lessons and now I drive an American Pontiac Silver Streak which our brigade 'acquired'. It drives really well and can take lot of supplies of medicines to the front. It also doubles as an ambulance.

I loved seeing the children you are helping to look after and the lessons you were giving, trying to make everything as normal as possible for them. You are all heroes in my book.

I don't know how I would have coped without the overwhelming friendship of the Spanish people. I'm especially grateful to your wonderful friends but above all of course I am especially grateful to you.

I don't know what's going to happen in the coming days but I want you to know how much I admire you and hope that we can meet again.

Please write soon if you can.

Take good care of yourself and the children. Give my regards to Carmen and Maria.

Your friend, Emily.

Monday, February 8, 1937

138 Calle de Nueva, Plaza Segovia Nueva, Madrid

My dear friend Emily,

How happy I was to receive a letter from you. How much I look forward to them. I hope you receive this letter as we know that the battle for Jamara valley has started. We get reports every few hours in Madrid. I am so grateful to you. You say I am a hero for working with the children but you are the real hero. You and all the others who are fighting for our freedom. The defence of Spain is the defence of Britain too. If Franco breaks through in Jamara then the road to Madrid is open for him and he can cut off the road from Madrid to Valencia. I know you will stop him. I have faith for you and all those around you.

You talk about the bombing. It has been very bad for the past two days. Sometimes I can't look at people because I worry what I will find in their eye. Sometimes I am so mad that tears run down my cheek.

You remember there are a lot of spies and saboteurs in the city setting off explosions and starting fires and there can be bad days of violence. All of the priests and nuns have left or are in hiding and the burning of churches is normal here just like Barcelona.

The children are very brave and have a wonderful spirit. Many of them have lost everything when their villages have been bombed or when the Francoists have killed and looted. But still, they smile and sing and try to be normal. It is me who is learning from them.

I too wish that we were all together again in our café. We have such good times there.

I hope that we can meet again.

'Keep your eye peeled', 'use your loaf' and keep out of trouble.

Your friend,

Isabel.

Tuesday March 2, 1937

138 Calle de Nueva, Plaza Segovia Nueva, Madrid

My dear friend Emily,

I am very worried. I have not heard from you for four weeks. Please write to me if you are able. I know that the battle went well and that the fascists have been stopped. Please let me know what is happening. We have reports of terrible casualties. Please write soon.

Your dear friend Isabel

Saturday March 6, 1937

Torremocha de Jamara,

Dearest Isabel,

I am well.

I am sorry for not writing but the battle was very long and hard and we did not have time for anything apart from eating and sleeping. There were a lot of casualties and everyone was running about like mad trying to help. I have also been wounded. Nothing to worry about. It wasn't serious and I was in the field hospital for only a week. The car I was driving was nearly hit by a shell. The explosion knocked the car over and I had a small amount of shrapnel in my shoulder. They got it all out and I am fine now and back to my work in the dressing station.

Some of our comrades have miraculously been returned after being captured. Mainly British and French. But they are in a bad way and need a lot of care. We think that it is to try and appease the British and French governments, to get them to hold to their non-intervention pact and keep out of the war. They are very lucky because we know that a lot of captured soldiers are shot. We are all very scared of being captured and we are all angry at our governments not helping more. The British government has just recently passed a 'Foreign Enlistment Act' which makes it illegal for British national to fight in Spain. It makes my blood boil to think how our politicians don't understand the importance of this struggle.

They are pulling our brigade along with some others back to Barcelona and we will have some leave. But only for a few days. It would be lovely to see you there. I am staying in the same place off the Rambla.

I hope you can make it.

Viva la Republica!

Your dear friend,

Emily

X

Monday, March 15, 1937

138 Calle de Nueva, Plaza Segovia Nueva, Madrid

My dear Emily,

Thank God that you are well and alive. It was a great relief to get your letter.

I am writing this as soon as I arrive at my apartment. I have been to see the children and they are well too.

I cannot put into words how much I loved the three days I spent with you last month. All the words in the world are not enough. It needs sky and air and heat. I want to hold you again. I want to hold you so tight that it hurts. The day is always dark without you.

I love you in your uniform and your baggy pants. I love that you are strong. I love that you care about us. I love your small careless kindnesses. I love your funny Spanish accent. I love your eyes when you laugh. I love dancing with you. I love that you try to dance but are hopeless. But still you try. I love that you always try.

I miss you and I love you.

I did not want to fall in love but I was wrong and could not help it. In these terrible times we need each other. When this is all over, I hope to share my happiness with you. With so many bad things around it is incredible that I found you.

You are always in my thoughts and in my dreams.

I miss you and I love you.

I will end now and send this to you quickly before I lose my nerve.

I miss you and I love you.

Isabel

Xxx

Ps Don't you dare get yourself killed.

Ana put the letter down, took off her reading glasses and blew out a long breath. She looked at the photo of her ninety-year-old gran alongside a dozen other small, framed, family pictures jostling for space and attention on the wall behind the kitchen table 'Wow,' she said addressing the photo. 'I never knew. I didn't know anything about this.' She pushed the chair back and went to the fridge. 'I need a drink.' She poured a large glass of wine then turned and raised the glass to her gran's photo. 'Here's to you Emily.'

She sat back down at the table and picked up the next letter. 'Blimey Emily, what the hell are you going to say to that?'

Saturday, March 20, 1937

Tarazona de la Mancha, Albacete.

Dearest Isabel,

We are back at camp. We have some new equipment and we need an extra few days here for training. Your letter was sent on and brought to me today.

Thank you for your letter. Thank you. Thank you.

It means so much to me and I cried when I read it.

I love you too and that's all there is to it. When you are not here, I am reduced to a thing that just needs you. Everyone needs a reason for their existence and I can start living again only when I am with you. I just miss you in a terrible, desperate human way.

It was your lightness that drew me. The lightness of your talk and your laughter. This thing is ruthless. It blazes through me. It taunts me and leaves me helpless. I find that I am floating through the times when I am not with you, unable to connect with everyday life.

I do not know where they are sending us next but I will let you know as soon as I find out. I can't tell you how much I need to see you again.

There is so much violence yet to be done but we will meet again, against all odds, we will meet again.

I had these thoughts many weeks ago but was too afraid to tell you. The dreadful thought that I might scare you away was too much to contemplate.

I love you,

Emily

Xxx

ps I think you've got a funny accent too.

pps I'm not planning on getting myself killed any time soon. You watch out for those bombs (keep your eyes peeled). We both have to stay alive now.

'Okay. Well, now we know then.' Ana sat back and stared out of the window for a long time. She took a sip from her glass leaned across the table and started to read the next letter. It was short and she had time to scan it. 'Oh no! No! Oh no! That's terrible.'

Friday, March 26, 1937

138 Calle de Nueva, Plaza Segovia Nueva, Madrid

Dearest Emily,

I have awful news. Maria is dead. I can't speak the words. I can barely write them. Her medical convoy was attacked bringing supplies and wounded back to Madrid. Italian planes machine gunned the trucks. She has no family here. Carmen is bringing her home. I have to meet her as soon as possible to help with arrangements for a funeral. She was twenty. Only twenty years old. We don't want her in an unmarked grave.

I am sorry to have to tell you this but I know how much you liked Maria. We all did. I can't believe she has gone. This horrible, horrible war.

I miss you so much. It seems bad to say that because we have each other, and we have life but we do not have Maria now.

I love you,

Isabel.

X

Ana put the letter back in the box. She didn't want to continue reading. She went into the living room and began tidying the books on the bookshelf. She stopped and stared at the ceiling. Then she began putting the books in alphabetical order. She pulled out three books but let them fall out of her hands onto the floor. Then she sat on the sofa and cried. Deep, gulping, overwhelming gasps of hot breath forced her head back. She could feel her heart heaving

The doorbell rang and she took a few moments to sit still. She inhaled a last big breath, filling her lungs. Then she dragged herself up, wiped the tears away with a tissue from the box on the coffee table and answered the door. It was Xavi.

'Where've you been?' said Ana, her voice husky and dry. 'I've been calling you all morning. Come in. I'm glad you're here. I want to speak to you about something.' She began walking to kitchen.

'I had my mobile stolen,' Xavi blurted out as he followed her.

'What? Oh no. Where?'

'In the flat. I've been burgled. They took the hall phone as well. Got in through the back door.'

She turned abruptly and looked straight at him. 'Oh no. Don't say you were still there?'

'Yes, fast asleep in my bed.' He didn't want to tell Ana that he was drinking too much and regularly fell asleep and crashed out in his armchair or that he had forgotten to lock the back door and they hadn't needed to break the window. He didn't want to add this list of blunders to what he knew he had to say to her in a few minutes.

'Did they take much?'

'Bits and pieces. It's okay. It's all covered by the insurance.' He sat down at the end of the table, trying to think of the best way to broach the subject of Axel. He knew he had to tell her. 'It's a bit strange though,' he said tentatively.

'What d'you mean?'

'I had a visit yesterday.'

'Visit?'

'Yes, from three young people … two boys and a girl … said they were Portuguese students up from London where they're studying. They wanted to take a photo of the flags that Emily was given in Paris when she had to come home from Spain.'

Ana wrinkled her brow. 'Why? Why would they want to do that?'

'They said it was for a thesis on politics or something. It wasn't a very comfortable visit. I was glad when they left. One of them was a bit aggressive … I didn't like him at all. Seemed like a bit of a weirdo. He really, really wanted the flags. Desperate to know where they were. The other two seemed to be okay … I think. At least not as crazy as him. I don't mind admitting I was a bit scared.' He pulled at his beard and rubbed his neck. 'And then this morning I discovered I'd been burgled.' He looked at Ana. 'Quite a coincidence.'

'You think it was those three?'

'I do. I think they came back to look for the flags and tried to make it look like a normal burglary.'

Ana flipped her hands open and gave a small shake of her head. 'The flags? What's so special about the flags. I haven't seen them for years. Why on earth would someone break into your flat to get them? It's weird. There must be something about those flags for them to risk a break-in.'

'It seems that way.'

'And you think these people are dangerous? Aggressive?'

'Yes.' He was going to say *definitely* but thought *yes* was enough for now.

'So, they didn't get the flags?'

'No, I haven't got them.' Xavi shifted his weight and flicked his tongue across his upper lip.

'Do you know where they are?'

Xavi stared at the wall. He knew it would come to this. He said, 'your gran gave them to Axel,' and then waited, still staring at the wall. 'She knew he'd look after them.'

Ana's lips arranged themselves as though she was going to speak but nothing came for several seconds. She was frighteningly silent. Her whole body tightened. Xavi darted a sideways look at her. He could see that she was trying to avoid looking at him. At last, she took a deep breath. 'Well, that's not good. Not good at all. Is it? Dangerous, aggressive nutcases on the loose wanting to find something that Axel has got. Who knows what violence they could get up to. We need to find him and warn him about these people. Who knows what they'll do to him.' Eventually she whipped round and scowled at Xavi. 'You should have bloody told me about the flags,' she said, her voice getting louder, just under control. 'You should have bloody told me!'

Xavi pulled at his beard again and gave her a glancing defeated look. He paused, thinking of what to say to redeem himself. 'I think that's going to be a problem … finding Axel I mean … since he's been sleeping rough for the past few months. The good thing is that it'll be a problem for those three as well. They don't know where he is either.

We'll just have to start looking as soon as possible and scour the area. Maybe we can ask about. There's plenty of homeless kids to ask in Newcastle. They'll know where he might be staying.'

Xavi went to stroke his beard again but then stopped, folded his arms and gave a strange clucking sound with his tongue.

'Yes,' said Ana, the scowl had turned into a glare. 'I know what you're thinking. I should have looked for him as soon as he left. But it was difficult. He needed to go somewhere. He wasn't getting on with Amber. An understatement. He didn't like living here. His great gran's death affected him badly.' She spread her hands out. 'What was I supposed to do?'

'Good Lord, I'm just as much to blame,' said Xavi, glad to join her in confessing to general errors in judgement. 'He needed help. I should have done more as well. Who knows where he is now … and what he's doing on the streets.'

'He's a sensitive boy, and I failed him. It's not your fault. I should have been tougher on Amber and made this house a calmer place. She treats this house like a hotel. Doesn't come in until the early hours. Sometimes she doesn't come in at all. She's definitely getting some bad influences from somewhere and he just needed support while he sorted himself out. I failed him … and her.'

'Well, we can talk about this later,' said Xavi. 'We need to find him first. I don't think those three would take no for an answer if they get to him.' He winced. He knew he shouldn't have said that.

Ana gave him a cold hard look. 'Have you been to the police?'

'I contacted them about the burglary this morning. I need the police report for my insurance claim.'

'Did you tell them about the three Portuguese?'

'No,'

'Why not?' Ana said quickly. 'It's important that they know in case anything …' Her voice trailed off; she didn't want to finish the sentence.

Xavi hesitated. He didn't want the police getting involved in anything that happened all those years ago and he certainly didn't want them digging around and coming up with a Paris connection. 'Okay,' he said. 'I'll let them know.' He placed a hand on the cardboard box on the table, looking for a distraction. 'What's all this?'

'These are the letters I told you about weeks ago. Richard, Isabel's grandson brought them for me to look at. You remember Isabel?' Ana pursed her lips and gave him a sour lop-sided smile. 'You know, *Isabel*, gran's *friend* from Spain.'

Xavi stared at the box wanting it to disappear. He tried to disguise his rapid swallowing by stroking at his throat. 'Anything interesting?' he asked. But he guessed there would be.

'Oh yes, I think so. Fairly interesting,' Ana said, forced casual. She gave Xavi the March 15th letter to Emily and her reply to Isabel on the 20th.

Xavi put his glasses in and took his time reading the letters. He wanted some breathing space and time to think. He would be asking the same questions that she was about to ask if he were in her position.

Finally, he knew that he couldn't stretch the silence out any longer he handed the letters back to Ana.

Xavi puffed out his cheeks. 'Mmm,' he murmured.'

'Mmm? Is that all you can say?'

'It happens,' said Xavi, trying and failing not to sound flippant.

'Of course, it happens,' snapped Ana. 'And I don't mind. But don't you think I should know ... so I could understand.'

'What is there to understand?' Xavi said thinly. Even he knew he sounded pathetic.

'That my grannie was a lesbian,' Ana's voice was rising and she took a breath to get it back under control. 'I want to know what happened. How it happened? What happened to Isabel? I haven't heard of her before her grandson gave me these letters.' She took a long drink from her glass of wine and flicked some hair behind her ear. 'Did it end in Spain? Did it carry on?'

'Can I have a glass of wine?'

'No. What happened? Tell me.'

Xavi sat as still as he could. Answers were thundering around in his head and he was trying to catch the right ones. He turned them over, looked at them and then threw them back. Whatever he said he knew they wouldn't be the right ones but he would have to say something. Something as near the truth as he dared. He decided he didn't want to complicate matters. Things were complicated enough for now. The truth would have to wait.

'Your mum loved Isabel,' Xavi began, 'and she, as you can see from the letters, loved your mum. Isabel came to this country with Basque refugees in late 1937. They were in Tynemouth actually, just a dozen or so miles from here. She was their teacher. As you know I was one of the refugees. Isabel looked after me until your gran was discharged because of her pregnancy, although they covered it up by saying it was battle fatigue. They stayed together secretly and then Isabel had to go back to Spain with the children when they were repatriated at the end of the war. I had nowhere to go and so Emily took me in.' He gave his best *lost* look. 'Can I have that glass of wine now?'

'No. Why didn't gran follow Isabel?'

'I'm not sure. Probably, the simple answer is that she didn't want to or rather didn't need to. It was difficult for her. Emily confided in me a little many years ago when I asked the same questions.' Xavi gladly settled into the routine of words spilling out. 'She said she loved the idea of being in love. She loved the yearning and expectation. But she couldn't quite get it right face to face after those first few months of being together. At least that's what she said … whether it was true or not is a different matter. She said she truly loved Isabel and would always love her and she felt a deep sense of guilt at not being able to be with her and causing her pain. It was wonder and expectation outwitting pain and disappointment. What was it Emily said? Oh yes … she said she had a feeling of continuous melancholy but didn't mind it as it was her penance. That's how she put it … it was her penance.'

'What happened to Isabel?'

'She continued as a teacher in Spain. She married and had a child. A marriage of convenience. Apparently, her husband was a good man who understood and knew all about your gran. They were together only for a short while. She carried on writing to Emily for many years until her death. I don't know what happened to him.'

'I found out from the letters that their friend Maria was killed in the war, do you know what happened to Carmen?'

Xavi looked around the room, unsure of what to say. 'I know that Carmen survived the war. She was captured and imprisoned but then released. I think she might have gone to France. I'm sorry, I don't know what happened to her either.'

Ana went to the fridge to refill her glass. She picked up another glass and brought the bottle back for Xavi. Xavi filled the glass, took a long drink and waited patiently for the question.

Ana looked carefully at Xavi. He knew she was looking for honest answers.

'So,' said Ana. 'If she was a lesbian, how did my mum come to be born? I thought the family story was that grannie had an affair in Spain. That seems unlikely now after what I've just read.' She threw her arms out. 'What happened? You say they covered up her pregnancy when she left Spain. Why?'

'She was raped.'

Ana sucked in a breath. 'I thought it might be that.' She let her fingers play on the table. 'What happened to him? Do you know who he was?'

'He died. That's all we need to know Ana.' Xavi answered her as quietly as he could. *Please don't ask me why or when or how. I don't want to lie any more to you. I've already told too many lies to you today. Please don't ask.*

'And he gave my mum the disease?'

Xavi nodded. 'It's all in the past,' he said quickly. 'We have more pressing matters now. We need to find Axel.'

Arthur stood beside Felipe in the living room of Will Roddy's house. There were two leather armchairs and Valentina and Ramos were sitting on those. The rest of the room was crowded with two tall bookshelves, two sets of drawers, a large circular table with one wooden chair, and a plastic stool, heavily strapped and held together with Sellotape. An old juke box stood behind the door. It was a cloudless, sunny day and the light in the room was provided by a small table lamp set on top of one of the bookshelves and from a ten-centimetre gap in the curtains which were usually pulled right across to prevent anyone looking in and finding three strangers using Will's house.

Arthur held up his phone showing the family photograph that Felipe had emailed to him using Will Roddy's laptop.

'Did you find anything?' asked Felipe.

'Yep, good news,' said Arthur. 'I've asked around and shown the photo. We obviously knew about this Emily character from Facebook and the newspaper reports of her funeral. Her daughter is Rosa and we're not sure where she is but we know the address of the granddaughter, her name's Ana. And you know the address of this one, Xavi. We don't know where the young lad is. But even better news is

'…' he paused theatrically, 'that we know a lot about this girl.' He pointed to the expressionless face of Amber in the photograph.

'How? How do you know about her?' said Felipe.

'Because,' Arthur replied, 'she's one of us. Or at least she says she is.'

Ramon looked up quickly. 'What do you mean?'

Arthur nodded to the picture on his phone. 'She likes what we say and do.'

'I don't understand,' said Felipe, looking at the similar puzzled expressions on the faces of Ramon and Valentina.

'Okay,' said Arthur, grinning. 'Here's how it is. One of our group was trying to chat her up in a pub in Newcastle. It didn't work out but he got talking to her for quite a while. Turns out she hates the lefties as well. So, he invited her to come to one of our meetings, which she did. That was a few months ago. She's been to a lot of the meetings and a few demonstrations. We tend to keep her at arm's length for the moment as we're still not entirely sure of her. We get a bit nervous about *plants* so special meetings are reserved for the inner circle. Only five of us in the inner circle.' He gave a loud snorting laugh. 'I wanted to call it the star chamber but I was outvoted … we are a very democratic group.' He laughed again. 'Anyway, we like to keep it small and confidential. One or two of the things we're planning are a bit… high risk, shall we say. And we don't want any Special Branch boys and girls poking their noses in and spoiling the fun. So, this Amber, she might be able to help you.'

'She'll inform on her own family?' asked Valentina, frowning.

'I know what you mean but she seems like a bit of a hard case,' said Arthur. 'Hates the family. Hates her mother. Hates her brother. She's mentioned him a couple of times to different people. Always with something bad to say about him.'

'Good, very good. That's very good news,' said Ramon. 'How can we meet her?'

'Well, as a favour to our international friends,' Arthur said, smiling and waving his arm buoyantly at them. 'We've arranged a meeting tonight. We made sure that she knew about it and could come. A nothing meeting. We'll just go through some administrative junk for show. I'll introduce you three as visiting fellow travellers, soldiers of the cause, y'know, all that kind of stuff ... and to be fair, I'll have to call you something, but of course I won't say why you're really here. A few of us go to the pub afterwards so you can get all cosy with her there and see if she knows anything. I'm sure she does.'

'Excellent,' said Felipe.

'And you can do us a favour as well,' said Arthur, putting his phone back into his pocket and looking at each of them in turn. 'See what you make of her. See if she's genuine. Let me know what you think.' He handed Felipe a small piece of paper. 'This is the address of the house we're meeting at. See you at seven, okay?'

'We'll be there,' said Felipe.

Arthur suddenly clicked his heels together, threw up his right arm and called out, 'Sieg heil'. The three Spaniards looked at each other in surprise. After a few seconds Valentina jumped up and gave the fascist salute back. Felipe and Ramon stared at her as Arthur left through the back door and closed it quietly behind him, glad to be outside, unable to keep the broad smile hidden any longer.

'I didn't know we were *sieg heiling*,' said Felipe.

'I suppose it happens from time to time,' said Valentina. 'When in Rome ...'

'But this is great news,' said Ramon. He started pacing the room trying to contain his excitement. 'Exactly what we want. We should be able to get some information from this Amber girl tonight.'

'And when we get to this pub you can do the talking Felipe,' said Valentina.

Ramon shook his head. 'Why can't we all talk to her?'

'Because it might be too much for her, the three of us asking questions. It might scare her off. She might think it's an interrogation,' said Valentina. She looked directly at Ramon. 'And this time we need to know what is going to be said. We don't want anyone getting over excited. We need to go carefully.'

'I can get her to talk,' said Ramon. 'I understand I lost it a bit with that Xavi but I can be delicate. We need that information.'

'I think you need to back off this time,' said Valentina. 'Leave it to Felipe.'

'Why him?'

'Because Felipe can talk politics better than any of us. He knows what to say. His English is better than yours. And if she's interested in our views like Arthur says then she'll be interested in what Felipe has to say. He'll be able to reel her in, gain her trust. And besides that, he's the prettiest.'

'So, actually I'm just chosen for my looks,' Felipe sniffed.

'No, not at all,' said Valentina smiling. 'But they do give you a good advantage. If she's not taken by what you say. She can't help to be taken by you.'

Ramon shrugged and frowned at Valentina. 'Let's hope she's not too fussy then.

*

Later that night, at nine o'clock, the meeting had ended and a few of Arthur's group headed to the Crown Posada pub near the quayside in Newcastle. The pub was long and narrow with a high, ornate moulded ceiling and the walls were heavily textured. Dark mahogany panels with colourful leaded glass separated the two red leather fixed seating areas either side of the bar, one of which was screened off to make a small sitting room for five round tables, the other a long thin seating area with seven tables in a row at the far end of the room. The low wall lamps gave an orange glow. Two, long pre-Raphaelite style, stained glass windows were at the front of the room leading on to the street, one window depicted a lady in a long dress pouring a drink and the other a man in Tudor clothes about to consume it. At the end of the bar was an ancient seventy-year-old turntable record player providing quiet retro pop music. The Beatles, *With a Little Help from my Friends* wafted through the pub.

Arthur led the way in. The place was only half full and some of the group found seats at the back of the room while others ordered drinks at the bar.

Arthur stood beside the three Spaniards. 'You'll like it here,' he announced. 'Lovely old pub with real ale. And there's a lot of things to remind you of home. Legend has it that the pub which was originally called the Crown was bought by a Spanish sea captain for his mistress. And I believe I'm right in saying that *Posada* is the Spanish word for resting place or inn. And behind that wallpaper,' he pointed to a panel to the left of the bar, 'are some old wall paintings claimed to date back to the Spanish Civil War which only see the light of day when the pub is redecorated once in a blue moon. Now, what can I get you?'

Pints were ordered and Valentina, Felipe and Ramon sat in the corner at the furthest table from the bar. along with Arthur, George and two others. Amber sat a few tables away and was talking to an older man and woman from the meeting.

After ten minutes the man and woman left and Amber began to drain her glass. Valentina nudged Felipe and nodded towards Amber. 'You're on. Now's your chance when she's alone. Hurry up before she leaves.'

Felipe picked up his drink, strolled across and sat down on a low stool in front of Amber. She pulled back and furrowed her brow both in surprise and as a question.

'Hello,' said Felipe.

'Hello. What's up?'

'I just thought I'd come across and talk to you. My name's Felipe, I was –'

'Yes, I know. You were introduced at the meeting. From Spain.'

Felipe smiled. 'So, you remember me?'

'It was only an hour ago. It's hard to forget. My short-term memory loss hasn't kicked in yet.'

Not going well, thought Felipe. 'I can leave if you want me to.'

'Suit yourself.' Amber gave him her customary indifferent look.

Felipe stole a look at Ramon and Valentina as Amber began to pick up her coat. They looked nervous.

'Okay,' said Felipe looking up at Amber as she stood. 'Well, it was nice meeting you.'

'Was it?' Amber feigned a look of surprise.

'Yes, of course. We're trying to make as many contacts as possible … for our special project.'

'And what would that be then? Your special project.'

'We're trying to find something to take back to Spain. Something very important that can help us disrupt the Catalan independence referendum.'

'Again, what would that be then?'

'Sorry. It's very secret. I'm not sure I can tell you— yet.' He made sure Amber saw him giving Valentina and Ramon a furtive look. 'But it's something that we think could help tip the balance. You have heard of the Catalan referendum … next year?'

'I've heard of it,' Amber shifted her weight and pulled her shoulders back defensively. 'But I don't know much about it.'

'Well, if you let me buy you a drink, I can tell you about it and what it means for Spain.'

Amber put her coat back on the seat beside her. 'If you want,' she said. 'I like to find out as much as I can. I want to learn as much as I can. And I don't mind a free drink.'

Twenty minutes later Felipe had given her information in great detail about the referendum scheduled for early the following year and its importance for the whole of his country. A passionate description of the dangers of breaking up the country which he could see impressed her.

'So, you see,' said Felipe rounding off his diatribe. 'If Catalan votes to go it will be a huge blow for Spain and will have consequences right across Europe. Selfish self-interest, promoting materialism and extravagant liberalism.'

'Nation above the individual,' said Amber. 'It has to be.'

'Exactly. You see it exactly.' He nodded sagely and then gave another killing smile. 'The right needs more people like us. You understand the importance of what we are doing. We are the new generation and we can get things done. But in a quiet, intelligent way, not the old way. Not like *The Old Shirts*, carried away by wine and violence. First, we must get control. Then, if we need to … the old way,' he laughed.

'Sacred violence,' said Amber solemnly and then she laughed with him.

'Ha, you understand perfectly. You have obviously learned a lot.'

He could tell that she was intrigued by what he was saying and enjoying their conversation but he gave her an extra beaming smile complete with crinkled eyes just to make sure. He had a quick look round and was pleased to see Ramon and Valentina chatting to Arthur and other members of the group and looking relaxed.

Felipe took a sip from his drink and moved to the wall seat next to Amber. 'The socialists say the public welfare comes first but we've been saying that for decades. We defend the people. Hold their values true.'

'A single party,' said Amber. 'No bickering. No argument. Everyone for the common cause. A strong nation.'

'Yes, yes, yes,' said Felipe. 'We need discipline and regulation. We need to bring stability and national honour. And are we equal? Of course not. There is a natural hierarchy. Your Darwin explained that two hundred years ago. Competition, competition. The survival of the fittest, the strongest. No place for weaklings. That is how we survive as a country and as a people.' He moved closer to her and noted that she didn't move away. 'And remember, most fascist groups and far-right parties are not put there by coups or military takeovers. They are put there by democracies. People vote them in. They are wanted and needed. The pendulum is swinging our way. The far-right is gathering strength.' He held up his hand and began touching each finger, ticking off a list. 'In the last year alone: Freedom Party, Austria, twenty five percent of the popular vote; Belgium, New Flemish Alliance, twenty percent of the popular vote; Netherlands, Freedom Party thirteen percent; France, National Rally thirteen percent; Germany, Alternative for Germany, twelve percent; Spain, Vox Party, fifteen percent.' He sat back and took another drink. 'It is our duty to lead. We must be strong for everyone. We must be proud of who we are and where we come from, you British, me, Spanish. The others in our countries are invaders.'

He paused for a moment to let his words install themselves, pleased with himself and warming to the task. *She wasn't bad looking either.*

Amber gazed at him. 'It's the only way,' she said softly. 'Everything has to change. Neo liberalism fails every time. Too muddled. Too slow.'

'Of course. You know it and I know it. Authority ... hierarchy ... order ... duty ... tradition.' He used his fingers again to emphasise each point.

Amber smiled and nodded enthusiastically. 'A natural hierarchy to bring stability.'

'Yes, yes. Our way is the rational way, the only way. It gathers all the benefits of competitive struggle. Fascism gives the masses the chance to express themselves through spectacle, through devotion to their nation and race. And in return for strong leadership the people give their obedience. It's a bargain ... a deal between the masses and the hierarchy. And we must be continually acting on our beliefs, action for action's sake gives us strength. We need an intellectually gifted elite who will understand a country's real national interests and therefore has the right to call for strict obedience. *For Us Against Others* ... that is the call we must take to the people ... *For Us Against Others.'*

'For us against others,' said Amber. 'I like it. Simple and straight to the point.'

'Exactly. Just so. It's our duty. Our solemn and spiritual duty. We cannot let the people down.' He returned Amber's earnest gaze. 'It is our duty not to let the people down.'

This is the time, it has to be now, thought Felipe. He took a long drink of his beer.

'We need propaganda,' he said. 'We need something to help us. Especially now with events in Spain and the left pushing to split up the country. That's why we've been sent here. It's vital … for the cause … that we find this thing and take it back with us. It will really help with our propaganda.'

'But what is it?' Amber shook her head not trying to hide her frustration. She wanted him to know she was keen to be involved. 'You still haven't said.'

'It's a big thing for us. But also, a big secret. We can't let too many people know.'

'But what is it? You can't just leave it at that.' Amber began to raise her voice but then brought it under control quickly.

'I know. I understand. You are one of us. You understand. I know you see the importance of what we are doing.'

'So …?'

Felipe hesitated for a moment for effect. 'It's a painting. It's vital that we get it to aid our propaganda.'

'A painting?'

'Yes.'

'A painting of what?'

'It's a painting by a Spanish … no, Catalan artist. It doesn't matter at this moment to those helping us what it is about. Only that it is critical that we have it. We think it can help a lot. Arthur is trying to help but

215

he is not finding much.' He looked at her carefully. *If she knows anything she'll tell me now.* 'We don't know where it is but we know where it is hidden.'

Amber shrugged. 'That doesn't make sense.'

'Yes, I know, I know it doesn't seem clear. I know it sounds like a puzzle.' He leaned back in his seat and took a breath. 'We know the painting is hidden between two flags.'

'What!' Amber sat up. The words sizzled. 'What did you say? What kind of flags?'

'Two flags from the civil war. An International Brigade flag and a Spanish Republican flag.'

Amber jumped up but then sat down again quickly and put both hands to her head. 'Oh my God!' she said, almost spluttering. 'Oh, my God!'

'What is it? Do you know something?'

'Oh my God. Oh my God. I know where the flags are. I know who has them.'

'But this is fantastic. I can't believe it. Where? Who?'

'It's my brother. He was given those flags. He showed them to me weeks ago when we were nearly speaking. It's got to be them. It all fits. My great gran was in the International Brigade. It has to be them. And they were still sewn together so he obviously hasn't found the painting.'

'This is amazing,' said Felipe and he genuinely could hardly believe it. 'We'll have to talk to him. Where is he?'

Amber blew out a breath. 'Hard to tell. He left home. He squats around. Lives on the street.'

'But still in this city?'

'Yes, oh yes. He's not that brave. He's not far from home and mummy.'

'Do you have any idea where we could find him?'

'Follow me.'

Amber walked to the front door of the pub and Felipe followed her out into the street. Ramon and Valentina exchanged glances as they watched the pair leave the building. Amber took Felipe to the opposite pavement and then pointed to a massive double level bridge spanning the River Tyne. A train was just crossing the upper level.

'There,' said Amber. 'The High Level Bridge. That's where he usually stays, under one of the arches. I think it's the second one from the Gateshead side. You might find him there but he has other places he knows, where he can sleep. I can try and find him and get them for you, he always has them with him. Like a baby's special blanket.'

'No, no,' said Felipe quickly. 'You've done enough. It's up to us to get them. We have to do it ourselves. You understand?'

'Okay. But I don't think he'll just hand them over. That could be a problem. And what if he's not there. I'll write down some of the other places I've heard about, where he sleeps.'

'Okay that's great but don't worry. If he's under the bridge we'll get it. I know that Valentina can be very persuasive. And if he's living on the street, I'm sure he'd appreciate some cash in exchange.' Felipe shivered. 'I think we'd better go inside,' he said before Amber could say anything else.

Back in the pub Amber went straight to the toilet at the far end of the room, Felipe sat down next to his drink and gave the thumbs up to Valentina and Ramon.

Chapter thirteen

Thursday, 27th October, 2016

High Level Bridge, Newcastle, Northern England.

After the Crown Posada pub the three Spaniards went back to Will Roddy's house and waited for the city to quieten down and also to take time to sober up.

It was two o'clock in the morning when they drove the short distance to the Gateshead side of the High Level Bridge and parked in a deserted car park at St Mary's Church, just beside the bridge. They stayed in the car for a few minutes so as not to be seen by the one or two solitary figures who were making their way home. They walked to the end of the bridge, gave a quick look round, waited until there was a gap in the taxis coming across from Newcastle city centre and then clambered over the two concrete balustrades and began the steep slope down to the first arch, their feet sliding on the loose grit.

It was a mild night, dry and cloudy. They negotiated their way as quietly as possible through the bushes and the mess of litter: empty cans, food boxes and plastic bags, discarded by late night revellers and thrown over the side of the bridge.

Soon they were alongside the first arch and peered through the iron railings in the gloom at its concrete floor. A movement at the back of the floor in some bushes caught their attention but it was only two small rodents squabbling over an empty pizza box. They couldn't make out if they were rats or mice. They had their torches with them but they didn't want to turn them on.

Satisfied that the base of this arch was empty, with no signs of anyone sleeping rough, they hung on to the railings and sidestepped their way to the next arch, hands pressed against the cold concrete wall to help them avoid slipping.

'Smell that?' said Felipe, leading the way.

At the back of the three, Ramon smiled. 'Someone's smoking dope,' he whispered. 'He's there.'

Valentina put a hand on Felipe's shoulder. 'Let's try and sneak in,' she said softly. 'Grab what we need and get out again as quick as we can. We don't want any trouble.' She eyed the tall iron railings partitioning the arch with their thick spikes. 'This is going to be difficult enough. Let's hope he's asleep. Try not to wake him.'

Felipe gave one small nod. 'No torches yet.'

He made a back for Valentina who scrambled awkwardly over the railings and landed quietly on the other side. He continued bending over so that Ramon could haul himself up and over. Then he went to the concrete wall to get some leverage with his feet and after a few moments of frantic scrabbling he too was across and landing as quietly as possible.

They scanned the area and its debris of empty cans and bottles and cigarette butts. At one end beside a stone wall were two unrolled sleeping bags either side of a small, still burning makeshift fire built inside a ring of bricks. Felipe and Valentina picked their way across to inspect the bags.

At the other end of the space, between two bushes growing out from the wall was a large cardboard box with *Panasonic* written in big black letters on its side. The end of a sleeping bag was poking out of the box and trails of smoke were escaping from cracks in the cardboard. Ramon spotted a full plastic bag beside the box and began to quietly empty the contents. Suddenly the cardboard box was flipped to one side and revealed a figure propped up on one arm staring up at Ramon.

'Hello,' said Leon still with his joint hanging down from his mouth. 'And may I ask, who are you?'

Ramon froze. Valentin and Felipe stood still, held their breath and stared at the figure.

'I'm sorry,' said Leon, looking at Valentina and Felipe and then at the mess all around. 'If I'd known I had visitors I'd have tidied up. I feel so embarrassed.'

Ramon leaned over him. 'Are you Axel? Axel Edelman?'

'Unfortunately, not,' said Leon. 'Fine fellow though he is.'

Felipe came across. 'That's definitely not him,' he said to Ramon, and then to Leon. 'So, you know him?'

'Yes,' said Leon, and immediately winced at being so careless.

'And he stays here?' said Ramon.

'Sometimes,' Leon blinked rapidly. He knew he shouldn't have said that. He shouldn't be saying anything to these people. He was feeling very slow. *I'll have to sharpen up a bit*, he thought to himself.

'When will he be back?' said Ramon.

Leon shook his head and sat up straight. 'No idea,' he said, trying to redeem himself. 'Sometimes I don't see him for weeks.'

'We need to talk to him,' said Ramon. 'It's very important that we talk to him.'

'Very important,' added Felipe.

'And why would that be then?' said Leon. 'Why do you want to talk to him so urgently? Does he know you? I can give him a message … if I see him in the next week or so.'

Ramon and Felipe looked at each other.

'Whose are those sleeping bags over there?' said Felipe.

Leon glanced at the sleeping bags that Axel and Sami had left behind as they didn't want to carry them around all night. Axel was taking Sami to meet some friends in Newcastle to find out if she could get somewhere to crash for the next few days. He knew they'd be back but he didn't know when.

'Whose are those bags?' repeated Felipe.

'One of them's mine, a spare one, drying out by the fire,' said Leon. 'The other one's my mate Tony's. He kips here from time to time.'

'Kips?'

'Sleeps here,' said Leon. 'Dosses down, crashes out, sofa surfs. Snoozes the night away.'

'Are you trying to be funny?' said Ramon.

It usually helps, thought Leon. *Usually gets me out of trouble although sometimes it gets me into trouble. Like now.*

'Not at all, old boy,' said Leon. 'Merely translating the vernacular for you visitors to our fair city. I assume from your accents you're not from these parts.'

'So, you think he won't be coming back soon?' said Valentina.

'Definitely not.' Leon went to take a drag from his joint but then half turned and flicked it against the wall. 'Weekdays, I know he likes to spend at his country retreat.' He noticed the glaring looks from Ramon. *Damn it, can't stop myself.*

There was a long pause and a breeze could be detected now further freezing the already icy atmosphere.

Felipe folded his arms. 'Do you know if he has any flags with him?' he asked roughly. 'And if he –'

Ramon grimaced and stopped Felipe with a withering look which Leon made a careful note of.

'Flags?' blustered Leon. 'Never seen any flags. What kind of flags? Jolly Roger? Union Jack? Star spangled banner? Papal flag of the Vatican City? Why would he need some heraldic device with him? Maybe to hoist it over the railings there to let everyone know he's at home, like the queen at Buck Palace. But as you can see there's no flag there so he's obviously not here.'

Ramon continued glaring at Leon.

What more can I do? thought Leon. He averted eye contact with Ramon. *Dangerous animal that one. Need low voice and slow, slow movements.*

Ramon looked at Felipe and Valentina. Felipe shrugged and flicked his head towards the railings. Ramon nodded and then walked across to the two sleeping bags. He picked them both up and then turned back to Leon. 'You've got one already so you won't be needing this one and your friend's not here so he won't be needing his.' He held both sleeping bags lengthways over the fire until they caught alight and then dropped them on to the flames.

Leon flopped back, lay flat on his makeshift cardboard bed and clasped his hands behind his head. 'Ah, now,' he said quietly. 'That's a really mischievous thing to do. Really rascally behaviour.'

'Let's go,' said Valentina. 'There's nothing for us here.'

'Agreed,' said Felipe. 'I'm tired anyway. Let's go back to the house. 'We'll continue tomorrow.'

The three of them walked across to the iron fence.

'Adios,' Leon called after them. 'And a very buenas noches to you.'

They all turned quickly and looked at him.

'What?' said Leon. 'Hit a nerve? Just a guess. I didn't think you'd mind.'

Valentina gave a small shake of her head and then she and Felipe clambered over the fence and began scrambling up the slope to the street level of the bridge.

Ramon gave them a few seconds to get out of sight and then ran across to Leon, kicked him on his side, dragged him off the cardboard and sat across his chest with both knees on Leon's arms so he couldn't move. He grabbed his hair and pummelled his head three times on the hard concrete floor, then he put his hands around Leon's throat and squeezed as hard as he could.

Valentina and Felipe had nearly reached the street when they noticed that Ramon wasn't with them. They looked back down the slope and heard muffled gasps and rasping squeals coming from the arch. They realised at once what was happening and raced back down the slope.

They reached the railings just as Ramon was shoving the palm of one hand across Leon's mouth to stifle his groans and then continued strangling him. They could see Leon's legs kicking wildly trying to free himself. There was a retching, gurgling sound coming from Leon.

'Ramon! Ramon!' shouted Valentina. 'Stop! Stop it! What the hell are you doing?'

Felipe hurled himself across the fence first but Valentina was not far behind. Both snagged jeans and jackets in their desperation to get to Ramon and Valentina yelped as she wacked a knee against the concrete before rolling over and then scurrying on, almost falling again.

Felipe reached Ramon, put both arms around his chest and pulled him away. Ramon fell over and jumped to his feet but Valentina and Felipe stood between him and Leon.

Ramon made an attempt to get back to Leon but Valentina and Felipe barred the way, holding their arms up ready to fight him if necessary. In their anger they resorted to shouting in Spanish.

'What the hell was that all about?' yelled Valentina. 'What do you think you're doing? You could have killed him!'

'He knows!' ranted Ramon, spit flying from his snarling mouth. He shook himself and whirled about, desperately stabbing a finger at Leon. 'He knows! He knows where they are! He's lying! He knows where they are! The bastard knows! And we need to get him to tell us where they are!' He glared at them as Felipe and Valentina stood open mouthed, glancing at each other, momentarily stunned by the poison in his voice.

'So, you're going to kill him!' shouted Felipe. 'You're actually going to kill him. What good would that do? We certainly wouldn't find out anything then, would we?'

'You're not making any sense!' Valentina waved both arms out wide, her eyes blazing into Ramon. 'This is stupid! How is killing him going to help us?'

'I was going to make him talk!' Ramon clenched his fists. 'I was going to get him to tell us where they are! He knows where they are!' He glared at Leon. Valentina and Felipe both spread their legs a little wider and made themselves as big as possible, ready to push Ramon back if he tried to get past.

'I didn't look like that to me!' yelled Felipe. 'It looked like you were trying to kill him! You had your hands around his neck! It's a good thing we heard him choking! No, it certainly didn't look like you were trying to make him talk. Just the opposite. Idiot!'

'We have to have the flags!' Ramon pointed at them both furiously. 'We have to have them. Whichever way we can! We have to get them! Everything depends on it! I was going to get him to tell us and he would have done if you two hadn't come back!'

They stared at each other, taking a few seconds to cool down.

'Not like this,' said Valentina forcing herself to speak slowly. 'He couldn't speak anyway with your hands around his neck. It definitely looked like you were trying to kill him. And that would be incredibly stupid.'

'I'm not being stupid!' Ramon began yelling again. He pointed at Felipe. 'He's the one who's stupid! He's the idiot. He told him we were after the flags! He knows now! We can't let him tell anyone! He'll drive them underground and we'll never get them! We have to –'

'So, you *were* going to kill him,' Felipe cut in. 'You were going to silence him. You were going to make sure he didn't talk. You've just admitted it.'

'Not like this Ramon,' repeated Valentina. 'Not like this. 'What's got into you? We can't go around killing people in a foreign country. What do you think they'd do back in Madrid if they knew that we were killing people and leaving a trail back to them — they'd kill *us*, that's what they'd do. Our people wouldn't like this. This thing has to be done quietly, secretly, no fuss. We can't risk being found out. You have to get a grip.'

Leon listened to all of this as in their temper they resorted to their incredibly fast language which he had no chance of understanding with his secondary school Spanish even if they slowed it down to idiot level. He understood nothing, that is, apart from the fact that one of them wanted to kill him and the other two were stopping him.

He felt his throat as they continued to shout at each other. He was breathing with difficulty and his windpipe seemed like it had cracked. He tried to swallow but it was too difficult so he let the saliva slide out from the side of his mouth and allowed his arms to flop down to the cold floor. *Damn Spaniards. Moorish bastards*, he thought to himself.

Then a blackness covered him, sweeping up from his legs, crawling across his chest to the soreness of his neck, settling behind his eyes, and he fell unconscious.

Valentina came across, knelt down beside Leon and felt his pulse. 'He's alive,' she said. 'Let's get out of here.' She looked at Ramon. 'We'll find this Axel guy tomorrow.'

*

Hours later dawn was breaking with a beautiful, clear ice-blue sky. Leon was sitting by the railings keeping a careful watch. He had already packed his things an hour ago when he came round. He was breathing in small, shallow gasps flinching every now and then and massaging his neck. He had been sick when he woke up and still felt sick but it was too painful to keep on retching.

Axel and Sami came slithering down the gravelly incline, threw their bags over the railings and then clambered across. They both noticed Leon sitting on his rolled up sleeping bag with a small rucksack and a bulging carrier bag beside him. They went straight across to him.

'You don't look too good mate,' said Axel. 'What's up?'

'I'm off,' said Leon. His voice crackled. 'I'm off. Just been waiting for you two,' he croaked.

'Blimey,' said Sami. 'How many ciggies have you had? You sound terrible.'

'It's not with smoking. I've been strangled.'

'Eh? Strangled?' Axel put his hand on Leon's shoulder. 'What d'you mean – strangled?'

'Some nutters came last night,' Leon looked at Axel. He was speaking in whispers. 'They were looking for you.'

Axel produced a can of lemonade from his pocket. 'Here, have a drink mate. You sound like a broken radiator.'

Leon waved the can away. 'No, can't mate. Too painful to swallow. It's all I can do to breathe.'

'What d'you mean they were looking for me. Why would anyone want to look for me. What have I done?'

'I dunno',' said Leon. 'They said something about flags? Three Spanish guys. Two blokes and a girl. The one called Ramon attacked me. Tried to bloody kill me. No joking. Tried to kill me. If the other two hadn't come back he would've finished me off. I've been sat here for an hour watching for them in case they came back.' He took a moment to try and clear his throat. It was hurting with so many words. 'I was waiting for you two, to warn you. You can't stay here. They might come back.' He pointed at the fire still smouldering. 'And you need sleeping bags, they burnt yours.'

Axel and Sami exchanged puzzled looks.

'Okay,' said Axel. 'Don't worry about me. I can go to –'

Leon twisted round. 'No, don't tell me.' He said it quickly and then grimaced as his whole neck seemed to be on fire. 'Don't tell me. I don't want to know. I want nothing to do with this and definitely nothing to do with those three nutcases. I tell you, they're dangerous. I mean nasty dangerous.'

'Did you tell them I had the flags?'

'No, of course not. Absolutely not. But they seem to think that you have them. Have you got them?'

Axel pulled the zip on his backpack, put his hand down deep and came up with a plastic bag. Out of the bag he produced the double-sided flag of the International Brigade and the Spanish Republic flag. 'These are the flags,' he said. 'These are what they're talking about.' He gave them to Leon to hold and told him about them and where they'd came from.

'But what's so special about them?' said Leon, still trying to massage his throat.

'No idea,' said Axel.

Sami took the flags and turned them over. 'Well, there must be something about them,' she said. 'Why would three people come all the way from Spain for them. There must be loads of these things you could get on eBay for a few quid.'

'Anyway,' whispered Leon. 'I'm off. I don't want anything to do with flags or Spaniards thank you very much.'

'Hang on Leon,' Sami looked at them both. 'Shouldn't we go to the police. I mean, you've been assaulted. These psychos are still out there. Shouldn't we report them. Can't have nutters running about all over the place.'

'Well, keep out of their way then and warn as many people as you can about them. No police for me,' said Leon. 'I make it a strict rule of mine never to get involved with the police. Don't want all that statement stuff and then getting myself put on the system. No thanks.'

'What do you think Axel?' said Sami.

'I don't know,' Axel took back the flags pushed them into his bag. 'I don't know. Maybe we should think about it.'

'Well, you should at least go home, warn your family,' said Sami.

'I don't think so,' there was an edge to Axel's voice. 'It's me they're after. I'm not going to lead them to my mother, am I?'

'Okay, okay,' Sami held up her hands. 'It's your call, the two of you. Whatever you say.'

The three of them stood in a tight triangle staring at the cigarette butts on the ground.

Leon broke the silence. 'Anyway, I'm not hanging about here, I'm offski.' He looked at them for a few seconds and shook his head. 'No hugs? Special goodbyes?''

'Hey, look after yourself.' Axel smiled at Leon.

'You too,' said Leon trying to stifle his croaking voice. 'I wouldn't mind seeing you again … in one piece. And you too Miss Sami. Look after yourself.' He began to climb the railings. 'Not be doing this for a while anyway.'

'You look after that throat,' Axel shouted. 'At least it'll keep you off the booze for a few days.'

Leon dropped down on the other side, held his throat with one hand so he could call out, 'Live well and prosper.' Then he grinned at them both, gave a quick wave and disappeared up the slope.

Sami picked up her bag. 'Don't you think that maybe you should give them the damn flags?

'No, not happening. I promised my Eldergran Edelman just before she died that I would look after them for her so that's what I'm going to do.'

'Okay,' Sami nodded. 'So, where are you going to go Axel? If you're not going home. You can't hang about here. Where are you going to stay? Great name by the way, Eldergran Edelman.'

'I know some garden allotments in Low Fell about an hour's walk from here. I've stayed there before. It's easy to get into. There's a shed. Dry enough. I can stay there until I figure out what to do. Nobody goes this time of year, so it'll be quiet.'

Sami held both arms out as wide as they could possibly go. 'What about me?'

'What about you?' Axel squinted at her in surprise. 'I thought you sorted a place out to crash last night.'

'Well, that was before, wasn't it.' Sami shook her head from side to side and pulled a face in pretend indignation.

'Before what?' Axel wrinkled his eyebrows and stood very still waiting for her to answer.

'Before I knew you were a hunted man.'

'What d'you mean?'

'Well, it's exciting, isn't it?' said Sami. 'Better than hanging about the streets. We're being chased and we have to find out what the hell is going on. I want to find out what's going on. I can't just leave now without knowing.'

Axel shook his head and gave her a long look. 'This is serious Sami. Very serious. If what Leon said is true then these people are ugly and it could get nasty if they find us. I definitely don't want to be around if they catch up with us and you shouldn't either. It could be very dangerous. Axel gave another shake of his head and pulled his bag on to his shoulder. 'Your choice,' he said without looking at her. 'You can do what you want.'

'Okay, let's go then,' said Sami, smiling.

They scrambled over the fence and began climbing up the slope to the street level then pulled back behind a stone pillar as two cars with early morning workers came past.

'Who d'you want to be then?' whispered Sami standing just behind Axel.

'What?'

'Who d'you want to be? Bonnie or Clyde?'

Axel turned and stared at her. 'Hilarious,' he said quietly. 'Absolutely hilarious.'

Chapter fourteen

Thursday, 27th October, 2016

Newcastle, Northern England,

Ana's house.

Later, in the early evening, on the day that Axel left the bridge, Ana returned from searching for him in Newcastle. She had gone with Xavi to try and find him or at least get some information about where he might be. He had to be warned.

They had been walking the streets for hours asking every homeless person they could find if they knew him or had seen him. The photograph she had with her was looked at carefully by them all but it drew a blank. She and Xavi widened the search and called in at the various shelters: the YMCA on Walker Road; Crisis Skylight on City Road; The people's kitchen on Bath Lane; The Salvation Army temple on Brunswick Place. They had even gone to each of the largest foodbanks in Newcastle and Gateshead and showed as many people as they could the photograph but no-one could tell them where Axel might be. They would try the rest the next day.

Xavi drove her home and pulled up outside the house. 'See you tomorrow then. Continue the search?'

'Okay,' said Ana hesitantly. 'But I can't think of what else we can do. We've been everywhere I can think of.' She stared into the distance. 'I didn't realise he has hardly any friends to ask. He's disappeared. It's impossible. Can you think of anywhere else?'

'Police? Missing persons?'

'He's gone of his own free will though. There haven't been any strange circumstances. They'll not take any notice.'

'The only other option of course is …' Xavi glanced at her and stroked his beard.

Ana finished the sentence for him. 'Hospital,' she said. 'I've been thinking about that too but didn't want to say the word. I don't want to think that way.' She squeezed Xavi's shoulder. 'I'll see you tomorrow. Something will turn up.' She stepped out of the car and was about to leave but then turned back. 'And make sure you lock all your doors in case those three come back.'

Ana went inside the house, threw her coat over the banister and kicked off her shoes. It had been a long, fruitless and frustrating day. She was exhausted as well as worried sick.

And the day was about to get worse.

Amber suddenly appeared in the passageway.

'Oh,' Ana said, jerking her head back in surprise. 'I didn't know you were in. Haven't seen you for what? About three days? Where've you been?'

'Mate's house. Just came to pick up a few things.'

'Is that it? Which mate? Where does she … or he … live? Are you staying? Want something to eat?'

'No.'

'No, what? Not staying or nothing to eat.'

'Both.'

'How long will you be gone for?' asked Ana, failing to separate concerned from accusatory. It just sounded awkward.

'Don't know. No idea.' Amber dashed the words out, spilling them all around.

'Days? Weeks? Months? Years?'

'You look frazzled,' said Amber.

She didn't know it but it was the kindest thing she had said to her mother for a long time and Ana took it as a kindness.

'I – we – have had a rough day. Xavi and me have been looking for Axel. He's disappeared. No-one seems to know about him or where he is. I knew he was a bit of a loner but … no-one …' She rolled her eyes.

Amber made a noise somewhere between a snort and a guffaw. 'Loner? Hopeless and friendless would be better words to describe your *son* … maybe outcast.'

'Your *brother*,' Ana said sharply.

Amber ignored her mother, folded her arms and pretended to be thinking hard. 'Yes, I quite like outcast … or pariah … or … oh, I don't know, there's so many that would fit him perfectly.'

'Even if you don't like him Amber …'

'Don't like him, ha,' Amber snorted. Her mouth curved up into a huge ironic smile and her eyes widened. 'That's an understatement.'

'Even if you don't like him Amber,' Ana continued. 'He's still your brother … and we think, or rather we know, that he's in danger. We have to find him. Do you have any idea of where he could be? Where he could be staying?'

Amber widened her eyes again. 'No … *Ana.* I've no idea.'

Ana took a step back from her daughter. Out of slapping range. She didn't want to start doing that. That would surely signal the end. She pulled herself up, stared at Amber and gave herself a moment. 'So, you're cutting yourself off then,' she raised her voice. 'Is that it? No brother and no mother. No family. Is that what you want?' The words flew out, harsh and thickly venomed.

Amber stared back and gave a long, laboured shake of her head. 'It's been that way for years,' she said in an equally lazy voice that was meant to show she was getting bored with cutting remarks but yet still managed routinely to stab home, inflicting just the right amount of pain.

'No, it hasn't,' Ana rasped, her voice on the edge of quivering. She pushed her hands deep down into the pockets of her jeans. 'And if it has it's because of you. You decided on this. You decided to shut us out. Even though you live here. You decided to make it this way. You did this. You!'

'Well, whatever. I'm going to leave now,' Amber said quickly. She tilted her head and did something with her mouth as though she had just tasted something unpleasant. She looked all around the passageway. Her gaze brushing against both walls, hovering above the door then moving along the carpet and up to the ceiling before landing on Ana. As slow as she could. As innocently as she could. Her eyes sparkling. Accentuating the finality of the moment. Taunting.

Don't smile, thought Ana. *Don't smile. I don't know if I can control myself if you smile.*

'I'll see you around,' said Amber. She gave Ana the biggest smile she could as she pushed past her, scooped up her coat and bag from the peg by the door and swept out, leaving the door wide open.

Ana stood still for twenty seconds breathing deeply. She stopped herself shaking and then ran to the door and shouted. 'Mother! My name's mother! My name's mother! And you're my daughter! You little shit!'

She slammed the door shut and then paced angrily to the kitchen, flung open the fridge and grabbed a half full bottle of white wine. *At least I can rely on you.* She sank down at the kitchen table angrily unscrewed the top and took a long swig from the bottle. 'A long soak, that's what I need.' She announced to the bottle. 'And you're coming with me old friend. I've had a hell of a day.'

An hour later Ana lay on her bed wrapped in a huge bath towel staring up at the ceiling, the empty bottle standing proudly on the bedside table, glad to have helped. She felt better. The drink had revived her and the long soak in the bath had eased her throbbing muscles.

She wondered whether to get ready or just climb into her pyjamas. She decided on getting ready and pulled on her jeans and a green sweater. She was about to go into the bathroom when she heard the doorbell. She gave a loud heartfelt tut, turned on her heels and went downstairs. *Can't be bothered with this but it might be some news on Axel.*

She opened the door and found a tall fair-haired man standing there with an unwavering wide smile.

'Yes?' said Ana.

'Hello again,' he said. The smile became unbelievably bigger.

'Hello again,' said Ana, trying desperately to recall where she had seen him before. She suddenly snapped her fingers. 'Of course, the letters. Isabel and Emily. I'm sorry I've forgotten your name.

'Ah, no problem. Richard. Richard Stevens.'

Drop the smile, Richard. Way too big. I've had enough of smiles today.

'Yes, yes, I remember now. Come in please. Wasn't it London? Have you come all that way today? You should have called. Oh, of course we didn't exchange numbers.' She stood back to let him come in to the hall. 'This way. Let's go into the lounge. Can I get you something to drink?'

'No thanks, I'm fine.' He went to sit in a large armchair by the window, unbuttoning his cream-coloured trench coat as he sat down.

Ana sat in the other armchair opposite. *That's disappointing*, she thought. *I could do with another drink. Would it be impolite of me to have ... no, can't be done.*

'So, what brings you here Richard? What can I do for you?'

'It's about the letters.'

'Oh, you want them back? I haven't finished reading them but ...'

'No, not at all,' Richard sat forward, perching on the edge of the chair. 'I was just wondering how you were getting on with them. Maybe have a chat about them.'

'I *have* been reading them.' She turned and flicked a hand at the door leading to the hallway. 'They're actually on the kitchen table as we speak. But as you said at the time, there's a lot of them. All very interesting but I haven't finished reading them.'

'No worries. I found they give great information about the feelings of so many in that terrible war. We should always honour their memories. The struggle still goes on.'

'So, are you socialist? Like your gran and my gran.'

'Of course.' Richard nodded. 'It's the only way forward. We need a fairer world.'

'Of course.'

'So, you find the letters interesting?' He looked at her steadily. 'In what way?'

It was Ana's turn to smile. 'Oh, I think you know, Richard. About the affair. My gran and your gran.'

'Yes,' Richard nodded again, enthusiastically. 'That was interesting, very interesting ... and very moving.'

'It was beautiful. I was very moved by it. The emotion in their writing made me glad that they found each other and had such happiness in those difficult times. I was very, very moved by it all.'

'They trusted each other.'

'Completely,' agreed Ana.

'And they confided in each other completely.'

'I would think so,' Ana settled back and folded her hands across her lap. 'They were very much in love.' *Where is this going?*

'How far have you got?'

'Up to near the middle of the civil war, I think. About late thirty-seven.'

'Oh, I see, that's as far as you've got.' Richard tucked the smile away to make room for a grave, serious expression. 'Believe me, it gets better, much better,' he added earnestly. His eyes seemed to light up.

'What do you mean?' Ana shifted her weight and placed both hands on the arm rests.

'I can't really say,' said Richard.

She thought he had a self-satisfied, triumphant look about him and was fully expecting him to wink at her furtively any moment. *I haven't got time for this. I need to be thinking about Axel.*

'Well, it all sounds very intriguing.' Ana pulled her eyebrows up and moved her head forward an inch, asking the question again without saying the words.

'You need to open up package ten and read two letters,' said Richard. 'One from Emily to my gran on February the ninth, nineteen seventy-seven and the reply from my gran to Emily on February the sixteenth, nineteen seventy-seven.' He sat back, burrowed into the chair, taking a long time to make himself comfortable and produced his smile.

I certainly haven't got time for this. And there's that bloody smile again.

'What?' said Ana, with as much surprise as she could muster. 'You want me to read them *now*?'

Richard nodded slowly. 'Please, if you wouldn't mind. I would be extremely interested to hear what you think about them.'

'They must be very interesting if you can remember the exact dates.' Ana realised that he was starting to make her feel uncomfortable.

'I have a good memory for dates anyway, but these are extra special.' He glanced at the open door to the kitchen. 'Well worth a read.'

Ana shrugged and sniffed. 'Okay. If that's what you want.' She strung out the words trying to make them sound as condescending as possible and then eased herself out of the chair and went into the kitchen. She was relieved to be away from him.

She opened the lid of the box she had bought specially to keep the letters in and brought out the pack with a large black *ten* in felt tip written across the piece of paper wrapped around them. She pulled at the elastic band holding them together and found the two letters that Richard had mentioned.

'Take your time.' She heard Richard call from the living room. 'No rush. I've got plenty of time.'

Oh well then, that's very kind of you, thought Ana. *And if we've plenty of time ...* She went to the fridge and poured herself a large glass of wine, brought the bottle to the table and then sat down and started reading the letters.

25 Albert Terrace, Newcastle.

England

February 9, 1977

Dearest Isabel,

I'm sorry that I haven't written to you for a long time but I have important news. I remember telling you that it would be my life's ambition to find the Hungarian man who raped me. Well, I found him and tracked him down to a brigade conference in Paris last week.

I killed him there.

The details don't matter. The main thing is that he is dead. I had to tell you. You know how much this meant to me and I know that you agreed with me that it was a thing that had to be done.

I feel cleansed. I feel that justice is done. I feel almost happy if that's not a morbid thing to say. I don't regret it one bit. He ruined my life as well as others and now we know he has ruined my daughter's life.

You and Xavi are the only two people who know about this now. I know I can trust you both. Xavi, as usual, has been wonderful. I didn't want him to go to Paris but he insisted. He didn't know that I was going to kill the Hungarian but when he found out he was supportive and kind and of course secretive.

I made it look like an accident and up until now I haven't heard anything about it, fingers crossed.

I'm sorry that I could not tell you this in person but I wanted you to know and it helps me, if I'm honest, to get it off my chest. I'm free of the beast. At last.

Take great care of yourself,

love,

Emily

X

248 Calle de la Peanya,

Valencia

February 16, 1977

Dear Emily,

I have just receive your letter this morning. So, it is over. Thank God. It has hung over you for many years. You are finally got rid of him. I am glad for you. I am so glad that you write this letter because I think of you often. I am glad that you honour me with this information. I am humbled by your courage.

I do not think it is the right time to tell you all the news. I will write later. It is enough for now to let you know that I support you in this. It was the right, brave thing to do and you know that your secret is safe with me.

Love always,

Isabel x

Emily put the letters down and pushed them away. 'Shit,' she murmured. She picked up her glass but put it straight down again. She felt dizzy and could hear the pistons in her heart thundering and chugging, like a train picking up speed. Her mind became blank and crowded with tiny butterflies dripping with black ink. She shivered to try and rid herself of the words she had just read. Her head throbbed as the information sank deeper. 'Oh, shit. Oh, hell. Oh, bloody hell shit.'

Richard came into the kitchen and sat down at the table. 'Good read?' he asked with a casual deadpan face, then quickly changing it to an exaggerated puzzled expression. He pushed strands of his fair hair behind his ears and then looked at his hands, turning them over, inspecting them thoroughly.

Ana couldn't think of anything to say so just sat quietly looking down at the table and began stroking her own hair. She let her chin drop to her chest. All she could think of at the moment was the desire to start clawing at her face.

The space became muted, foggy edged. A voice came to her from somewhere, relaxed and easy. 'I did say it was very interesting.' She understood that it was Richard talking. She wondered why he was being so flippant.

Ana looked at him for a few seconds then let her eyes dart around the room trying to find some words, any words.

Finally, she whispered, 'it's unbelievable.'

'I know it's hard to get your head round it, isn't it?' Richard let his fingers tap on one of the letters. His blue eyes seemed to glint. 'But there it is. In black and white. All those years ago. What a secret to keep. What a thing to hide away. You have to take your hat off to them, especially your gran. What a woman.'

'You think?' said Ana. She wanted to frown at him but couldn't get it right, concentrating everything on controlling her eyes seemingly independent of her mind, still flitting about everywhere. She didn't want him to be like this, all glib and breezy.

'Definitely. Of course. You read what they said. The man was a beast. He deserved everything he got. It's not every day you find out that your gran was a hero. In military life and personal life.'

'It's not every day you find out your gran's a murderer.' Ana felt her cheeks burning with anger. *More secrets. This bloody family. What else don't I know?*

'I'm sorry that it's upset you,' he said softly. 'But I thought you needed to know.'

'Yes, yes, of course, thank you,' Ana replied, still unable to make direct eye contact. 'It was very good of you to let me see them. I wish you hadn't of course. At least the last bits. I suppose all of them really, I think. I don't know ... maybe if the first one had been the end, then ... I don't know. I suppose it's for the best. I realise it's ... oh, I don't really know what I think.' She realised she was rambling and directing her mumblings in a brisk monologue to the wine glass, which was ignoring her completely.

'Ana, listen,' Richard bent sideways to her line of vision. 'Ana, listen ... and look at me. Look at me. This takes time to take in. I think you've had a terrible shock. I'm sorry that I can't undo it. But the facts are there. We just have to live with them.'

Ana finally managed to stare back at him and shook her head. She made a huge effort to put some thoughts together. 'I know. I know what you're saying. It's just been a big shock to the system. Hard to take it in.'

A long pause.

They heard a click from the boiler as the central heating turned on and then a tapping at the window as a branch waved about in the wind and slapped against the glass.

'But you know,' Richard broke the silence. 'I know it's probably not appropriate to mention it … but both Isabel and Emily are dead, so that in a sense is a good thing.'

'What?' Ana jerked her head back. 'Oh, I see …'

'Yes, if you think about it,' continued Richard in the same matter of fact tone. 'Neither of them can face any charges. Emily for the killing and Isabel for complicity in the killing. Complicity … is that the right word? Collusion? Collaboration maybe?'

'You seem to be taking this very much in your stride. Don't you think it's a little too serious for that kind of talk.' *I don't like you, Richard. And I don't like your tone.*

'Oh, sorry. I only meant that the secret can be allowed to be a secret.'

'Agreed,' said Ana. 'I hope we can rely on each other keeping quiet about this. It wouldn't do to let it out. My gran and your grandma's name would be dragged through the mud.'

'Definitely,' Richard nodded severely. 'But of course, they weren't the only two involved, so we have a bit of a problem … a dilemma … a conundrum if you like.'

Ana looked up quickly. 'You mean Xavi?'

'Exactly.'

'You're not suggesting that we hand Xavi over, after all these years. I know him. He couldn't exist in prison. It would kill him.'

Richard sat back and looked at Ana. 'Xavi was there and he is … *implicated,*' he said. The word floated about the room.

'No way!' Ana blurted out.

'It's difficult isn't it,' he said evenly. 'Because there has to be justice of some kind.'

'I thought you agreed that the man was a beast, a rapist.'

'Yes, yes, he was. And we obviously have to keep Xavi away from the clutches of the law.'

'So, what on earth are you talking about? We just keep quiet, that's all. Protect him … and them. That's what we'll do.'

'Well, it's not as easy as that is it? We live in a complex world.'

'I don't understand. What? What do you mean?' Ana wanted her wine but she wouldn't have time to drink it, she needed to listen carefully to this man and concentrate. She didn't know what he was driving at.

Richard folded his arms and brought his smile back into action. 'Actually, on the other hand, when I think about it, I live in a very *simple* world. No job. Thrown on the scrapheap because of my age. No chance of another job. A simple one-bedroom flat in London. Tiny. No prospects. No *money*.'

Ana stiffened and glared at him. *Oh yes, I think get it now.*

'I don't think you can blackmail me Mr Stevens,' she said tersely. 'Your gran is implicated as well.'

'She's dead.'

'You're implicated! You've known about this for months now since you discovered the letters at your mother's house.'

'Only found them three days ago. Brought them straight round to you when I knew what they were … without reading them.'

'That's a lie.'

'I know.'

'Xavi knows when you brought them to me.'

'Ah yes, Xavi. Will he be contacting the police about me?'

'I'll burn them.'

'I've had the interesting ones copied.'

They looked at each other for a long time. Ana, glaring, poisonous. Him, easy, relaxed.

Ana reached for the bottle and poured more wine into her glass. 'You're a wonderful specimen of humanity Mr Stevens. What happened to a fairer world?'

'Ana,' he leaned forward and looked straight at her. 'This couldn't be fairer. I've been dealt a bad hand. This evens things up a bit. With a bit of justice thrown in for good measure. Perfect.'

'And what about me? Where's the fairness for me? Where's the fairness for Xavi? He didn't know what she was going to do. He was just being loyal. He wanted to protect her. Justice was done in Paris. It should end there.' She knew she was wasting her breath but she needed to keep talking otherwise she would start throwing things. She looked around for something heavy in case she ran out of words. 'It's not fairness. It's meanness. Vindictiveness and greed. Pure greed.'

'No, like I say it's all about trying to even things up.' He pulled back and gave her a mock indignant look. 'Please don't look at me like that Ana. I'm just trying to do what I think is right. I only want –'

'No! No! I don't think so.' Ana stopped him and shouted across the table.' You need to go now. Get out!' Her eyes darted to a large bottle of olive oil on the edge of the table.

'Okay Ana, I'll go if you want me to.' He sounded almost apologetic. 'But you know you have to talk to me.' He took his wallet from his coat, pulled out a small piece of paper and placed it gently on the table. 'My mobile number. We need to speak again.'

'I don't have anything to say to you.'

'You do. You know you do.' He walked to the open living room door but then turned back as he was about to disappear. 'You've got my number there. Shall we say, speak in two or three days. Give you a chance to get the money together. Ten thousand should do it.'

He turned to go, just in time to avoid the bottle smashing against the wall near the door only a few inches from his head. He didn't look back but hurried along the corridor brushing glass from his shoulder and left without closing the front door.

Ana stared at the bottle of olive oil on the table and then at the white wine snaking its way down the wall. Her shoulders sank and she thumped her back into the chair.

'Oh, bugger,' she muttered. 'Wrong bottle.'

*

Twenty minutes later Ana was sitting on the wooden swivel desk chair at the small writing table in Xavi's living room, gently turning from side to side and sucking at the cut on her index finger. She'd tried to pick up the shattered glass from the wine bottle she'd thrown at Richard but she'd given up, partly because she was hurrying and was making even more mess with drops of blood on the carpet and partly because she had to see Xavi immediately. The finger was still bleeding and she re-wrapped a piece of kitchen roll around it.

'I've got some plasters in the kitchen. I'll just get them.' Xavi started to get up from the armchair at the other side of the room.

'Doesn't matter,' said Ana curtly. 'Just stay where you are.'

Xavi did as he was told. She hadn't needed to say anything. The look on her face was enough to stop him in his tracks.

Ana gathered herself. 'That bloke Richard came back today, less than an hour ago. You remember? The one with the letters.'

'Yes. I haven't met him but you told me about him. Isabel's grandson.'

'He asked me to read to read two letters. One from Grandma and one from Isabel. He knew the precise dates.'

Xavi said nothing. He tried to make himself small so that he could disappear into the armchair. *What now?* he thought to himself.

Ana continued. 'More secrets.' She shook her head but still managed to keep her eyes blazing into Xavi as she slowly swung about in the chair, back and forth, back and forth.

Xavi wanted to continue in silent mode. It seemed to be the safest way. Instead, *I'll regret this*, he thought. 'What were they about?' he asked. He wanted the words to come out lazily almost indifferent and he tried hard but he couldn't quite hide the slight faltering and hesitancy.

'The murder,' said Ana coolly. 'Grandma told Isabel what she'd done.'

Xavi nodded very slowly. He slurped in air, closed his eyes then opened them quickly as if remembering something important, more important than a murder being revealed. He got up and went to the kitchen. He came back a minute later with two plasters and laid them on the table in front of Ana. 'One spare,' he said. 'Always best to have a spare.'

Ana studied him as he returned to his seat. She watched his easy, plodding walk and the sag of his shoulders as he sank back into the armchair and set his jawline at the fireplace. Right at this moment he looked older than ever. There were deep creases everywhere, from brow to cheek, from chin to neck. He looked like he needed a good ironing.

'I understand it,' said Ana. 'And Isabel understood it … and gave her blessing.'

Xavi looked up at her. 'She shouldn't have written that letter. It was foolish to put that down in writing.'

'She obviously wanted to confide in someone apart from you. She said she hadn't wanted you to go with her to Paris. She didn't want to involve you. Who better to confide in than her lover?'

'Isabel should have burned those letters.'

'But she didn't.' Ana stopped swinging about on the chair.

'It wasn't murder. It was an execution.' Xavi buried his gaze deeper into the fireplace. 'I didn't like it but I agreed with her. It was something that had to done. It released her. She killed her monster and could live again.'

'Actually, this is one secret I wish you'd kept to yourself.' Her voice was soft, childlike, almost appealing. 'I really wish I didn't know. It's too much. This is all getting too much.'

Xavi looked up quickly. He wasn't expecting this. There should be chaos and shouting. Because of her words he expected to see her shrinking but instead her gaze was stern and unflinching and he noted a tiny twitch of a vein at her temple as she glared at him, fighting hard to maintain composure.

'I'm glad you know,' said Xavi.

'Really?' Ana began swinging again, faster. Now she began to raise her voice. 'Really? You're glad. You're *glad* are you? You want to involve me in an … assassination. From years ago. A killing. Why?'

Xavi tried to think of what to say. He folded and unfolded his hands. After a few seconds, he said. 'Selfishness I suppose. Just like Emily. Someone to confide in.' *No, no, no, wrong thing to say. Wrong thing to say.*

'Well, thank you Uncle Xavi. That's very kind of you.' Ana swung in a complete circle and then came round and glared at him again. 'It's been quite a few days. Quite a few days of revelations. My gran's love affair. My son is in danger. And now a family murder. Quite an interesting few days, don't you think? I thought I was doing quite well with the affair and the fact that my son is in danger and I can't find him. I hadn't considered a murder. But as long as you feel glad that I know about it!'

Xavi pulled himself to the front of the armchair, folded his arms, put a thumb to his mouth and chewed at the nail. He held on to the tip of his nose for a few seconds. It looked like he was sticking it back on. 'Well, maybe, on reflection, I'm not glad that you know.'

Ana shook her head and snorted. 'I really, really, want to cry now,' she said. Her voice was quiet, submissive.

They sat absolutely still for long seconds. No tears but a deafening silence between them. They could hear each other's shallow breathing.

'If only Richard didn't know,' said Ana eventually.

'What does he want?'

'Money. Ten thousand.'

'Can't be done,' snapped Xavi. He shook his head. 'Out of the question. We wouldn't be able to pay for Rosa's care home fees.' He stood up, walked to the fireplace and rammed both hands in his pockets. 'And what if we don't pay?'

'He'll go to the police. He'll tell them that you knew of the murder. You'll be arrested as an accessory. Jail.'

'I'd rather go to jail than give him ten thousand.'

'No. You're not going to jail.'

'We can't raise ten thousand!'

'I know.'

'So, what do we do?'

'I don't know,' said Ana. 'We'll just have to think of something. Come up with a plan.' She looked at him. 'You should be good at that. You're the master criminal here.'

Xavi stroked his beard. He wanted to do something with his lips. He couldn't think what was appropriate and ran out of time so he settled on continuing to stroke his beard.

'How long have we got?' he said.

'Two or three days. Enough time to get the money together he said. He gave me his number so I could contact him.'

'Good Lord, that's not much time.'

'No, but it doesn't matter how much time he's given us. We can't think about it at the moment. We need to concentrate on finding Axel.'

'Of course. And all we can do is repeat what we did today. And hope that someone knows something.'

Ana nodded and shrugged. 'I'll pick you up tomorrow, early. Let's hope we have better luck.'

'Don't worry,' said Xavi. 'It will all be okay. We'll work it out.'

Ana stood up and walked across to him. She put a hand on his shoulder. 'You think so Uncle Xavi? You really think so? I hope you're right.' She began a deep frown but then reconsidered and gave a small shake of her and head.

They walked to the front door. 'That bloody war. If only she hadn't gone,' Ana blurted out. 'And those damn flags. Whatever they mean. Why did they give them to her? They should have given them to someone else then all this might not have happened.'

Xavi nodded, he gave her a smile, intended to be indulgent, calming, comforting. Then he wrapped her in his arms and they hugged each other until it was enough to let each other know it would be all right. It was worth it even if they both knew they were deceiving themselves. But there had to be hope.

Xavi went to open the door for her but noticed a piece of paper on the floor. He bent down to pick it up and showed it to Ana. 'No specs,' he said. She read it out loud.

'This is where Axel likes to stay.

High Level Bridge, Gateshead arch,

Jesmond Dene, derelict watermill,

Abandoned building, Central Snooker club, city centre,

Abandoned Salvation Army building, City Road,

Saltwell Garden Allotments,

Saltwell Park, wooden gazebo, corner of big field,

He needs your help. Find him.'

Ana looked at Xavi and then back at the note. 'Who? I don't get it. Who could have done this? And who was meant to get it? You or me?'

'Or both of us?' said Xavi.

'But how could that be? Who knew I was here? No-one knew. Unless I'm being followed.' She blew out a long breath. 'This is crazy. It's freaking me out.'

'But it's a breakthrough,' Xavi took the note and read it again. 'Someone wants to help us. And now we know where to look for him.'

'We have to go now,' said Ana.

'Of course.' Xavi took two coats from the hooks by the door and gave one to Ana. 'Take this. It's going to be cold and we could be out all night. Let's start at the top of the list and work our way down.'

'Okay,' Ana said, stepping out of the door. She looked up at the deep red slashes across the black sky. 'Bloody flags,' she muttered into the night.

Chapter fifteen

Friday, 15th October, 1937

International World's Fair,

Paris, France.

Javier and Luis had met Emily at the Gare d'Orsay railway station in Paris, situated on the Rue de Lille. Javier, tall, blonde with round spectacles, Luis, also tall with long, dark unruly hair and deep brown eyes. They were Spanish agents assigned to the Spanish Pavilion at the World fair and were tasked with taking Emily and the three other International Brigaders she was travelling with to a hotel near the pavilion. The hotel Gustave was located on the Rue Viala only a few minutes' walk from the Eiffel tower and the accommodation was paid for by the Comintern (the Soviet controlled Communist International). The following day there was to be the customary short ceremony of farewell reserved for departing International Brigaders, thanking them for their service to the Spanish Republic in the war, discharging and honouring them with military honours. Then they would leave for home.

They weren't to know that the International Brigades would be entirely disbanded the following year by Spanish Prime Minister Juan Negrin in the ill-advised hope that if he removed foreign fighters on the republican side, then Italian and German troops fighting on the nationalist side would be forced to withdraw through international pressure.

Emily was three months pregnant. It was decided between her and her unit commander that it would be better if she returned home before questions were asked about her pregnancy. She was with an American, a German and a Swedish volunteer. All had minor injuries but bad enough to need them to go home for convalescence.

Javier was driving them the short distance from the train station to the hotel, the four brigaders squashed into the back seat of the Citroen Traction Avant, but first he made a detour to show them the pavilions of the World's Fair Exhibition. He pulled up at the corner of a wide boulevard flanked by dozens of fountains spouting huge columns of water and pointed to a simple, modern, rectangular building situated at the edge of Trocadero square in the shadow of the Eiffel tower. 'That's where Luis and I work,' he said, in fluent English. 'The Spanish Pavilion, built by Josep Luis Sert. Modest but very modernistic inside.'

'Unfortunately, it wasn't finished in time for the opening,' laughed Luis, sitting next to him. 'So, they had to drape a massive republican flag over the front to hide the building work. It missed the wide publicity of the fair's grand opening and didn't receive a lot of recognition. It wasn't even shown on the official maps.'

The German volunteer leaned forward form the back seat. He winced as he caught his bandaged shoulder on the door handle. 'But you're young,' he said in English.

'What do you mean?' asked Luis, although he knew well enough what he meant.

'Shouldn't you be back home ... fighting?' The German stared at the back of Luis's head.

Javier and Luis exchanged glances. 'We're on special duties,' said Javier.

Luis turned to face the German. 'And there's just as much danger here,' he said pointedly.

Emily sat scrunched in the corner and glanced at the two Spaniards and the German. She was expecting fireworks but none came. The German pulled back into his seat and Luis turned to the front, his face a picture of studied indifference.

After an awkward few seconds Javier again waved an arm towards the exhibition pavilions and resumed his role as tour guide. 'Forty-five countries taking part. It's supposed to show important dualisms for France: Paris and the provinces; France and her colonies; socialism and capitalism; fascism and democracy. You know that last year's elections gave the communists and socialists a dramatically increased representation in the French parliament. The right wing are not happy.' He leaned forward, wrapped his arms around the steering wheel and stared at the scene in front of him. '*Peace and Progress* is the theme, advancing national prestige for the French. And here's an interesting thing, another theme is to help relieve the widespread and growing poverty among artists … an embarrassment to the city which prides itself as the home and centre of fine art. So, the city of Paris commissioned seven hundred and eighteen murals and employed over two thousand artists to decorate the pavilions.'

'How do you know all this?' asked Emily.

'It's our business to know,' said Luis. 'It's our job. Makes things easier if we know what's going on and why things are the way they are.'

'Definitely makes things easier,' Javier looked at Luis and then pointed again to the pavilions in front of the Eiffel tower. 'For instance, look at the far end of the plaza. See the two huge windowless pavilions reaching up into the sky. Those are the German and Soviet Pavilions facing each other like competing giants across the fountains. The German building was designed by Albert Speer, Hitler's favourite architect ... in fact Hitler wanted to pull out of the whole thing but Speer persuaded him to take part. And then Speer had a bit of luck. He accidentally saw the plans for the Soviet building ... or so he says. But we know that German intelligence agents had supplied Speer with a description of the Soviet design. And so of course, Speer decided to make the German Pavilion bigger so that the massive imposing building is topped off by a German eagle, its talons clutching a wreath encircling by a huge swastika. Fifty-three metres high! You can just see at the bottom, a Teutonic couple staring out at the Soviet building with its group of striding Russian figures holding up the hammer and sickle symbols of communism.'

Luis nodded and turned to the back of the car. 'Of course, Nazi Germany just staged the Olympics last year and is riding on its own wave of international attention. It was a major public relations success for Germany and so they are intent on similar success here in Paris. They are also helped by growing anti-semitism. Last year the French conservatives attacked the socialist leader Leon Blum because of his Jewish ancestry and his strong anti-Nazi stance. There's a popular slogan going round at the moment, *Better Hitler than Blum*, but we don't think that French Fascism will take root.'

'And also,' said Javier, taking out a cigarette and lighting it. 'When the Soviets had their pavilion built, they used Parisian workers but the

Germans brought a thousand of their own workers to build their pavilion and of course it was the perfect opportunity to bring in their own agents and spies as well.'

'So, you are operatives for the Spanish Republican government then?' said Emily flatly.

Javier blew out a long plume of smoke. 'Yes, that's correct, but we don't like to advertise it. We can tell you because you'll be gone soon and anyway … we're all on the same side, aren't we?'

'I hope so,' said Emily smiling. 'But it's hard to tell these days.' She gazed out of the window at the huge crowds walking between the pavilions. She thought back to fighting the Stalinists in the Comercio Gratuito bar with Isabel and Carmen and Maria, of the different leftist factions and infighting on the streets of Barcelona And she thought of Lazlo.

She brushed a hand against her stomach and filled her lungs trying to slow down her rapid breathing which had become more common during the past couple of weeks. Nausea hadn't been a problem but she often found herself out of breath.

Javier's cigarette smoke drifted around the silence in the car.

'So,' Luis announced. 'Let's get you to your rooms and we'll pick you up again in a few hours to get something to eat. We'll take you to Le Procope on the left bank. It's a favourite of ours. You don't have to worry about paying, we've been given some money to buy you food and drink.'

*

At seven o'clock Luis, Javier and the four brigaders were seated around a long table at Le Procope. They were joined by two young French women and an older Spanish man. The café was dimly lit with gas lights and each of the ten tables was covered with a crisp white cloth. The place was packed and filled with the smells of cooking and cigarette smoke.

After an hour of eating and talk about the exhibitions and the pavilions the group split up into more earnest conversational huddles. The Spanish man spoke mainly to the Swedish and the German volunteers because he didn't have much English and they had picked up a little Spanish from their time in Madrid and Barcelona and also with fighting alongside Spanish regulars. The two young French women fell into a serious debate in English with the American volunteer and Javier about the role of women on the front line and the depictions of women in the German and Soviet exhibitions.

Luis moved from the end of the table and pulled a chair up alongside Emily. He took a long drink from his wine glass.

'So, what do you think of Paris? First impressions?' he said.

'It's very beautiful,' Emily replied. 'It's nice to be somewhere that hasn't been bombed.' She took a sip from her bottle of beer, trying to make it last. 'I'm sorry,' she shrugged. 'That was a crass thing to say. It's very beautiful. I really like your city.'

'Don't worry,' Luis threw up both hands. 'You've seen a lot of bombings?'

'Enough.'

Luis gave her a long steady look.

'Mainly at the front,' said Emily. *He needs more*, she thought. 'Lots of bombing from the Italians and the German Condor Legion. And my friend Isabel ...' she checked herself and swallowed. 'My friend, Isabel, has seen a lot of very bad bombing and air strikes in Madrid. Worse than I ever saw.'

'Yes, we heard it was bad in Madrid. Is she safe?'

'I don't know. I'm not sure.'

'I hope she got out of there.'

'It's not like that,' Emily said sourly. 'She has to be there.'

'I'm sorry. I didn't mean anything by ...'

'She looks after the refugee children. She's a teacher and she knew she had to be with them. She has to help them. That's the kind of person she is. They have nothing. She wouldn't just leave them' She thought hard about the next sentence. Discarded it but then brought it up again because she was annoyed with him. 'She didn't have an art gallery to look after.' Emily thinned her lips and sucked in air. She took a few seconds to think. *That was really underhanded. Cheap and heartless. He didn't deserve that. He must think I'm an ungrateful snake.*

Luis shook his head and pushed himself against the back of the chair. 'Again, I'm sorry. I didn't mean to offend you ... or your friend. I can see how much she means to you. I just meant that it is good for ... for ... I don't know what I meant. But I didn't mean to say that she was running away. I can see that she has an important job to do. Everyone has to do what they can if we are to win this war.' He looked directly at her and held her eyes. 'Madrid is my home. My family are there.'

Oh no. Please no. Don't tell me they're missing. Not that. Not after what I've just said.

Emily could feel her breathing quickening. She felt a fluttering in her stomach and pressed down on it with her right hand but could feel nothing more. 'Are they safe?' she said. Her voice sounded small and brittle.

'I believe so,' said Luis. 'At least they were a week ago. But the bombing continues and you never know …'

Emily didn't reply. She turned away to watch the others in their animated discussions. She let her eyes roam about the swirling atmosphere of the room: noisy, smoky, lots of laughing, loud talking.

'Can I ask a question?' Luis said.

Emily turned back slowly and kept her face impassive, uncertain of how they could be with each other now. 'Of course, ask away.'

'Are you glad to be going back home?'

'I've been asking myself the same question. And the answer is yes and no.'

'Yes?'

'Because I will be glad to see old friends again. To be able to sleep properly. To be able to sleep not fully clothed. To be able to listen to the sound of an engine and not jump. To be able to read a book.' She fixed her gaze on the bottle of beer and stroked the condensation with one finger. 'And have mashed potatoes and cabbage and peas and gravy.'

Luis smiled. 'All very important … and no?'

'Because I will miss my new friends. I will miss their enthusiasm and passion. I will miss their courage.' She frowned, recognising the strain in her voice. She didn't want to be emotional. She gave a short sucking noise, rolled her tongue against her front teeth and then was able to continue. 'I will miss Spain and the wonderful bravery of the Spanish people. I will miss the camaraderie of the brigade, the solidarity, the fellowship. I'm sad that I won't be there for the final victory.'

'You believe in the International Brigades?'

'Of course,' Emily bridled. 'Who couldn't believe in them.' She stiffened and frowned at him. 'Thousands of people coming together to protect the world from fascism. To try and make it a better place. I loved being in the brigade. Why do you ask such a question?'

'It's just that some people ... some Spanish people ... disagree with the International Brigades. They say that foreigners shouldn't be coming to fight their war. If it wasn't for the foreigners then maybe the Germans and Italians wouldn't have joined in. The republicans think they could beat Franco if he wasn't backed by Germany and Italy ... that's what some people say.'

'A lot of good foreigners died.' Emily shuffled in her seat and thought about glaring at him but then decided to look around the room again, composing herself, avoiding his eyes. She wanted to say something more but snapped her mouth shut. She didn't want to be angry.

'I know,' said Luis, his eyes were round and kind. 'I know.' He took a drink from his glass. 'I agree with you. It is important for the world to see that people care. That friends will come and help.'

'They did care.' Emily said quickly. 'They do care. And they leave their bones in Spanish soil, far away from their homelands.' The words sizzled around them trying to escape the stifling stillness that followed and tangled everything up.

They both took a drink and managed to give each other fleeting glances.

Eventually. 'What was it like? At the front?' asked Luis.

'Not very nice.'

'You were a nurse?'

'Yes, I suppose I was, but not fully trained.' Emily stared at the table gathering her thoughts. She didn't want to speak about it but she needed to. She needed to speak it out loud for herself as much as for him. She needed to hear the words to the nightmares she was having. To put the text to the images to hopefully try and exorcise them. 'I started with a rifle,' she began. 'Then I was asked to drive an ambulance, a car really, but it served its purpose. Then I was attached to a medical unit.' She tilted her head, turned and spoke to the wall. Her voice monotone and distant. 'There was so much ethanol. It made me sick. At the battle of Jamara, often, we had no running water but we fixed up big metal containers to boil water. And sometimes we had to fix up our own electricity from the car motors if there'd been a bad raid and the lights had been blown out. We were supposed to be a dressing station but often the worst cases had to be dealt with immediately because they wouldn't make it back to the main hospitals in Madrid and Barcelona. It was constant at Jamara. Just as you thought you had finished; another group of wounded were brought in.'

'Once,' she continued, still not looking at Luis. 'We were thinking of finishing but still had some cases to deal with. Suddenly there were loud crashes and the sound of things being broken and flying about. Then came the sound of folk running. Our doors were open and before we knew it there was a chaotic stampede in the dark. Folk rushed into our unit which was already full of wounded. It was pandemonium. Lots of shrieking and wailing and moaning and cursing. A man bumped into me and as I put my hand out to push him off it came back clammy and damp. When the lights suddenly came on again, I saw that he was an older man missing the flesh on his left cheek, his mushy lip hanging loose on to his chin. Others were in an equally shocking state. It was a mess. Most were being helped into the unit by their friends. Some ripped by shrapnel. Some with arms and legs missing, or half blown off. Half-naked women, gashed and bleeding with clothes shredded by the blast. I was tripping over, stumbling over falling people. I picked up a young woman. Don't know where I got the strength from. She regained consciousness and I struggled to hold her. It was difficult because one leg had been blown off. For a second, I just stood there. I couldn't move. It was just plain horror. One of the doctors saw me struggling and took her off me. My legs were so weak I could hardly move but he got someone to push me outside for a moment. Outside I kept tripping over bodies, some dead, some unable to move with their injuries.

Going back to the entrance I stumbled over a man and fell on top of him. I said sorry. He didn't answer and I realised that my hand was on his face and it was cold as stone. It must have been many hours before that he died … we'd missed him. Completely missed him. He just lay there… quietly, not making a sound. Someone probably thought he was already dead. We were so busy, you see. It was frantic. Every second. He probably shouldn't have died. I remember looking round at the chaos and shaking. Every muscle twitching, uncontrollable. I went through the door thinking of the icy touch of the man. He shouldn't have died. I looked around at the blood and gore inside. I couldn't hear any screaming anymore. I was deafened by the shock. I remember everything seemed blurry and slow. A soldier nudged me and gave me a mug of coffee. It was hard to hold on to and kept slipping because there was so much blood on my hand. He sat me down in a chair and I just shook and shook and shook.' Now she turned to look at Luis's frozen stare. 'There were other times like that. It wasn't that unusual. It was exhausting.'

She wanted him to say something but he just continued staring at her, so she cleared her throat and carried on.

'Sometimes,' she said. 'We had to be a bit ... inventive? Pragmatic? If the situation was desperate and we didn't have time to set up a proper camp we operated under bridges, in railway carriages ... in a disused railway tunnel at Brunete. I remember working in a cave in Jamara valley. The cave was infested with rats. We were giving blood transfusions by candlelight and the flickering flames of cigarette lighters while others took it in turns to stand with a big stick to chase away the rats.

At the end of the battle for Jamara we had a proper tent set up, a sort of marquee. There were dozens of wounded inside, mainly Spanish, probably three quarters, the rest were British, American, Germans, Russian, every country you could think of that the volunteers came from ... French, Yugoslavs, Hungarians ... all for the red side. Late in the day we took in a young, wounded fascist officer ... a high-ranking type. The wounded Spanish Republicans were shouting at us, "Let him die. Leave him to die" But of course we were there to treat anyone and everyone, all the people. It was what was expected of us. He waited patiently for his turn and we did what we could but he died in the night. We weren't sorry when he died. His body was disposed of without any great degree of kindness. The Spanish lads cheered when he was carried out.'

She waited again for Luis but still he sat looking at her intently.

'Of course,' continued Emily. 'At first the language could be a problem when you were in stressful situations and had to act quickly. It wasn't possible to check everything, people just didn't have the time. I remember another English nurse; Jennifer I think her name was. She was told to write a note urgently requesting ten more pans —*sartenes*— to boil water for sterilisation. *Nosotros necisitamos diez sardinas* she wrote after the order was dictated to her. Of course, *sardinas* is sardines. The following day we received ten boxes of sardines in assorted sizes.'

At last Luis sat back, gave a tentative smile and then laughed.

They allowed the seconds to pass. Luis took out a pack of cigarettes. He took one out and offered it to Emily but she shook her head. He put the cigarette back into the packet and placed it on the table in front of them so that he could twirl it round with his fingers as a needed distraction.

'What will you do when you get home?' Luis said.

Emily puffed up her cheeks and blew out a long breath. She raised her eyebrows, glad to be thinking of something other than war. 'I don't know. I'm not sure. I'll need to get somewhere to stay. My parents aren't exactly supportive. I'll need to get some sort of job. I don't know what though. I was training to be a nurse before all this.'

'And you'll have a baby to look after.'

Emily couldn't hide her surprise. 'Yes. Is it obvious? I didn't think I was showing. How did you know?'

'You can't tell from your belly. But you're out of breath quite a bit. And to be honest the biggest giveaway is the reports that came with you four. I can see that the others have physical injuries … but battle fatigue for you? I'm not saying you're tired of battle but after what you've just told me you don't strike me as the type of person who would willingly leave their comrades. So, it had to be something else. How far on are you?'

'About three months.'

'Will he look after you?'

'Doubt it.' Emily gave a small shake of her head as she unwillingly recalled excited green eyes, leering lips and burning tarpaulin. 'I don't want him and I don't need him.'

'Good for you. The world is changing rapidly. Women are more … powerful?

'And now I have a question for you,' Emily smiled. She knew she hadn't done enough smiling. It was time to end the awkwardness. She needed to be affable. It was her last night as a brigader and she wanted the evening and the following day to be peaceful so that she could get through the farewell ceremony. She knew it would be difficult for her.

'Yes, of course. I'm sorry if it's seemed like an interrogation.' Luis returned her smile. 'What would you like to ask?'

'In the car this morning you said there was just as much danger here. What did you mean?'

Luis took a cigarette out of his packet. 'Okay if I smoke?'

Emily nodded and glanced at the others as Luis lit his cigarette.

'You know that Andres Nin,' said Luis. 'Leader of POUM, the Workers Party of Marxist Unification was murdered in July, executed by Soviet agents.'

'I'd heard something about it. But we understood, or rather it seems, that it wasn't definitely Soviet agents.'

'It was.'

'How can you be sure?'

'This is a huge exhibition. Lots of people want it to succeed and lots of people want it to fail. Discredit it. Embarrass the republican government of Spain. There are lots of agents here, from all over the world. It's easy to infiltrate. Franco's people have offices in Paris but they weren't allowed into our exhibition. However, there is a Spanish Right-Wing exhibition in another area. The nationalists have their own exhibition there but it has to be under the Vatican flag.' He took another long drag on his cigarette. 'We get reliable information from the French and British intelligence agencies as well as our own. They let us know what's going on and what may or may not happen. We know that the Soviets are trying to take control of the republican movement.'

Emily leaned forward and took another sip of her beer. 'What do you think is going to happen?'

'Don't know. It's all a bit confused at the moment. Events in Moscow are dictating what's going on. As you probably know less than a month after the civil war started the Soviet show trials began. Anyone who criticised Stalin or the stance on Spain was accused of being a crypto-fascist. They call it the Great Purge. Many old bolsheviks were accused of treason and being western spies. They were quickly found guilty and were executed. The Great Purge has been going on all across the country eliminating anyone who supported the likes of Trotsky and getting rid of any threat to Stalin. We know that Alexander Orlov has been appointed by Stalin as Soviet Politbureau adviser to our country's Popular Front government. Of course, in Soviet terms that means they're supporting the Spanish Communist party, not the socialists and anarchists.'

'So, what will he do? This Orlov.'

'We know there are mobile brigades set up with direct orders from Stalin to eliminate supporters of Trotsky who have gathered here and in Spain from all over the world. It's considered too risky to leave up to locals. They have already started. Comintern agents accuse Trotskyists of espionage.' Luis tapped his cigarette on the ashtray and sat back. 'In Spain they execute them immediately. No question of letting them put up any sort of defence or political trial. We already have dozens of instances. So, you see, we have to be on our guard. They want to make life as difficult as possible for people like Javier and me.'

'It's a mess,' said Emily. 'It's making our victory very tough.'

'Impossible I would say. We're winning the propaganda war but not the actual war. That's impossible.'

Emily frowned at him. 'No.'

'Yes. I think so. And that's not all,' said Luis. 'We have reliable information that French Fascists are around the pavilions. There is a

273

particular group call *La Cagoule*, in English, The *Cowl* … particularly nasty, bankrolled by some very prominent businessmen. They perform assassinations, bombings, sabotage and other violent activities, some intended to make people suspicious of communists and add to political instability by blaming the Left. In June they assassinated the Italian Jewish Rosselli brothers. They were socialists. They'd been in Spain to help the fight. In Italy they had founded one of the first anti-fascist newspapers and had to go into exile in France because they were under observation by the Mussolini regime. They were betrayed by one of the members of their own small organisation and in the spa town of Bagnoles-de-L'Orne they were killed, stabbed and then shot by *La Cagoule*.

For this act *La Cagoule* received one hundred semi-automatic Beretta rifles from Italy. *La Cagoule's* declared aim is to overthrow the French government and we think that they'll try this year … and these rifles will help them. They've been infiltrated by French police and we know that a small group are being accommodated in the German Pavilion. They aim to do something … we don't know what … to our exhibition. Our best guess is that they want to destroy some of the artworks for their own purposes, to show that they can hurt us even in this leftist pavilion. All except one of our artists are Spanish and supporters of the republican government and so it would be good propaganda to spoil the displays in some way.'

'So, what are you doing about it?'

'Tightened security. Trying to screen visitors, but that's difficult as we have hundreds every day. We've put a ten-foot cordon around the three big exhibits, Picasso's *Guernica* painting, Calder's *mercury fountain* and Juan Miro's *Reaper* mural. It will be difficult for anyone to get near enough to slash the paintings or break the fountain.'

'Then you just wait? Is that all you can do?'

'That's all we can do at the moment. We wait to see what precise information our friends can give us.' Luis took another drag on his cigarette and inhaled deeply. 'So, you see, it can be tricky here too.'

They were interrupted by a loud bell and a sudden gust of wind as the restaurant door was opened wide.

'That looks like the end of the evening,' said Luis. 'They have an interesting way of telling us to go here.'

'Thanks for that,' said Emily as she stood up. Luis offered his hand and she leaned forward, smiled and shook it. 'I'm glad that you can trust me ... and good luck.'

*

Half an hour later, Luis and Javier sat smoking in the car parked outside the hotel where they had deposited the four brigaders. It was starting to rain, the windscreen was misted over with condensation and speckled with raindrops. The roof rattled with the force of the heavy shower. They were on to their second cigarette and the inside of the car was thick with smoke.

'She's definitely the one,' said Luis.

'The English girl ... Emily?' said Javier, struggling to wind open the window to release some smoke.

'She's the one. Easy to get it back after the war if anything happens to Miro's mural. It would be difficult to get it back from the German,

275

and the American and Swede would be too far away. Also, she's pregnant so she'll more than likely stay home at least for the foreseeable future … and she loves the International Brigades so she's certain to take care of the flags.'

'We've got her address?'

'In her report, on file,' said Luis. 'Everything's taken care of. Miro agreed to let us have his practice painting. I explained about the threats and that we needed to make sure we had a colour copy, in case anything happened. He's got black and white photos but the colour photography is too expensive for him and anyway we need the exact pigmentation if the mural needs to be reproduced. Picasso didn't want to give us anything so the security has been doubled on his painting and Calder's mercury fountain. To be honest, the mercury fountain would be the obvious target … it's dangerous enough as it is.'

'So, she'll be given it tomorrow?'

'They'll all get a double-sided flag each at the ceremony, but hers will have the practice painting stitched inside. She can get it out of the country safely and we can collect it later and give it back to Miro when we're sure that his mural is safe. As we discussed … it's no good us hiding it, we're being watched constantly.'

'And we are the only ones who know?'

'Of course, we have to keep this as small as possible. We can't trust anyone. These exhibits are very important for our government. We are the only ones who know what's going on. It's up to us to safeguard the painting … and her.'

'And she's the one,' said Javier smiling. 'She's the one.'

'I've already said that. She's the one.' Luis stared at Javier's beaming face for a few seconds then tutted loudly, shook his head and looked away.

Javier's smile became even bigger.

Chapter sixteen

Saturday, 16ᵗʰ October, 1937

Spanish Pavilion, Paris World's Fair Exhibition, France.

The following morning Emily and the other three brigaders were led into the Spanish Pavilion, standing on the edge of the central avenue. They walked up the long staircase leading to the second floor where the tours began. On the way they passed the twelve-metre-high statue topped by a star, erected outside the entrance with the slogan *The Spanish people have a path that leads to a star.* It was a cold day and the ground was still covered with puddles from the previous night's heavy rain making the wooden stairs slippery.

Luis and Javier pointed out the art works on the second floor, all by Spanish artists. They paused for several minutes to look at the photographs of Catalan peasants and the massed ranks of Franco's troops marching in perfect order alongside photographs showing the aftermath of bombings by the nationalist planes: broken buildings and broken bodies. In the bookshop the main bookstand was covered with pamphlets about Frederico Garcia Lorca, the Spanish poet assassinated by fascist troops the previous August.

They were led down an internal staircase to the ground floor. The rooms were high with light grey walls and bright red beams. Dozens of red, yellow and purple paper streamers were hung across the ceiling. Near the bottom of the staircase was Miro's huge five-metre-high mural, *The Reaper.* The far end of the room was dominated by Picasso's monumental painting, *Guernica,* inspired by the bombing of that town by the German Condor Legion in April. It was a shocking surrealist anti-war plea, painted by Picasso in twenty-four days in his workshop near the Seine.

Installed next to Picasso's painting was the mercury fountain sculpture by Miro's friend, the American artist Alexander Calder. The assembly of steel shapes and rods propelled by the fountain pumping pure mercury, provided swaying mobiles above a deadly glistening pool.

As Emily came down the stairs, she noted the young men standing about at various corners and vantage points in the room, oblivious to the magnificence of the exhibits but eyes darting about continually, scanning the crowds. Because of her conversation with Luis the night before she knew they would be the extra security brought in for these three most important artworks in the exhibition.

As they reached the bottom of the stairs a group of about thirty well-dressed men and women suddenly burst into spontaneous applause. The dozens of visitors admiring the sculpture and paintings stopped and turned to see what was going on as the officials from the Spanish embassy continued to clap.

An older man with a neatly cropped moustache, wearing a smart double-breasted suit and vivid red tie strode forward and beckoned the four brigaders to stand on a small wooden platform.

Emily climbed up with the other three, trying to look as inconspicuous as possible. She noticed that her boots were scuffed and the right boot had a tear along the seam which turned into a hole at the heel. She looked at the others: the German frowning slightly; the American, folded arms, hands clasped tight on to upper arms, adopting an indifferent slanted stance; the Swede, looking back at her and nodding briefly.

Let's just get this over with, she thought. *Whatever it is.*

'Camaradas.' The moustache bristled as the smart double-breasted suit faced the audience and began to speak, his voice booming around the walls. 'saludamos a nuestra companeros internacionales.'

Emily understood that he said, *'we salute our international comrades'.* But after that he spoke far too fast for her. Her command of Spanish was by now good, but only if the conversation was unhurried and measured. She looked back along the line and saw that her brigade friends were equally unsure because of the speed of the speech.

The speech went on for another six minutes and was followed by loud applause. The four brigaders clapped too although they didn't know exactly what had been said. Then Luis came forward and presented each of the brigaders with a double-sided flag, taking great care to make sure Emily was given the correct one. The brigaders smiled, accepted the flags unfolded them and held them up to receive further applause.

The moustache and double-breasted suit stepped back along with Luis and they were replaced by a short balding man with a large protruding stomach, wearing a dark brown overcoat. He took out a piece of paper from his inside pocket and put on his reading glasses. He bowed towards Emily and the other three and then turned back to the crowd which had grown considerably as more visitors to the pavilion came to see what was going on.

'Comrades,' the bald man began, reading from his notes in Spanish. 'We salute our international comrades as we gather here in the magnificence of this building and surrounded by the magnificent art work on display.'

He glanced up at them on the platform. 'You are our history. You are the solidarity which we craved. You will not be forgotten. Comrades of the International Brigades. You came. You came in your thousands. And we salute you and your heroic bravery. It is a rare thing to come from so far away. From the far corners of the world to help a country that you may know nothing about. Yet you came and we salute you. You who stand before us today are the bright stars that will bind us together in solidarity and brotherhood. We applaud your glorious efforts and your self-sacrifice.'

Emily shuffled uncomfortably but tried to keep as still as possible. Again, she could understand very little of what was being said, only catching a few words and phrases here and there. She saw Luis and Javier smiling. There was nothing left to glance at on the walls and so she returned to her boots.

The bald man continued. 'When you walk into this building instead of seeing the glories of technology you are shown the photographs of children. Children, whose world is torn apart and is being torn apart by the savagery and brutality of nationalist forces under Franco. It may be uncomfortable viewing but it is necessary. It is necessary to show the world what is being perpetrated on to a people and their rightfully elected government.

Behind you and to my left you see the magnificent paintings of Picasso and Miro depicting the savagery, the brutality, the tragedy and the futility of war. Especially a war deliberately waged against civilians. In the middle of this room, you see Calder's mercury fountain.

A special message. An Homage to the town of Almaden. Even as we speak it is still under siege from Franco's troops. It is under siege because it is no ordinary town. It delivers most of the world's mercury, an essential ingredient in the making of detonators for bombs. It is of crucial importance for the nationalist army, and of great importance to big business which can make big profits from war machines. Also, of course it is a vital commodity for Franco's friends in Germany, where it can help produce the bombs that kill our countrymen.'

The bald man turned and with a grim expression spoke directly at the four brigaders. 'It is against this background that we salute these four individuals. Their greatness will live on in the minds and hearts of our people and our struggle. We will never forget what they have done for us. We gift them these flags to remember us and remember their time of comradeship and solidarity.'

At the top of the steep wooden stairs two men watched the ceremony with great interest. Nicolas and Gabriel were Frenchman. They were also members of *La Cagoule*. A third Frenchman, Marcel, was waiting at the main entrance.

Two hours before they had been in one of the heavily guarded storerooms in the German Pavilion. It was there they received their final instructions from the German agents. Nicolas was to have the petrol bomb to throw at Miro's painting of *The Reaper* and destroy it. Gabriel was given the pistol to deter any chase and Marcel was to be at the main door with a smoke bomb to create a distraction for their escape. In the confusion they would make their way back to the German Pavilion one hundred and fifty metres away across the central avenue. There they would be hidden until everything had died down. The police would not be given access to the German building. At the end of the day, they would be disguised as German workers and taken out of Paris. On no account, said the German agents, on absolutely no account, could they be seen to be going into the German Pavilion. There would be German agents in the avenue to give assistance if needed.

The speech was still going on when Nicolas gave a small nod to Gabriel. Gabriel went to lean on the top stair rail while Nicolas swung his shoulder bag across his stomach. He undid the two buckles and felt for the cotton wick at the top of the glass wine bottle. The petrol in the bottle swished about as he made his way slowly down the stairs step by step. He knew the Germans had put plenty of sugar in the bottle to make sure that it stuck to its target. With any luck the whole of Miro's mural would be engulfed in a fireball but at the very least it would be severely damaged and he was told that a German agent was in the building to take photographs and make sure that the images of the destruction were seen around the world. This ceremony for the International Brigaders would be an added bonus for the propaganda photos.

Gabriel pushed his right hand deep into his inside coat pocket and folded his fingers around the Czech CZ pistol. Just fifteen centimetres long it was perfect for concealing in a coat and was a favourite of the German agents.

The bald man was just finishing his speech as Nicolas reached the bottom stair. He wanted to be on the floor so that he could throw the bottle up at a certain angle and make sure that the fire splashed down on to as much of the mural as possible.

'And so,' the bald man raised his voice to emphasise the climax of the speech. 'We say again, thank you to our brave ...'

Nicolas eased the bottle from his bag and took out a cigarette lighter. He flicked it three times but could get no flame. He shook the lighter and tried again, turning his back on the crowd to hide what he was doing.

But Luis had heard the click and rasp of the lighter and moved across from beside the platform breaking into a run when he saw a man desperately trying to light something hidden from sight.

Nicolas finally got the lighter to work and lit the cotton fuse hanging from the neck of the bottle. He turned and pulled his arm back to throw the petrol bomb just as Luis arrived. Luis flung himself at Nicolas pushing him against a column at the bottom of the stairs. Nicolas just had time to release the bottle but it spiralled into the air heading for an empty wall across the room.

As the bottle looped its way over the heads of the crowd, everyone stood transfixed and watched. The bald man put his hand to his mouth. The room became still and hushed. At last, the bottle completed its lazy arc and smashed against the wall. The fireball was ignited immediately and gusts of flame were flung on to the ceiling, the wall, the wooden floor, and across the coats of two women at the back of the crowd. The paper streamers caught fire, broke loose and wafted about over the heads of the crowd.

The screaming started immediately.

Two men helped the women tear off their coats and then flung them across the room only adding to the confusion as they landed among the Spanish Embassy officials. The four brigaders ran for the open-air theatre at the far end of the long room. Now there was complete mayhem as figures scattered anywhere they could to get away from the flames and burning streamers flying around them. But the stairway offered no escape as Luis struggled with the Frenchman and blocked that exit. Nicolas broke free and kicked at Luis's face as he tried to hold onto the Frenchman's leg. Nicolas stumbled and staggered up the stairs as Javier came running across to help followed by three more security men. Luis and Javier and the security men were only a few steps behind as Nicolas reached the top of the stairs. Gabriel let Nicolas run past him and then pulled out the pistol.

Gabriel wanted them to halt when they saw the weapon but they kept on racing up the stairs. He pulled the trigger twice to stop them, not aiming at anything and trying to shoot above their heads. The pistol shots calmed the mad frenzy below as the crowd ducked for cover and hid behind whatever they could find. Luis and the security men stopped near the top of the staircase and then turned, incredulous, to watch Javier tumbling backwards down the stairs. A bullet had ricocheted off the iron stairway rods and had gone through his throat. He was dead instantly.

Gabriel now raced after Nicolas and both leapt down the outside steps. Marcel was waiting for them. He pulled the ring on the smoke bomb and flung it at the bottom of the stairs. Immediately thick black smoke spouted out, spreading quickly along the pavement and now causing panic outside the pavilion. The three Frenchmen ran between the terrified crowd, racing to get away from the smoke and the sound of shooting. They split up, running in different directions.

Luis jumped through the smoke and spotted them. He shouted to two security men to go left and follow Marcel, the other one to follow Gabriel to the right. He raced after Nicolas. As he ran, he saw that

Marcel and Gabriel were suddenly lost in the fleeing mass of people, but he was closing in rapidly on Nicolas.

Nicolas weaved his way between the crowd, heading for the safety of the German Pavilion only a few seconds away.

Luis vaulted over a bush at the side of the avenue. He ran past a group heading in his direction. A huge man suddenly loomed up in front of him, bent down and leaned his shoulder into Luis's stomach. Luis fell, sprawling on to the pavement, winded.

He wanted to stay there. He would have been safe if he'd stayed down but instead, he forced himself to his knees, sucked in air and continued to race after Nicolas.

Fifty metres from the German Pavilion, he noticed a young woman running alongside him to his left, her blond ponytail swinging about. She was keeping up with him. He glanced at her and frowned, trying to warn her off. He shouted at her in French and English. 'Aller! Va-t'en c'est dangereux. Go! Go away! It's dangerous!' But she kept on running alongside him. He frowned at her again, mystified. After a few more paces she pulled her right arm across her body and swung it back with a clenched fist into Luis's chest. The blow stopped him in his tracks and he staggered two more steps and then sank to his knees. He looked up into the woman's pale blue eyes as she quickly inspected him before replacing the paring knife with its short blade in her pocket. Then she ran off, disappearing into the crowds. For an instant he thought of Emily standing over her patients, checking them, making sure they were alright. He wished he could see her now. He wished he could see her again.

Luis realised his chest was on fire. He started coughing rapidly and looked down. The blood was already seeping through his shirt. He curled up and pulled his arms across his chest to try and stop the pain. He gave one short gasp and then slipped to one side and slumped on to the cold pavement unable to see or think clearly.

Emily and the Swedish brigader had ran to the top of the outside stairs to find out what was happening. They saw Luis lying on his side on the pavement near to the German Pavilion. They jumped down the stairs two at a time, pushed though the crowds and ran across to him but were forced back by the exhibition security guards. One of the guards was bending over Luis frantically loosening his shirt and trying to stem the bleeding.

'Luis! Luis!' Emily shouted over the shoulder of a security guard blocking her path. But there was no response.

He was declared dead one hour later at the Onteniente hospital on the Avenue D'Orsay.

Chapter seventeen

Friday, 28th October 2016

Low Fell Allotments, Gateshead, near Newcastle,

Northern England.

Axel Edelman flicked his eyes open and instinctively pulled his woollen hat down against the cold night air. Something was going on outside the shed. He could definitely hear something. It wasn't the rats with their usual foraging about in the middle of the night, scouring the allotment garden plots for food. This was a different sound, a kind of stiff breeze, difficult to detect, coming in short bursts and then a crack or two. He was fully awake now and propping himself up on one elbow, concentrating hard and focusing on the sounds but still unable to make out what they were.

Axel unclasped his arms from across his jacket and adjusted his sweater. He always slept fully clothed and ready. But with no sleeping bag now he had no choice anyway. He flopped out of the camp bed as quietly as he could and crawled across to the window, wincing as he stumbled into the cans of fence paint stacked under the small worktop only a short step away. He froze and stopped his breathing for a few seconds so that he could listen even more intently. This wasn't good, not at two in the morning.

He inched forward, avoiding the creaking floorboard next to that side of the shed. He allowed himself to unfold, crept up to the window and slowly drew back the sacking nailed to the wooden planks of the wall and used as a makeshift curtain. There was a full moon which gave him just enough light to see where he was putting his feet now. The four window panes were rain spattered and difficult to see out of. He put his face against the nearest pane but then carefully pulled back as the window steamed up with his breath. He realised he was panting in shallow bursts. The noises outside had stopped. He could feel the blood rushing in his eardrums and made a conscious effort to even out his breathing. Maybe it had been a fox. He knew it wasn't.

He crouched for a few more seconds holding every muscle in check. The sounds had gone. He relaxed and turned to go back to the warmth of his sleeping bag. He could already feel the cold seeping into him. He rubbed his hands together and then stopped in his tracks.

He heard the word.

It definitely sounded like *quiet.* It definitely sounded like a spoken word, hushed and urgent.

Axel swung round and eased the sacking aside again. He held his breath and pushed his face closer. His nose pressed against something. The corner cobweb gave way and broke. A fat short-legged spider swung onto his forehead and scuttled down to his chin. Axel instinctively brushed it away and swiped a hand across his face. At the edge of the window pane he could make out the end of a long, thin white line, then another, then another, distorted with the raindrops on the window, bending and splitting. The three lines were moving together in the same direction crossing over each other, skimming and darting.

He moved across to the bottom right-hand pane to get a better view. The glass was cracked and a small piece the size of a coin had fallen out. He put his eye to the hole, blinked as the icy air wafted in through the gap and found the beginnings of the three beams of light slashing through the darkness.

Axel squinted and tried again, moving the side of his face against the cold glass to get a better view. He scanned the allotments to his left. There, there beyond the neat bushes and the compost heaps and the bramble hedges he found what he was looking for. Behind the beams were the silhouettes of three figures. The figures crept forward, only making the slightest noise as a footstep landed too heavily or a twig was missed and cracked as it was stood on.

There were twelve allotments on the site. He thought they must have started at the top and were coming to his place at the end. He could make out the figures easily now as they climbed over a small fence. They shimmied effortlessly over the fence and slunk along the narrow flagstoned path towards the large garden shed, two allotments before his.

He heard a grating, snapping sound and then a faint voice hushing, again urging quiet. The door of the shed had been jemmied open and Axel saw the beams of light disappear as the figures went in. Axel backed away and pulled at the crumpled red coat on the far side of the camp bed squashed up against the side wall of the shed.

Sami's head came up. 'What? Wassamatter?'

Axel put a finger to his lips. 'Sshh … Shush. Come on get up. We're leaving.'

'What? What d'you mean? It's freezing.'

'We've got to go. C'mon. There's something happening outside. Three people. We've got to go. Hurry. Come *on*.'

Sami sat up instantly and wriggled off the camp bed. She too was fully clothed, for warmth and for speed. They both quickly put on their trainers.

Sami sneaked a look out of the window. 'D'you think they're looking for you?' she whispered.

'Dunno. Probably. I didn't see them carrying anything so it looks like they're not here to rob anyone. But I'm not taking any chances. Come on, let's get out of here.'

Sami snatched a pack of candles and a box of matches from the window ledge and began to fill her pockets.

'No, leave that stuff. Just grab your bag,' Axel hissed. He didn't mean it to sound harsh, but there was a wave of panic starting to surge up through his chest. 'Leave it. We haven't got time. Let's go. C'mon. C'mon. Let's go.'

'But they'll know we've been here if they see our stuff. And the allotment owner will know we've been here.'

'Doesn't matter. Come on. *Come on.* Grab your bag. We can't hang about if it's them. We can come back for the other stuff if we get a chance. Leave everything else. If it's who I think it is, these people won't mess about. It must be those three Leon was talking about.'

Axel slung his backpack over his shoulder and stooped to the crack in the window. He could see the beams of light again, this time closer. There was only one more allotment between them and this shed. He gently pulled the bolt back on the door and grimaced as the metal rasped and gave a squeaking scraping noise. The door was on the end of the shed away from the torch beams and they would be hidden for a few precious seconds.

He tapped Sami on the shoulder, stepped out of the shed and nodded to the big bushes to his right. They would give them some more cover and they could run to the iron railings only a few yards away. He knew where the loose railing was. It had been his way in to the site many times and could be pulled aside and put back into position to cover their way in. But this time there was no need for secrecy, speed was all that mattered. They would be okay if they could get out on to the street unnoticed. There they would be able to run to and hide.

Axel heard a voice again, calling to the others, this time louder and more urgent. No need for silence now. Their hiding place had been discovered and they had been seen. He stood, frozen by the thousands of tiny electric charges racing through his body and stared at the dark figures, mesmerised by the beams of light slashing about his chest, searching for his face. He heard the nearest fence creak and the thud of feet landing heavily. Sami came alongside him, grabbed his arm, yanked him round and heaved him towards the bushes.

'Run,' she screamed. 'Run'

They launched themselves at the thick hedgerow and dense undergrowth beside the shed. They put their heads down and pushed on through the lower branches of the birch trees. Sami yelped as a branch whipped back and caught her on the cheek drawing a thin line of blood but she still kept a firm grip on Axel's arm and tugged and hauled him through until they were at the high iron railings topped with rusty barbed wire.

'Where is it?' yelled Sami. 'Where's the opening? Where's it gone?'

Axel pushed past her and pulled at three tall railings until he found the one he wanted. He twisted it to one side. There was just enough space. He threw his bag in the gap, motioned to Sami to do the same and then helped her scramble through. He stumbled after her and then took a moment to pull the railing back into place.

As they ran up the lane Axel glanced over his shoulder to see the three figures desperately searching for and failing to find the loose railing. The fence was too high and the barbed wire on top was a further deterrent. Axel watched them as they retreated back into the bushes to find their original way in at the other side of the allotments, giving Axel and Sami an extra minute to make their escape.

'Saltwell Park,' said Axel, his voice coming in fast breaths. 'We'll be okay there.' He led Sami along a narrow path beside more tall wrought iron railings until they came to wide wooden door. 'We can get in here and hide. There's a place I know.' He squinted up at the rain starting to fall and swirling through the lights of the lamp posts stretching through the darkness. 'It's a shelter. We can get out of this rain.'

Axel showed Sami the footholds at the side of the door. They scrambled over and started running to the south field, past the bandstand in the huge Victorian park near the urban centre of Gateshead, flanked on two sides by hundreds of terraced houses and on a third side by a large cemetery. The tall chimneys and turrets of the grandiose red brick Saltwell Towers mansion glinted in the rain as they raced across the field, past the imposing Boer war memorial with its angel holding aloft the peace laurel. In a few minutes they had reached the big northern field bordering the boating lake. Along the top of the field was a long broadwalk, at both ends of which were circular wooden shelters with a bench running around the interior walls. The rain was now lashing down, they were soaking wet and their feet flicked up splatters of water from the puddles suddenly appearing on the pathways.

'Here. Here we are.' Axel pointed to the nearest shelter and they ran in. They flung their bags on to the wooden bench, gave themselves a shake and pushed their dripping hair back. 'It's okay. I've stayed here lots of times. We're safe here. In the morning we'll figure something else out. As long as we're away from them. Let's try and get some rest.' He stretched out on a section of the bench and looked across at Sami's glistening face as she stared back at him with narrowed eyes. 'It'll be okay, honestly, it'll be okay. Let's try and get some sleep.' He scrunched himself up with his back to Sami.

'Glad to hear it,' panted Sami, sitting on the bench on the opposite side of the shelter, catching her breath and already arranging her bag as a pillow. 'For a moment there I was getting a bit worried. A bit too much excitement for one day. Especially after all the fancy places you take me to.' She pulled her mobile phone from her jacket pocket, flicked it on and looked at the screen. 'Two o'clock in the morning … still awake … and no mini bar.'

But it wasn't okay and they weren't safe at all.

Felipe, Ramon and Valentina were walking along the narrow path at the top of the lane. Felipe snapped his torch on and looked at the map Amber had hastily drawn for him at the pub, blue ballpoint pen circles heavily scribbled in and dotted about. Alongside the map a list of locations that Axel had used. The rain was already beginning to blur the ink.

'Here,' said Felipe. 'The park is right beside the gardens we've just been in. This is one of his places. This is where he'll be. Got to be. They can't have got far, especially in this weather. And that girl Amber said he uses this place a lot.'

Ramon wiped beads of rain from his brow. 'Let's go then,' he said quickly.

Five minutes later they went past the war memorial and were walking up from the boating lake to the top of the north field, keeping to the bushes and trees at the edge.

Sami lay back on the bench, eyes closed, arms firmly folded against the cold, hands tucked under her armpits, trying to get to sleep. The rain had stopped and there was a heavy smell of earth and grass all around. She heard a dull scraping sound. A grey squirrel appeared on top of the low wooden wall, stood perfectly still and looked at Sami. She sat up bolt upright, startled by the big black eyes staring at her. The two of them regarded each other for a few seconds, then the squirrel turned and bounded away towards the trees but suddenly stopped and changed direction, alarmed by something. Sami searched in the darkness for what had frightened the squirrel and saw two dark figures coming slowly forward. She stood up and was about to call out a warning to Axel when a hand was pushed roughly against her mouth stifling her cry and an arm thumped into her chest and dragged her back. She saw the two dark figures starting to run. They were only a few strides from the entrance to the shelter.

Sami twisted her neck and bit down hard on Ramon's hand. He released his grip and pulled his hand back, cursing under his breath.

Sami whirled around and pushed her elbow into his face at the same time shouting out her warning. 'Axel! Axel! Go! Go! Quickly! Go!'

Axel leapt up. His eyes darted about as he grabbed his bag. He hesitated for an instant as Felipe and Valentina ran into the shelter and Sami hurled herself at them, all three crashing to the concrete floor. Sami untangled herself and then dived at Ramon's feet, hanging on to his leg as he tried to get across to Axel.

'Go! Go!' Sami shrieked at Axel. 'Go! It's you they want! Go! Get out.'

Still Axel stood.

Sami was being dragged along by Ramon. He started to punch at her head. 'Go! Bloody go!' She shouted again. 'I'm okay! Run! Run!'

Axel leapt over the shelter wall and started to run. He stopped after twenty metres and turned to go back but he knew there was nothing he could do. Sami was already being held down and now the other two were coming fast. *They can't get the flags. They won't get them. I promised.*

Axel turned again and started to run, slipping on the wet grass. As he ran, he yelled into the blackness, 'Shit! Shit! Shit! Shit!'

Felipe and Valentina were coming fast but thanks to Sami he had a head start and as the rush of adrenalin kicked in, he easily outpaced them. He stopped at the bottom of the field, bent down, hands on knees, fighting for breath, and watched Felipe and Valentina as they gave up and returned to the shelter. He let them see him. Let them know he wasn't giving up. *Nothing I can do. Nothing I can do. Wait and watch. Sorry. Sorry. I'm sorry. There was nothing I could do.*

Ramon dragged Sami to her feet just as Felipe and Valentina came into the shelter.

'I can see he's still down there,' said Ramon. He pulled at Sami's coat and ripped it. 'Get your phone out. Get your phone and call him. If he wants to stop you getting hurt, call him. Now! Call him. Now. Just do it!'

'He doesn't have a phone!' Sami yelled and swung her arm round to break Ramon's grip. 'He doesn't have a phone. I can't call him.'

Ramon moved forward again; hand raised. 'Don't lie. You just call him.'

'Stop! Ramon stop!' Valentina moved quickly and stood between Ramon and Sami. 'I don't think she's lying. We'll just have to think of something else.'

'Okay, that's it,' said Felipe. He picked up Sami's bag. 'Let's get out of here. Let's get her back to the house. He can find us there if he wants this one back.'

Ramon flung his arms up. 'How? How's he going to find us? He doesn't know where the house is. He doesn't know where to go.'

Felipe turned and looked at the far end of the field. 'He's still there. I've got some paper. We'll leave him a note and make sure he finds it.'

Felipe pulled out the map Amber had drawn. 'We don't need this now.' He turned it over and began writing. When he had finished, he showed it to the others.

"All we want are the flags. That is all. Bring them to this address at noon today. The girl will not be harmed. NO POLICE. If you don't

bring the flags the girl will be in danger. She has a pretty face and we have acid.

36 Walker Road. NO POLICE"

Valentina looked at the note. 'Acid?'

'Bit of extra pressure to persuade him,' said Felipe. 'He doesn't know we haven't got any acid.' He took the note, went to the entrance to the shelter and waved it above his head. He could just make out the figure at the far end of the field. 'Read this Axel,' he shouted. 'Read this. If you want to help her, read this.'

The words skidded across the wet grass to Axel. He gave an involuntary shudder and then stared up at the shelter as the three Spaniards walked Sami back to their car. All four figures became distorted and blurred. The trees around them became bleary and merged into a single hazy line.

Axel wiped the tears away with the back of his hand and started to run back to the top of the field. He kept to the trees and watched as Sami was guided over a fence and then steered along the narrow path outside the park flanked by Valentina and Felipe and led by Ramon. He continued watching for a few more seconds to make sure they weren't turning back and then ran to the shelter.

He found the note on the bench he had been lying on weighed down by a stone. After reading it he turned it over and looked at the map. He recognised the handwriting immediately, carefully folded the paper and put it into his pocket. Axel unzipped his backpack, opened a plastic carrier bag and looked at the flags. *Why? What's so special? What's this all about*? He stared up at the deep black sky, the rain had stopped and now it was clear and studded with hundreds of stars. 'Sorry eldergran,' he murmured. 'Sorry. She wouldn't be in this mess if it wasn't for me. I have to let them go. I'm sorry.'

Chapter eighteen

Friday, 28th October, 2016

Xavi's flat, Newcastle, Northern England.

It was early morning. 'We need to get started.' Ana sat at Xavi's kitchen table nursing a cup of coffee. 'Hopefully we'll have more success than last night.'

'I know, I know.' Xavi pulled his chair, went to the sink and poured his coffee out.

'You didn't need to do that.'

'It's fine. I don't need it. We need to get going and try and track Axel down as soon as possible. We've still got half of the list still to cover. Whoever sent it ... we've got a lot to thank them for.'

Ana took a long drink from her cup. There was a buzzing sound. She picked up her mobile and looked at the display. She waited for a silence to settle in the room. 'He's coming today.'

'Who?' Xavi half turned as he rinsed his cup.

'Richard. He's just messaged. He's coming for his money. He'll be here at three. He said he'd give us a couple of days but he must have changed his mind. He's coming today.' She stared at the phone again and then looked at Xavi. 'I don't know what to do.'

'I do. I know exactly what to do.'

'What do you mean?'

'I don't care. He'll wish he hadn't tried to blackmail us.'

'No! Don't do anything rash. He'll do it. He'll go to the police.' She glared at him. 'And you're not going to prison. Not for something that happened decades ago, to someone who deserved it and that wasn't your fault. Grandma Emily wouldn't like that.'

'We can't pay him. Good Lord. Ten thousand. We haven't got that kind of money, and even if we did, we shouldn't pay him. You know we need the money for Rosa.'

'I know. I know that.' Ana pulled at an eyebrow and massaged her brow. 'We'll just have to stall him … until we can think of something else.' She glanced at Xavi. 'Maybe he'll settle for less. Maybe half.'

'Maybe he'll settle for a broken head.'

'That won't help.'

'It would help me.'

'It wouldn't help my mother and her care fees. And you wouldn't be able to help anyone because you'll be in prison. Richard sounded desperate. He'll go through with it. He'll tell the police. He's got nothing to lose. We need to make some sort of deal.'

They stared around the room trying to work out what to say next. A loud knock on the back door made Ana jump. 'Do you think that's him?'

Xavi didn't answer. He locked eyes with Ana for a brief second and then walked across, unlocked the backdoor and opened it. A tall young woman with blue hair and a long scar down the left side of her face stood facing him.

'You!' grunted Xavi. 'What do you want?'

'Just to talk,' said Valentina. 'I've got something you need to know.'

Xavi stepped to one side and motioned for Valentina to come in and then nodded to Ana sitting at the table. 'This is Ana,' he said.

'Yes, I know who you are,' said Valentina, looking at Ana. 'You're Axel's mother. I'm glad you're here. I didn't know how to contact you or where to find you. I was hoping you would be here.'

Ana shook her head. 'How do you know who I am? Who are you?'

'I have some important information about your son.'

'What?' Ana sat up quickly. 'Is he safe? Where is he? How do we get to him?' She realised she was talking too fast and slowed down, understanding that she had to let this woman speak but not yet quite ready. 'We haven't been able to contact him. He hasn't got a phone. He did have but he doesn't use it. We've just been going round in circles. We need to find him to know that he's safe.'

'Ana,' Xavi widened his eyes and flicked a hand at Valentina. 'Let her speak.'

Valentina looked at Ana. A serious expression. A chill went through Ana. *Oh no*, she thought *Oh no. don't say that. Please no.*

'It's okay,' Valentina said, speaking fast. 'He's okay. Please. Please let me explain.'

Xavi talked at Ana without taking his eyes off Valentina. His eyebrows came together like storm clouds and gave her an accusatory look. 'She was one of the three who came here … looking for the flags … probably broke in the same night. Am I right?'

Valentina nodded. 'Please let me explain. I haven't much time.' She pushed her hands into her jacket pockets and pulled her shoulders back. 'This is all going to sound very strange to you but please hear what I have to say. My name is Valentina. The other two I am with are Ramon and Felipe. We are all Spanish citizens.' She looked at Xavi. 'We are not Portuguese students. Ramon and Felipe are part of a far-right political group in Spain … not a terrorist group but quite influential in the work that they do to help other groups spread dissent in their efforts to destabilise our democratic government. They work behind the scenes … a long way back … to spread misinformation … shape different theories. Conspiracy theories if you like. They are extremely secretive. The group doesn't even have a name. They are very well hidden and have proved to be a valuable asset to those who wish to distort views and hope to bring down the government.'

Xavi eyed Ana. 'So, are you one of them?' he asked.

'No, I am not.' Valentina leaned back against the sink. 'I am with our government's security services. We only found out about this group a few months ago. I was given the task of infiltrating them. I've been doing deep operative work for years inside far-right organisations. We understood what they were doing but we didn't know where the funding for their operation was coming from. We identified Ramon as someone who might be a little more negligent and careless than the others because of his temperament … he can be aggressive, and lately because of his obsession with the flags. I am sure you are aware of the flags?'

'Oh yes,' snapped Ana. She stared at Valentina trying to concentrate. There were too many questions flying through her head. 'We know about the flags.'

'What's so special about them?' said Xavi. 'I don't understand. And why should we believe any of this?'

Valentina looked from Xavi to Ana and then back again. 'It's not the flags. It's what's sewn between them that is important to Felipe and Ramon, and seemingly especially to Ramon.'

Ana looked up. 'What's sewn between them?'

'It's a copy of a painting by a famous, Catalan left-wing artist,' said Valentina. 'The important thing is that the group, or at least some of the group think that it might be useful in the Catalan independence election coming up in a few months' time. It might help with the far-right propaganda to destabilise the election. However, I have to tell you that the painting hasn't actually been proved to be there yet. Hopefully we'll find out soon.

I was tasked with infiltrating far-right groups but there are others in the National Intelligence unit who have infiltrated leftist groups, and also specifically Catalan independence leaders and activists. The important thing for our security services... and our whole security ... is that we try and find out how the painting will be used. Who will receive it? What this group's sponsors will think about? Will they fund Ramon and Felipe and me if they think it is all worthwhile? Maybe it will lead us to the people who are providing the money for this group and ultimately to the extremists who plant bombs. We have two main objectives, one, to make a detailed map of who is where at the moment, and two, to do everything we can to demobilise them without revealing how we know about them.'

Ana stood up and leant heavily on the table. 'I know that Axel had the flags,' she said firmly. She darted a reproachful look at Xavi. 'But you still haven't said where he is. Is he in danger? Where can we find him?'

'We tracked Axel and his friend Sami to a place where they were hiding, Saltwell Park I think it's called —'

'Was it you who gave us the list of places?' interrupted Xavi.

Valentina nodded. 'Yes, I wanted you to find him first. But we found him in Saltwell Park. A contact told us where he stays.' She didn't want to mention that it was Axel's sister Amber who gave them the information. She didn't want them to know that Amber was helping them and make the situation more complicated than it already was. 'Axel escaped with the flags but we caught his friend Sami. She's being held as a kind of hostage in a house on the other side of town until Axel comes and exchanges the flags for her.'

'A *kind* of hostage?' said Ana. 'What different kinds of hostage are there? This is all getting too weird.'

Valentina ignored the questions. 'I have only a short time here. I said I was going out to get food. I thought it was important to let you know that Axel is safe.'

'Safe! Safe!' Ana stood up to her full height. She spoke the words slowly trying to keep her voice level. 'How the hell is he safe? As far as I can see he's walking into a trap. He's not bloody safe at all.'

'And again, how do we know all this is true?' said Xavi. 'And if it is true, how do we know we can trust you? Like I said before, why should we believe any of this.'

'Because I'm here,' said Valentina. 'What other reason would I have to come here? And would I really be able to make up such a fantastic story? The British security services know we are here and what is happening. They know about our project and have agreed to help where necessary and not to interfere, in exchange for information about any contacts and links with British far-right groups. Importantly, they don't want any … scandal … no that's the wrong word. They don't want anything finding its way into the press and causing any embarrassment … anything that would endanger the operation. They certainly have made it clear that they don't want any British citizens …' Valentina stopped and pulled her mouth into a tight thin line.

'Hurt? Killed? Is that the word you're looking for?' Ana shouted across the room unable to contain herself anymore. 'It's my bloody son! My son!'

'We need to find him,' said Xavi, he walked across and stood directly in front of Valentina. 'I think you thought I had the damn flags. I knew he was given the flags so it's my fault. My responsibility. We need to find him and make sure he's safe … and the girl'.

'We need to go to him now,' Ana said, lowering her voice into a soft growl.

'I'm sorry. That would be very difficult. I don't think it's possible.' Valentina folded her arms across her chest, emphasising the decision. 'I know you are worried. I understand. And I promise I will do everything to make sure that Axel and Sami are safe.'

'But this boy Ramon has a temper,' Ana glared at Valentina. 'That's what you said. He could do anything. He sounds like a psycho. I'm sorry this is not good enough. We need you to tell us where my son is or we'll go to the police about all this.'

'And I'm sorry. Again, that would be very difficult,' said Valentina. She tightened her jaw. 'This project around this group has been a long time in the planning. You have to believe me when I say it is a very, very big operation. It would not be good if it was put at risk. Too many things depend on it. It cannot be compromised.' Valentina watched them both carefully, ready to assess their reaction to what she was about to say. 'You have to know that when I knew I was coming here I was given a file on you and your family. To see if there was anything that could help us. Ana, obviously we know about your grandmother's involvement with the International Brigades and the civil war. We keep extensive records of all political involvement … and we update them when we can. So, we also know that she paid a visit to Paris in the seventies.' She tilted her head towards Xavi. 'Along with you Xavi. And there she had a … meeting … with another brigader, an Hungarian. We don't know exactly why she wanted to meet this man but we know the outcome and we have a good idea what happened … nothing conclusive of course … but we could dig around more thoroughly.'

Ana and Xavi looked at each other. They couldn't disguise their dismay.

The air stilled in the room as Valentina waited for any reply. Xavi broke away and walked to the window, stared out for a few seconds and then whirled round. 'I don't care. I don't care what you know. We want Axel back here – safe. I don't care what happens to me. We can't even be sure who you are. We're going to the police!'

Ana drew in a long breath. Her shoulders sagged and she gripped her hands together. 'No. It's no good Xavi. She is who she says she is. I believe her. We can't go to the police. It's probably too late for that anyway. And we haven't been able to find him. We have to trust her.'

'Thank you, Ana,' Valentina said. 'I *will* make sure your son is safe.'

'You have to. We're trusting you,' said Ana with a tone of resignation in her voice.

Xavi walked back to the table and sat down. He placed both arms on the table, stretched them out and stared at them. His mouth was set in a hard line. 'However, there is another problem,' he said quietly, 'that might put your *project* at risk.' He glanced at Ana. 'We have a person coming today … to Ana's house … who knows about the *meeting* in Paris. He's out to cause trouble and wants money to keep quiet.'

Valentina looked at Ana. 'What are you going to do? Are you going to pay him?'

'No,' said Ana. 'We don't want to and we can't anyway. But he seems set on getting the money or causing trouble. I'm sure he'll cause trouble if he doesn't get what he wants.' Ana quickly explained about Richard and the letters and how he knew about Lazlo.

Valentina rolled a finger down the scar on her cheek and looked across the kitchen. Eventually she allowed her gaze to settle on the table and finally Ana. 'Okay. Don't worry. I can solve this problem for you.'

'How?' Xavi glanced at Ana and wrinkled his forehead. 'You don't even know how much money he wants.'

'That doesn't matter,' said Valentina. She looked at a torn envelope on the table. 'Write down your address and his details … you've got his number? What time is he coming to your house?'

Ana reached into her bag slung on the back of a chair. She took out the piece of paper Richard had given her and searched for a pen. 'He said he'd be there by three. What are you going to do?' She looked up quickly. 'You're not going to kill him, are you?'

Valentina gave a big smile which unnerved Xavi. He thought she looked almost normal after all the things she had disclosed. 'No, no. we don't do that sort of thing,' she said softly. 'We leave all that kind of thing to other people. We have our own methods.' She waited for a few seconds. 'Do you believe that?' And then she gave a short throaty laugh.

Ana stopped writing on the envelope and stared at Xavi. He shrugged, looked away and pulled at the loose skin on his neck. She finished writing and then handed the envelope to Valentina.

'Thank you both,' said Valentina. 'We have a good agreement. I can repay your trust by dealing with this man.'

'And making sure that Axel and the girl are safe,' said Ana coldly. 'Making *absolutely* sure that they are safe.'

'Of course.' Valentina checked the details on the envelope and then looked at them both. 'Of course,' she repeated. 'But now I have to get some food for them and get back. I'll see you at Ana's house just before three. I'll find another excuse to get away.'

Chapter nineteen

Friday, 28th October, 2016

Newcastle, Northern England,

Will Roddy's house.

Valentina nudged the unlocked front door and went straight into the living room. It was dark. The curtains were closed and only a small crack of light was allowed in. Through the gloom she could make out Felipe stretched out on one of the armchairs. Ramon stood at the far end of the room. Sami was sitting on the floor with her back against the wall, her hands were not visible and Valentina presumed they were still tied behind her with the length of electricity cable Ramon had found in a cupboard.

'What took so long?' said Ramon. 'You've been gone more than an hour.'

Valentina walked across to the curtains and tugged at them until they were fully open. A brilliant shaft of light scorched through the room. 'It's not good to have these closed all of the time in the daylight,' she said. 'Looks suspicious.' She went back to the table and began unpacking the bags. 'I've got food. Had to find a supermarket. That's what took the time. I've got bread and coffee and cookies and cheese and eggs … and some other stuff.'

Felipe jumped up. 'Excellent,' he said. 'I'm starving. I'll make us an omelette.' He picked up the cookies, ripped open the packet and crammed a cookie into his mouth.

Valentina bent down in front of Sami. 'How are you?' she said. 'You okay?'

'She's fine,' said Ramon.

'Couldn't be better,' said Sami, giving Valentina a sardonic smile. 'I could do with the toilet.' She flicked a glance at Ramon. 'He wouldn't let me go. And if I don't go soon this place is going to smell a whole lot worse than it already does.'

'I think that would be a good idea,' said Valentina. 'She needs these free.' She pulled Sami to her feet and untied her hands. 'I'll need to go with you though.'

'Of course,' smiled Sami. 'Maybe we can talk about the boys when we're in there. See which ones we fancy.'

'Just go,' barked Ramon. 'And hurry up. You don't want us to get nervous if you take too long. Make sure you watch her Valentina.'

Valentina turned quickly to Ramon. She stopped herself from saying what was on her mind. She could tell that Ramon was on edge and she didn't want to make the situation worse. Everything needed to be peaceful so that Sami could be handed over to Axel in exchange for the flags and then they could get back to Madrid.

Twenty minutes later they were all eating the food that Felipe had prepared. Valentina and Sami sat at the table, Felipe was on his usual armchair and Ramon again stood at the other end of the room picking at his plate as he paced about.

Valentina glanced at Ramon. She was starting to get worried. *He's getting too agitated. He needs to settle down. We need to get this done as smoothly as possible.*

The room was quiet apart from the clink of plates and cups. The silence was broken by Sami. 'Well, this is nice,' she announced. 'I love a good party. Got any music?'

Valentina put a hand on Sami's arm and at the same time glared at Ramon as he started to walk across the room, stopping him. 'We don't need that Sami,' she said. 'We don't need you being clever.' She looked at Ramon again. It was enough, he returned to his part of the room.

Felipe put his plate on the carpet and wiped his hands on the arm of the chair. 'What was the time of the plane to Madrid?' he asked.

'Midnight,' said Ramon.

'You sure? Do we need to check it? Make sure it's still on.'

Ramon shook his head. 'We checked days ago. We can't check now. You know we can't use the cell phones. They could be traced. Can't risk it.'

'We could use Roddy's laptop again. Or we could use her phone.' Felipe flicked a hand in Sami's direction.

'Same thing, could be traced.' Ramon widened his eyes.

'By who?' said Felipe. 'Who knows she's here, apart from her boyfriend Axel?'

'*Excuse* me,' said Sami indignantly. 'We're just friends.'

'I think we should use her phone,' said Felipe. 'Just to make sure. Roddy's laptop is too slow. We don't know if the plane's been cancelled. We might need to get to another airport quickly. We can't stay here for longer than necessary. We need to make sure.'

'It will be fine,' said Ramon. 'We don't need to risk it.'

'No,' said Felipe flatly. 'We should make sure. Nobody knows about her phone. We need to make sure we can get back to Madrid quickly.'

Felipe stood up and walked across to the table. He took Sami's phone from the back pocket of his jeans and held it out to Sami. 'This is locked, yes?'

Sami nodded.

'What's the pin?' said Felipe.

'Isn't one,' said Sami.

'What then?'

'Fingerprint scanner.'

Felipe placed the phone on the table in front of Sami. 'Okay. Open it.'

Sami stood up from the table and took the phone. She turned her back to Felipe, quickly removed the back cover and put the phone on the floor. 'Actually, there isn't a fingerprint scanner,' she said quietly. 'I just don't want you using it. I don't want to help you with anything.' She stamped on it as hard as she could. Then stamped on it twice more so that it was completely shattered.

Felipe clenched his fists. 'Stupid. Stupid. Not a good idea.' He looked at Valentina. 'Don't worry. I'm not going to do anything. We need her.' He backed away and flopped down on to his armchair.

Valentina looked across at Ramon who remained in exactly the same position. His arms folded and his face impassive. *Why?* thought Valentina. *What's wrong with you? Why aren't you going crazy? What's going on?'*

The living room door opened. 'Okay. I'm here. Just as you asked.'

The three Spaniards and Sami spun round to see Axel standing at the door with Amber just behind him.

'The front door was open,' said Axel. He nodded to Sami. 'Are you okay?'

'Never better,' said Sami. 'I've had a lovely time. Made some really nice friends.'

Felipe went behind Axel and Amber and closed the door. He gave Axel a nudge so that he was in the middle of the room. Amber smiled at Felipe as he came past.

Felipe tilted his head to Amber and turned both hands over. 'What? How?'

'You gave me the address at the pub when I gave you the map,' said Amber. 'I came to see if you'd got the flags yet.' She pulled a face at Axel. 'Didn't know he was coming here too. Followed him down the street.'

Valentina stared at Amber and pursed her lips. *No, no, No. You shouldn't be here. You're messing things up. You shouldn't be here at all.*

Axel shook his head at Amber. 'So, it *was* you. I knew I recognised the handwriting on that piece of paper. *You*! Telling them where I'd be. I knew you were nasty but I didn't think you'd be this bad. What the hell are you playing at? I suppose I should have expected you to sell me out … but you put Sami in danger as well.'

'Some of us *believe* in things,' said Amber. 'You should try it sometimes dear *brother*. Instead of wasting your life away.'

Ramon moved quickly to stand in front of Axel. 'Forget all that. You can have your family argument later. Have you got them?'

Axel shook his head again at Amber and then turned to Ramon. 'In this bag.' He opened the top of his backpack and took out the flags.

Ramon grabbed them from Axel. 'Very good. Very good. Excellent.' He inspected the flags, turning them over and over and rubbing them between his finger and thumb. 'Excellent.'

Ramon went into the kitchen and came back with a long sharp knife. He lay the flags on the table and started to pick away at the seams holding the two flags together. 'Now we'll see,' he muttered to himself. 'Now we'll see. Now we'll see.' When a line of stitches were loosened halfway down the length of one side he put the knife down. 'Now we'll see.' He took a tight grip and pulled at the edges of the two cloths drawing them apart. 'Now we'll see. Carefully. Carefully.' He continued muttering and wrenching the edges until one side of the flags could be completely folded back.

'Yesss!' Ramon let out a howl. His eyes lit up and he punched the air. 'Yesss! I knew it!'

Everyone edged forward and stared at the flags.

'What's that?' said Axel. 'What is it?'

'This,' said Ramon. 'This, my friend is gold. Pure gold.'

'So, you were right,' said Felipe almost gasping the words out. 'You were right. Miro's missing painting.'

Ramon continued pulling at the seams until the painting was completely free. He pulled it carefully from between the two flags, pushed them into a pile to one side and lay the copy of Miro's mural gently on the table.

They could all see it clearly now. A surrealist cubist figure. The figure of a man Picasso-esque. A Catalan peasant, sickle in hand, wearing the characteristic red barretina hat of Catalonia with its expanse of wool flopping over to one side. The other hand of the figure made the republican clenched fist salute. His face was contorted into a cry of despair. The background was a pulsating green, blue and yellow. Two black stars to the right of the face. The peasant's chin, cheek, eye, ear, left arm and teeth were coloured white. The face, neck and right arm red. Bold dark blue and black circles swirling in the sky.

'Well done, Ramon,' said Felipe. 'You were right. This is excellent. A perfect idea. This will be great. A perfect drama and perfect publicity to show them what we can do.' He turned to Amber and gave her a beaming, warm smile. Amber's eyes gleamed as she smiled back.

Axel watched them both and narrowed his eyes. He pointed at the painting 'So, what is it? What is this thing that you are so excited about? Are you going to tell us? What's it for? What does it mean?'

Ramon took a deep breath and pulled his head back so that he was staring at a spot on the wall above their heads. He seemed to be visualising words on the wallpaper, remembering what he had read about the mural. After a few seconds he returned his gaze to the painting. 'This,' whispered Ramon, his voice trembling slightly, 'is a potent symbol of Catalan identity and a sign of resistance against the Spanish people and nation. The sickle is the reaper's symbol, his tool … and when he thinks his freedom is threatened, his weapon. You can see, the reaper has no legs, he is rooted to the ground like a tree. He represents the dream of rebellion, the dream of freedom. The colours have been missing for nearly eighty years. No one knew where the painting went. There were rumours. And now we have found it … after all these years. We have found the copy.' He gaped at Valentina and Felipe. His whole body seemed to be shaking and he fought hard to gain control. He squeezed his eyes shut, then threw his head back again and laughed at the ceiling. 'Unbelievable … unbelievable … unbelievable,' he muttered to himself over and over.

'This is fantastic Ramon. Well done.' Valentina deliberately interrupted Ramon's trance-like state and smoothed the painting with a soft hand gliding over the silk. 'Now we need to get this back as soon as possible.' *Let's get this over with. Let's get these three out of here.*

'I still don't understand,' said Axel. 'What does it mean? What do you need this for?'

Ramon breathed deeply and gave a caustic smile to Axel. 'You don't need to know.' His voice was slow and indulgent. 'But it is something that will be a big help. So, thank you for that.' He picked up the two flags and handed them to Axel. 'Here, you can have these back. We have no need of them.' He smiled again.

Valentina walked across quickly and pulled the door open. 'Okay, you three.' She pointed a finger at Axel, Amber and Sami. 'Get out of here,' she growled. 'Go home. Just go home!'

'Wait!' Ramon leaned heavily on the table and looked at Valentina. 'Wait. We can't let her go. Sami stays. They'll go straight to the police. She stays.'

'That was the deal,' Axel shouted across the room, panic in his voice. 'That was what was agreed. The flags in exchange for Sami.'

Ramon held his hands out, looking for support from Felipe and Valentina. 'We can't let her go. He'll go straight to the police. If we have her, he wouldn't dare.'

Damn, damn, damn. Valentina waited for Felipe to speak. *If he sides with me the three could still get away.*

'He's right,' said Felipe. 'We can't risk it. It's only another few hours and then we can let her go. There's too much at stake now that we have the painting.'

Axel raised his voice again, desperate. 'No! I won't. I won't go to the police. Let her go.' Then he added, 'I'm not leaving without her.'

'Suit yourself,' said Ramon coolly. He picked up the knife from the table and pointed it at Axel. 'You can stay too, but we don't want any trouble from you.'

No-one moved. All eyes were on the glinting blade of the knife.

'We don't need this,' said Valentina. 'This will cause more trouble. We don't need anyone to get hurt.' *Slow, slow and calm,* she thought to herself. *No rash words. No quick movements.*

'I'll stay.' A voice came from behind Felipe and Amber took a step forward. 'I'll stay,' she said again.

'What?' Ramon pulled the knife back and stared at her.

'I'll stay,' Amber pushed her hands into the pockets of her jeans. 'I'll take that girl's place. I'm his little sister.' She looked at Axel. 'He's so stupid. He won't go to the police if he knows something might happen to me ... even me.' She let here gaze fall on the knife and then looked at Valentina. 'I won't give you any trouble. You can rely on me. I'm on your side remember.'

Felipe glanced at Amber and then at Ramon. 'Okay, I think that will work,' he said.

Axel looked at Amber, raised his eyebrows and then pulled them down as tight as he could. He leaned to the side and stared at her.

'Don't worry Axel,' snorted Amber. 'This won't happen again. Call it a momentary lapse.' She nodded to Sami. 'She doesn't deserve this. It has nothing to do with her. I can rationalise things. No matter what you think.'

'We just need them all out,' said Valentina quickly. She turned to Axel. 'We can easily work out how to find your mother if the authorities are involved. We have contacts in this country who can carry out payback if you let us down.'

'Just let us all go,' said Axel. 'I won't tell anyone. I won't contact the police or anyone else.'

'No!' Ramon yelled. 'Not good enough. We need some guarantee.'

'I'm your guarantee,' said Amber. 'He won't go to the police if I'm here. He's soft. I know him. He wouldn't put mummy's little daughter in danger. He wouldn't want to upset mummy.'

At least I can look after her here, thought Valentina, *get these two out quickly before Ramon can say anything else. Come on. move, move.*

'Okay. That's settled then. Let's not waste any more time.' Valentina called out. She grabbed Sami's arm and pushed her towards the door and did the same with Axel. 'You two get out. And no police. No police or it will be worse for everybody. Go! Go!' She bundled Axel and Sami out into the street before anyone could argue. She grabbed Axel again just outside the front door and lowered her voice. 'Go home. Just go home. Speak to your mother.'

Axel gave Valentina a baffled look as she went into the house and slammed the door shut. He put the flags back in his bag. He didn't know the significance of the painting which had been sewn between them but he didn't care. He had the flags back. He knew his eldergran would be happy. Amber had made her choice and that baffled him too. He nodded to Sami, put his arm through hers and they began walking quickly along the street casting uneasy glances over their shoulders.

Chapter twenty

Monday, 20th December, 1937

The French-Spanish border.

It was snowing hard: big flakes covering the ground in a moonlit glistening white. Emily leaned out from the cramped cabin of the truck and stretched as far as she could to swipe the brush across and clear the snow off the windscreen for the hundredth time. She hauled herself back in, stepped over her backpack and sat on her shoulder bag. She never went anywhere without the shoulder bag. It had the flags in it, folded neatly and wrapped in a shirt. She called them her *jewels*, her lucky charms, and she didn't like them to be too far away. The driver, Arthur Williams struggled to keep the wheels on the narrow track. Emily and the two other passengers in the truck, Michel Tomas from Paris and their guide Alazne had to step out occasionally and walk in front of the truck to show the way and point out the potholes and ice patches for Arthur. They had to travel without lights.

An hour earlier Emily had taken her turn to walk in front of the truck and point out the ice on a steep slope. Holding up both arms to indicate a dangerous spot. It was bad outside, a mixture of sleet and snow with poor visibility. She was directing Arthur around a rocky crevice when she remembered she had her bag still around her shoulder. She didn't want the flags to get wet so she stumbled through the snow back to the truck and put her bag into the cabin. It was then that Arthur's foot slipped from the wet brake pedal and the heavy truck picked up speed and went sliding down the slope exactly across where Emily had been standing. It crashed off a huge boulder before straightening out on to the track.

'Hell, sorry about that everyone,' shouted Arthur. 'Good job you came back Emily. Sorry.'

She knew that her jewels had looked after her again.

Arthur, from Glasgow, had volunteered for the journey after visiting relatives in Newcastle and hearing that someone was needed to drive the aid truck. He thought this was more important than his work as a car mechanic. Frenchman Michel was going to join the French International Brigade, the Henry-Barbusse, commune de Paris 11th battalion and had asked them for a lift outside the Paris Communist headquarters. He spoke fluent English and Spanish and was a big asset to them for translating as Emily's Spanish was passable but she had only a few French words and Arthur even less. Alazne was Basque. He had fled Bilbao after it fell six months earlier when the republican northern army was all but defeated and the Basque region was in nationalist hands. He helped smuggle people across the border. He didn't give them his surname.

Emily was back in Spain. She had been home to Newcastle for only a few weeks, enough time for her to arrange a small flat to rent because she knew she would have to return soon to have the baby. She was nearly five months pregnant but still not showing and she knew she only had a short amount of time to complete what she needed to do.

The rest of her time in Newcastle had been organising meetings and fund raisers for the republican army and the International Brigades in Spain. She had spoken at all of the meetings and with the help of the Independent Labour party and the local Communist Party as well as the sympathetic Trade Union leaders and members, and ordinary locals, they had raised a good amount of money. Enough money to hire a Bedford five-ton truck for the journey to Spain. It was filled with medical equipment, donated clothes, dried food and cigarettes. Space was even found to carry a few dozen Christmas presents of toys and games for refugee children from the Basque region.

The foreign policy of the British trade unions was generally anti-communist. Support for the republican cause in the Spanish Civil War was widespread on the left, even including some Conservative Party and Liberal Party members. However, the national Labour Party distrusted the communists and rejected unity campaigns. The British Trades Union congress was split on support for non-intervention in the war but their leaders Walter Citrine and Ernest Bevin used their block votes to pass motions supporting non-intervention at the Trades Union Congress in September 1936. Most rank-and-file members of the unions and leftist parties would generally ignore directives from the leaders and would work as cooperatively as possible, so it was possible for Emily organise the truck in a short time.

Emily had appointed herself as map reader for the journey. The Communist Party had arranged papers and visas as far as Perpignan, twenty miles from the Spanish border. After that they would be put in touch with French republican sympathisers and smugglers who knew the legal and illegal routes across the border. France had its own non-intervention policy so travellers, especially those who tried to bring weapons, had to be wary. Franco's nationalist spies and agents were also in the French border towns and great care had to be taken so that you got to the right place at the right time and spoke to the right person.

They had travelled from Paris with only small stops along the backroads of France. The truck was powerful and sturdy and the only other major problem was when Arthur had to take an hour to realign one of the brake discs. The windscreen wipers had slowed down and even then, only worked fitfully, as they were in constant use dealing with the hail and snow when they were negotiating the towering white mountains of the Pyrenees.

It had become very difficult to cross the Spanish border from France legally. Visas were granted very sparingly and the French policy towards the war had ensured that international incidents seldom happened as the border was heavily guarded by French police.

To counteract the activities of the French government there had arisen a vast network of anti-fascist groups who conspired to work around the ban against entering republican Spain. On the other side too, there were committees and secret groups working to help the forces of Franco. This meant that France was honeycombed with secret supporters of both republican and nationalist combatants in Spain. The original plan for Emily and Arthur was to get to Marseille, try to get false documents and take the ferry to Barcelona across the Mediterranean Sea by way of the Golfe du Lion. However, they learned that Franco's nationalist ships were patrolling that route and had recently torpedoed a republican ship, the 'City of Barcelona' out of Marseille, with over a hundred lives lost, among them dozens of Americans. Another way had to be found and so they found themselves in Perpignan.

Their first difficulty had been to get in touch with the correct committee in Paris. Emily still had contacts and friends there and had experience of how the passage to Spain worked from her previous

324

journey to join the International Brigades. As soon as the officials of the Comintern found out that they were carrying much needed medical supplies, suitable letters and documents were provided.

Two days later they had arrived in Perpignan, a small town on the extreme south eastern edge of France about twenty miles from the Spanish border, the largest town before reaching Cerbere which the last stop on the French border, a dot on the map. They were heading for Figueres in Northern Catalonia where they would be met by republican agents and given safe passage to Barcelona where they would unload their precious cargo. Then the truck would return, hopefully by the same route, with as many refugee children as possible. At Perpignan they had been told to make their way to the café Vienne on the Place Francois Arago and ask for a monsieur Durand.

*

It was already seven o' clock in the evening when Michel wove his way between the tables and went to the back of the café Vienne followed by Emily. Arthur had stayed with the truck.

Michel went up to the bartender. 'Do you know monsieur Durand? I am his cousin from Toulouse.' It was the agreed signal. A password to introduce themselves.

The bartender eyed them carefully. 'Just wait here,' he replied. 'I'll see if he's around.'

'What did he say?' asked Emily.

'We have to wait here,' said Michel. 'They speak a type of Catalan here. I find it difficult to follow it. But I understood that we have to wait here.'

Meanwhile all of the customers put aside their card playing and chattering and studied Emily and Michel. Because they were supporters and collaborators for the republicans in Spain, they were always suspicious. They had to be. They were smugglers, taking goods and comrades to Spain. Arrests had been made in the past few weeks for anyone helping people to cross the border.

Five minutes later a tall gaunt man came from the back room. He inspected their letters and documents and then went across to one of the tables and spoke to the four men there. Emily and Michel were introduced to the four men, the tall thin man spoke to Michel and then stood back a little, arms folded, waiting for their response.

'What's going on,' asked Emily when he had finished.

'As far as I can understand,' said Michel. 'One of these four men are going to give us a room for the night. Apparently the two customs guards at the crossing were comrades but now they have been replaced by another two who are following orders and going by the book. It's too risky. Our papers won't stand up. So, they're saying they'll show us a mountain pass in the morning and get us a guide. He wants to know if we agree.'

'Of course. Of course, we agree,' said Emily. 'Anyway, we have no choice … but let him know we are very grateful.'

*

The following afternoon the main road was crowded with wagons and trucks heading towards Cerbere where they would unload their goods for the customs inspectors to examine.

In the evening, as soon as it was dark, Emily, Michel and Arthur were told to return to the truck. When they did, they had found Alazne, who was to be their guide, waiting for them. Alazne introduced himself and showed them a rough map drawn on to a piece of paper torn from a notebook. He pointed out various points on the map showing the steep inclines and twisting tracks they would encounter and the time it would take them. He also showed the areas where they could expect border patrols and where they would change the route if needed. He explained all this to Michel who translated as much as he could to Emily and Arthur. Emily had tried to follow what Alazne was saying.

'It's difficult,' said Michel. 'He's speaking a combination of Spanish and Euskara, the Basque language. But he's slowing it down and making it easier for me.'

After Michel had spoken to the other two, Alazne took a cigarette lighter from his overcoat pocket and set fire to the map before dropping it to the ground. He watched the map burn completely then walked across to the truck and banged on the side with his fist. He looked at Arthur and said in broken English. 'This is good. This is take us for Spain. A good truck.' He patted his nose with a finger. 'But a slow truck. Slow with careful, yes.'

Arthur smiled at him. 'Thank you,' he said. It hasn't let us down so far. And I will be careful.'

It was starting to snow again when they set off and after a few hours the Pyrenees were difficult to make out through the darkness and the near blizzard. The truck proved Alazne and Arthur correct and they made steady time moving cautiously towards the border without coming across any French patrols.

'This is good,' said Alazne. 'The snow is good. Good cover. Guards stay home. Good for us.'

Emily glanced at Alazne sitting next to Arthur. She knew he was risking a lot and she knew this probably wasn't the first time he had guided people through the passes. She nudged Michel, squatting on the cabin floor with his back against her knee and using her backpack as a cushion. 'Ask him why he's doing this,' she said. Although she already more or less knew the answer, she wanted to hear it from Alazne. It was important for her to find out the motivation for such a dangerous journey. She was hoping to write some articles about the war for her local paper to see if they could be used to raise more funds. She also thought about trying the London newspapers, at least the ones who were sympathetic to the republicans.

'What?' Michel half turned to Emily. It was difficult to hear with the roar of the engine and the wind hurling the snow in all directions.

'Ask him why he's doing this,' repeated Emily.

Michel nudged Alazne's knee with his elbow and asked the question. Alazne didn't answer but just kept staring ahead.

Emily waited for a minute then leaned forward until she was almost on top of Michel so that Alazne could see her face. She touched his shoulder and he turned to look at her. 'Tu,' she said. 'Por que – estas – acqui?' She spread her hands. 'Por que? Why? Why are you here?'

Alazne stared at her. Then he turned back to look out of the windscreen at the driving snow.

Emily sat back in her seat. Arthur put the truck in the lowest gear to climb a steep incline. The truck slithered for a few yards and then caught a good patch and gathered momentum.

'Damn!' said Arthur. 'The wipers.' He stopped the engine

'I'll get it.' Emily grabbed a brush from behind her seat and opened her door. A rush of cold air had everyone pulling up their collars as Emily jumped down from the cabin and swept the snow from the windscreen. She put one foot on the tyre and hauled herself up to tug at the wipers. They responded and started to move side to side with a lazy jerking motion.

'That'll do,' shouted Arthur.

Emily climbed back into the cabin, slammed the door shut and flicked the snow from her coat. Arthur was just about to start the engine when he heard Alazne say something.

'Gernika,' said Alazne. 'It is Gernika.'

'Guernica?' said Michel, glancing at Alazne.

Emily, Michel and Arthur looked at each other. They had all seen the newsreels about Guernica. The whole world had seen them.

'Ask him why?' said Emily.

Alazne didn't wait for Michel. He started to talk and Michel translated for them.

'He says he was at Guernica. That's what made him decide to help all that he can to defeat Franco.' said Michel. 'April twenty sixth. He didn't live there. He was going to the Monday market. He says the place was hollowed out. Just a place of big gaps and holes. Kitchens laid open to the wind and rain. Not one house with a roof. Everything was jagged. Everything pulled apart.

He says Monday was market day when most civilians would be out and about and hundreds more would come from the surrounding villages. Farmers came in with their cattle and sheep to sell. Crowds of people were there were there, swelling the population from seven thousand to more than ten thousand, including some refugees and demoralised troops retreating from the front line only ten miles away. The nationalists knew this. The German Condor Legion knew this. The Condor planes used the town as target practice. It started at forty minutes after four in the afternoon. One plane came over and dropped bombs to show the others where to hit. After the first bomb, people started running out, stampeding into the fields but more planes came and machine gunned them, driving them back into the town, herding them back to where they could be easily slaughtered. Then the heavy bombers came, Heinkels and Junkers. They bombed and bombed and bombed ... so many bombs. |He says incendiary bombs were dropped in aluminium tubes, sprinkling down like silver confetti.'

Alazne folded his arms and pulled at his cheeks. He was breathing rapidly. He took a few moments to stare out of the window again, gathering his thoughts. The cabin was silent except for Alazne's breathing. Even the snow had stopped. He started speaking again and Michel continued translating.

'The town was being used as a communications centre for the Northern Republican Army. He says they knew that. They didn't need to kill so many. They were only people going to market. Wave after wave came over the town. The bombing lasted for three hours ... until there was nothing left. The houses were mainly made of wood. He says you can imagine how they burned. Whole families were buried in the ruins of their homes. Charred humans staggered mindlessly in the streets. Blazing cattle and sheep ran between the burning buildings until they fell and died. Many died from lack of oxygen as the fires sucked up the life out of the air. The municipal water tanks and the fire station were the first targets … to make sure the fires couldn't be put out. He says he managed to get away, through the fields. They were all split up. He couldn't find his wife … his brother.' Alazne stopped. He gulped in a deep breath. They watched his eyes, dull and empty. His fingers groping at his knees as his jaw slackened, his face in a trance. Michel waited for him.

Alazne shook his shoulders and drank in cold air in a sudden gasping slurp. 'He says he found them later.' Alazne's voice was gruff and dry. Michel continued the translation. 'There was nothing that could be done. He couldn't take the bodies because Franco's troops came in immediately and occupied the town. They wouldn't let anyone in to the town for three days. They tried to clean it up. Cover up how the damage was done. How many bombs had been dropped. He couldn't find their bodies after that. They tried to say that retreating republican troops destroyed the city … can you believe it, he says? It was an assault. An assault on humanity. He doesn't do this for revenge. He says he does it for humanity.

When he returned days later, small fires could be seen in the bomb craters as some people came back to claim possessions, moving like shadows among the rubble. Most were cooking meals … some were burning the dead horses and dogs. Wherever you looked there was nothing but destruction. And then there was the terrible smell. Women, children, babies … they were only people going to market. There wasn't much left … Santa Monica church … a very few homes … the Renteria bridge, which must have been a big target for them to cut off the road to Bilbao … they completely missed it. This was the town where every Basque president takes an oath under an oak tree known as the tree of Guernica. The tree survived.'

Alzane turned to Emily and spoke in faltering English. 'This because I do it. I hate them. They kill everyone. The fascisti do not care of people. I hate them for what they do to whole world.'

They all sat for long seconds gazing away from each other into the darkness, not knowing what to say. Then Arthur started the engine and the truck slid off into the night. The snow had started again.

It was only forty kilometres from Cerbere to Figueres but the mountain passes were narrow and the snow made the driving dangerous so it took them six more hours to reach their destination. They arrived in Figueres just as the town was waking up. They had safely crossed the border into Spain. They didn't need to seek out their contact in the town as the truck had already gathered a small crowd. The local people knew exactly what it was and what was happening. Within a few minutes four republican agents turned up and checked the truck. A smiling woman came up and gave them coffee and sandwiches while the agents made a rough itinerary of what the truck contained. They were given papers to be handed over in Barcelona and then a motor bike appeared with a young soldier who was to show them the way.

In the middle of the afternoon, they parked the truck outside the republican army mobile unit depot on the Carrer de L'Oest by the harbour in Barcelona. Alazne stayed in the truck. His job was only half complete. He had to guide them back. The truck was unloaded by civilian dock workers and was to be kept at the parking bays at the headquarters until it was decided what was going to be done with it. Usually, trucks of this size were requisitioned as ambulances. A republican captain took the papers off Arthur and informed him of the decision.

'I don't think so,' said Arthur looking at Michel. He waved an arm across his chest in a slicing motion to emphasise the finality of his thoughts on the subject. He wasn't going to argue about it. 'You tell him Michel. We already know what's going to be done with it. It's going back to Britain. It's hired and I'm responsible for it. The plan is to try and take some refugees back with us.' He looked at Emily for support and she nodded, giving the captain the sternest face she could muster, given that she was exhausted. They were all exhausted and didn't need this but Arthur and Emily were determined that the truck would be returned. Michel translated but the captain merely shrugged.

'That's no good,' barked Arthur. 'Shrugging's no good!' He wagged a finger at the captain. 'You tell him Michel. The cargo in this van was donated after a lot of money was raised by comrades in Britain. If you want any more you'd better let me take this truck back. You can tell your superiors I'm not going back without it and if you want any more medical supplies, you'd better make sure we go back with it.'

The captain handed the papers back to Arthur. 'I understand,' he said. 'I'll see what I can do to get you back to your country … so you can bring more equipment.'

Michel left them after saying his goodbyes and profound thanks. He walked off in the direction of the city centre to find information about the French International Brigade.

Emily knew that she wouldn't return with Arthur and Alazne and the truck. She had tried to convince herself that she was doing this for the cause and to bring refugee children out of the war zone. That she was back in Spain to help with the rescue of as many children as possible. But she knew this wasn't completely, if at all true.

She was back in Spain to find Isabel. She hadn't written to her since she left Paris after the Spanish Pavilion killings. She hadn't known what to say to Isabel. She didn't know how to tell her she was pregnant. All she knew was that she loved her, missed her and needed her more than anything in her whole life.

She hardly knew how to begin to find her. Isabel's last letter was months ago and she had written that she was moving about the country fast helping to pick up children from the northern frontline and the Basque region. Emily's one and only hope was Carmen. From Isabel's letters she knew that Carmen was with the republican Eastern Army, 44th division which had been withdrawn from Madrid to defend the River Ebro at its eastern end in southern Catalonia. She knew that Isabel would keep in touch with Carmen and when Carmen was given leave Emily guessed she would almost certainly take it in Barcelona where she had a lot of relatives. If she could find Carmen she might be able to find Isabel.

The Spanish captain arranged a lift to take Emily, Arthur and Alazne to the centre of Barcelona, at the northern end of the Rambla, an area that Emily knew well. They were shown to the hotel Gotic, an anarchist run hotel just past the corner of the main square, the Place de Catalunia on Calle de Fontanella. Arthur and Alazne went straight to their room to get some sleep but Emily dropped off her backpack, hitched up her shoulder bag and went off by herself. She knew exactly where she was going and what she needed to do.

Twenty minutes later she was standing outside the Comercio Gratuito, the café where she had met Isabel and her friends. She pushed open the blue door with the crack running its entire length and walked into an almost empty room. Two old men sat by the fire and stopped their game of cards as she came in and looked at her for an instant before returning to their game.

Emily stared around the room. The end of the long mahogany counter near to the two old men was gone, part of it was neatly sawn off but she could see jagged pieces of wood and splinters jutting out between the beautifully carved panels. There was a gap of about two metres and then another metre of counter was propped up by two tables with wooden crates on top. The huge ornamental mirror behind the counter was cracked into dozens of pieces with a chunk the size of a football completely missing. Two brass wall lights were gone and the glass shelves behind the counter, where the rows of bottles had stood, were also gone. The ceiling and the wall opposite the counter were both scorched and one window was boarded up with planks.

A figure wearing a black apron and carrying a crate of wine appeared in the door behind the counter.

Emily recognised him immediately. 'Miguel,' she said. 'Do you remember me?' She spoke slowly, making sure she put the right words together.

Miguel tilted his head and thought for a moment.

'It's me, Emily. Do you remember. The fight. The fight with the Stalinists in here. Me and my three friends. Do you remember?'

Miguel put the crate down and pulled a pretend sad face. 'Of course. I recognise you now. I recognise you. The English brigadista. Your Spanish has improved.'

Emily waved an arm at the room. 'What happened? You'd think there was a war going on.'

Miguel laughed. 'Yes, you'd think so, wouldn't you.'

'So, what happened?'

'A Blue Angel, that's what happened. Have you heard of the Blue Angels?'

'I've heard mention of them but I don't really know who they are.'

'A hand grenade. Three days ago. At first, we thought it was those communists. They don't like this café.' He smiled at her. 'As you well know.' He pulled a bottle from the crate, uncorked it with a corkscrew hanging from his belt and pointed to the nearest table. The two old men glanced across again as Emily and Miguel sat down.

'She was caught,' Miguel said. He looked over his shoulder at the two old men. 'As I say, at first, we assumed it was communists, trying to teach us a lesson, but she was caught and ... interrogated. She was a Blue Angel. I'm surprised you have not heard a lot more about them. I thought all leftist women would have heard a lot about the Blue Angels.'

'So, who are they?'

'They are fascists. An organisation of fascist women. People think that because the fascist women follow traditional values ... home, family, church, a patriarchal society ... all that sort of thing, they think that fascist women don't fight. But they do. They are dangerous, doubly so because they are women and can retreat back into their *traditional* values when it suits them. Yes, fascist women can fight. They carry out undercover activities … spying, espionage … and throwing hand grenades. They are using the term fifth column in Madrid to describe nationalist spies. General Vidal has four nationalist army columns moving towards Madrid. He says nationalist supporters inside Madrid are his fifth column undermining the republic from within.

People underestimate the Blue Angels,' Miguel continued, 'and their acts of resistance against the republic, but they are everywhere. Hiding in plain sight. Everywhere. The Blue Angel almost destroyed this place. Luckily, we caught the fire in time. And luckily our Blue Angel seems to have had some respect for human life … she threw the grenade in when the place was empty. There was just me, stacking bottles in the back room.'

'Or maybe she just didn't know the opening times,' said Emily giving him a beaming smile.

Miguel laughed again. He took a drink of the wine and then handed the bottle to Emily. 'I try to use the glasses sparingly now that we haven't many left.'

Emily nodded, pulled her head back, gulped a mouthful of wine and then put the bottle on the table between them.

'So, why are you here?' said Miguel.

'I'm looking for my friends, Isabel and Carmen. They used to come in here a lot. Do you remember, our other friend Maria sang *Els Segadors* over there on that table.' Emily looked at the table in the corner. 'Unfortunately, I can't meet up with Maria anymore …'

'Yes, yes, I know. I was at her funeral. I spoke to Carmen there.'

'Have you seen Carmen lately?'

'I have. You're in luck. She's on leave for a few days. She was here yesterday.'

Emily sat up and stared at Miguel. 'Does she come in every day?'

'No, not every day.'

'Do you know where she lives?'

'Unfortunately, no. If you write down your address, I'll tell her if I see her. How long are you in Barcelona for?'

'I don't know ... long enough to meet her though. Maybe I should come here every day?'

'You can ... if it's that important, but it could be a long wait for you, better if I look out for her.'

*

The next day Emily went with Arthur and Alazne to the truck. When they arrived at the mobile unit depot they saw a group of twelve children and two adults, one male and one female. At their feet were a collection of small battered suitcases, backpacks and brown paper parcels. Some of the children were sitting on a wall, hands jammed in overcoat pockets and the rest were walking about stamping their feet and blowing on their hands to try and get warm. The children, five girls and seven boys, looked to be about eight or nine years old and each one of them had a piece of cardboard cut into the shape of a hexagon tied around their neck with string. On the cardboard was the name, date of birth and birthplace of each child.

The Spanish captain was there. He came over as soon as he saw Arthur, Alazne and Emily. 'Good morning,' he said. 'We've got you some passengers. We're just waiting for one more girl. She'll be along in a few minutes I hope.'

'Well,' said Emily. 'Didn't take you long.'

The captain shook his head. 'No, it doesn't take long. There are so many of them. Hundreds arrive every day. And these children haven't got the correct papers so we have to use ... informal methods to get them to safety. The only stipulation is that they must not be separated. They have to be kept together ... wherever they end up after Paris when the Communist Party headquarters have registered them. These *expedicionares* must be kept safe'

Emily told Arthur what was going on.

'Okay,' said Arthur. 'Well, let's open the truck for them. It'll be warmer inside.'

'And one more thing,' said Emily as Arthur was unlocking the rear doors. She took a breath. 'I'm sorry. I'm not coming with you.'

Arthur turned slowly and scrunched up his face. 'What?'

'I'm sorry. I'm really sorry I'm not coming back with you. I have something to do here.'

Arthur shook his head. 'What do you mean? What kind of thing? What kind of thing is more important than this?'

'I have to find somebody.'

'Who?' Arthur threw his arms wide and raised his voice. Everyone near the truck stared at him, wondering what was going on.

'Somebody,' said Emily, keeping her voice deliberately low. *Come on Arthur. We don't need to argue. This is bad enough as it is.* 'Somebody I know very well. Somebody very dear to me. I have to do this. I don't know if they're alive or dead.'

Arthur took a step closer to her and gave her a steady look. 'You talking about love?'

'Yes.'

'Alright,' said Arthur quietly, following Emily's lead. 'We can wait for you. Until you find him or find out what's happened to him.'

It would just complicate matters if I told you who it was. 'No, you can't. I don't know how long it'll take.'

Arthur blew on his hands and then folded them under his armpits. 'Okay then. We have to reach the French border in darkness so it doesn't really matter what time we leave here. It'll take about six hours to get there so I can hold things up for a couple of hours if that's any good. Until about one o'clock.'

'Thank you, Arthur. That's very kind of you and very understanding of you but I don't think I'll find out by then. You take care of yourself.' She walked up to him, shook his hand and kissed him on the cheek then went across to a puzzled Alazne and hugged him. 'Gracias,' she whispered to him. 'Muchas gracias.' She turned quickly, trying not to look at the children, gave a final wave and walked away.

Chapter twenty-one

Wednesday, 22nd December, 1937

Hotel Gotic, Calle de Fontanella, Barcelona, Spain.

It took Emily forty-five minutes to get back to the hotel Gotic. The trams weren't running and she had to walk all the way from the harbour. She was desperate to get back to see if Miguel had left any information about Carmen.

She went through the heavy main door, having to push hard as it was closed to keep out the cold air. As she reached the top of the third flight of stairs, she noticed someone sitting on the floor outside the door to her room, smoking a cigarette.

'Carmen!' Emily shouted as she ran down the dark corridor.

Carmen stood up and let Emily hug her but kept her own arms by her side.

Emily let go and took a step back, frowning. 'You okay? It's good to see you.'

'You're lucky to find me,' said Carmen. 'I have one day left of my leave before I return to my division. I saw Miguel last night and he told me you wanted to see me. He gave me your address here.' Her face was hard, unfriendly. 'What is it that you want?

Emily took a few seconds trying to read Carmen's hostility and work out how to respond. 'I'm trying to find Isabel,' she said at last.

'Why?' The word was razor sharp.

'I need to explain something to her.' She took out her key and unlocked the door to her room. 'Let's go inside.'

Inside the room, Emily threw her shoulder bag on to the single bed with its thick woollen blankets. The room was sparse but neat, with a small table, one set of drawers and one wardrobe with a long mirror fixed to one of the doors. Carmen took the one wooden armchair next to the table. Emily took out a cigarette and lit it.

'You need to explain a lot,' began Carmen. She sucked hard on her cigarette and inhaled deeply. 'She was hurt. Very badly hurt. You left Paris and didn't contact her.' She glared at Emily. 'What had she done to you? Why did you just leave like that?'

Emily stared around the room and settled on her reflection in the mirror. *Who are you? You look very small and scared.*

Emily watched the girl in the mirror talking. 'I didn't know how to tell her,' the girl said.

Carmen flicked ash on the floor. 'Tell her what? What couldn't you tell her.'

Emily looked at Carmen. 'I couldn't tell her what happened to me in Brunete … when we were retreating.'

'What?' Carmen almost hissed the word, firing it at Emily, hoping to wound her. She stared at her cigarette, blew out a long deep breath, composing herself, pushing down the anger. 'What happened?' asked Carmen. 'What happened that was so awful that you couldn't tell her.' The words were measured and icy and the cold room became colder with each syllable. 'What happened? She was in love with you. You should be able to tell her anything.'

'I was a coward. I ran away. I didn't want to deal with it. I just ran.'

'Deal with what? You're not explaining. Deal with what?'

Emily turned to the girl in the mirror. *You'll have to tell her. I can't do it.* The girl gave Carmen a steady agonising look. Emily could see the girl was fighting back tears. The girl opened her mouth. 'I was raped at Brunete.'

Carmen pushed back into the chair and gave a tiny shake of her head.

Emily wanted her to say something but Carmen remained still and quiet, her face blank.

'And now I'm pregnant,' Emily said quickly. An involuntary hand went to her stomach. 'I didn't want Isabel to deal with that. All this bloodshed and fear and looking after refugee children … and Maria. I didn't want Isabel to deal with that too.'

Carmen stubbed her cigarette out on to a plate on the table. 'So, how did you get here? You were in England, yes?'

'I helped bring medical supplies across the border. The truck we have will take refugees back to France.'

'When do you leave?'

'The truck leaves today at one. But I'm not going with them. I'm staying here until I find Isabel.'

'And what will you tell Isabel?'

Emily looked at the girl in the mirror again. She gave an encouraging nod. 'I'll tell her that I'm sorry. So very sorry. I was stupid. I'll tell her I'm sorry … and that I still love her.'

Carmen pulled at a strand of hair then brushed a hand across her forehead. 'She was hurt, almost broken. Isabel is a strong woman. I have seen her strength. I could not do what she does ... the endless supply of devastated children. I could not do that. I have seen her strength ... but you almost broke her. You almost broke her.'

The words punched her in the throat and Emily took two stumbling steps backwards. *You almost broke her.* She didn't know what to say. She looked for support from the girl in the mirror but she was gone.

'Do you still love her? Really?' Carmen whispered. Emily could see her eyes glistening.

'Yes. Yes ... I made a big mistake. I was a coward. I was stupid. I still love her. I need to tell her that.' Emily stared at her shoulder bag on the bed. She was too afraid to look at Carmen. 'I owe her that. I know she won't forgive me but I owe her that. To tell her the truth.'

Carmen stood up, walked across to the window and looked at the street below. 'You need to tell her. She will forgive you. I have seen it in her eyes. The pain is still there but ... you need to tell her. She still loves you. I am certain.'

Emily's cigarette had burned right down. She looked at her fingers. A thin line of smoke was coming between two of them and she could feel the skin burning but she continued staring at them. Carmen's words were searing through her body and she was oblivious to everything else. Eventually she opened her fingers and let the stub fall to the floor.

'Where can I find her?' said Emily at last. 'Do you know where she is? Here in Barcelona? Madrid?'

'I'll have to write and tell her you're coming.'

Emily could feel a pulse throbbing at her temple and her voice clogged. 'But where is she?'

'She volunteered to leave the country. To help with a group of twenty Basque refugees. They left on the SS Habana from Bilbao just before the city fell to the Francoists. She didn't have to go.'

'Out of Spain? But where? Where did she go?'

'You don't know?'

'No, how could I?'

Carmen waited for a moment. 'Yes, stupid question.' She gave Emily a hard look and pulled her head back. 'She's in England. A place called Tynemouth. A place not far from your city, Newcastle, is that right?''

Emily flicked her head up, threw a hand to her chest and gave a gasping breath. She could feel her heart thudding against her ribs. 'WHAT?' The girl in the mirror was back. Emily saw the girl's eyes widen with her mouth hanging open, helplessly shaking her head.

'Her last letter,' said Carmen, 'about a month ago, says that she was in a town called Portsmouth in southern England. The hundreds of children on board the SS Habana were being redistributed around the country. She organised to go with some children to Tynemouth.'

Emily tried to say something but she couldn't arrange the words. They were just a scrambled mess in her mouth. She felt dizzy and sick, as though someone was shaking her from inside, and not stopping. *What are you saying? What's going on? What do you mean?*

'She wanted to try and find you and help with the children at the same time. She had contacted your brigade. She knew you had left for

Paris. She assumed you would go home. The brigade gave an address for you but it was the wrong one.'

'I found a different flat when I went home,' Emily blurted out. She concentrated on her breathing. 'A new place to live for when I have the … the baby. No-one knows the address. I haven't had time to …' She shook her head slowly from side to side in ever widening arcs and getting even slower. 'I can't believe it. She must have been in Tynemouth when I was in Newcastle. It's only about ten miles.'

'So, what are you going to do?'

'I'm going straight back home. I need to see her.'

'To tell her that you still love her.'

'Yes.'

'Very well then.' Carmen dug her gaze into the floorboards. 'I'll give you her address.'

Emily nodded. She wanted to smile but it didn't seem right. She glanced at the clock on the set of drawers. Twenty past twelve. Arthur was leaving at one.

'I'll have to hurry,' said Emily. 'I think I can get a lift back.' She began scurrying about the room, grabbing clothes and throwing them into her backpack.

Carmen wrote down the address on a slip of paper and placed it on the chair. She walked to the door and opened it.

Emily stopped with an armful of clothes when she heard the doorknob being turned and looked at Carmen. 'Goodbye … and thank you. I hope we meet again when this is all over.'

Carmen stared at Emily. She made to go through the door but then stopped and looked at Emily again. 'You weren't a coward,' she said quietly.

'What?'

'You weren't a coward. It was a just the opposite. It was a brave thing to do … to protect someone you love. It must have broken you too.' Carmen didn't wait for any reply. She closed the door behind her as she left.

'Thank you,' Emily whispered to the door. 'Thank you.'

Minutes later she was running down the street outside the hotel Gotic with her back pack and shoulder bag. *Stay Arthur. Stay. Just give me enough time. I need this ride.*

She reached the mobile unit depot by the harbour just as the Bedford truck was clearing the main gate. The truck picked up speed and Emily could do nothing but watch the children hanging out of the windows waving to a group of soldiers and dock workers who had gathered to see them off. Emily was sweating. She stopped running and bent over, breathing heavily, cursing under her breath. She had missed Arthur by seconds.

Arthur changed gear to negotiate the steep curve on the road out of the harbour. He glanced in his rear mirror and saw a figure about a hundred metres away, bent double. He smiled to himself and changed the gear to reverse.

As the truck pulled alongside her Emily. Arthur wound down his window, laughed and called out, 'Hello, fancy seeing you here. Can I give you a lift?'

Emily put one foot in front of the other, gave a low theatrical bow, then straightened and laughed with Arthur. 'That would be very kind of you my good man,' she shouted above the engine. Alazne pushed the cab door open for her and she squeezed in between him and Arthur, placing her back pack and shoulder bag on the floor.

Arthur reached cross and patted her on the shoulder. 'Glad you could make it,' he said. 'You seem in good spirits. Everything okay?'

Emily gave him a beaming smile. 'Everything is absolutely and totally fine. Just hand me my brush. I'm ready for the snow.'

'No need,' said Arthur. 'Had the wipers fixed.' He darted a glance at her as he hauled on the steering wheel and turned the truck into the steep curve. 'So, you found out about him then?'

'I did,' said Emily, staring at the road. 'I certainly did.'

'So, I take it he's … okay. Alive?'

Emily continued concentrating on the road. 'Yes … *she's* alive and okay. And I'll be meeting up with her in England.'

Arthur gave her another sideways glance and smiled.

Chapter twenty-two

Friday, 31st December, 1937

40 Percy Park, Tynemouth, Northern England.

Nine days later, on New Year's Eve, Emily and Arthur arrived back in Newcastle. It had taken a long time to get back. The winter had deepened in the Pyrenees, much worse than a few days earlier when they crossed into Spain. And they had to cope as best they could with the unbelievable cold and icy roads. Arthur had to drive most of the way in bottom gear. They stayed in Perpignan for a few days, worried about the safety of the children in the extreme conditions. They spent Christmas day in a hotel in Perpignan. The hotel provided a free Christmas dinner and local people brought gifts for the children.

It was raining heavily as they handed the truck over to the Newcastle, 'Aid Spain committee' run by the local Labour Party. The truck would be loaded up as quickly as possible for the next delivery of supplies bound for Spain and the republican movement. They had parted company with Alazne in Perpignan. He had been a big help to them. They couldn't have done the trip without him and they told him how grateful they were.

The refugee children were handed over to the French section of the Communist International in Paris where they would all be given a safe place to stay until more semi-permanent accommodation could be found. Many children had already been sent to Britain, other European countries, the Soviet Union and Mexico. Careful documentation was kept to ensure that the children would be returned to Spain when it was safe for them.

Emily said a long goodbye to Arthur at the railway station in Newcastle. He was going back home. She saw him to his train to Edinburgh where he would catch a connection to Glasgow. Emily wasn't going home to her flat just yet.

She took the next train to Tynemouth, a short journey of only thirty minutes. She left the beautiful Victorian station and headed for the centre of the town. The heavy rain had subsided to a steady drizzle. Her hair was soaking wet within seconds but she didn't care. She continued walking for a hundred yards, her steps becoming slower and heavier. Her backpack and shoulder bag seemed to be dragging her down. Her whole body sagged with the dread and anguish of anticipated disappointment.

After another minute she turned into Percy Park, an open, grassed area of about three acres, roughly the size of two football pitches. The area was flanked by two rows of large three storey Victorian houses. She could see the North Sea just off the bottom of the park.

On the green a football match was in progress with stones for makeshift goalposts. A mixture of adults and children dashed about, sliding on the wet grass, shouting and calling for the ball, completely oblivious to the rain, their dark hair glistening.

At the edge of the field, about fifty yards away, a woman stood, swathed in bright coloured scarves and holding a big umbrella. She was shouting encouragement to the players. Emily could see clouds of icy breath billowing from her mouth. She was shouting in Spanish. Beside her was a small boy, perhaps five or six years old. The woman had one gloved hand on his shoulder, the other hand using the umbrella to shelter them both. Emily watched the woman bend down and say something to the boy. Emily couldn't hear what was being said but she knew it would be encouraging words with a big smile.

The woman suddenly stood up and glanced in Emily's direction, then completely turned to her and stared.

It was Isabel.

Emily's heartbeats instantly became too loud and too fast. She could feel the thumping in her chest like a giant bird stomping around and flexing its wings. The rain came down her face in streaks, cascading, mixing with her tears. She could feel her face tightening and her breathing stopped.

They stared at each other for a long time, both frozen to the spot, each waiting for the other to move, their eyes locked.

A dog ran across the field chasing a smaller dog. They ran in between the football players. The two dogs then ran between Emily and Isabel, stopped and faced each other in a stand-off, panting heavily. Then they raced back across the field in and out of the players again before retracing their steps back between the two women and finally disappeared into an alley.

The small boy at Isabel's side noticed Isabel looking away and followed her line of vision. His eyes settled on the other woman. He looked up at Isabel, tugged at her arm and said something. Isabel didn't reply. She continued staring across the edge of the field. The billowing breaths came faster.

Another half minute passed.

Emily opened her mouth and finally breathed. She drank in the rain. She couldn't quite work out where Isabel was now. The rain and tears blurred her vision but then she was suddenly aware of a tall dark shape coming closer, walking towards her.

Emily rubbed her eyes and tightened the grip on her shoulder bag.

Isabel was only twenty paces away and walking steadily, still holding the hand of the young boy. She stopped in front of Emily and they subjected themselves to an unblinking wide-eyed gaze, peering at each other with expressionless faces.

The small boy gave a deep frown and stared up at the two women. The sound of the soft pattering of rain on the umbrella mixed with the shouting of the football players. He looked at Isabel for some sign, some explanation for her silence and awkwardness, but she wasn't aware of him. He turned his attention to Emily and held up his hand, then waved it at her so she couldn't ignore it.

'Kaixo,' he said.

Emily turned to the voice, coughed and took deep breath. 'Kaixo. Perdon, no hablo Euskera. I'm sorry I don't know the Basque language. Hello is all I know.'

'Okay,' he said. 'Buenos dias senorita.'

'Buenos dias senor.' Emily gave a small bow.

She smiled at him then looked at Isabel again. She saw the tears running down Isabel's face and she knew with a relieved gasp that it was going to be alright. She coughed again to clear her throat but her voice cracked when the words came. 'Y tu … Isabel? C-como estas. H-How … how are you?'

Isabel didn't answer. She threw the umbrella down, let go of the boy and grabbed Emily by the lapels of her soaking corduroy jacket. She pushed her face up as close as she could to Emily's. Emily could feel the warm breath on her cheek. The rain was heavier now. It splattered off Isabel's nose and went into Emily's open mouth.

'Where the hell have you been?' Isabel shouted. 'Where the hell have you been, eh? English Brigadista! Where the hell have you been?'

She let go of Emily's coat and gave her a heavy push with both hands. They stared at each other and then they fell into each other and wrapped themselves around each other and squeezed and squeezed, holding tight. Their breath came out quick and gasping and the freezing clouds swam together like one small cloud of vapour until it was lost in the heat of their faces and their tears.

Then they broke away and stood staring again, shaking their heads and smiling and the smile turning into a keen, breathless gaze. The rain lashed down, whipping into them. They hugged each other again with the rain streaming down their hair. Emily glanced across Isabel's shoulder, she nudged her and nodded to the field and then turned her.

The football game had stopped and the players stood motionless witnessing the scene. They were Spanish and at this particular time in their country's history they knew all about loss and parting and the amazing wonderment and pure joy of lost friends and lovers found again. They started cheering and clapping and waving. Their cheers muffled by the rain.

'Come, come with me,' Isabel shouted to Emily. She laughed and waved back to the football players. 'Come with me Emily. I'll show you where we are living.'

Isabel picked up the umbrella and gave it to the young boy at her side. 'Here you are Xavi. You take this. This lady is a friend of mine and I'm going to show her our home.'

Xavi took the umbrella, smiled at Emily and then ran back to the field.

The two women walked the short distance to number forty Percy Park, overlooking the field. Once the main door was closed behind them Isabel pulled Emily to her. 'So, where have you been Emily? What took you so long?'

Emily didn't reply. She took Isabel's face in her hands and kissed her. They held each other and kissed again. Then Isabel took Emily's hand and led her into the living room.

'So, this is where you are,' said Emily. 'I met Carmen in Barcelona and she gave me your address. I couldn't believe it. Here all this time.'

'How is Carmen?' Isabel motioned to Emily to sit with her on the sofa.

'She seems fine. Worried about you. Angry with me.'

'I'm worried about her and angry with you too. Why didn't you tell me what was going on? The last I heard from you was that you were in Paris.'

Emily opened her mouth to speak but the words jammed in her throat and so she gave a hopeless shrug softening it with the most miserable face she could produce.

Isabel reached across and put a hand on Emily's shoulder then slid her hand down, unbuttoned Emily's jacket and felt Emily's stomach.

'Don't worry. I know. I received an express letter from Carmen yesterday. She told me what happened. It's not your fault.'

'I didn't know what to do … how to tell you. I didn't know how you would react. I was scared of losing you.'

'You can tell me anything Brigadista. You were raped. It wasn't your fault. Carmen told me what you said. Who was it? A fascist bastard?'

'No. Socialist bastard. Hungarian. International Brigader.'

'Same thing. Men are all fascist bastards if they do this.' Isabel leant her face forward and smiled at Emily. 'One good thing though.'

'What's that?'

'Well, at least it was forced and you hadn't gone straight. I was worried. I thought I'd have to fight off men as well as women.'

Emily peered into Isabel's face and laughed. A long, relieved bellowing laugh and Isabel joined her.

'Don't worry,' Isabel said softly. 'There's no need to worry. We are together. And we will care for this baby together.'

Emily rubbed her eyes, shook her hair with both hands to get rid of the raindrops and then took her coat off. She focused on the pattern of the carpet and gathered her thoughts. 'So, this is where you call home now.'

'Yes, it is. And not so bad,' said Isabel, glad to be changing the conversation too.

'So, not so good then?'

'No, it's fine. We are looked after very well. The house is mainly run by your Labour Party. We have everything we need. The neighbours were a bit weary … wary?'

'Wary,' said Emily. 'But probably weary as well … tired.'

'At first, they were suspicious. But we put on concerts for them at the church hall. The children sing old Basque songs and I do my best to join them. I think we are winning them round. The Duke of Northumberland owns these houses. He wanted us out when we first came here. Didn't want his houses turned into hostels. But I think we are winning him round too.' She glanced out of the window to the football game which had started up again. 'We get lots of visitors. Those men out there are from my country … Spanish sailors. They call in whenever their ship comes to the area. They give the children any news they have about what is happening back home. I know they make it up sometimes … for the children. And on rare occasions they actually do have news of the families.'

'I have a home now,' said Emily. 'A flat in Newcastle. You must come and stay with me. When you can. I know the children must come first.'

'I would like that … very much.' Isabel sat back, swept a hand across her wet hair and looked at Emily. 'I can't believe it,' she said. 'I can't believe how happy I am.'

And for sixteen months they both were. In love, content, and grateful just to be together.

Chapter twenty-three

Friday, 28th October, 2016

Newcastle, Northern England,

Will Roddy's house.

After Valentina had bundled Axel and Sami out of the house, she walked back to the living room. She was desperately trying to think of a way to leave and go to Ana's house to meet with Richard without raising suspicion. She had already made plans to stop him before he got the chance to get further involved, found out what was going on and ruined the whole operation.

It was crucial that she got to Ana's house and she was about to be handed the means to go there. In a totally unexpected and brutal way.

'I think we need to get going as soon as possible,' said Felipe as Valentina entered the living room. 'And remember to speak in English.' He nodded at Amber. 'She needs to know what's going on. She's given herself up so she at least deserves that.'

'But what about her?' said Valentina.

'We can drop her off on the way to the airport.' Felipe glanced at Amber again. 'Make sure she's safe. We don't want any trouble now that we've got what we came for. And maybe … if she's interested in what we are doing, maybe she can join us in Madrid in a few days. See what we're going to do with Miro's mural.'

Amber raised her eyebrows, tilted her head and gave Felipe a deep smile which she tried to hide but couldn't.

Ramon tutted. 'Or maybe there's another way to do things,' he said. 'We need to be … clever … not too hasty.'

Valentina eyed him carefully. 'What do you mean, clever?'

Felipe held up his hands. 'We need to get the mural back to Madrid as soon as possible. They'll need time to prepare the best way to use it. Not to mention the credit we'll get from the whole thing. Especially you Ramon. You're the one who pushed for this. You're the one who found it.'

'Thank you,' said Ramon. 'But we all came here, didn't we?' We all helped. We all gave our time … and you two gave money, for which I am really grateful.'

'So, again, what do you mean Ramon?' Valentina raised her eyebrows.

Ramon sat down at the table. He moved the knife he'd used to cut open the flags to one side and stroked his hand across the copy of Miro's mural. 'I did a bit of research. Back in Madrid.'

'We know,' said Felipe quickly. 'You told us. You told us all about how you found the Facebook picture of the brigade woman with the flags. You told us about the art book about the civil war and the theory of a copy being smuggled out of Paris. You told us how you were always searching out anything on the International Brigades. We know you did some great research.'

'I did more research into Joan Miro.' Ramon's words came measured and quiet. 'He is, as you know, a very famous artist.'

Felipe blew out a long breath. 'We know all this. We know he was a famous artist. This is just wasting time. We need to get going. We need to get to the airport and book tickets.'

Valentina stood very still and continued staring at Ramon. *I'm not sure where this is going but it doesn't sound good.* 'So, what's your point Ramon? And what do you mean by *research?*'

'I'm saying,' Ramon looked around the room and let his hand crawl across his ear and chin, looking for somewhere to rub. 'I'm saying that Miro's paintings are worth a fortune. They sell for thousands of euros, hundreds of thousands and more.' He returned his gaze to Valentina and then to Felipe. 'And we have the best of them. The only known painting of *The Reaper,* showing the true colours. Imagine what you could get for this.'

Felipe gave a serious nod, his forehead corrugating. 'So, you're saying that instead of destroying the mural copy, we sell it … for the cause. That's not a good idea. We came here to find a way to help destabilise the Catalan referendum. That's what we're here for. Selling the painting would complicate everything.' He looked across at Valentina. 'Although the funds would be very welcome to the Madrid group.'

Valentina let the silence in the room settle. *So, that's what you're up to Ramon. I didn't see that coming.* She looked at Felipe. 'I don't think that's what he's saying Felipe. I think Ramon has something else in mind. Is that right Ramon?'

Ramon pushed his chair back and stood up, leaning on the table with both hands. 'This is a once in a lifetime opportunity. We have to take it. The thing is worth a fortune.' He began waving his arms about. 'And what have the Madrid group done for us. Look what they did to me. Humiliated me. We owe them nothing. We can sell the mural and split the money. We don't have to go back to Madrid. We can go anywhere we like.'

Felipe shifted his ground, put both hands to his head and turned once on his heels. His mouth opened a little in amazement like he was trying to blow smoke rings. He filled his cheeks, blew out a torrent of air and finally exploded. '*Whaaat!?* What the hell are you talking about? What about the cause? Y'know, the thing we're supposed to believe in. We have to stop those bloody lefties. That's what we're here for. We have a duty to –'

'We don't have a duty,' Ramon interrupted. His voice was silky and overly quiet. 'We don't have a duty to them. We only have a duty to ourselves. Us. Us first. We look after ourselves. No-one else will. They don't care about us. We only have a duty to ourselves.'

Felipe's face reddened, he screwed his eyes up and pointed at Ramon with a stiff arm. 'You bloody traitor! Traitor! You're worse than the commies.'

Valentina stood back as Felipe raged. She wasn't sure what to do. Intervene and try to calm things down, or let them go. See what happens. See if she could use anything here.

Amber stood beside her looking equally unsure.

'Don't be stupid,' Ramon said, still with the quiet voice. 'Think of yourself for once. You're just worried that you won't get your medal. Your certificate to show what a good fascist you are. Grow up. We're on our own. We don't owe anybody anything. Grab this opportunity.'

'But that's not true is it, Ramon?' Felipe growled. 'That's the whole point. We're not on our own. There's a whole movement. A whole movement wanting to straighten out our country … straighten out the world.'

'Well, let *them* do it,' Ramon said. 'Think of yourself'

'And what about your little speech, eh?' Felipe bellowed, spit flying. 'Your little speech in Antoni's apartment in Madrid. You seem to have a short memory, but I don't. Remember? Remember what you said? You said, if we find it, we can destroy it … show everyone that we have a long reach … that we have a history too … to make sure that what happened eighty years ago is never forgotten … that Franco is never forgotten … you said we owe it to that generation. What about that, eh Ramon?'

Ramon gave the tiniest of smiles and shrugged. 'Things change,' he said.

'Lies!' Felipe yelled. 'Lies. All lies. You've just been using the group. Using us. You're just out for yourself. You're showing *your* true colours now … black … black for treachery.'

'Isn't that just what I've been saying Felipe. I am out for myself … you're not paying attention.' He waited a few seconds. 'And what about you Felipe. Look at you. On some kind of crusade. Get over it.'

'I won't betray what I believe in.'

'Good for you.'

'And I'm not a liar and a traitor.'

'I have my reasons.'

'What? You're poor? A lot of people are poor. They don't sell their friends out.'

'I don't need to explain to you.'

'Yes, you bloody do! You planned this all along. You used Valentina and me.'

'This is my one chance. I'm not some rich boy. And yes, I did plan this all along. Of course. As soon as I found out about the missing mural and saw that picture of Edelman. But it doesn't have to be like this. There'll be plenty of money for us all.'

Felipe shook his head and cursed under his breath. He turned to Valentina. 'You're quiet Valentina. What have you got to say about this.'

Valentina looked at Felipe. 'I'm with you Felipe. This is bad. We're here for a reason. We should finish what we set out to do and bring the mural back.'

'How are you going to do that?' said Ramon.

Felipe and Valentina exchanged glances.

'We'll take it … if we have to,' said Felipe.

'Oh, you'll have to,' said Ramon. He faked a smile. 'I need this.'

Amber waved a hand at the three of them. 'Look, this is getting out of hand. Just do what you said you were going to do Ramon. Get it back to Madrid.'

'She's right!' Felipe shot forward to grab the cloth but Ramon was ready for him. He turned sideways and kicked out with his right leg catching Felipe off balance and making him stumble into the armchair. Felipe pulled himself up and stood facing Ramon with clenched fists.

Ramon shook his head slowly, without looking he grabbed the kitchen knife from the table and held it at arm's length, gently waving it a few centimetres side to side aiming it directly at Felipe's stomach.

'Don't,' said Valentina, keeping her voice low.

Ramon looked at her without moving the knife from its target. Felipe glanced at Valentina, trying to work out what she was going to do.

'This is mad,' said Amber, starting to come forward.

Valentina looked at her. 'Stay where you are.' Then turned her attention back to Ramon. 'Don't, Ramon.' She held up both palms of her hands. 'She's right. This is mad. You don't want to do this.' Valentina took a deep breath. 'It's so easy to lose control Ramon. It's too –'

'I'm not losing control. I'm perfectly *in* control.' Ramon interrupted without taking his eyes off Felipe.

'Don't do it,' said Valentina quietly. 'Listen. Listen to me Ramon. Have you ever killed anyone? Have you? I have. Believe me it's not what you want to do. You'll replay it every day for the rest of your life. You'll wish you had the time over again. You'll wish you hadn't done it. It will eat away at you. You'll never –'

Ramon took his opportunity while Felipe was concentrating on Valentina. He straightened his right arm, lunged forward with his right leg and slid the knife into Felipe's stomach. Felipe's shocked face was visible for only a moment before he began falling forward, clutching his stomach, and stumbled into Ramon. Ramon steered him away with his left hand and as he did so he expertly turned the knife and eased the blade into Felipe's left side as he fell. Ramon made it look effortless. Felipe crashed into the table and lay cradling his wounds with the blood already spurting through his fingers.

Everything in the room stopped. The air. The breathing. Time. Everything became still and dense, waiting. Waiting for whatever it was to pass.

There was a scream from somewhere. A wild, high-pitched wail came from just behind Valentina and Amber started to run to throw herself at Ramon. Valentina caught her by the neck of her sweater, pulled her back and pushed her away to the far end of the room. Amber twirled about, bounced off the wall but then quickly recovered and ran at Ramon again. Ramon turned to face her, the reddened knife held loosely, ready.

Valentina jumped across Amber and punched her in the chest with the heel of her hand. Amber fell back winded and sank to her knees. Valentina spun round, pointing at Ramon. 'Enough! That's it! Enough!' She took two steps to her left so that she stood between Amber and Ramon. 'Let me get an ambulance for him, and then we'll go. You can have the damn painting.'

She looked down at Felipe, he still wasn't groaning which she knew wasn't a good sign. But she could see his chest pumping up and down rapidly.

'No,' said Ramon coolly. 'You can go Valentina but I need Amber with me.' He brought out the words unhurriedly and strolled across the room.

Valentina watched him. *You've done this before. I knew you were dangerous.*

Ramon walked over to Amber and dragged her up. He flung his arm around her neck and held the knife at her back pressing it against her so that she flinched and gave a loud gasp.

'I'll take the car keys Valentina,' Ramon said. 'You can go wherever you want. Amber stays with me. A bit of security. But I'm sure you won't do anything crazy. Of course, if you do, then Amber ...'

Valentina realised it would be pointless trying to reason with him. *You're too far gone aren't you. You're blooded and desperate.* She took the keys from her pocket and placed them slowly on the table. She nodded to Felipe. 'He needs help. He'll die if he doesn't get help.'

Ramon prodded the knife more firmly into Amber's back making her gasp again. He sniffed and the corners of his mouth turned up. 'And she'll die if you get him help. Once I'm out of here you can do what you want. I like you, Valentina. I thought we made a good team. I don't want to hurt you. You can go. I'll take her to the airport with me. She'll fit in the car boot easily. Don't do anything stupid. You know what will happen to her if you do anything stupid. I've come too far to be stopped now. Now you go. Collect what you need and go.'

Valentina looked at Amber. She seemed calm enough, resigned to whatever was going to happen.

'Don't give him any trouble,' Valentina said. 'It'll be okay.'

Amber didn't reply. Her breathing was strained with the pressure of Ramon's arm across her neck. She gulped and stared at Valentina, her face blank.

Valentina raced upstairs and came down two minutes later carrying her small bag. She looked at Felipe, still motionless on the floor but she could tell, still taking shallow breaths. She glanced at Amber, nodded to her and then opened the front door and was gone.

She would have to call a taxi to get to Ana's house as quickly as possible. It was important that she met Richard. Her command unit had told her in no uncertain terms that her project could not be jeopardised. Richard could certainly do that if he found out what was going on. He was the most important person at the moment.

She had to make sure that she remained undercover. *The important thing is information. We need everything we can get. We can't have anything undoing the work we've already done. It's too important. It's too ... I'm sure she'll be okay. He's got too much to lose to harm her, hasn't he? Hasn't he?*

Chapter twenty-four

Friday, 28th October, 2016

Newcastle, Northern England,

Ana's house in Heaton.

There were three quick loud knocks on Ana's back door. Ana looked at Xavi. 'That must be her, she's early.'

'Unless it's Richard, early,' said Xavi.

Ana pulled a face. 'Don't say that. That's all we need. It must be Valentina.' She opened the door and found Valentina there. 'Good,' she said, unsmiling. 'You made it. Xavi's here.'

Ana showed Valentina into the large square kitchen. Xavi pulled a chair out for her and she sat beside him.

'Everything okay?' Xavi asked unsmiling. 'Coffee?'

Valentina nodded and Xavi poured a mug of coffee for her from the pot at their end of the table.

'I think I'd better have one too,' said Ana. 'I've already had two glasses of wine I'm so nervous.'

Valentina was going over in her head what she was going to say to Ana. She took a long drink of coffee and looked around the room. The place was a mass of colour with multi-coloured patterned tiles along one wall, orange, blue and plum coloured kitchen cabinet doors, and a big red fridge in the corner. Beside the fridge was a circular, brown, red and black Turkish rug decorated with Islamic patterns.

Valentina looked up at Ana. 'Are Axel and Sami here? They left about –'

'They're here. In the other room,' Ana snapped. She glared at Valentina. 'They told us what happened at that house.' A small vein began twitching at her neck. 'I told them we wanted to speak to you alone.'

'Yes,' said Valentina. 'Amber was very brave, volunteering to take Sami's place.'

Ana's eyes drilled into Valentina. 'So, you left her.'

'I had no choice. I had to get back here for that man Richard.' Valentina looked around the room again for inspiration. 'It was important that I came here.'

'What will happen to Amber?' Ana clenched her jaw.

'Nothing will happen to her,' said Valentina. 'I'm certain of it. Ramon's just trying to make sure that you don't go to the police or security services. That's all.'

'So, when will she be released?' Ana said, her voice still sharp.

'Tonight, when …' Valentina struggled to find the right words. 'When they go to the airport. She'll be released, then let go somewhere that will give time for the plane to take off.'

'Are you sure?'

Valentina hesitated for only a split second. 'Yes.'

Ana eyed her suspiciously. 'I'm trusting you Valentina … *again*. With another child of mine. You ask a lot. Brave or not I want Amber back. Safe and unharmed.' Her voice was simmering, about to boil over. 'I don't want to think that I didn't do enough to save her. If anything does happen to her …' She pointed at Valentina. 'I'll hold you responsible.' She went to the fridge and poured herself a glass of wine. 'I need another drink.'

Xavi straightened in his chair. He looked pointedly at Ana. 'Axel said they cut the flags open and there was something between them … a painting. You mentioned this before. So, you found it. What was it? Remind us, why is it so important that it's brought you all the way from Spain.'

'It's important to them. To this far-right group. It's the only perfect copy of a mural by Joan Miro that went missing eighty years ago. They'll use it as more propaganda to try and destabilise the referendum.'

Ana sat down heavily in her old chair where she had first read the letters of Emily and Isabel. She took a long drink from her glass.

Xavi looked at Ana. 'Good Lord, but this changes things, doesn't it. You weren't sure if you would find the copy but now that you have … they need to be stopped, this Ramon and Felipe. The Catalans have a right to a fair referendum. You can't let these bloody fascists dictate what happens – again.' He scrunched his face up with anger and the creases on his face became even deeper. His voice rose and the folds of his neck rippled as he rapped the table with his fist. 'You – we – can't let this happen. My family died because of people like these. I won't stand by and allow them to do this. I won't!'

Ana looked up quickly. 'But Xavi. Amber. We can't risk it. We need to get her back.'

Xavi turned on her. 'So, you'll let them get away with this. Poisoning people's lives … again … poisoning people's thoughts.'

'We have no choice,' Ana said firmly. 'You know we have no choice. What do you expect me to do? Choose your principles over my daughter.'

Xavi flinched. 'Not just my principles Ana. My family. The whole family. Murdered by people like these bastards. I can't … I won't …'

A long pause.

Valentina watched Xavi fight back the tears.

'You know there's nothing we can do,' Ana said quietly.

Xavi pulled his head back and stared at the ceiling. The first tear dropped and he quickly swept it away with a finger. 'I know,' he murmured and let his head drop to his chest. 'I know it's a choice between memories and the living.' He scanned the room with an empty, helpless look. 'The truth is … I find it hard to remember. The faces went long ago. I only know what happened to them. I was there and I saw it … but I have tried to forget and I have succeeded. I can't remember what they look like.' He rubbed a hand across his forehead. 'I have to look after my new family now. You're right.'

Ana waited for a few seconds. 'Thank you, Xavi,' she said and then turned to Valentina. 'Have you any idea at all where they will leave Amber?'

'Like I said, probably near the airport somewhere,' said Valentina. 'I have no way of knowing where.'

'But you can contact them,' said Ana. 'And when you meet up with them you could let us know, couldn't you? That's the least we expect. Surely you can do that since we've agreed not to go to the police.'

Valentina didn't answer.

'You can at least find out what time,' said Ana. 'We could get her as soon as possible.' She looked at the large clock above the fridge. 'We can look for the times of the plane to Madrid. Will you go straight back to Madrid? Or will you just get any plane that's available?'

'I'm not sure,' said Valentina.

Ana pointed at Valentina with her glass. 'We can drive you to the airport after you've met Richard so you can join them. Discreetly of course. I know you don't want them knowing what you're up to.'

Valentina stared at the floor, and then stared again, for a long time. Ana looked at Xavi with a puzzled expression.

Suddenly. 'I don't need to be there,' Valentina announced. 'You need to know this.'

'What do you mean?' said Xavi.

'I don't need to be there.'

Ana's eyes darted towards Valentina. 'Why?'

Valentina slid the words out. 'Ramon has gone … rogue … on us. I believe that's the English expression.'

'What about Felipe?' asked Xavi. 'Him too? Has he gone *rogue* too?'

'No. There's a problem there.'

'*What* problem?' Ana snarled.

'It seems that Ramon wanted to keep the copy of the mural all along. He wants to sell it for himself. It seems he has no interest in the politics of it.'

'What about the other lad, Felipe?' repeated Xavi. 'Him too? Does he want to sell it?'

'No,' Valentina said. 'Felipe wanted to stick to the original plan. In fact, he tried to get the painting off Ramon.'

Ana studied Valentina carefully. 'So, what happened?' she said slowly.

Valentina wanted to pull back, as far back as she could. She didn't want to say the words but she knew she had to be honest. She took a long time to speak. *This is only making it worse.* 'Ramon stabbed Felipe,' she said eventually, directing her words into her coffee mug. All she could do now was wait.

It didn't take long.

Ana and Xavi exchanged looks. Xavi frowning, Ana's eyebrows shot up. They both turned and shook their heads and then looked at each other again.

Valentina froze, waiting. *Come on, get on with it. Get it over with.*

Ana jumped up from her chair and banged her glass down on the table, so hard that the stem broke off. The bowl of the glass fell from her hand and the wine spilled on to the table.

'What!? What have you done!?' Ana wasn't shouting yet. She was revving up.

Valentina looked up into the glare of Ana's fiery eyes. She kept her face expressionless. Her jaw set tight.

Now Ana started to shout, almost shrieking.

'What the …! Are you telling me you just left her there! Just left her with this bloody maniac. A maniac with a knife who's just stabbed someone! Are you frigging stupid?'

'I'm sorry,' said Valentina trying to be practical. 'There was nothing I could do.'

'You could have bloody stayed!' Ana yelled again. She was panting now, trying to control her breathing. 'You should have bloody stayed!'

Valentina stood up, taking her time. 'Look. I said I'm sorry. I had no choice … and I don't think Ramon will hurt Amber.'

'THINK!' Ana roared. 'You don't *think*!

Xavi pushed his chair back and stood up between the two women. 'Let's keep calm Ana,' he said softly. He turned to Valentina. 'What makes you so sure she's going to be safe with this man? What do you think is going to happen now?'

'He'll have to contact me,' said Valentina. 'I left a note in his bag telling him I've got his passport. I took it from his bag in his room when he ordered me to get my things upstairs. He can't leave the country. He'll have to contact me so he can get it back. We can make an exchange –'

'Another exchange!' Ana, now pacing the room, shouted over her shoulder. 'They don't seem to go very well … these exchanges.'

373

'He needs the passport,' Valentina said. 'And he knows he won't get it if he harms Amber. Trust me. She will be safe.'

'Trust *you*.' said Ana. She had recovered her breathing and her voice was calmer.

Valentina walked across the room and stood directly in front of Ana. 'You have to trust me Ana, you have no choice. I will get Amber back. And I can get rid of this Richard guy. You have to trust me.'

'What about your other friend, Felipe,' asked Xavi. 'How is he?'

'He was breathing when I left,' said Valentina. She sat back down at the table. 'Ramon wouldn't let me call for help there but I called on the way here. Our British security colleagues will go and get him as soon as Ramon leaves the house. They won't intervene as long as Ramon is in there. They have instructions not to put my assignment at risk.'

'But he might die,' said Xavi.

'He might,' said Valentina.

'What?' Xavi shook his head. 'I can't believe you're just going to let him die.'

'That's up to Ramon,' Valentina said flatly. 'If he leaves soon, they can get to him. They won't go in until he's left. If Felipe is still alive, he'll know that I've contacted British authorities. But we can work that out later. We can keep him here until after the referendum. We can't let an ordinary ambulance deal with this. We have to find out who this group is working for. It's important for both our governments. Ramon mustn't know I'm not really part of the group. There's a chance that he might contact them. He'll know if the British authorities go in.' *I know it sounds callous but what choice do I have? I have to explain.*

'This is madness,' said Xavi. 'I can't believe that you're willing to sacrifice that boy.'

'We have to find out who this group is working for,' said Valentina. 'It's vital for both our governments. I have explicit instructions ... very explicit.'

'But *you* could go back,' Ana hissed. 'You could go back and make sure the boy is alright ... and Amber.'

Valentina took a deep breath and stared at Ana. 'I could,' she said. 'But I have to be here for Richard. He could spoil everything if he finds out what's really going on. He could endanger the whole project. He could get Xavi sent to prison. At the very least he could cost you thousands of pounds. Your choice.'

'No,' Ana raised her voice again. 'Don't put this on me. It's not my choice. You've already made your decision. You can't have Richard messing up your precious *assignment*.'

'We're agreed then,' said Valentina.

'Not quite,' snorted Xavi. 'If you won't go ... we will. Axel has told us where the place is. We can be there in a few minutes. It would be perfectly normal for us to go and get Amber back. Ramon wouldn't suspect you were behind it. He would know that Axel told us.'

'No, it's too risky,' said Valentina.

'I don't think so,' snapped Ana. She nodded at Xavi. 'We can go now.'

Valentina took a sip of coffee. 'No,' she said firmly. 'That can't happen. The house is already being watched by British security. They wouldn't let you anywhere near the place. It would be dangerous for you. There's too much at stake. And you might panic Ramon ... make it worse for your daughter.' She looked at them both. 'We have to be patient and wait. It's the only way.'

*

Late in the afternoon Ana spotted Richard coming through the back gate and walking up the garden path. She recognised his cream-coloured overcoat. He had a small backpack slung over his shoulder. The wind was picking up, some leaves blew up from the grass. She called Valentina from the living room and pointed him out. 'That's him,' she said. 'Where do you want to talk to him?'

'He can stay outside,' said Valentina. 'This won't take long.'

Valentina pulled the back door open before Richard had a chance to knock. He took a step back in surprise.

'Hello,' he said. 'Who are you?'

'Friend of the family,' said Valentina. 'I said I'd meet you for them.' She closed the door behind her.

'Oh,' Richard tried a smile and tilted his head.

'You're Richard, eh? Have you come about the money?'

Richard's eyebrows almost danced about. 'They told you?'

'Of course.' Valentina noted the first shadow of concern cross Richard's face.

'Well, this is all a bit embarrassing.' He tried the smile again, but it just wasn't working. 'I was just expecting to see Ana, Emily's granddaughter. We had a little chat a while ago and agreed a ... sort of fee ... a payment. About the letters ... well, you know, don't you? ...

the letters between my grandmother Isabel and Emily, Ana's grandmother.'

'Yes, I know. She told me all about it.' The breeze caught Richard's heavy scent of aftershave and wafted it to Valentina. She flared her nostrils.

Richard shook his head. 'Sorry, but who are you exactly? This is quite confidential. I really think I should be talking to Ana.'

'Like I said, I'm a friend of the family. I just want to make sure that everything is okay and that everyone gets what they deserve.'

'Has Ana agreed to —'

'Your demands?' Valentina broke in.

'Hardly demands. As I say ... a small fee to help me out ... and to help her.'

Valentina looked at him over the tip of her nose. 'I'm so sorry Richard, but you won't be getting any money today. You needn't have brought your bag.' Valentina ran a finger down the length of the scar on the left side of her face and pulled at her lip with a finger and thumb.

'So, that's it, is it? That's what Ana says. I don't want to appear rude but I don't want to talk to you. I need to talk to Ana. She knows what will happen if she doesn't come up with the money.'

'And I don't want to appear rude, but there'll be no money for you today ... or any other day. We find your values a bit ... suspect.'

'My values,' Richard laughed softly. 'So, she's willing to risk this getting out, is she? She's willing to risk Xavi being locked up as an accomplice to a murder.'

'There's no risk involved.'

'How's that?'

'Because you won't be doing anything about it.'

Richard began blinking … for a long time. He shifted his weight. 'So, you're calling my bluff.'

'No.'

'So, what makes you think I'll just walk away. Just forget it. I'm sorry but I need that money.'

'If you continue with this, you'll regret it.'

'Are you threatening me?'

'Yes, of course.'

'What are you going to do? Beat me up?'

'No, there's another way to persuade you. Come here, beside me.'

Richard shrugged, gave a small shake of his head and hesitated at first but then went to stand beside Valentina.

Valentina reached into her coat and took out her phone. 'I have a lot of friends … especially in those services where their work often goes unnoticed.' She pressed two keys and the screen lit up. She showed the screen to Richard. 'A video taken two hours ago. Recognise this?'

Richard peered at the video: two figures in a room with their backs to the camera, one kneeling on the wooden flooring, the other standing by a cabinet. He threw his head back, darted a glance at Valentina and then looked at the screen again. 'How …? What …? That's my house. How did you …?'

'I got your mobile number off Ana. Easy to trace the address.'

'What's going on? What's all this about? Who are those people?'

'There are people who don't want you anywhere near here. And they certainly don't want you taking money because you'll probably come back for more. So, for one reason or another ... and I won't go into details ... you have been designated a high security risk. You will be watched. Those people in the video are planting high quality drugs in your home. You won't be able to find them ... they're experts. But they can contact the police at any time and they'll find them. It won't look good for you when your family and friends find out you're dealing.'

'You can't do that. It's illegal.'

Valentina smiled. 'Oh, there's a lot of things my friends can do. They can go into bank accounts, alter figures.' She smiled again. 'You're renting, aren't you? They can have a word with the landlord. See if they need a different tenant.' She waited. 'Impressed yet?'

'What if I don't care? I could show the letters anyway. I've nothing to lose.'

'I don't think you understand Richard. You've got everything to lose. Literally everything. The police won't help you ... not when they find out you're a security risk. Doesn't really matter what for. And they will find out. This is up to counter intelligence level now.' Valentina paused again. She could see Richard's eyes darting around, looking for some question or some answer.

'Still not impressed?' she continued. 'Look at your phone. Check your photos.'

Richard glared at her, fumbled in his pocket and brought out his phone. He turned it on, went to his photo store and then gave an explosive gasp. 'What the ...?'

'Nasty, eh? They can put them on your Facebook as well. Show all your friends what you're up to.'

Richard's eyes dulled. 'Bastard,' he whispered.

His face suddenly resembled a barn owl, huge eyes made even bigger with incredulity, it only needed his head to swivel to complete the image. Valentina wanted to laugh. Instead, she took a step closer, leaned into him and sniffed. 'Nice aftershave,' she said. And then. 'If you don't agree to drop this there are other things they can do. Believe me, you don't want to ignore them.'

Richard shifted his feet again and moved back a step. 'So, what happens now?'

'Nothing ... it's up to you. Nothing will happen unless you make it happen. Agreed?'

Richard twisted his mouth into a tight frozen circle and kept it like that for several seconds. His face tightened; she could see the effort he was putting in to work out his response. She could see his chest heaving. Then his face suddenly crumpled and he blew out air, deflating.

'I'll leave it then,' he said abruptly. He jammed his hands into his coat pockets, turned and walked down the garden to the gate.

As Valentina went back into the house Ana pulled away from the window. 'It's done?' she asked.

Valentina sat at the table again. 'Yes, it's done. He won't be back. He won't be coming for any money.'

'What did you say to him,' said Xavi.

'It wasn't so much what I said. More what I showed him.'

'He looked scared,' said Ana.

'That was the plan,' said Valentina. 'He didn't like what I showed him. Counter intelligence services have certain powers. They can destroy you if you don't play their game. I know that ...' Valentina's phone started buzzing. She took it out and looked at the text message on the screen. 'It's Ramon. He's going to meet me tonight.' She read the text to herself. *At one a.m. On the High Level Bridge. Come alone. Bring the passport. I'll have the girl. Don't be clever. She'll be safe unless you do something stupid.* She looked at Ana. 'I knew he had to contact me.'

'Where and when?' said Xavi.

'One a.m.' Valentina noticed Ana giving Xavi a furtive look. She put the phone away quickly. 'He'll tell me where later. He says Amber is okay. I have to go alone.' She looked at them both. 'I have to go alone. Everything will be fine.'

Chapter twenty-five

Thursday, 27th April, 1939

Newcastle, Northern England,

Emily's flat.

It was eleven o'clock on a beautiful Spring morning. Emily tucked Rosa into her second-hand wooden cot, pulling the blankets tightly around her. She checked underneath to see if the cockroaches had reappeared and then sprinkled some more powder around the room, mainly in the corners and along the skirting boards. She stopped when she heard a knock at the door and replaced the lid on the jar.

'Isabel,' she gave a big beaming smile as she opened the door. 'Come in, come in.'

They went into the living room. Isabel had brought seven-year-old Xavi with her.

'I wasn't expecting you until tomorrow,' said Emily. She looked down at Xavi. 'And you're most welcome too.'

'I know,' said Isabel. 'I had to come and see you. It's very important.' She walked across the sparse room, a brightly coloured Tyneside proggy mat covering the wooden floor in front of the fireplace, a big mirror on one wall, two maps on the other wall, one of Spain and the other of the whole of Europe. 'How is little Rosa today? She didn't sleep much last night.'

'Exhausted. She's having a nap in the bedroom. She's under that blanket you made her. She always likes sleeping under that. She loves it.'

Isabel nodded at the jar of white powder Emily was still holding. 'And how are our cockroach friends?'

Xavi looked up quickly then glanced around the floor.

'Under control I think,' said Emily. She pointed at a worn brown sofa. 'Come and sit down? I'm glad you came. What a lovely surprise.' She tapped Xavi on the shoulder. 'You're in luck. I've just bought some biscuits yesterday. I'll go and get some. And wash my hands after dealing with those pesky creatures.'

Isabel had been living with the Basque refugee children for almost a year and a half. She saw Emily nearly every day and split her time between Emily's house and forty Percy Park in Tynemouth as much as she could. It had been a blissful time. That's the only way they could both describe it. They had tried hard to keep their relationship secret for the first few weeks after Emily had returned from Spain but they couldn't help themselves. It must have been the way they looked at each other that caught the stares. Maybe their closeness, keeping a safe respectable distance yet somehow still managing to be together: a touch on the arm, a hand in the small of the back, a helpful hand fastening a coat or smoothing out wayward hair, an overwhelmingly warm, knowing smile.

Emily brought a tray into the living room with a plate of biscuits and three glasses of orange juice. She handed the plate of biscuits to Xavi and was about to place his drink on the small round table in front of him.

'I've had a letter,' said Isabel abruptly. There was a tightness to her voice.

'Letter?' asked Emily.

'From Carmen.'

'Oh my God. How is she? We haven't heard from her for months.'

'I know,' She explains everything in the letter. She couldn't find a way to send it. She's been in one of Franco's prison camps. It was smuggled out.'

'What? Is she okay? Is she well? Those places are notorious.'

Isabel brought out a piece of paper from her pocket. 'Here it is. You can read it. It's in Spanish. I'll help you if you with any words you can't read.'

Emily took the letter, sat down by Xavi and began reading.

Wednesday, April 12ᵗʰ, 1939

Albatera concentration camp.

To my good and dearest friend Isabel,

I am writing this letter to you and I hope that you can show it to Emily. I know that you are together and I would like for you to read it together. My friend Sofia says she can take it out for me.

First. How are the children? I hope that they are good and have enough to eat. They have been through bad times but I am glad they are not here.

Second. I hope that you and Emily are well. I am glad that you are together. I am glad that you are not here.

I was captured after the fall of Barcelona in January and have been in this camp since then. We are not allowed to write letters but Sofia is to be released tomorrow and she says she will do her best to get this to you. She will have to smuggle it out. I am writing as much as possible by candlelight because we have heard that Sofia will be released very soon and I need to tell you what has been happening in our country.

Yesterday Franco's army entered Madrid so our great cause is finally defeated.

In the last days of Barcelona there was constant bombing. Thousands were fleeing across the border into France where they were put into French camps. We also heard that the French authorities were overwhelmed. They did not expect such huge numbers, hundreds of thousands crossed the border so holding camps were set up on the beaches. In Barcelona there was famine and disease. People in rags searching for scraps. There are lots of informers in the town and in the country so even the language has changed and people no longer greet each other as comrade. The Ministry of Justice started executions immediately. The black market was everywhere. You needed 12 pesetas to buy a kilo of flour instead of the usual 2 pesetas. Beans, meat, olives, all three times more.

Also, more bad news. Our café, the lovely Comercio Gratuito is no more. It took a direct hit from a bomb. The place is flattened. The singing has stopped.

I hid as long as I could but was soon captured along with hundreds of others. We were paraded around the streets and the people were told to come and see the criminals but people came forward and pressed cigarettes and any food they had into our hands. We refused to give the fascist salute but were told we would be shot if we did not do it. We did it.

Executions are normal. We hear that in other towns and villages, widows of nationalist victims take part in line ups to identify anyone suspected of being involved with the death of a husband or son. Those identified were shot immediately. No trial or justice. People are disappearing every day.

I was lucky. I was captured by a unit of the Italian 'Black Arrows' division. They took pity on us. They didn't like the way we were treated. They took our republican papers from us and burnt them so that Franco's internal security forces couldn't tell if we were communists or socialists. Instead, we would be just common criminal soldiers. They saved us from a beating and made sure we had food and water. We were later given a meal and an apple and paraded before the world's press.

I watched the 'Lister Division', the cream of the Spanish working class told to stand in sixes until they dropped and then were replaced by another six. We know that German prisoners from the International Brigades are handed over to the German authorities and they will have an equally hard time, if they survive at all.

In this camp it is not so bad. We have to work in labour battalions, as cheap labour in the construction of dams, bridges and irrigation channels. We also have to tear down bombed buildings so that there is no trace of bombings remaining. We hope to be released very soon and go home to our families.

Sorry. I have to leave this now. It is early morning and I can hear the guards coming for the next batch of prisoners to be released. I must get this to Sofia.

I hope this letter reaches you. I will give your address to Sofia. Do not worry. I am well. Take good care of yourselves.

Emily folded the letter and looked up at Isabel. 'She must have had a terrible time. I hope she gets released soon and gets back home. We should contact her. Do you know where her family live? We could send her a parcel and maybe ...' Emily's voice faded away as she watched Isabel take another piece of paper from her pocket.

Isabel handed the paper to Emily. 'This came in the same envelope. It was written by Sofia, who smuggled Carmen's letter out. You need to read it.'

Emily took the paper.

Hello Isabel. This is Sofia writing. I know you are a good friend of Carmen. She often talks about you and your times before the war. I feel I must tell you about Carmen. She is putting on a brave face. She didn't write that letter to you. She dictated it to me and I wrote it down for her. She was too weak to write. She is thin and malnourished. She is not well. She is in a very bad way.

The camp is brutal. They allow relations of victims of the republican army in to beat us. The guards are vicious pigs dedicated to torture and humiliation. There are beatings every day in the camp. Yesterday was Carmen's turn, again. They accused her of being a communist spy. They hit her so hard that they broke her eye socket. She cannot see out of her left eye and it is probable she never will. When I left she had pneumonia and there is dysentery in the camp. They do not give us medication.

I feel it is a bad thing to do, to betray the words of a friend but I felt I had to tell you the truth about her situation. It is my duty to Carmen.

They are releasing prisoners every day. I don't know when Carmen will be released but I know she will not be going home to her family. Her brother is missing. The rest of her family were killed in the bombing. Only her mother survived but she has been injured and needs a lot of help. I know this because I was there when Carmen received the letter telling her about her family.

I am sorry to write with bad news but I felt you must know the truth.

Regards Sofia.

Emily closed her eyes and dropped her head. She sat like that for more than a minute trying to focus on an image of Carmen when she knew her at the start of the war: graceful, funny, a free spirit, and what she must look like now. She imagined her gaunt, crushed and defeated. She opened her eyes and found Isabel staring at her with a strange, troubled look.

'Listen, Isabel,' Emily said softly. 'Try not to worry. They're going to release her soon. She'll get better. I know she will.'

'The letter came two days ago. I've been thinking about how to show it to you.'

'I knew there was something on your mind.'

'I keep taking it out and reading it. I've done a lot of thinking. I can't think of anything else.' Isabel's words came out achingly slow.

Xavi stopped eating his biscuit, stared at Isabel and then at the floor.

'We have to contact her,' said Emily. 'We have to let her know that *we* know. That we understand. We can send food, money, anything she needs.' She spoke quickly, trying to fill the space. The faraway, troubled look was still in Isabel's eyes. It worried Emily. She glanced at Xavi still staring at Isabel. *What's happening? What's going on?*

Isabel's voice became suddenly brusque. 'I have to go and see her.'

'Of course,' said Emily. 'You must go. See that she's okay. Help her.'

'I have to go soon.'

'Yes, I understand ...' A slow panic hovered and then eased into Emily's throat, clamping around a deeply swallowed gulp forcing her cheeks to tighten.

'No. No, you don't understand Emily. Now the war is over we have been ordered to take the children home. I wanted to tell you this yesterday but I was concentrating on the letter. I have to tell you something ...'

'What? What is it?'

Carmen's voice faltered. 'I don't know how to say it. I don't know to ... the words get in the way.'

'Say it.'

'It's difficult. It's too hard.'

Emily stared through Isabel trying to avoid her eyes. She wanted her mind to race but it was numb. *No, no, no, no, no, please not this. Please no, not this. Anything but this.* 'What is it you have to tell me?' Her voice was too strong, trying to be unafraid.

Isabel looked away. 'I have to take the children back. Those that we have letters for. Letters that tell us who will look after them. No children can go without a letter.'

'Of course.' Emily looked at Xavi. She knew there was more. She could tell by Isabel's face, the way she was moving, as if her whole body was gradually slowing down. 'So, I suppose Xavi has no letter.'

'That's right. He has no letter. We have to make alternative arrangements for him.'

'And what about you Isabel?' There was a slight crack in Emily's voice. She coughed and swallowed. 'Have you made alternative arrangements.'

'You know I love you.'

'And I love you.' *Just tell me. Get it over with. Please.*

Now Isabel looked at Emily. She pulled her head up. Her voice became even softer. 'When I go back, I will find Carmen. She needs me. I have to look after her.'

'How long for?'

'It will be a long time.'

Emily wanted to stop Isabel speaking. She wanted to interrupt by saying something but the words became glue in her throat. *I need you. I need you.*

'She has no-one,' said Isabel. 'I have to look after her. I have to find her and look after her.'

'But what about us? Our …' Emily stopped. She hoped she didn't sound pathetic. 'Are you in love with her?'

Isabel nodded slowly, her nose dipping only a centimetre or two. 'It's a different kind of love.' She looked away. 'Not like the love we have.'

'Did you love Carmen before the war?'

'I don't know. I think so. Yes. But it wasn't like us. It wasn't. But I loved … love her. And now she needs me. She has no-one. She must be so desperate … so lonely.' Isabel took a firm grasp of both hands to stop them shaking.

'But what about me?' Emily could hear a strange buzzing noise in her head.

'I love you.' Isabel whispered. She pulled both hands to her chest trying to stifle the speed of her heart. 'I love you.'

'Is it possible to love two people at once?'

'I think so … I do. But it's different.' Isabel slowed her breathing. 'But now Carmen … she needs me. I need to help her … and her mother.' She pulled at her fingers again. 'I'm sorry. I'm so sorry.'

'You won't come back, will you?' Emily took one shuddering intake of breath and then held it, waiting. Her body seemed to shimmer. She felt herself falling, but inside, falling into herself, drowning. She didn't want to hear the answer. She wanted to faint and end all the words.

'I don't know. I don't think so.' Isabel brushed a hand across her eyes. 'This is so hard Emily. It is breaking my heart. I'm torn apart. I love you so much but Carmen needs me so much. I have to go to her. She has no-one.'

Silence.

You don't think I need you? You don't think it will tear me apart?
Emily wanted to speak. She moved her lips but no sounds came. The
buzzing was still there.

'You have Rosa,' said Isabel. 'You have someone to care for. And I
will miss Rosa too.'

'Yes, I have Rosa.' Emily looked at Xavi, still sitting on the sofa,
frozen, staring at the floor. In the last few minutes she had completely
forgotten about him. 'And I suppose I have Xavi?'

'He doesn't want to go back. There's no-one there for him. He loves
you. He wants to stay with you.' Isabel concentrated on smiling at Xavi.
Glad to be talking of something else.

Now Xavi moved. He turned and looked at Emily. His eyes were the
saddest she'd ever seen.

Emily held his gaze. *You know what's going on. What's that look
for? You or Isabel or me? Or all of us?*

Emily smiled at Xavi. 'Of course, you can stay with me Xavi. It
would be an absolute honour to have you here.' She made the smile
even bigger. 'And I love you too.' She turned back to Isabel,
expressionless. 'When do you go?'

'In two days.'

Emily gave a rasping gasp. 'So soon.' She watched Isabel closely.
She loved the way she rolled her shoulder self-consciously and tilted
her whole body when she was uneasy or embarrassed. She fixed the
image in her head. She would miss that.

'I suppose that makes sense,' said Emily distractedly, recovering. 'Now that Hitler has invaded Czechoslovakia last month there's probably going to be another war and it'll be difficult to get the children across Europe to Spain.'

'Yes, that's it,' Isabel said flatly. 'I'll come back tomorrow with Xavi's things and the paperwork that's needed.'

Emily and Isabel now committed themselves to a long examination of the walls and furniture in the room.

Eventually. 'You left me once, remember?' said Isabel.

'I was afraid. I couldn't tell you. I was afraid that I'd lose you.'

'I'm afraid too.'

Emily shook her head. 'Of what?'

'That I'll lose your love.'

'You'll never lose my love. I'll always love you. You must know that. You have to take that with you. I care about you too much to do that. It was wonderful. Unbelievably wonderful. I'll never forget.' Emily straightened. 'Do you think we'll ever see each other again?'

Isabel didn't answer.

There was only two metres between them but they both kept their distance, standing like mannequins, unsure of what would happen if they touched. They both knew that would be unbearable.

'What did I do wrong?' Emily said. She had to say something. It wasn't a plea. She knew the answer. She just had to say something.

'You did nothing wrong. You did everything right.' Isabel's eyes glistened. 'But she needs me.'

'Will we see each other again?' Emily repeated her question.

'I don't know. They've closed down the country. 'Anyone thought to have helped the republican cause is not allowed to leave.'

'Will I hear from you again? Will you write.'

'Of course.'

Emily patted Xavi on the shoulder and stood up. She walked across to the kitchen door. As far away from Isabel as she could. She struggled to control the burning sensation behind her eyes. She turned back and looked at Isabel. 'Well, I've got two bottles of beer in the cupboard. This calls for a celebration, don't you think?' She paused, holding on to the doorpost to steady herself. 'Xavi coming … and you going. To your new life.' She suddenly blew out a long breath. 'I'm sorry. I didn't mean it to sound like that.'

'I know you didn't,' said Isabel. 'It's just too hard.'

'How am I supposed to stop dreaming of you?' said Emily. 'You'll be there every night when I go to sleep.'

'You won't sleep. You'll be too busy with Rosa and Xavi'

Emily smiled. Her eyes gleamed, shining bright: not with tears but with admiration and love.

'You always make me laugh Catalan girl,' said Emily.

'Good.'

'It's a good way to end … if there's such a thing.'

'I know.'

'I love you.'

'I know,' Isabel pulled her shoulders up and started to breathe more deeply, sucking in air in big gulps. She managed a short tight-lipped smile and put her head to one side, crinkling her eyes at Emily. 'I'm not going to cry. I'm not.'

'Shame on you girl,' said Emily, desperately trying to give a pretend frowning face, her voice again too strident, attempting to veil the tightness in her throat. 'Shame on you. You tear my heart out, smash it to pieces, yet you won't shed a single tear.'

Isabel gulped again, her facial muscles straining, rippling around her jawline. She glanced at Xavi. 'I'll save it for later. When I can have a proper breakdown to myself.'

Emily nodded and tried a smile. 'Me too,' she said hoarsely as something seemed to crumble way down inside her.

There was a sudden wailing cry from the bedroom. They all looked round.

'You get the beers English brigadista,' Isabel said softly as she started walking across the room. 'I'll – get – Rosa … one more time.' Her eyes were still dry as she reached the bedroom door but the tears were in her words.

Chapter twenty-six

28th October, 2016

Newcastle, Northern England,

Ana's house.

'I'm going now,' Valentina checked her watch and called through to the kitchen.

Xavi and Ana came in to the living room.

'Aren't you going to tell us where you're meeting?' asked Ana.

'No. It's best if I meet him alone.' Valentina grabbed her coat and started for the front door. 'We don't want him getting all nervous and jittery if he sees too many people there.'

'Jittery?' said Ana.

Valentina looked at her. 'You know what I mean. We all want this to go as smoothly as possible. As long as we get Amber back, he can do what the hell he likes with the painting.'

'We're counting on you,' said Xavi. 'This is a precious package you're going to get. We need you to make sure everything goes well.'

'Absolutely I will. And one bit of news that you need to know is that Felipe is fine. He's in a military hospital. They collected him when they saw Ramon and Amber leave. They'll keep him there until we can work out a story.' She turned back as she opened the door and looked at Ana and Xavi. 'I know that you're worried but I will get this done. Alone. Thank you for helping us. Your grandmother Emily would be proud of you Ana. We're on the same side. And don't try and follow me. I'm trained to spot and avoid anyone following. I'll know. And it will just make things more difficult … and waste time.' She gave them one last serious look, impressing on them the importance of what she had just said and then opened the door and stepped out into the darkness.

It was quarter to midnight. Valentina had been on her phone most of the evening. She knew it would only take her forty-five minutes to walk across town to the High Level Bridge and she wanted to be there in plenty of time to meet Ramon and Amber at one a.m. There were things she had to sort out according to which side of the bridge Ramon would be coming from. She guessed the Newcastle end but she couldn't be sure. It was important for her plan. She didn't want anything to upset her arrangements so she made sure that Ana and Xavi didn't know where the meeting would take place. It was for their own good. It wouldn't be fair on them to witness what was going to happen.

As soon as the door closed Ana turned to Xavi. 'What do you think? Follow her now or in a few minutes.'

'It'll be difficult. She's clever. Like she says, she'll know we're following her.'

Ana shook her head. 'You're not saying that we just sit here?'

'Of course not,' said Xavi. 'I think I know where they'll meet.'

Ana shrugged, widened her eyes and flipped her hands over impatiently.

'Well,' began Xavi. 'It'll have to be a place that he's familiar with. He knows she hasn't got transport, so it can't be too far away. That rules out Saltwell Park. The Crown Posada is too central and that part of town is busy even at this time of night.'

Ana tilted her head. 'So, where do you think Xavi? Get to it. Just say!'

'He knows the High Level Bridge. He's been there, Axel told us that. It's quiet this time of night. Also, they've started work reinforcing it so there's no cars allowed over from today. He knows she can get to it easily. That's where he'll go.'

Ana nodded. 'I think you're right.' She checked the clock on the wall. 'I'll give her a few minutes and then I'll drive to the bridge before her. Find somewhere to hide so I can see what's going on.'

'Okay. I just need to get something from my car.'

Ana put a hand on Xavi's arm. 'I'll do this alone Xavi. You don't need to come.'

Xavi pulled back in surprise. 'What? Why do you say that?'

'I don't know. It's just that ... it could be dangerous. He's dangerous ... and that girl Valentina looks like she could definitely handle herself. She looks as though she could easily do something nasty. And anyway, didn't you do something like this all those years ago. Got yourself involved in something when you didn't have to. We can't have history repeating itself.'

'If it's dangerous then all the more reason for me to be there ... with you.'

'Xavi, you're eighty-four. We might have to move fast.'

'I think I can keep up.' Xavi bristled and then looked at Ana. 'Why do you think it's so dangerous? All she has to do is hand over his passport and walk away with Amber.'

'In theory.'

'What d'you mean?'

'D'you think she'll just let him walk away? She's always banging on about how important her *assignment* is. Ramon must know a hell of a lot about their group. They won't want him wandering about Europe trying to sell the painting. Having to explain how he got it, attracting all kinds of suspicious authorities. And she has to make sure that they know she's done everything to stop him so that she keeps her cover. I doubt that they'll just let bygones be bygones … forget the stabbing.' She looked at him and spread both palms out. 'It could be very dangerous. That's why I've told Axel and Sami to stay here. Anything could happen. But I need to be there to make sure anything doesn't happen … if I can. I've told them to contact the police if I'm not back in two hours.'

Xavi rubbed his eyes for a few seconds. 'I know what you're saying. We'll just have to be extra careful. I'm coming. No arguments. I just have to get something from my car. I have to go Ana. I need to be there.'

'I'm not happy about this.'

'I'm not happy about any of it,' said Xavi as he walked towards the door. 'And now you've told me your thoughts on Valentina, I'm even more unhappy.'

Ana pursed her lips as though she was about to say something but then sucked in a deep breath instead.

Two minutes later Xavi came back into the room wearing his heavy jacket and carrying a pistol.

Ana gave him an incredulous look and then pointed at the pistol. 'What!? Where the hell did you get that? What are you going to do with it? You'll get us all killed!'

'Stop us all getting killed, I think. Emily gave it to me when she came back from Spain the first time.' Xavi turned the pistol over in his hand. 'It's a TT-30, commonly known as the Tokarev, after it's designer Fedor Tokarev. It was –'

'I don't bloody care who designed it,' Ana spluttered. 'What d'you think you're going to do with it?'

'Just for scaring purposes,' said Xavi with the hint of a frown.

'You can't go round shooting that thing off. I won't let you take it.'

'Don't worry, it's harmless.' He waved the pistol in the air before pushing it into his jacket pocket. 'No bullets.'

Ana shook her head. Stared at him then shook her head again. 'Okay then … if you're so determined to go, let's go. But keep that thing out of sight.'

'Wait.' Xavi pulled on his beard and looked around the room.

'What is it now? we need to go.'

'It's important.'

'What is?'

'In case anything happens on the bridge. To me … or you.'

'Well?'

'You need to know.' Xavi stopped pulling his beard but still searched around the room. 'It's about your mother Rosa ... and me,' he said gravely.

Ana put on her long, hooded coat slowly and then turned to face Xavi. Waiting.

Xavi Blew out his cheeks and stared at Ana. 'I've been wanting to tell you for a long time. And now it seems appropriate ... in case anything goes wrong tonight. I've wanted to tell you for years ... but I couldn't. At first it was because I was part of the family but somehow separate. When Isabel went away, Emily moved to a small house. A new beginning. New friends. New neighbourhood. Everyone thought of me as Rosa's big brother. It was never advertised that I was a refugee. And I picked up the language quickly.' He dragged his eyes away and stared at his hands, turning them over, studying them. 'As the years went by, Rosa and I ... grew closer. Then the inevitable happened and you were born. We had to make up a story. We said it happened when Rosa was on a short holiday to Scotland. A one-night stand. A brief affair. That's what we said. We loved each other. Still do. Although your mum doesn't know much about that now. I helped look after you ... as a caring uncle ... or so everyone thought.' Xavi puffed up his cheeks and blew out a loud breath. 'Rosa started to become really ill when you had left home, but we still kept up the pretence, for the family's sake.' He looked up briefly and Ana could see the tears in his eyes. 'I'm sorry Ana. I should have told you a long time ago. It was a cruel thing to do. To keep this from you.'

Ana fastened the zip on her coat and pulled herself up to her full height. 'We have to go,' she said quickly.

'What?' Xavi wiped the tears from his cheek and stared at her. 'Aren't you going to say anything?'

'What? About you being my dad?'

Xavi nodded, his face crumpled and the creases on his forehead rippled as he tried to control his shaking hands. He suddenly looked ancient, like an old book, well-thumbed with the cover worn. He gave a bewildered shake of his head.

Ana smiled at him. She went across and held his hands. 'I've known for years,' she said quietly. 'I guessed it at first because you spent so much time looking after mum and you looked after her so tenderly. But then I persisted in asking Grandma Emily and eventually she told me. And she also made me promise never to reveal what had happened. She was worried about you. She didn't want you hurt in any way by malicious gossip or anything else.'

Xavi stared at her. His head started to quiver as if the information was too much for it to take in and it was trying to sort it out before his neck gave way. His breathing started coming in quick bursts but he opened his mouth wide to gulp in a huge amount of air to steady himself. His mouth remained open and hung there with his tongue working its way around his lips.

'Are you coming Xavi?'

'Yes,' he muttered, still gaping.

'We have to go now,' said Ana briskly. 'Let's go. We can talk about it later. We haven't got time now Xavi. You don't mind me still calling you Xavi, do you?

*

402

Valentina turned into Shields Road. A long straight road leading directly into the centre of Newcastle. The numerous pubs had emptied but there were still stragglers weaving their way home. The wind had picked up from the afternoon and was now a full-on gale, whistling along the street. Litter blew across the road: plastic bottles and empty cans rolled around and clanged into lamp posts. She heard a glass smash as it crashed against brick wall. Valentina pulled her hood up and hurried on. In another half an hour she had reached the High Level Bridge, looming over her, nearly forty metres above the inky blackness of the River Tyne, the freezing waters choppy and frothing, whipped up by the gales hurtling along the river banks.

Valentina climbed up the steep High Bridge Street and walked past the Norman castle to the entrance to the bridge. She stepped over the yellow emergency diversion signs which had blown down and then under the red and white tape stretching across the twelve-metre width of the bridge, cordoning it off to the public. She walked along the left footpath, climbed over a low stone balustrade and found a sheltered spot behind a huge iron girder supporting the stone arches holding the railway line above. There was plenty of time. All she had to do was wait and hope that her plan worked out. *Come on Ramon. Come on. Be a good boy. Step into the trap.*

At exactly one o'clock Valentina heard a car engine. She leaned out and watched the car park under the castle walls. Ten minutes went by and then she saw Ramon leaving the car and leading Amber under the tape. She had guessed right; he had approached the bridge from the Newcastle end. She climbed back over the balustrade so that Ramon could see her. When he was a short distance away, she saw that Ramon had a small backpack and Amber had a length of rope attached to her right wrist. Ramon gripped the rope with his left hand and she could see the knife he had used to stab Felipe hanging down from his other hand, ready. *I'll have to watch out for that knife. You're very good with it.*

Valentina nodded to them both. 'Hello Amber … you okay?' She had to shout to be heard above the wind so she moved closer.

'Fine,' Amber called back. She looked at Valentina with wide anxious eyes. 'How's Felipe?' she shouted. 'How's he doing? Is he okay?'

Valentina didn't answer. She knew she couldn't.

'That's far enough,' said Ramon. He looked much older than his twenty-nine years. His combed back blond hair flayed about in the wind and his carefully managed stubble had thickened. He smiled in a strange way and eyed Valentina with steady dark blue eyes. 'Just give me the passport and we can get this done.'

'I'm sorry it has to be like this Ramon,' said Valentina. 'I wish there was some other way …'

'Don't be stupid,' Ramon shouted. 'Don't try anything clever.' He glanced down and flicked the knife over in his hand. 'Let's just do this quickly and get out of here.'

'Okay,' said Valentina. 'Just let Amber walk over here and I'll give you the passport.'

'No, that's not the way it's going to happen. You give me the passport and I'll let her go when I get back to the car.'

Valentina paused for a moment. 'I don't think you can get back to the car Ramon,' she said.

'What are you talking about?'

'I think these gentlemen want to talk to you.' Valentina directed her gaze behind Ramon.

Ramon glanced over his shoulder and started with surprise as he saw two figures approaching. One was tall and completely bald and the other one was small and slim with a long ponytail waving about in the wind. He recognised them immediately and turned back to Valentina. 'Bastard!' he snarled. 'You bastard.'

'I'm sorry Ramon,' Valentina called out so that the two figures could hear. 'I had to let the group know what was going on. Your behaviour was just too erratic. You're a danger to us.' She nodded to Antoni and Vincente as they came up and stood directly behind Ramon.

'Hello,' said Vincente, raising his voice against the wind. He looked at Amber. 'You must be Amber,' he said in perfect English. 'We've heard a lot about you. You did the right thing, Valentina. We can't let things get out of hand.' He turned to Ramon. 'I said back in Madrid that I didn't think you would find the painting, but you did, so well done for that.' He gave Ramon a big smile. 'Do you have it with you? Let's see it.'

Ramon hesitated, desperately thinking of a way out. He realised he could buy some time by showing the painting. He pulled his bag from his shoulder still keeping the knife in his hand and a tight grip on the rope attached to Amber's wrist. 'Take it out,' he said to Amber. 'Take it out and show them … and then put it back.'

Amber bent down, opened the bag and pulled out the copy of Joan Miro's mural. She unfolded it, held it up with both hands and showed it to Antoni and Vincente. The mural flapped in the wind making the stars leap and the surreal Catalan reaper sway about as if striking the enemy with his sickle.

'Again, well done Ramon,' said Vincente, leaning forward to study the figure on the mural copy. 'An excellent job.'

'I said this wouldn't work,' said Antoni with his thick Catalan accent. 'But it did. I got it wrong.' He dropped the tight smile he had put on and scowled at Ramon with narrowed, unblinking fierce eyes. 'However, Valentina tells us that you have other thoughts on what to do with the painting. But, do you remember, I also said we have to be hidden. Not attracting attention. We demand total secrecy, and if we don't get that ... of course there have to be consequences ... you do understand, don't you?'

Ramon pulled on the rope and dragged Amber nearer to him, the top of her head touching his chin. He put the knife at her throat. 'We have to leave now,' he said calmly. 'Give me the passport Valentina and I'll let Amber go when we're out of here.' He pricked the knife into Amber's throat making her wince and then he looked at Antoni. 'We don't want any incidents, do we?'

'You need to let her go!' A voice came from behind Valentina. Everyone spun round to see Xavi walking quickly along the footpath, closely followed by Ana. 'Let her go,' repeated Xavi. They all took a step back when they saw the pistol in his hand pointed at Ramon's head.

'Who the hell is this?' shouted Antoni. 'Put that gun down old man. You'll hurt someone with it.'

'Let her go,' Xavi roared. He moved the pistol five centimetres to the right and pulled the trigger. A loud crack echoed around the bridge as the bullet ricocheted off the iron girders behind Ramon kicking up sparks and flakes of metal.

Ana raced up alongside Xavi. 'Bloody hell, Xavi!' she shouted at him. 'No bullets! You said you had no bullets!'

Xavi pointed the gun back at Ramon's head. 'Bit of a lie,' he said, not taking his eyes off Ramon.

'Who the hell are you?' Vincente growled.

Ramon looked at Xavi. 'How did you get here?' he said. A thought suddenly struck him and he stared at Valentina.

Valentina could see in Ramon's eyes that he was thinking fast. *He's working it out. He knows. He knows I've been in contact with the family all along. He knows if he can divert attention to me, he has a chance. He's going to tell them I'm undercover. He's going to –'*

Ana noticed the way Ramon was looking at Valentina too. 'It was him,' she shouted to Antoni and Vincente, pointing at Ramon. 'He called us. He said he wanted witnesses. He said he was worried what Valentina would do to him.'

Valentina glanced at Ana. *Well done, Ana. Thank you for that. All we need now is to get Amber.*

Valentina knew she would get a reaction from Amber which would give them a chance to grab her. 'He's dead Amber,' she yelled. She jabbed a hand towards Ramon. 'Felipe's dead. Ramon killed him. He didn't recover.'

Amber's whole body seemed to shudder and she let out a choking gasp. She howled, flung her free arm round and punched Ramon in the face then yanked her right hand up and pulled herself free. She ran to

Valentina but Ramon went after her, pulled her round and snatched the painting from her. Amber was only a footstep away. She glared at him and punched him again.

'Stupid little bastard,' he yelled. He pulled his arm back to slash the knife across her throat but another warning shot rang out from Xavi, stopping him in his tracks, making everyone duck down. Ramon grabbed his chance and leapt over the balustrade with the mural copy in his hand. He jumped on to the narrow parapet and started scrambling along the outer edge of the bridge shifting his weight carefully and using both arms outstretched to steady himself. Valentina came after him. Antoni and Vincente ran to the next girder to block his escape.

Ramon saw that there was no way out. He decided to climb back over the parapet just as Valentina reached him but a sudden huge gust of wind blew the painting into his face. He lost his balance and tripped on an iron spike. The painting caught on the spike and as Ramon fell over the side he clung on to the cloth and started clawing at it, trying to pull himself back up.

Valentina reached the spot and saw Ramon dangling just below her. He was swinging about: his legs kicking to try and gain a foothold on the bottom lip of the parapet. His weight started to tell on the cloth and little by little it started to rip. Within a few seconds it came apart, Ramon lost his lifeline and he fell, his body hurtling forty metres down and crashing against the base of one of the massive stone arches before tumbling into the river. There was no scream or yell. No noise except for a faint splash carried away by the wind. They all raced across and leant over the parapet to see if Ramon had survived. Ana gave a short gasping, 'No!' They waited for a full minute but his body didn't surface. The copy of the mural, now in two jagged torn pieces danced and flapped about in the wind before wafting into the choppy waters and being carried away through the darkness. They could just make out the trailing pools of colour briefly caught in the street lights along the quayside before vanishing among the rippling waters

The wind moaned around them as Valentina walked across to Antoni and Vincente and spoke to them quickly in Spanish. Antoni nodded, jerked a hand up towards Ana in a quick dismissive salutation and then he and Vincente started to walk away to the Newcastle end of the bridge. Valentina came back to Ana, Xavi and Amber.

'I have to go now,' she said. Her voice was remarkably calm. 'We are driving up to … well, it doesn't matter where … you don't need to know. We need to get an early flight out of the U.K.' She spoke as quietly as she could against the wind, even though she was well out of hearing of Antoni and Vincente. 'I told them I'd have to speak to you to make sure you kept this to yourselves. That you would be in danger if you spoke out.' She raised one eyebrow. 'However, I don't think I have to say that to you. You know how important this is for me and my government … and you don't want to be implicated in Ramon's death.'

She looked at Amber. 'You can relax Amber. Felipe is fine. He's alive and in a military hospital, being looked after for a few weeks. They'll probably try to deradicalize him. I've arranged for someone to take you to him next week. If you want to, of course.' Amber nodded, her shoulders sagged, she let out a long breath and closed her eyes. 'I told those two that Ramon changed his mind and contacted the police.' Valentina was about to say something else but was stopped by Ana's raised hand.

'You could have saved him,' Ana said with a loud measured voice. The words clattered between them. The wind picked them up and hurled them about. 'He wasn't that far below. You could have reached down and saved him.'

Valentina straightened, she pulled her collar tighter around her neck, looked at Ana and pursed her lips. 'I don't think so. The cloth was already ripping when I got there.'

Xavi waved an arm, slapping away her words. 'You slowed down,' he shouted. 'All three of you did. We watched you. You could have got there and helped him.'

Valentina pulled some windswept hair back from her brow and stared at Xavi but said nothing.

'You and your *friends* could have saved him,' repeated Ana.

'And then what?' Valentina shot back. 'Take him to the British police so he could have a nice chat about what he was doing here and what he was doing in Madrid.'

'You could have got your contacts in British security to hold him,' barked Xavi, his eyes blazing. 'Make sure he didn't talk about your group.'

'Not with Hugo and Vincente here.' Valentina kept very still.

'But you must have sent for them,' Ana eyed her angrily. 'Only you knew what was going on. You knew what would happen if they came. It was all your ... *plan.*'

'They needed to be here,' Valentina said. 'To see for themselves what was happening. To know that I could still be trusted.'

'Trusted to let him die,' said Xavi.

Valentina looked at Xavi and shook her head. 'He was too far gone. He couldn't be helped.'

'Do you mean on the bridge, or for what he'd done?' asked Ana sullenly.

Valentina tilted her head at Ana and gazed at her blank faced. 'I thought you understood. I've been telling you how important this is. I told you we can't let anything get in the way ...' She began blinking rapidly, realising what she had just said.

'Oh, yes, yes, we understand. We understand you couldn't let anything get in the way,' Ana scowled. 'Including my son and daughter.'

'We ... I ... wouldn't have let that happen,' Valentina tried to backtrack.

'If it wasn't for Xavi,' shouted Ana. She stole a glance at Xavi, still cradling the pistol. 'And that bloody gun.' She shook her head but then puffed up her cheeks. 'Amber could have been knifed. She could have ...' Her face shook as she gulped and sucked in air trying hard to control herself.

Amber stared at her with deep round eyes.

'I wouldn't have let that happen,' Valentina repeated.

'You gambled,' Ana forced her voice to be steady. She clenched a fist and jabbed it at Valentina, directing her rage along the length of her body. 'You gambled with my daughter's life. You didn't know what was going to happen.'

They stood in a tight circle. Each of them needing the silence to continue and let their thoughts be carried away in the wind whirling through the bridge.

Eventually Valentina flicked a hand to signal that she was leaving. 'I have to go now,' she said tersely. 'They're waiting for me.' She glanced towards the spot where Ramon fell. 'I've still got his passport but they'll work out who he is sooner or later. But not what he is ... or was. And we'll all be long gone by then.' She turned to go but then stopped and looked back at Ana. 'But whatever you think Ana. Thank you for your help and what you said before. That saved me ... saved the whole project.' She looked at Xavi. 'And thank you Xavi. Thank you for what you did. But those shots will have been heard and you need to get rid of the pistol.' Finally, she looked at them all. 'I'm sorry you were mixed up in this. You need to go quickly now. Get away from this place and just try and forget what happened. There was nothing anyone could do to save Ramon. He wouldn't have made it back to Madrid anyway.' She leant in closer to Ana. 'It looks like the copy of the mural decided not to go home after all.' She nodded once, as a kind of formal reverential acknowledgement of their help, and then began walking along the bridge to catch up with Antoni and Vincente.

Xavi waited for a few seconds and then took the pistol and hurled it between the iron girders into the river.

'I suppose it was a good thing you had that gun after all,' said Ana. 'To give those warning shots.'

'Actually, I was aiming at him for the second one,' said Xavi. 'Good job I'm a bad shot, eh?'

Ana shook her head, gave a derisive snort and then looked at Amber. She studied her, trying to work out what she could possibly say. After all that had happened, she just wanted Amber to come home. She wanted to apologise for not doing enough to protect her. She needed her to come home. She wanted to be her mother again.

'Let's go,' said Xavi quickly. 'We have to go now. We have to get away from here.'

Amber didn't move. She was looking at the ground in front of her. She exhaled a long shuddering breath.

'Just a second Xavi,' said Ana. She went across and tentatively held out a hand to Amber. Amber didn't respond so Ana gently touched her arm. Amber looked up and when she didn't pull away Ana put her arm around her.

'You're shaking,' said Ana.

'It's cold,' said Amber. 'I'm cold, that's all.' By habit she dredged up a resentful stare but quickly turned it into a look of indignation and then finally a short nervous twitch of her lips that looked remarkably like a smile.

Ana pulled her arm tighter around Amber. 'We thought we'd lost you. I don't want to go through that again. I don't want to lose you. Come home. Will you come home?'

'Ye-es,' said Amber.

'Good,'

''Cos I need the toilet.'

'Oh,'

'And I smell from being stuck in the boot of that car.' She arched an eyebrow. 'And I need to see that stupid brother of mine to thank him for nearly getting me killed.'

'So, he's still your brother?'

Amber gave a small nod.

'We heard about what you did at the house Amber,' said Xavi. 'Taking Sami's place. That was a brave thing to do. A good thing to do.'

'And we'll make sure you get to see Felipe,' said Ana. 'I can see he means a lot to you. Maybe he won't change but it's your decision.'

'Yes, I'd like to see him again … maybe for one last time.' Amber said. She looked carefully at them both. 'I've been a bit of a bitch, haven't I?'

'More like a whole bitch,' said Ana. She gave Amber the warmest smile she could.

'You've had a shock Amber,' said Xavi raising his eyebrows. 'We all have.' He glanced at Amber. 'Maybe you should have had that shock a few years ago.'

'Don't push it uncle Xavi,' said Amber

'Let's go then. We need to get away from here,' said Ana. She stole a look at Xavi. 'And I've got some interesting news to tell you about Uncle Xavi.'

'Okay,' Amber said. 'But I hope it's not about flags. I don't want to hear about flags.'

Chapter twenty-seven,

Wednesday, 10th July, 1996,

Newcastle, Northern England,

Emily's house.

Dear Isabel,

I know this will probably be the last letter I will write to you. Carmen has told me that you are very ill.

I am so sorry, but I am happy that you and Carmen have had a full life together. I will always treasure our time. Sometimes beautiful things can come out of the most terrible circumstances.

I think of you often. You haunt my dreams. Our time together burned bright, perhaps too bright and maybe it was inevitable that we parted. I don't know. But I need you to understand that I have always loved you and will always love you. It was just not meant to be but I have no regrets.

Thank you for being you. Thank you for loving me. And thank you for keeping my secrets all these years. The secret about Paris and the secret about the flags. I still have them. They are my guardian angels, just as you were. I sleep with them under my pillow every night. They have looked after me all these years. A reminder of the wonderful Spanish Republic and the wonderful people who came to help. The flags scare me sometimes with the secret they have kept hidden. I don't want to lose it and I don't want to give it back. All three are a part of me. I couldn't bear to lose them. I open them up occasionally to let them all breathe. And so that I can draw strength from them.

Thank you. Thank you. Thank you and farewell my beautiful friend.

Emily put her pen down. She would write more later, but she had an important job to do before she finished the letter.

She walked across to her kitchen table, placed a new bobbin on the spool feed of her sewing machine and turned it on. She finished off sewing Miro's silk mural copy back between the two flags with neat running stitches.

Notes on events mentioned in the novel.

The Spanish Pavilion at the Paris Exhibition

An exhibition coming to London in January will attempt to recreate the impact of the Spanish pavilion of 1937, a little gallery built as cheaply as possible at the Paris International Exposition by Spain's Republican government at the height of the civil war.

It opened late and stood literally in the shadow of two of the biggest pavilions at the fair: one built by Russia and directly opposite, another built by Germany, each topped with a gigantic symbolic sculpture.

At the end of the fair, the organisers jointly awarded the prize for best pavilion to those two hulking monuments of totalitarian politics and art, while the young Spanish architects, Josep Lluis Sert and Luis Lacasa, fled into exile.

Spain's pavilion ... unveiled extraordinary works by two of the most famous artists of the day.

One was Pablo Picasso's Guernica, a howl of rage at the virtual obliteration of a small Spanish town by German bombing.

The other was The Reaper, a towering mural painted on the stairwell wall by Joan Miro, which has not been seen since the pavilion was demolished. Although it could have been cut free by some canny dealer, it may have been broken up with the rubble from the pavilion. The painting was personal and political to Miro, he said "El Segador (The Reaper) reflects the pain, suffering and revolutionary angst of the Catalan people on seeing how their identity, their language and their culture risked being engulfed by a nationalist victory."

While Guernica was painted in grey, white and black, The Reaper is assumed to have blazed Miro's trademark crimsons and yellows – but there is no colour photograph of the original. The work has therefore been recreated by scanning, enlarging and stitching together the best surviving images of it, in black and white. It is huge but slightly under the original height of 5 metres because of space restrictions.

Punyet Miro still hopes his grandfather's work may resurface one day. He says, "For many of us born in the 50s and 60s, the pavilion continues to have very special meaning. We lived during the latter years of the dictatorship, the transition period and the arrival of democracy. Despite Spanish and foreign scholars studying the pavilion in detail, there are still mysteries to be uncovered, like where is Miro's work, The Reaper, still missing today."

Maev Kennedy Sat 24 Dec 2016, The Guardian newspaper.

*

Joan Miro's highest selling piece of Art

At Christie's last Friday, Joan Miro's painting *Peinture (Femmes, lune, etoiles)* sold for €20.7 million (roughly $ 22 million) – making it the highest selling piece during the Paris auctions this fall and one of the highest priced pieces to date in France.

'It epitomises Miro's post-war style, full of poetry,' Valerie Didier, an impressionist and Modern art specialist at Christie's in Paris said. 'Miros of this scale and quality, and with such extraordinary provenance, rarely come to the market.'

Peinture (Femmes, lune, etoiles) is one of the most paramount examples of the Catalan painter's art practice.

Shelby Black, October 27, 2023 galeriemagazine.com

*

The Spanish second Republic and the International Brigades

The Spanish Second republic was founded on 14 April 1931. However, despite the introduction of democracy, the forces of reaction continued to oppose reform as violently as they had done for over a century.

Government attempts to introduce reforms in land distribution and to limit the powers of the Catholic church and the army provoked a powerful reactionary coalition of landowners, army officers and clergy. A new law giving women the right to vote was also opposed as was the granting of autonomy to Catalonia in 1932 and to the Basque country in 1936. Meanwhile, some on the left, especially the powerful anarchist movement, launched revolutionary actions in search of faster and more radical change.

Over 35,000 volunteers from 53 different countries came to fight in the International Brigades. In the course of the war nearly 20 per cent of the international volunteers died and most suffered wounds of varying degrees of severity.

Despite the British government's policy of non-intervention, polls taken show that there was overwhelming support among the British people for the Spanish government. Committees sprang up throughout the country, involving people from all walks of life. Although left-wing activists were in the majority, the campaigns attracted support from a wide political spectrum.

When the first British Medical Unit left for Spain on 23 August 1936, huge crowds gathered at London's Victoria station to bid them farewell.

During the Spanish Civil War, medical units with the Republican army were working closer to the front than ever before in an assortment of hastily converted buildings. Mobile units were organised using lorries, specially equipped to act as operating theatres wherever needed. Railway tunnels were sometimes used as temporary hospitals. Most foreign medical workers were withdrawn from Spain together with the International Brigades in September 1938.

Democracy was finally restored to Spain after Franco's death and free elections were held in 1977 for the first time since 1936. In 2007, the Spanish government passed a law conferring Spanish citizenship on the surviving volunteers of the International Brigades.

Antifascistas, (British and Irish Volunteers in the Spanish Civil War). Richard Baxell, Angela Jackson, Jim Jump. 2010

*

Catalonia

Catalonia is one of Spain's wealthiest and most productive regions and has a distinct history dating back almost 1,000 years. Before the Spanish Civil War, it enjoyed broad autonomy but was suppressed under General Franco. When Franco died, the region was granted autonomy again under the 1978 constitution and prospered as part of the new, democratic Spain. The 2008 financial crash and Spanish public spending cuts fuelled local resentment and separatism along with widespread feeling that the central government took much more in taxes than it gave back.

The Catalonia region had its autonomy suspended for almost seven months by Madrid after a failed bid to break away in 2017. In October 2019, Spain's Supreme Court sentenced nine Catalan politicians and activists to jail terms of between nine and thirteen years for the independence bid. In the referendum on 1 October 2017, declared illegal by Spain's Constitutional Court, about 90 % of Catalan voters backed independence. The turnout was 43%.

The ruling separatists in the Catalan autonomous parliament then declared independence on 27 October. Angered by that, Madrid imposed direct rule by invoking Article 155 of the constitution – a first for Spain.

The Spanish government sacked the Catalan leaders, dissolved parliament and called a snap regional election on 21 December 2017, which nationalist parties won.

BBC World News, The Catalonia crisis. 14 October 2019

*

The Basque Refugee Children in Tynemouth

Throughout the Spanish war Franco's most ferocious assaults on the civilian population were carried out in the Basque provinces. Between April and August 1937, as these provinces were subjugated, German and Italian aircraft destroyed the town of Guernica in one afternoon; towns and villages were bombed and shelled, the ports blockaded by warships and the roads became blocked by refugees fleeing towards the coast.

In these conditions the Basque regional government made an international appeal to other countries to shelter the refugee children. Mexico, France, Belgium and the Soviet Union readily did so, whilst in Britain the National Joint Committee for Spanish Relief managed to persuade the Home Office to admit 4,000 Basque children – on the strict understanding that no public expenditure was to be involved. At the end of May 1937, the children and some adult companions arrived in Southampton on a ship escorted from Spain by a British destroyer … during the next few weeks efforts were made to establish 'colonies' for the children around the country amidst a furore in the popular press with wild stories about theft, vandalism and communist rioters.

North Shields like most of the North East of England, was active in support of the Spanish republic through its Spanish Aid Society. By May 1937 the Society was raising funds and storing food and medical supplies at 15 Windsor Gardens in the town. This was the home of Nell Badsey, a former nurse who was a member of the Communist Party and secretary of the Spanish Aid Society. The Society had received five offers to adopt Basque children from Tynemouth families by June 1937 – offers which were turned down because the Basque government wished to keep the children in 'colonies' to preserve their national identity – and pledges were coming in to raise the required sum of ten shillings a week to support one.

In early 1937 a mass meeting at the Albion Assembly Rooms in North shields (attended by a large party of Spanish sailors from the Tyne ports) heard the Duchess of Atholl, who chaired the National Joint Committee for Spanish Relief, make an appeal for support of the

Basque children. Despite the success of the meeting doubts were expressed about whether the North shields area, itself with poverty and problems of its own could raise and sustain enough donations to make a hostel for the children viable.

Nevertheless, by the end of the month the local Spanish Aid Committee had decided to go ahead. On the weekend of 1st August 1937 twenty Basque boys between six and thirteen accompanied by a young woman teacher, Carmen Gil, arrived from Southampton for accommodation the Society Committee had arranged at 40 Percy Park in Tynemouth.

Some problems were immediate. There were boys who slept in their clothes, hoarded food and lived out of the bundles they carried until gradually they accepted that they would not have to leave in the middle of the night or take cover as they had to do so often in the past. Only a few of the eldest spoke English.

But the most pressing problem was summed up the *Shields News* front page report which announced their arrival under the headline 'Basque Refugees On Way to Tynemouth Despite Residents' Protests'; *In spite of a bid by Percy Park residents to ban one of the houses ... from housing 20 Basque refugees it is expected that the children will be in occupation tomorrow ... Objection had been raised to the property being converted into a hostel and residents in Percy Park claim that conditions governing the property stipulate that it must be maintained as a private residence ...*

Very quickly, either through genuine feeling or after skilful managing by Nell Badsey, the local press began to carry supportive and sympathetic articles on the hostel – one of the very few hostile letters it oriented was quickly exposed as part of a national letter writing campaign organised by the British Union of Fascists.

The hostel was run by a committee as broad as the Aid Spain movement itself. Besides Communist and Labour Parties those involved with it included Liberal Councillor Anderson, a retired army Commander Barret and two prominent local clergymen.

Apart from the North Shields area, support groups were established in several different towns in the North East. In Gateshead for example one was chaired by Mary Bell who was to be post war mayor of Gateshead. The jumble sales, raffles, street corner collections, concerts socials and door to door collections could now add the Tynemouth Basque refugee children to other Spanish Aid causes.

One obvious route to raising funds was through the visual presence the boys could provide as living examples of what Aid for Spain and the Republican cause was all about. Angel Perez Martinez (now Angel Badsey) was twelve when he arrived with the others at Percy Park. He was a member of the concert party which was formed by the children and soon became a familiar aspect of Spanish fund-raising events around Tyneside.

Spanish sailors visiting the Tyne ports would drop in to Percy Park, sometimes able to bring news of particular families ... news from the Basque provinces was never good. Letters from boys' parents spoke of no work, no money and no food, fathers and elder brothers missing. Their gratitude to the hostel was profound and they made it clear that there was no other way under the prevailing conditions at home that the boys could be looked after.

An Inspiring Example: North East of England and the Spanish Civil War 1936 – 1939

By Don Watson and John Corcoran

*

Evacuation and Repatriation

The land route for evacuation was blocked but the sea route was a possibility. Some 70,000 elderly, women and children were evacuated to France, Belgium, Britain, the Soviet Union and Mexico – 27,000 of whom were unaccompanied children The campaign organised in Britain by the Tory Duchess of Atholl, the Liberal M.P. Wilfrid Roberts and Labour's Leah Manning persuaded the British government to reluctantly agree to nearly 4,000 refugee children and their accompanying adults entering Britain. The majority of children returned to Spain by the outbreak of the Second World War whilst 400 remained. Most of the adults did not return to Spain.

The number further reduced up to 1945 with 250 remaining. These were the children who were most at risk, if they returned to Spain, of being taken by the state and entering into forced adoptions by Franco-supporting families. The adults were facing trial for rebellion, punishable by capital punishment or life imprisonment. The Basque government was in exile.

Simon Martinez, trustee for the Basque Children of '37 association U.K.

Magazine of the International Brigade Memorial Trust No. 60 February 2022

*

Els Segadors (The Reapers)

The Tough living conditions of the peasants and the billeting of 10,000 soldiers in Catalonia during the winter and spring of 1640 caused a popular revolt in Catalonia. On 6 June that year, hundreds of reapers led a large-scale rebellion in Barcelona. The peasant revolt led to political revolution ... The events were described in a popular song, Els Segadors (The Reapers), which was passed on orally from parents to children. Made an official anthem by the Republican Generalitat, it became a battle hymn for opposition movements during Francoism ... In 1993 by decision of the Catalan Parliament, Els Segadors, once again became Catalonia's official anthem.

Museu d'Historia de Catalunya

SOURCES

The Battle for Spain by Antony Beevor, a phoenix paperback 2006.

The Real Band of Brothers (first-hand accounts from the last British survivors of the Spanish Civil War) by Max Arthur, Collins 2009.

Antifascistas (British and Irish Volunteers in the Spanish Civil War) by Richard Baxell, Angela Jackson, Jim Jump. Lawrence and Wishart 2010.

The Thirties (An intimate History) by Juliet Gardiner, Harper Press 2010.

Making Spaniards (Primo de Rivera and the Nationalization of the Masses, 1923 – 30, by Alejandro Quiroga, Palgrave Macmillan 2007

A People Betrayed (A History of Corruption, Political Incompetence and Social Division in Modern Spain 1876- 2016) by Paul Peston, William Collins 2020.

International Brigade Memorial Trust Newsletters.

An Inspiring Example: The North East of England and the Spanish Civil War, 1936 – 1939

By Don Watson and John Corcoran, published by McGuffin Press 1996

*

Acknowledgements

Many thanks to: Pauline Wilson, Judith Johnston, Kate Pearson, Lyn Pearson, for their editing skills, proof reading, comments and advice for this novel.

Front cover illustration by Tom Pearson and Eric Johnston

Printed in Great Britain
by Amazon

47743691R00243